PRAISE FOR

*30 Things I Love About Myself*

"I adored everything about this hilarious, clever, uplifting novel! A truly gifted storyteller... Sanghani's charmingly flawed characters are so lovable and authentic you'll feel like you're part of the Mistry family. In turns uproariously funny and tenderly touching, *30 Things I Love About Myself* is the perfect antidote for today's stressful world."

—Lori Nelson Spielman, *New York Times* bestselling author of *The Star-Crossed Sisters of Tuscany*

"Absolutely charming! Touching, clever, poignant, and hilarious. Readers will cheer for Nina as she discovers the most important lesson in life—to love yourself. A brilliant and timely read!"

—Jenn McKinlay, *New York Times* bestselling author of *Wait For It*

"Laugh-out-loud funny." —The Associated Press

"This comedy-drama is unafraid to tackle difficult subjects amid the often hilarious saga of a British Indian journalist and her journey toward self-love and acceptance."

—Shelf Awareness

"A heartwarming read about self-acceptance and the idea that it's possible to learn to love your imperfect self."

—*Kirkus Reviews*

"A sweet and funny contemporary novel about learning to embrace yourself, flaws and all. Discussions on racism and depression add depth, keeping the tone from becoming saccharine. Readers will be inspired to create their own self-love lists."

—*Booklist*

"This! So good!! Funny, fresh, touching. I'm completely in love with Nina the heroine. I love the way Radhika writes."

—Jane Fallon, bestselling author of *Worst Idea Ever*

"Witty, warm, and, most of all, brave and important."
—Catherine Gray, bestselling author of
*The Unexpected Joy of Being Single*

"A heartwarming and uplifting read, exactly what we all need right now.... This is going to fly!"
—Nikki May, author of *Wahala*

"A treat. Just lovely, funny, life-affirming storytelling."
—Lauren Bravo, author of *How to Break Up with Fast Fashion*

"Takes you on a heartwarming, affirming journey of what self-love looks like beyond the social media one-liners. An ideal read for any young woman struggling to see her worth and wondering how choosing herself might look."
—Megan Jayne Crabbe, author of *Body Positive Power*

"Felt like a big, warm hug! This book is filled with lots of gems, heartfelt moments, and plenty of LOLs. I rooted for Nina all the way. Well done to Radhika for writing such an unconventional rom-com. We need more of these!"
—Lizzie Damilola Blackburn,
author of *Yinka, Where Is Your Huzband?*

"I absolutely loved this book.... A witty, relatable, and heartwarming novel about the obstacle course of adulthood and learning to, in time, be your own compass, self-help guide, and best friend."
—Emma Gannon, author of *Olive*

"A charming novel. I loved spending time with Nina, Meera, Rupa, Auntie Trish, and the whole gang. Typical Sagittarius."
—Nell Frizzell, bestselling author of *The Panic Years*

"It is PERFECT—funny and charming and moving all in one.... I honestly believe everyone will be touched by Nina's story.... I loved it!"
—Harriet Minter, author of *Working from Home*

## TITLES BY RADHIKA SANGHANI

*I Wish We Weren't Related*

*30 Things I Love About Myself*

*Not That Easy*

*Virgin*

# I WISH WE WEREN'T RELATED

## RADHIKA SANGHANI

BERKLEY

New York

BERKLEY
An imprint of Penguin Random House LLC
penguinrandomhouse.com

Copyright © 2023 by Radhika Sanghani Ltd.
Readers Guide copyright © 2023 by Radhika Sanghani Ltd.
Penguin Random House supports copyright. Copyright fuels creativity,
encourages diverse voices, promotes free speech, and creates a vibrant
culture. Thank you for buying an authorized edition of this book and for
complying with copyright laws by not reproducing, scanning, or
distributing any part of it in any form without permission. You are
supporting writers and allowing Penguin Random House
to continue to publish books for every reader.

BERKLEY and the BERKLEY & B colophon are registered
trademarks of Penguin Random House LLC.

LIBRARY OF CONGRESS CATALOGING-IN-PUBLICATION DATA

Names: Sanghani, Radhika, author.
Title: I wish we weren't related / Radhika Sanghani.
Other titles: I wish we were not related
Description: First Edition. | New York: Berkley, 2023.
Identifiers: LCCN 2022058276 (print) |
LCCN 2022058277 (ebook) | ISBN 9780593335062 (trade paperback) |
ISBN 9780593335079 (ebook)
Subjects: LCGFT: Novels.
Classification: LCC PR6119.A569 I9 2023 (print) |
LCC PR6119.A569 (ebook) |
DDC 823/.92—dc23/eng/20221209
LC record available at https://lccn.loc.gov/2022058276
LC ebook record available at https://lccn.loc.gov/2022058277

First Edition: July 2023

Printed in the United States of America
1st Printing

Book design by Katy Riegel

*To Coco—the best cat I know*

# I WISH WE WEREN'T RELATED

## CHAPTER 1

### Day 1

REEVA MEHTA PUSHED open the double doors and walked out of the courtroom feeling like the heroine of the movie that was her life. She stood at the top of the stone steps in the glaring sun, beaming down at the world through her oversized sunglasses, allowing herself this one moment of pure, unadulterated success. Because she'd done it. She'd *won*. Her client wouldn't have to walk out of her marriage to that abusive asshole with barely any funds to raise her three kids. Instead, she'd get everything she deserved.

Reeva was still fuming that the shitty Mr. Khan had tried to funnel all his money away to his brother, pretending he was practically broke. She knew she should be used to it by now—she'd been working in divorce law for a solid decade—but every time, the injustice of it all floored her. Only this time, she'd stopped it. She'd found out exactly what Mr. Khan was doing and had successfully applied for the court to undo the transfer of assets, meaning her client would get her fair share of what was rightfully hers: £3.5 million. Justice had been served.

When the judge had made his ruling, the former Mrs. Khan had hugged Reeva with tears in her eyes. And in that moment, Reeva had remembered exactly why she did this job. She could still feel the warmth of the hug as she strode down the street now toward the office in her new fuchsia heels. She knew she should swap into the trainers she carried everywhere, but this was Reeva's moment. The shoes added to her heroine vibe. She needed a soundtrack too. Something bold. Celebratory. The kind of song they'd play in the finale of a feminist film. She pulled out her phone and went straight to the "Boss Bitch" playlist Lakshmi had made. She scrolled down, looking for something to match her mood, and laughed out loud when she found it: "All I Do Is Win."

Reeva walked back to her office listening to DJ Khaled on repeat. She doubted he knew the unique feeling of having saved a woman from financial ruin by using the power of the law, but she still felt very seen by his lyrics. Because right now, that was Reeva. Despite the best efforts of Mr. Khan's lawyers, she'd won, won, won.

"I'm so proud of you," cried Lakshmi, bursting into Reeva's office and wrapping her arms around her. "I can't believe you did it! I mean, I can. Because it's you. But you know what I mean."

Reeva squeezed her best friend tightly. "I know. And it felt amazing."

"We need to celebrate," said Lakshmi. She opened the bottom drawer of Reeva's desk and pulled out their chocolate stash. "Which are the most expensive ones?"

Reeva pointed to the Rococo pack. "They're from Felicity Howard-Jones."

"The double-barreled ones always give the best chocolates."

Lakshmi pulled out a couple and passed the pack to Reeva. "We need music."

"I've been listening to your playlist on repeat ever since I walked out of the courtroom," said Reeva. "Well, just one song. 'All I Do Is Win.' Don't judge."

"As if I would! I play that every time I have an orgasm."

Reeva laughed. "Of course you do." She selected a white-chocolate truffle and sighed loudly as she slowly devoured it. "I'm just so relieved," she said, her mouth still full as she reached for a dark chocolate praline, "that we managed to get Noor her money. I don't know what she would have done if we hadn't. And the poor kids. They didn't deserve *any* of this. Their dad is so selfish."

Lakshmi smiled kindly. "Are you doing that thing again?"

"What thing?"

"The one where you overempathize with the kids whose lives are ruined by their parents." She paused. "So, all the kids."

"I'm not overempathizing! I care about them a normal level."

"And you're not projecting your childhood onto them? Selfish, wealthy parent? Neglected kids?"

"Stop therapizing me," protested Reeva. "I'm meant to be celebrating."

"Sorry, sorry. But it's true. And it's probably why you're so good at your job. Unlike the rest of us, you seriously care, Reevs."

"I can't tell if that's a good thing or not." Reeva caught sight of a short figure striding toward them through the glass door and winced. "Oh god; don't look now, but Lee's coming."

Lakshmi grabbed the open box of chocolates and shoved them into a drawer. "What? He always takes the best ones."

"Girls." Lee stood at the door with his arms spread out. "I knew you could do it, Reeva. Well done."

"Thanks, Lee." Reeva smiled politely at her boss.

Lakshmi rolled her eyes. "You mean 'women,' not 'girls.'"

"What are you going to do, sue me?" He ignored Lakshmi's expression that suggested she was going to do exactly that. "What about you, anyway? How's the duke?"

"As entitled as ever," said Lakshmi. "But don't worry; I'm getting him everything he wants. The prenup I drafted protects his inherited assets. His ex's claim will be confined to her reasonable needs. In other words—she's not getting the estate."

"Good." Lee nodded. "Keep up the good work and you'll have a real chance at partnership."

"A real chance? We both know it's mine. Who else wins as many cases as I do?"

"Reeva," said Lee, jerking his head toward her. "I don't know why you're not going up for partnership too. You could have fought it out between you."

She shrugged. "I just want to focus on the cases I care about. Being partner takes me further away from the stuff I love."

"All right, Pollyanna," he said. "There's champagne—well, prosecco—downstairs. May as well celebrate your win."

"Nice move," said Lakshmi, nodding approvingly. "I hope you've ordered enough for when I get made partner."

Lee scoffed and muttered something to himself about "women" and "the death of me" as he walked out of the office.

"That man," said Lakshmi. "I swear, if he makes Maria partner over me, I'll fucking *kill* him."

"As if he'd dare."

Lakshmi hesitated. "You know, I just, uh . . . I hope you're not not going for the partnership because of me. I'd be fine with it. The competition, I mean. And if you were made partner over me, I'd be genuinely happy for you." She paused. "Well, eventually."

Reeva smiled. "I know. But I promise, it's not about you. I just don't want it. I'd rather go sideways than straight up the career ladder, you know? Build up a rep on the cases I want, and then maybe go out on my own one day."

"Which you would be *incredible* at, though you know you'd also have to take on the cases you don't like. Where you rep the bad guys. And don't just palm them off onto me."

"Hey, I've represented my fair share of dickheads."

Lakshmi sighed. "True that. Well, at least our resident dickhead got us some prosecco. Coming?"

"I'll meet you there," said Reeva. "I just want to finish up the paperwork."

"Only you celebrate a win by doing paperwork. Remind me why we're friends again?"

"*Because* I celebrate a win by doing paperwork. See you down there!"

WHEN LAKSHMI HAD gone, Reeva pulled down the blinds of her office door and rushed over to the mirror. The paperwork was a lie; she needed to see if things had gotten worse. Lakshmi knew everything—what was the point of a best friend who didn't?—but Reeva couldn't bear the pity that appeared in her eyes whenever they spoke about it. She needed to do this alone.

She took a deep breath and looked straight at the woman in front of her, in her ecru silk blouse, wide-legged charcoal trousers, and pointed heels. Her wavy hair, dyed in various shades of browns, was cut above her shoulders, gently framing her slightly too-angular face. It was, as reflections went, a pretty good one. But Reeva was too focused on her task to notice.

Slowly, she used her little finger to push a large chunk of her hair over from the left to the right side of her head. It revealed a perfectly round bald patch. Reeva felt the sickening lurch in her stomach that hit her every time she looked at her bare scalp (at least twenty times a day) in the hope that it had shrunk. But it hadn't. Instead, it was now so large that with the LED office lights shining straight onto it, it looked like a round lightbulb poking out the side of her head. Trying not to cry—or think about the fact that she now resembled a human lamp—Reeva reached for her ruler.

Just then her phone rang with a FaceTime call. Reeva looked down at the screen and frowned. Her mum. The last time they'd spoken, she'd forced Reeva to sit through a guided video tour of her villa on a private island in the Seychelles "right where George proposed to Amal!" It had lasted thirty-seven minutes. Reeva's finger hovered over the reject button. She had too much going on in her life to deal with her mum right now. But at the last second, her finger slid over to "Accept." She sighed in resignation; no matter how much she tried, Reeva was incapable of taking her younger sisters' lead and rejecting their mother's calls.

She quickly pushed her hair back to cover the patch as she held up the phone in front of her. The last thing she needed was for her mum to notice that she was going bald.

"Darling?" Her mum's perfectly made-up face slowly appeared, pixel by pixel, on her phone screen. "Can you hear me?"

Reeva nodded. "Yep. Is everything okay?"

There was a dramatic silence before Saraswati replied with a pregnant monosyllable: "No."

Reeva waited expectantly for the ensuing monologue on the latest crisis—last time, a Bollywood actor had dared to (accurately) suggest that Saraswati was in her sixties—but the sound cut out and the screen froze. She sighed, placing the phone down on a shelf so she could see her mum, but her mum couldn't see her. Then she picked up the ruler. It was time.

"Reeva, where are you?" The pixels slowly rearranged themselves back into her mum's familiar Botoxed face.

"I'm here, Mum," she called out, looking at the ruler with trepidation. "Shall we just talk later? I'm quite busy and your connection isn't great."

"Oh, the bloody Taj," muttered her mum. "I don't know why they can't fix their Wi-Fi." As Saraswati began ranting about the five-star hotel's poor facilities, Reeva focused on her task. She quickly flicked her hair back and reached up to measure the diameter of the patch. She gasped out loud—6.5 centimeters. It was growing.

"I know," said Saraswati. "It's shocking. Anyway, I suppose I should tell you why I'm calling."

Reeva rummaged around her bag for her makeup. She had a date that evening—her twentieth with Nick, not that she was counting—and she wanted to look perfect. "Please do."

"Okay . . . The thing is . . ."

Reeva pulled out her mascara and began applying it onto her lashes, her jaw falling slack as she focused on her task.

"Darling . . . your dad's dead."

"Uh-huh, and?" Reeva's mouth was still open as she put on her mascara, so her voice came out lisping. "Ith there a reathon you're bringing up thomething that happened when I wath five?"

"Don't talk like that, darling," said Saraswati. "You sound like you've had a stroke. And of course there's a reason. It's just . . . well . . ."

Reeva put away the mascara and pulled out a fuchsia lipstick that perfectly matched her shoes.

"I suppose I'd better just say it."

Reeva was only half listening. Her mum probably wanted to talk about her latest realization in therapy, one that would doubtless focus on her own struggles and avoid the phrase "I'm sorry." Reeva wished this new therapist wouldn't encourage her mum to share all her supposed breakthroughs with her daughters. It was fine when you were being paid more than £100 an hour to hear them, but not when you were forced to listen for free.

"You see . . . Your dad didn't actually die back then. He was alive. And he has been—all this time. Until today."

Reeva's hand slipped and smudged fuchsia lipstick across her cheek. "I'm sorry. What?" She grabbed the phone and stared into her mum's shifting face.

"It was a heart attack in the middle of the night yesterday. All very sudden." Her mum looked down at her nails (dark red Shellac—her trademark) and began fiddling with her ridiculously large diamond ring. "I'm sorry to not be able to tell you in person, Reeva. But this latest movie, it's just taking up so much of my time."

Reeva wiped the lipstick off her cheek and stared at her reflection in the mirror and then looked back down at her mum. "I'm sorry; are you kidding? Are you trying to tell me that Dad's been alive all this time?! Until last night?"

Her mum nodded guiltily. Reeva scanned her face for some kind of explanation, but none came. "So why did you tell us he was dead?! Mum—you need to explain! What's going on?!"

Saraswati coughed awkwardly. "I know it's a lot to take in. It's a real shock he died so young. Only sixty-four." A series of muffled shouts erupted on Saraswati's end, and her face brightened momentarily. "Darling, I'm so sorry, I have to go in a minute. That's the producer calling me. We're getting a flight up to the Himalayas today—I have no idea why these directors are so obsessed with getting the mountains into every song sequence. I think the Wi-Fi will be even worse there. Honestly, these hotels—"

"Mum!" Reeva cried out, forgetting her own therapist's advice to avoid raising her voice when dealing with members of her family. "What about Dad?"

Saraswati started twirling her diamond around her ring finger again. She held her hand up to the light and gave it an admiring glance before turning her attention back to the phone screen. "Look, it's all very complicated. I don't want to explain it on the phone. My lawyers will give you and your sisters a call later to talk you through the details. Your dad used the same lawyers, which makes it all less complicated. That's one thing he did right, I'll give him that."

"What details?" demanded Reeva. "Why do I need to speak to lawyers?"

"Well, it's just . . . your dad's last wishes were for you and your sisters to be at his funeral and perform the Hindu prayers for him," explained Saraswati. "Seeing as he couldn't spend time with you in life and all, he thought he'd do it in death. I suppose it's quite poetic, really. I get you when I'm alive; he gets you when he's dead. Perhaps more families should do things this way."

"I'm sorry, what prayers? When is his funeral? And—and where did he even live?!" Reeva felt her breath constricting again. "Mum, I need answers!"

"Oh, he's just a couple of hours away from London. In Leicester. You'll need to go for the full two weeks, I'm afraid." Saraswati looked somewhat apologetically at her daughter. "It's written in his will. You girls are inheriting everything so long as you turn up for all the prayers—oh, you know, they happen every night after someone dies? We did it for your ba, remember? Oh, yes, you girls were at school . . . Well, it's not as big an ask as it sounds.

You won't have to organize it all; you just need to be there, clean his stuff out and sing for an hour every evening. He wants the prayers all the way up until the kriya ceremony, though, when he finally goes."

Reeva blinked in total incomprehension. "Goes? What's a kriya ceremony?"

Saraswati sighed in impatience. "Darling, you really should know more about your culture and all our traditions. It's when the soul leaves the body. On the thirteenth day. Look, Reeva, my lawyers will call you to explain it because I really am needed elsewhere. Hemant was only an optometrist, so I doubt the house will be all that, but he never spent much, so there's probably a pile of cash for you all to inherit. It'll be helpful, I'm sure. Anyway, it was his last wish! You can do that for a dead man, can't you? And you never seem to take any holiday, so I'm sure your job won't mind. Perhaps you could take some extra time off and come visit me afterward? Oh, it would be so fun; we could go to a retreat in Kerala."

Reeva shook her head rapidly. She knew she had only a matter of seconds before her mum did what she did best and disappeared on her. "Wait. Mum. Why did you tell us he was dead when he wasn't? What's going on?"

There was an awkward silence before her mum's face started to blur. "Reeva? Reeva?"

Reeva leaned in closer to the screen. It looked like her mum was deliberately moving the phone herself.

"Sorry, the connection's failing again! I'll explain everything soon, I promise. Just do what the lawyers say, go to his house and spend thirteen days there with your sisters. Your aunt Satya— that's your dad's sister—will be there to sort it all out. And I'll be back before you know it."

Reeva's mouth dropped open in shock. She didn't have time to register the fact she had an aunt she'd never known existed; she was still reeling from her mum's revelation that she was expected to spend thirteen days with her sisters. Not to mention the Dad news. "Wait, they're going to be there too? No, no, no. I'm definitely not going if they're there. No. You can't make me. Nope."

Saraswati's arched eyebrows made a valiant effort to narrow. "Reeva. You're an adult woman. Grow up and stop acting like a child. They're your sisters. Go and spend time with them. It'll be good for you. You can bond over all this business with your dad." She paused thoughtfully. "You know, he's probably left some letters for you that will explain everything better than I ever could—that's just the sort of sentimental thing he'd do."

"No, Mum, no." Reeva's face tightened. "You can't just tell me Dad's dead—again—and then disappear. You need to come home and explain it all. Right now! And you cannot expect me to spend thirteen entire days with Jaya and Sita after everything that's happened. You *can't*."

Her mum's face started to blur suspiciously again. "Sorry! It's the connection. I'll call to check in on you soon. Love you! *Mwah*."

## CHAPTER 2

### Day 1

REEVA STARED IN silence at the blank screen on her phone. This was bad. Really, really bad. Her mum was no stranger to dramatic life-changing announcements: "I've got a job as a playback singer in Bollywood!" "I've bought a house in Mumbai!" "You'll love boarding school!" And most recently, "Come over and meet your new stepdad!" But this was next level, even for her.

All Reeva's life, she'd known her dad was dead. It was what she'd been told by her mum, and it was what she'd read on Wikipedia. She practically knew the entry by heart.

Her mum, Saraswati Acharya (known to her fans simply as "Saraswati"), had been born in Mumbai to a wealthy family in the music business and had impressed them all with her acclaimed voice. She'd been expected to go on to have a successful classical singing career, but at the age of nineteen she'd ruined everything by running off to have a love marriage with a Gujarati man studying in London. She'd gone on to have three daughters with Hemant Mehta, but when they were just five, three, and two years old, he'd tragically died.

Following a few years as a single mum in London, Saraswati had decided to make peace with her family, which resulted in reverting to her maiden name and her parents helping her launch a career singing in Bollywood films. Fast-track a few years and Saraswati had become a household name in India, while her daughters had become accustomed to spending all their time at boarding school. Saraswati's voice had featured in dozens of box-office hits and she was now so famous she'd occasionally been asked to actually appear in the films as an actress. Four years ago, Saraswati had remarried, and her wedding to film star MJ Shah had been so major that it had made British headlines as well as Indian ones. The happy couple now lived between Mumbai and London, where Saraswati's three daughters—Reevanshi Mehta, thirty-four; Sita Parmar, thirty-two, wife of entrepreneur Nitin Parmar and mother to twin daughters; and Jaya Mehta, thirty-one, lifestyle influencer—were still based.

This was the family history that Reeva had been brought up with and occasionally tried to amend online so it included her job title and omitted the nine-letter horror she'd been burdened with at birth (one that had been discarded when her kindergarten teacher had decided it was too complicated to pronounce). It was everything she knew; it was her life as much as it was her mother's. She was the five-year-old in the story, the teenager who'd been chucked into Wycombe Abbey, and the thirty-year-old who'd taken a week off work to awkwardly hover in a sari at her mum's five-day celeb wedding. A wedding that had subsequently ruined Reeva's life and destroyed her relationship with her sisters forever.

But Reeva couldn't think about that now. She was too busy trying to process the fact that everything she'd been told up until now was a lie. Her mum hadn't been tragically widowed at

thirty-two; she'd had a husband all along. And he'd been working as an *optometrist* of all things, just two hours away from London in *Leicester*—a city Reeva had barely heard of. Had they
divorced? Was her mum's new marriage even legal? And why had
her mum kept her dad's existence a secret from them for all these
years? Had her dad played a part in it too—or had it all been a
cruel trick of her mother's?

There were so many questions Reeva needed to find the answers to. Only she had absolutely no idea where to start. There
was no way she was calling her sisters, not after everything that
had happened. No. She'd let her mum—or, more likely, her
mum's lawyers—handle that. She'd just have to do what she always did and figure things out on her own. Reeva looked into the
panicked deep brown eyes of her reflection and reminded herself
she could handle this. She'd broken British legal history by getting a wronged billionaire's wife more than half his worth. And
last month she'd managed to get full custody for a man whose
wife had tried to kidnap their kids and take them to Utah to become Mormons. She could handle a dead dad.

All she had to do was think of her family situation as though
it were a case at work. There was no way she'd have to actually *do*
what her mum wanted and spend thirteen days with her sisters,
grieving a man she'd never known. No. She'd simply call the
lawyers to find out everything, then use her brains to get herself
out of this ridiculous will stipulation in the same way she would
for any of her clients: with minimal stress. Even if it meant defy-
ing her dead dad's last wishes.


"Guess you're going to Leicester!" Lakshmi gave her an apolo-
getic smile as Reeva groaned, theatrically dropping her head into

her hands. "Oh, come on, it might not be that bad. At least you get two weeks away from all the fucked-up drama of this place."

Reeva slumped into the brown armchair in Lakshmi's office and looked down at the brown carpet and brown furniture. They'd been asking Lee to update the decor for years, but he refused. Apparently the color brown projected an image of trustworthiness. "Are you kidding? I'm going to be *surrounded* by fucked-up drama. And I won't be getting paid for any of it. Surely there's got to be a way out?"

Lakshmi scrolled again through the document on Reeva's computer that Saraswati's lawyers had sent over and shook her head. "Sorry. It's airtight, Reevs. If you—or your sisters—want to get his inheritance, you've *all* got to go. Like, tomorrow, latest. You should probably be there right now."

"But it doesn't make any sense! He didn't even know us. Why would he want us to do his prayers for him?"

"Maybe he was religious?"

"No. None of it makes any sense. If we can't legally get out of it, then I think I should just leave it and turn down the inheritance."

"Oh, come on, you heard what the lawyers were hinting! He'd paid off his whole mortgage. You get a third of everything; you can't turn down money like that. At least give your share to charity." Lakshmi waved her pen in the air. "And it's not just about you, remember? You've got to be there so your sisters can get their share."

"I don't think they need the money either. Sita definitely doesn't—her house is amazing. And judging from what I've seen on Insta, neither does Jaya."

"You still follow her?" Lakshmi raised an eyebrow. "Is that healthy?"

"Is *any* of this healthy? How can this be happening, Lux? I don't understand why Mum told us Dad was dead when he was alive all this time. And why didn't she tell us *before* he died so we could actually speak to him?"

"I have no idea, but I cannot wait to find out," said Lakshmi. "You're going to have to go to his house to get answers."

"Uh, I'm not spending thirteen days with them hunting for clues. We're not the Hardy Boys."

"Yeah, they actually liked each other. And I'm pretty sure none of them slept with any of the others' fiancés."

Reeva shuddered. "Don't. I can't bear to think about it. I just . . . I've finally moved on. Things with Nick are going well. He likes me. I like him. It's the miracle I've been waiting for. And I hardly ever think about . . ." She took a deep breath. "Rakesh. Or Jaya. They're dead to me."

"Apart from when they pop up on your Insta feed."

"They're muted. Mainly. I just don't want to go and lock my-self up in a house with them in the middle of Leicester. It's going to bring it all back up. I want to leave it in the past where it be-longs."

Lakshmi nodded sympathetically and took a swig of her pro-secco. "I know. But, Reevs, you can do this."

Reeva went quiet. "I'm scared," she said eventually. "To face them again. It's all so humiliating."

"Hey!" Lakshmi walked over to Reeva and grabbed her shoul-ders, crouching down in front of her. "You've got nothing to feel bad about. It's Jaya who should feel awful. She's the boyfriend-stealing slut; not you."

"But it's so embarrassing that he chose her," whispered Reeva. Just talking about it all made her feel like an awkward teenager again; the tall, gangly girl who was always overlooked in favor of her prettier younger sisters. They'd all gotten on well enough at home—as kids, they'd spent hours rehearsing gory enactments of *Pocahontas* and *Mulan* with Reeva directing their performances ("Sita, more ketchup!," "Jaya, scream louder—you've just been murdered!"). Even as teenagers, they'd had a mildly companionable existence during the school holidays, bonding over their mother's ridiculous behavior and swapping CDs for their Discmans.

But it had been different at school, where Reeva was constantly referred to as "Jaya and Sita's sister." It was mortifying. *She* was the big sister; she should have been breaking rules, gaining a reputation for being cool, and paving the path of rebellion for her younger sisters. But instead, she'd always felt more like a lost middle child—an oddity, with a nine-letter name no one could pronounce compared to her sisters' cute four-letter ones and dark brown skin that stood out against her sisters' lighter complexions. It didn't matter so much in England, but every time they went to India, everyone spent the whole time gasping over how "fair" her sisters were while mouthing their condolences to Saraswati over Reeva's dark skin. It wasn't surprising that a young Reeva had internalized their colorism and concluded that she would never be as beautiful as her sisters.

Adult Reeva knew it was time to let go of all these insecurities and recognize her worth. At least that was what her therapist had been telling her for £60 an hour for the last four years. And if she was rational about it, she could recognize that comparing herself to her sisters wasn't healthy—they were all different. Back at school, Jaya had been voted "Most Likely to Be a Model" and Sita "Most Likely to Be Prime Minister," while Reeva hadn't made any of the "most" lists at all. But she had surpassed her sisters academically, getting straight A's while they brought home a collection of B's and C's, and she'd eventually carved out her own

corner in Model United Nations. Her friends there weren't popular enough to make any of the "most" lists either, but they'd been
loyal, kind, and smart, and she still saw them to catch up—well,
when they could get time away from their partners and children.
And Reeva had never managed to have a stream of boyfriends at
school like her sisters had, but she'd gotten there at university.
When she'd met Rakesh.

"It isn't embarrassing," Lakshmi replied firmly. "Jaya's a basic
Barbie. Rakesh is a cliché. End of. You're better off without him,
Reevs. I mean, who chooses some dumb influencer over *you*?
Think how shit their lives must be. Rakesh has to spend the en-
tire time taking endless photos of her, while she can't ever eat a
single carb."

"It doesn't look so shitty when they're both traveling the
world, wearing Dior in waterfalls," commented Reeva. "I don't
own *any* Dior. And I don't remember the last time I had enough
holiday leave to go anywhere near a waterfall."

"Uh, Dior's overrated. As are waterfalls. They're so much
colder than they look. Jaya probably photoshops the hell out of
her nipples. And . . . you've got Nick. A music agent is so much
cooler than a—sorry, what did Rakesh even do before he became an Insta husband?"

Reeva smiled despite herself. "Mergers and acquisitions. And
as much as I wish I did, I haven't exactly 'got' Nick. It's only been
three months. We haven't even had the 'what are we' chat yet.
God, the whole thing makes me feel like a teenager—I have no
idea what I'm doing."

"You'll have the chat soon," said Lakshmi confidently. "Maybe
even tonight. Once you tell him you've got a secret dad who just
died."

Reeva looked at her in alarm. "I can't talk to him about all this! He'll think I'm mad. His family is so . . . normal and stable and *British*. Whereas I've got a famous mum who's married to one of India's most loved actors, a sister who's marrying my ex, another sister who helped her do it, and as of the last eight hours, a dead dad I never knew about. It sounds like the plot in one of Mum's movies."

"Ooh, it would make such a good Bollywood film!" Lakshmi clapped her hands in delight. "Like if he was, I don't know, a major criminal whose actions were going to get you all killed, so he faked his death to protect you."

Reeva raised an eyebrow. "He worked at Specsavers. I don't think he was a criminal mastermind."

"Specsavers would be the ideal cover if he was, though," pointed out Lakshmi. "But it's fine, I've got more. How about . . . your dad was gay, and people were starting to find out, so he had to leave your lives to go and live his own?"

"Nice plot, but it's not 1950 anymore. And you know my mum loves everything LGBTQ+. She's been tweeting about it for years. She would have been thrilled to have a gay ex-husband to drink mimosas with."

"Yeah, your mum definitely isn't the average Indian," agreed Lakshmi. "She's more liberal than we are."

"Uh, I subscribe to *The Guardian*," said Reeva, looking down as her phone vibrated. "Oh, it's Lee. I guess I should go. What am I going to tell him about all this? Can I really just leave for two weeks? What about the Sherwood-Brown case?"

"Reevs, you're allowed a break from work. And you're allowed bereavement leave when your dad has died. Just . . . maybe leave out the fact that you never actually knew him."

Reeva sighed. "Okay. But, two weeks of prayers? Isn't that overkill? I thought they lasted a day."

"In St. John's Wood, maybe."

"What?

Lakshmi shook her head. "I forget how you grew up without a proper Indian community. Basically, everyone does it differently. My very Gujarati cousins in Leicester always do a full thirteen days of prayers, with the funeral in the middle and the kriya at the end—like your dad's having. But my relatives in Harrow only do a week of evening prayers with no kriya. And our Sindhi friends who grew up near where you did in St. John's Wood just do the one day."

Reeva raised an eyebrow at her. "There's a postcode lottery for grief?"

"Sure. The more affluent you are, the less time you have to mourn."

"Well, that's my privilege checked."

"And all before nine a.m.! Nah, I think it's just different family traditions. It's all pretty confusing. And I guess because your parents are from different parts of India, it's even more confusing for you."

"Great. So what else should I expect if I go?"

"Dhal and rice. A lot of it."

"Not paneer and chaats?" asked Reeva in disappointment. "The street food is my favorite part of Indian events."

Lakshmi shook her head. "Sorry—not for the first week. Your dad's family might do it differently, but mine don't eat fun food until after the funeral. Week one is basic staying-alive grub, then in the second week, you're allowed to eat all the dead person's favorite meals."

"What? That doesn't make sense. Surely you'd want to comfort-eat delicious carbs when your loved one has just died?"

Lakshmi shrugged. "At least this way you don't end up putting on extra weight. Combine the food with all the crying and it's basically two weeks of extreme dieting. They should really use that to sell the extended version of prayers to people. 'Two weeks of bereavement, and ooh, look, you've lost a dress size!'"

"Well, that'll make a change from everyone telling me how 'healthy' I look."

"Ah yes, the Asian synonym for *fat*."

Reeva stood up and checked her phone. "Great. Well, let me see if Brian's gotten back to me about— Oh fuck!"

"What is it?!"

Reeva looked up from her phone, stricken. "An e-mail. From Sita. It looks long."

"What's the big deal? I thought you spoke to Sita all the time? Don't you FaceTime the twins every week?"

"Every two weeks, but Sita and I don't 'speak.' We discuss logistical details on WhatsApp, and I get the twins every third Sunday. We don't e-mail, and we never write messages longer than a sentence." Reeva glanced anxiously at the phone. "This doesn't look good."

"Here, I'll read it." Lakshmi grabbed the phone from Reeva. "Okay. Ahem." She raised her voice an octave and began reading. "'Reeva, why are the lawyers saying you're considering not coming to our dad's house? I know you're a hotshot lawyer who doesn't need the money, but spare a thought for the rest of us. Jaya has a wedding to plan, and I'm a mother of two. I thought you at least cared about the twins. This money could make a huge difference to their futures. Can you stop being so selfish? We're heading up to Leicester tonight and expect to see you there. Hopefully we can figure out this gaping hole in our family history while we're at it. Sita.' Wow, she is *co-old*."

"See why I don't want to go?" cried Reeva. "I can't bear it. I know I'm the oldest sister, but I just feel kind of . . . pathetic around them. They're so confident and *scary*. Every time I go to Surrey to pick up the twins, I have to put on your playlist. It's the only way I can face Sita."

"Hey, you're a 'hotshot lawyer,' remember? And I've seen you at work; you're scary too. Reevs, you can handle your sisters. And isn't it all worth it to get to the bottom of this whole mystery about your dad? You've got to be desperate to know why no one told you about him."

Reeva sighed. "Obviously. I just . . . Me, Sita, and Jaya? Together for almost two weeks? Even before the Rakesh thing we would have killed each other."

Lakshmi put an arm around her. "In that case, I guess we'd better write your will too."

REEVA PUSHED THE front door shut behind her and Nick, almost tripping over the doormat in the process. She was drunker than she'd thought.

Nick followed her into the living room. The walls were painted a very pale pink with gray wooden molding, and the sofas were navy velvet. There were a few photos on the alcove shelves—a series of Reeva and Lakshmi through the years, from selfies on the beach to drunk dancing at weddings—nestled among brightly colored books with "Booker Prize" and "Women's Prize for Fiction" stickers on them. Everything was arranged immaculately, from glass art deco lamps to slate coasters, and there was zero clutter. It all looked like it was straight out of the pages of an interior design magazine—apart from the enormous wicker cat tree planted in front of the window.

Nick slipped out of his navy blazer to reveal a soft white

T-shirt and sat down on the armchair as he unlaced his vegan leather trainers. He watched Reeva in bemusement as she went over to stroke the black-and-white cat installed on the middle of its perch. She stroked the cat twice before it tried to bite her.

"Progress!" said Reeva. "Last time she only let me stroke her once."

"So . . . your cat still doesn't like you?" asked Nick.

"Hey, she tolerates me," said Reeva, turning back to him. "Which is embarrassing because I did a *Daily Mail* quiz the other day called 'What relationship do you have with your cat?' and it turns out we're codependent. Only it's not mutual."

Nick smiled politely. "I'm going to have to admit I'm not really a cat person."

"Oh, neither was I," Reeva assured him. "Until Lakshmi shoved Fluffy Panda onto me. And now here I am. In love with a cat that hates me."

"Poor Reeva. Come here." He opened his arms and Reeva walked into them, tiptoeing to kiss him. He wrapped his hands around her shoulders, slowly sliding them up to cradle her head. Nick always kissed her like it was the finale of a rom-com and Reeva loved every second of it. She leaned in happily, temporarily forgetting about wills, sisters, and dead dads—until his hand almost reached her bald patch. She pulled away with a start.

"Sorry, uh, I should feed FP." She turned away quickly and walked into the kitchen. FP leaped out of the tree to follow her, snuggling up against her legs as she opened the food cupboard.

"Cats are so fickle," said Nick. "It's why I prefer dogs."

Reeva frowned—it was not a good sign that the guy she was dating did not like the best thing in her life. She forced herself to remember that pre-FP, she'd been the same. Or even worse. She used to tell people she wasn't an animal person. But when

Lakshmi had turned up on her doorstep almost three months ago with a kitten christened Fluffy Panda, everything had changed. "It's to help with the alopecia," Lakshmi had explained, dumping the scrawny cat into Reeva's confused arms the day after she'd found the bald patch (1.7 centimeters). "I read an article on how pets can help with stress; stroking them is calming. And I figured it would stop you from feeling so depressed about how much hair you're molting all over your flat. Because now the cat can molt its hair with you!"

As expected, FP did molt all over Reeva's flat. Her black-and-white fur relentlessly found its way onto every single item of her owner's, including her predominantly black-and-cream wardrobe, which meant Reeva now spent several extra hours a week cleaning. This was just one example of FP failing to lower Reeva's stress levels and instead managing to do the exact opposite. Because FP did not like being showered in hugs, strokes, belly rubs, or anything that would release stress-busting oxytocin in her owner. She'd accept three hugs a day from Reeva—all before six a.m.—before asserting her boundaries and biting her. Her favorite hobby appeared to be turning up her little wet nose at all of Reeva's efforts to make her life better, like bulk-buying the overpriced organic food she was currently refusing to eat.

Which was why Reeva was now on her knees on the kitchen floor, waving a bowl of Chicken Princess at a cat who was completely ignoring her.

"She . . . doesn't eat her food?" asked Nick.

"She only likes the cheap stuff," explained Reeva. "But I can't let her eat it. It's only five percent meat and ninety-five percent unknown substances."

"You sound exactly like my friends who have kids," Nick said, laughing. "The ones that shop at Waitrose."

Reeva suddenly realized she was crouched on the floor of her flat like a crazy cat lady while an incredibly attractive man—a man who did not like cats—was watching everything. She stood up quickly. "You know what, she can eat the cheap stuff for once." She pulled out a pouch of processed lamb and let the firm jelly plop satisfyingly into a bowl. FP instantly ran over and began gobbling it up at record speed, purring loudly. Reeva shook her head. "Wow, I wish a bowl of twenty-five-p meat could cheer me up that much. I'd eat five pounds' worth."

"I didn't realize you needed cheering up so badly. Am I not doing my job properly?"

"Oh, no, it's just . . . uh, I've had a tough day."

"Really, what's wrong? And why am I only just hearing about all this now?"

Reeva hesitated. She had avoided mentioning her dad drama throughout the whole dinner, instead choosing to share funny anecdotes about her clients, making Nick laugh so much he'd almost choked on his tuna taco. He'd called her hilarious and said she was the most interesting woman he'd ever dated. Reeva hadn't wanted him to switch those adjectives for *unhinged* and *dramatic*, so she hadn't said anything. "Um . . . I just have some family stuff going on. But it's a lot, and there's no need to go into it with you, honestly. I mean, it's intense."

"Of course," said Nick, leaning against her dove-gray cupboards (with gold handles; they matched the gold frames of the *Vogue* prints hanging on her walls), looking so perfectly at home in her flat that Reeva was starting to wonder how she'd ever enjoyed being there without him. "You don't have to say anything at all. But I'm here if you want to."

Reeva bit her lip. She was so aware of not wanting to fuck this up. Nick was the best guy she'd dated in a long time, even though he hardly ticked any of the boxes she'd been so obsessed with in her twenties. Like the fact that he was divorced. At forty-three, he was also nine years older than her. And his lifestyle—jetting around the world to manage famous singers—was not conducive to the calm family setup that Reeva had desperately craved ever since she'd been shuttled off to boarding school. But after four years of dating in her thirties, she was now aware that this stuff didn't really matter. What mattered was that Nick came closest to hitting the Holy Quartet—the relationship checklist she'd invented with Lakshmi—out of any guy she'd been with since Rakesh. When she was with him, she felt (1) true desire, (2) genuine interest in him, (3) a fun lightness, and (4) the safety to be herself. Well, almost.

Reeva knew that the safety normally came with time, but it had been three months, and she was still scared to show Nick even 10 percent of her crazy. She knew she had to try and show him her authentic self by being more vulnerable with him—only then would she be able to see if he was right for her. Or at least, that was what a podcast on "Feeling Safe in Relationships After Childhoods Filled with Abandonment" had told her.

"Okay, well, um, my mum called me this morning from Mumbai to say my dad is dead," said Reeva. "No, it's fine, you don't need to look so sad for me! I thought he'd already died. When I was five. But it turns out, nope, he only just died today. They'd kept him a secret from me and my sisters. And, yeah, so now I have to obey his last dying wish and go spend thirteen days at his house, grieving with my sisters. It's one of the stipulations in his will, for his inheritance." She paused. "Does that make sense?"

"Uh, wow." Nick looked taken aback. "Yeah. That is a lot.

God, I can't believe your mum pretended he was dead, and . . . now he is. It's so dramatic."

"Welcome to my family," said Reeva, suddenly aware that she didn't feel as safe as she'd hoped she would. Was it her fault? His?

"So are you going to go to his house? And your mum, is she coming? To explain it all?"

Reeva snorted, then tried to cover it up with a cough. "Uh, no. She's conveniently stuck in Mumbai on a film set, so she can't come over. Her lawyers were the ones who properly explained the whole thing to me. I guess I have to go. My sisters won't get the money unless I turn up."

"Your mum's on a Bollywood film set?"

Reeva flushed. She'd purposely evaded telling Nick about her mum. But now it was too late. "She mainly just sings playback. She only acts occasionally."

"Wait." Nick's face lit up. "Your mum's not . . . Saraswati Acharya?"

"You know of her?"

"Of her!" cried Nick. "She's major! One of my artists wanted her on his backing track, but she was too busy."

Reeva shrugged awkwardly. "That's Mum."

"That's amazing! I can't believe I didn't realize until now— you look so similar! But you have different surnames?"

"She went back to her maiden name once my dad, well, didn't die."

"Isn't she married to MJ Shah? How come you never mentioned it before?!"

"I . . . don't really like to make a thing of it. But yes, they're married."

"Wow. She's a total legend. You must be so proud of her."

Reeva forced herself to smile. "Right." This was why she hated talking about her mum—people always made so many assumptions about how she must feel about it all, when the truth was she wished she had a mum with a normal job. It was at times like this she felt the loss of not speaking to her sisters—they were the only ones who knew how she felt.

"Are you okay?" asked Nick. He took her hand and led her over to the oval glass table with its teal suede chairs. "Let's sit a moment. This is all pretty big stuff. You must be so overwhelmed. I can't imagine how I'd feel if I found out that the dad I thought had died when I was a kid had been alive all this time."

Reeva felt tears springing to her eyes. She blinked them away in alarm. She hadn't cried once since her mum had called—she hadn't even felt the *need* to—but hearing Nick repeat the facts to her made everything feel more real. And his obvious shock made Reeva realize the enormity of what had happened. She just hadn't let herself recognize it until now.

She laughed in embarrassment as she ran her finger under her eyes. "Sorry. I guess it is a lot."

"You don't need to apologize."

"Sorry," said Reeva automatically. "God." She put her head into her hands. It was all just too much. Growing up, all she'd ever wished was for her dad to still be alive. She couldn't really remember him, and even though her mum didn't speak particularly highly of him ("Oh, we had nothing in common; no idea why we ever thought marriage was a good idea"), Reeva had idealized this man she'd never really known. Every time her mum let her down, promising she'd read her a bedtime story and then blowing kisses and apologies at her as she went out to a last-minute party, or sending her PA to parents' day because she was still on set, Reeva had fantasized about what life would be like if her dad were still alive. He would have read her stories, he would have turned up to parents' day, and he definitely would have remembered she hated raisins.

And now, all these years later, she was finding out that he *had* been alive. He'd been living just two hours away, and no one had told her. She could have had a dad. But she'd been denied her biggest dream, and she had no idea why. Had he not wanted her? Did he have another family? No, the lawyers had told her he'd never remarried or had more kids. But then why hadn't he come back to the kids he'd already had? Reeva's lips trembled. She'd thought she'd already been dealt a lifetime's worth of rejection from her mum and then Rakesh, but now she was being given a whole new dose: a dad who'd rejected her for twenty-nine years.

"What are you thinking?" asked Nick. "It must be a lot to process."

Reeva swallowed and forced herself to lift her head up and smile. She didn't want to break down in front of Nick. It was way too soon for that. "Yep. Families."

"I can't even imagine. Mine is painfully normal, I'm afraid. But I'm happy to offer up a sympathetic ear."

"Thanks, Nick. I appreciate it. But don't worry. I'll be okay."

"I don't doubt it. You're so strong—it's one of my favorite things about you. My exes were always emotional wrecks. They couldn't handle anything. But you're always so calm when you talk about your life. I feel like you can handle anything."

Reeva glowed. She felt so lucky to be with Nick—someone who effortlessly complimented her and made her feel special. When she'd broken up with Rakesh and her life had fallen apart, she'd found it impossible to believe she'd ever be happy with a man again. How could she when Rakesh had been so right for her? They'd loved doing all the same things—long heath walks on the weekend, cozy pub dinners, organizing fun trips away with their friends (well, his, but they'd become hers too)—and most importantly, they'd always understood each other. Rakesh had been the one person she'd never had to explain herself to because he just got it. How lonely she could feel sometimes. How the law made so much more sense than her emotions. How her family meant the world to her no matter how they treated her. Until he'd ruined everything.

Nick wasn't anything like Rakesh—he was much more of an extrovert, and his life was so glamorous that she couldn't imagine he'd ever be content with the quiet stability she'd had with Rakesh. But he was kind. Interesting. Fun. A lot more fun than Rakesh, actually. And she had a connection with him. After all the bad first dates she'd gone on, she'd given up hope of ever having that again. But now that she'd found it, she was desperate not to lose it—especially not by crying on him about her dad.

She cleared her throat. "Anyway. I probably shouldn't have too late a night. It looks like I'm going to have to go to Leicester tomorrow."

"Leicester?"

"Where my dad lived. I have to sort his house out with my sisters. And, you know, grieve him, and figure out the whole family secret. I am *not* looking forward to it."

"I'm sorry," said Nick, with an expression that did genuinely look sorry. "Are you going to go for the full thirteen days?"

"I think I'm going to have to. But it's not great timing. One of my clients is desperately trying to stop his ex from taking their kids abroad. But he's a struggling artist while she's insanely rich—which means she's got all the power, and he could go from seeing his kids weekly to once a year. It makes me so angry to think she'd ruin her kids' lives just for her selfish means!" Reeva paused then grinned. "Which is why I hired a private investigator who found out she has a coke habit and turned up to parents' evening high."

Nick laughed. "Of course you did. I love how into your job you are. And it sounds like you do it for all the right reasons rather than just the money."

Reeva blushed. "Oh, that's just how it works with family law. You can't help but feel for your clients because you end up knowing every detail of their personal lives. Even the things neither of you want to know."

"I wish you'd been my divorce lawyer; that would have made the whole process a hell of a lot less painful." Nick suddenly shook his head. "I'm sorry! I can't believe I'm bringing up my divorce on a date. Sorry. So you were saying you're going to be in Leicester for two weeks?"

"Thirteen days. Although"—Reeva's face brightened—"it started today, so I'll only be there for twelve days."

"Maybe . . . I could come up and visit? Moral support?"

An image of Jaya flirting with Nick while Sita grilled him about his extravagant lifestyle flashed into Reeva's head. She swallowed an urge to gag. "Uh, no, you don't have to. I think it's going to be pretty intense. And, you know, family time." Then she remembered Lakshmi's top piece of advice with men: thank them every time they offer to do something for you, even if it's the total opposite of what you want, otherwise they may never offer again. "But that's a really lovely thought. Thank you."

"Sure. Well, you know where I am if you need me. Do you want to head to bed?"

"Yes, please. I need today to end. No offense."

"None taken." Nick stood up and reached out a hand. "Coming?"

"You go ahead. I just need to turn FP's robot on so she can play with it. I'll come soon."

"Oh yes, you will. If I have anything to do with it . . ."

Reeva couldn't help smiling as Nick leaned in to kiss her again. It was perfect timing. She was done talking about her family—so done—and if there was one thing that was going to take her mind off it all, it was climbing straight into bed with Nick and his very sizable appendage.

## CHAPTER 3

### Day 2

REEVA PULLED UP outside a compact semidetached house in a quiet cul-de-sac. Her father's home. It looked surprisingly normal. All the houses on the road—and the surrounding maze of Elizabeth Streets, Victoria Roads, and Edward Places that Reeva had gotten lost in—were identical. Light terra-cotta brick, bright white window frames with symmetrical net curtains, and a little green front lawn with a singular apple tree bang in the middle. They all looked like the kind of house a child would draw, complete with a chimney and car in the driveway. Reeva pushed her '90s tortoiseshell sunglasses high up onto her head so she could better inspect the house. It looked surprisingly cheery considering it belonged to a man living a secret existence from his three daughters. She wasn't sure what she'd been expecting; something more Gothic, depressing? But this just looked ordinary. The only noticeable oddity was that her father had lived there alone. Judging by the plastic bicycles and balls in the adjacent gardens, it was very much a family neighborhood. But Hemant Mehta had chosen to live there without his family—without even having the courtesy to tell his family, or even let them know he was *living* anywhere.

Reeva forced herself to leave the safety of her car. She still couldn't believe she was doing this. But here she was, standing outside her father's home, next to her black Mini Cooper, with two weeks' worth of clothing in her suitcase. Lakshmi had agreed to move into her flat to take care of FP, Lee had been left with no option but to tell her to take as much time as she needed after Reeva had cc'd HR in an e-mail, and Nick had given her a post-coital kiss goodbye that morning, promising to call as soon as he got to work. Reeva checked her phone in case she'd missed his call. She hadn't.

With a sigh, Reeva put her phone away and dragged her leather carry-on up the paved stone drive. She could do this. Everything would be fine. She took a deep breath and reached out to press the old-fashioned bell, but before her finger could touch the plastic, the front door swung open to reveal a young woman in thick, black square glasses. Her dark hair was pulled into a messy bun, and her arms were crossed firmly across her oversized gray jumper. "Took you long enough."

"Sita. Hi," said Reeva, lugging her stuff onto the porch step, noticing her sister made zero effort to help. "So, this is it, huh? Dad's house."

Sita stepped back so Reeva could navigate past her in the narrow corridor. "Yep. Jaya and I got here last night, so we've taken the spare bedrooms. You'll have to stay in Dad's bedroom."

Reeva dropped her suitcase and looked at her sister in horror. "You're kidding! I can't stay in his bed! Isn't that where he . . . you know?"

"Died? Yeah. Heart attack in the middle of the night. Didn't see it coming. There are clean bedsheets though. I left them on the bed for you. And there's not exactly anywhere else for you to sleep."

"I'll just take the sofa. Is it through here?" Reeva pushed open the only door in the hallway and found herself in a small square living room with glass French doors that led into a kitchen. A two-seater white sofa was pushed against the back wall. Next to it were a chrome floor lamp and a small pine side table. The only other piece of furniture in the room was a wide television on a stand against the opposing wall. Propped up against the screen was a blown-up photograph of a serious-looking Indian man in wire-frame glasses. A homemade garland of garish fresh flowers— the bright yellow and pink ones that were always on offer in supermarkets—was draped over the photograph.

"Meet Dad," said Sita. "He doesn't look exactly like the pics Mum had of him and us as kids, does he? To be honest, I wouldn't be surprised if he was a different person than the man she told us about. I wouldn't put anything past her."

Reeva stopped in her tracks. As a child, she'd gone over every single photograph she could find of her dad. But they'd come to an end after her dad had turned thirty-five. That was it. He was frozen in her memory as that young man—practically the same age she was now—with his wavy brown hair and big smile. She knew his face by heart. But if she'd walked past her father in the street days earlier, there was no way she could have recognized him. It made her heart clench. She took a step toward the photo, examining it closely. His expression was serious, but his eyes were kind. And the wide nose and strong jaw were the same as the ones she'd studied as a child. "It's definitely Dad. Look at the eyes." Sita shrugged in response. "Hey, who did the flowers?"

"An elderly woman who knew Dad from the mandir. There's a lot of them around."

"Right," said Reeva, looking around the room. The sofa was shorter than she was, and she wasn't sure that sleeping in front of a huge photo of her dad's face was much better than sleeping in his room. "Where are the twins? I bought Alisha a vampire book she's going to love. And soldiers for Amisha."

"I'm trying *not* to encourage their obsession with war and murder."

"Sorry. I just wanted to get them things they want rather than dumping dolls on them like Mum did with us."

Sita lowered her arms. "Well, at least you didn't buy an actual gun like Nitin did. I mean, it's a kids' gun. But still."

"So are they upstairs?"

"They're at school. I can't just drag them out."

Reeva's face fell. She'd been counting on her nieces being there. They were the only members of her family who seemed to like her—and she, in turn, adored them. There was no way she'd be able to survive the next twelve days without them. "What? I thought they'd be here. Can't you just take them out of school?"

Sita shook her head in annoyance. "Only someone who doesn't have kids would suggest that. You can't just pull them out of school these days. It gets marked down on their record."

"For bereavement? Their granddad's dead."

"Granddad? None of us knew he existed," scoffed Sita. "Anyway, it's October half term on Monday. Nitin's bringing them up tomorrow."

Reeva's face relaxed in relief. "Oh, thank god. I mean, cool. Can't wait to see them."

"Right. So are you going to take your stuff upstairs or what? You obviously can't sleep here."

Reeva took one more longing look at the tiny sofa, calculating whether discomfort beat sleeping in a deathbed. She would give anything to be back in her king-size bed with its natural fiber mattress—perfectly shaped to her body after four years—and soft bamboo sheets. "He has a double bed upstairs?"

"Yup. IKEA's finest."

"Fine."

She dragged her belongings up the stairs—yet again Sita hadn't offered to help—until she reached the landing: a narrow cream-carpeted space framed with four brown doors. She opened the first. Bathroom. Clean. White. Sad-looking bathmat. The second: a sparse double bedroom with brightly colored kids' toys in it that suggested it was already claimed by Sita. The third: a single bed with a young woman in a crop top and tight jeans sprawled across its maroon bedsheets.

Reeva froze.

She hadn't seen her youngest sister since Rakesh had chosen her over Reeva. And now here she was. Scrolling through her phone, less than two meters away.

Reeva felt sick. She couldn't do this. It was too much. She wasn't ready. She tried to back out of the room and close the door before Jaya saw her, but it was too late. The floorboards creaked and Jaya's head whipped around. Reeva locked eyes with her sister and swallowed. Before she had time to react, Jaya squealed loudly.

"Reeva!" she cried, springing off the bed. "It's been forever!" She wrapped her arms around Reeva, embracing her tightly.

Over the last four years, Reeva had imagined endless scenarios of what it would be like to meet her youngest sister again—from icy coldness to blaring arguments to flat-out silence—but never once had it occurred to her that Jaya would do something as outrageous as *hug* her. She stood in rigid shock as Jaya squeezed her. She could smell her sister's perfume—the same sickly sweet one she'd been wearing for years. Baccarat Rouge 540, that was it. By Maison Francis Kurkdjian. She'd given Reeva some for Christmas once. Before everything, obviously. Reeva had been touched that her sister had spent so much on her, but then Jaya had let slip that the luxury brand had gifted it to her. Of course her sister hadn't actually paid for it. Jaya always got what Jaya wanted with minimal effort. Whether it was perfume or other people's boyfriends.

"How have you been?" asked Jaya, finally pulling away from her sister's stiff frame, widening her annoyingly green eyes. "You look great. This jumpsuit is amazing. The khaki looks so good on you."

"Um, thanks," said Reeva, unable to bring herself to pay Jaya a compliment in return. Why was her sister acting like everything was fine? They hadn't seen each other since the biggest betrayal imaginable, and now Jaya was exchanging pleasantries? But she felt satisfied that Jaya had noticed her outfit, especially after she'd spent an embarrassingly long time choosing it for this very moment.

"God, this is, like, completely crazy," said Jaya. "I don't even know what to say." Reeva nodded slowly, glad that Jaya was finally acknowledging the enormous elephant in the room. "I mean, as if Dad was alive all this time!"

Reeva blinked in surprise. Was Jaya really going to skip straight to the Dad stuff and ignore her treachery? She should be groveling for forgiveness!

"It's just so sad," continued Jaya. "How could Mum deny us a lifetime of having a father? Especially when he seems so normal and sweet. Look at his little house. Isn't it cute?"

Reeva felt her head spinning. None of this was panning out the way she'd thought. She should be the one in control of this conversation, making Jaya feel small and stupid. But instead, it was happening in reverse. Why was Jaya acting like she hadn't stolen Reeva's boyfriend and ruined her life? And why wasn't she doing anything about it?!

"Typical Mum." Reeva swung around to see Sita standing behind her in the doorway, arms crossed. "Dropping this on us the day he dies. Because it never occurred to her that we might like to visit him while he was still alive."

"I know, right," agreed Jaya. "She's the worst."

Reeva cleared her throat and forced herself to speak. She needed to get out of her head and act normal. "Yeah. It was not what I expected when I took a call from her at work."

Sita's eyes narrowed. "You still speak to her?"

"Wow," gasped Jaya. "What did she say? I didn't know you guys spoke. I haven't spoken to her in years!"

"Uh, well, we don't exactly speak every night. We just Face-Time sometimes."

Sita shook her head. "Obviously you still speak to her. You always were her favorite."

"That's not true," protested Reeva. "She barely even remembers what my job is."

"At least she recognizes you have one," pointed out Jaya. "She thinks being an influencer is a hobby."

"You think that's bad; she doesn't even know the names of her only grandkids," added Sita. "She texted me asking how Alisha and Anisha are! Is it really that hard to remember Alisha and *Amisha*?"

Reeva was impressed her mum had got only one letter wrong, but now didn't feel like the time to voice that thought.

"She's never been a real mum to us," continued Sita. "I'm twice the mum she'll ever be, and I spend most of the time sleep-deprived, wishing I'd waited another decade before I had kids."

"Well, I've long given up any expectation of her being any different," said Reeva lightly. "So speaking to her doesn't really bother me. She is what she is."

"Yeah, a full-blown narcissist," declared Sita. "It took her *six months* to come and visit the twins after I gave birth. And when she deigned to grace us with her presence, do you know what she gifted us? Therapy."

"Amazing!" cried Jaya. "I'm totally going to get therapy when I have kids. I mean, if. It's really important to heal your blockages before you raise children."

Reeva closed her eyes and tried not to imagine a day when Jaya and Rakesh had a child together.

"It is an insulting and inappropriate gift," said Sita. "And she didn't hold the twins *once*. But I still made the effort to go to her wedding. And then you know what happened . . ."

Reeva frowned; how was Rakesh cheating on her linked to Sita cutting out their mum?

"She spent the entire speech going on about MJ's grandkids— some average toddlers who spent the whole time crying—without even *mentioning* the twins," continued Sita indignantly. "That was when I vowed to never speak to her again."

"My moment was when I posted a photo of me and her on Mother's Day," said Jaya. "I wrote the nicest caption, and it got loads of engagement. But then Mum calls me screaming, asking why I posted it without asking her! As if you need your mum's approval to share a picture of her holding you minutes after giving birth! Honestly, I can't deal with someone as vain as that."

Reeva raised an eyebrow but decided not to say anything.

"Well, seeing as you're the only one of us who hasn't been forced to cut off ties with her, what did she say?" asked Sita. "When you spoke to her about Dad."

Reeva smiled tightly. "You know what she's like. It's impossible to get anything out of her that she doesn't want to share. I just got the basic facts—that she's in Mumbai on a film set for the next few weeks. Minimal signal, naturally. And that Dad died suddenly and his last wishes were for us to come here. Oh, and he's an optometrist."

"We already know all that," said Sita. "Did you not ask her *why* she hid all this from us?"

"Of course I did! She was her typical self about it. Avoided it all. Said it wasn't easy for her, and it wasn't something she wanted to discuss on the phone."

"No wonder you're the only one who's still in touch with her. You accept everything she says without pushing back."

"I do not!" cried Reeva, stung.

"Well, none of this is a surprise, really, is it?" continued Sita. "We'd better just do what we always do and handle this alone."

"Satya Auntie can help," offered Jaya. "She's such a babe; you'll love her, Reeva. Ultimate Gwyneth Paltrow vibes."

"That's Dad's sister?"

"Yes," said Sita. "Which you'd know if you were here last night. Oh my god, chill, you don't need to look so upset—I was just saying it would have been good if you could have been here. Anyway, go freshen up or whatever, and we'll fill you in on what we know."


REEVA SAT DOWN in the middle of her dad's bed and closed her eyes. She'd been in the house for only twenty minutes and already she felt nothing like the thirty-four-year-old woman she was meant to be. Instead, she felt exactly like the teenager she thought she'd left behind. She'd spent a fortune on therapy; how was she *still* battling the same insecurities that had plagued her since puberty? This was not how things were meant to go. But then again, nothing was really turning out how it was meant to.

On second thought, Reeva wasn't sure it ever had. She'd been so naive when she'd gone to university, thinking that finally her life would start to take on the same shiny appeal that Jaya's and Sita's had. But it hadn't. She'd felt just as out of place at Cambridge as she had at school. It didn't make sense; she'd had as privileged an upbringing as most of the people there, and she was just as smart as them. But for some reason, Reeva had never felt comfortable around those confident beings who all seemed to know how to make pithy yet intellectual comments in seminars, exactly what one was meant to wear to an all-night ball, and most daunting of all, how to start sexual relationships with each other.

It had only been when Reeva had met Rakesh at the end of her second year that things had started to improve. With him, she'd finally felt seen. He was an only child, and with no experience of what complex families looked like, he'd calmly accepted her bizarre family setup as normal. He'd never judged her or expected her to be a certain way—even though his mum had all Saraswati's albums and could be described as a legit superfan. He'd quietly taken Reeva under his wing, introducing her to his friend group and encouraging her to apply for internships at Magic Circle firms. When she'd succeeded, he'd been truly thrilled for her. The only downside had been that he hadn't gotten along with Lakshmi—the best thing to come out of said law internship. But Reeva hadn't particularly minded; she didn't need her boyfriend and best friend to like each other. What mattered was that she finally had a boyfriend and a best friend and that they'd never leave her.

Until nine years later when Rakesh had cheated on her with her little sister. Just thinking about it brought the brutal agony straight back to Reeva. She couldn't believe how much it still hurt. The pain was as physical as it was emotional. She hugged her knees into her chest and squeezed her eyes shut. She didn't want to relive the memory, but she didn't have a choice. Her mind was replaying it yet again.

Her mum's wedding. Udaipur. They'd all been at a fancy hotel in the middle of the lake. Even though it was a weeklong celebration, Reeva had been having a surprisingly good time. It was just so beautiful, and the whole setting shouted romance. She felt grateful to have Rakesh by her side, and she loved how well he got along with her family. They'd been a little group of their own—Reeva and Rakesh, Sita and Nitin, and Jaya—sitting together at all the events, with Reeva happily spending afternoons curled up with Sita and the babies.

But while she'd been bonding with her nieces, Rakesh had been bonding with her sister. Reeva had been so embarrassingly naive. She'd thought it was sweet that he was hanging out with Jaya, who must have felt lonely without a plus-one. It wasn't till the last day that she'd found out the truth. They'd been having a goodbye brunch on the Sunday morning after the official wedding when Reeva had seen a message from Jaya flash up on Rakesh's phone. He'd been getting her dosas from the buffet, so she'd opened his phone to read it. She'd known his passcode for years—he'd never bothered to hide it from her—and Reeva had assumed Jaya wanted something from the breakfast. When she'd seen it was a picture message, her stomach had tightened. And when she'd opened it, everything had changed.

Reeva had run to the bathroom, with the phone still in her hand, and projectile vomited. Her sister had sent her boyfriend a nude. And when she'd scrolled up their messages, she could see it wasn't a mistake. Jaya and Rakesh had been meeting secretly the whole week. Their messages before Udaipur had been practically nonexistent, but after the pool party on the first night, they'd started arranging to meet. In secret. The man she'd been with for almost a decade, who'd become a part of her family, was fucking her actual family.

Everything was a horrible blur from that moment on. Rakesh had tried to deny everything, as though Reeva was that stupid. Jaya had sobbed hysterically and made the whole thing about her. Reeva had locked herself in the bedroom, no longer caring about missing her flight home. She'd stayed there for three days, sobbing and barely eating. She was at rock bottom and things couldn't get worse. Until she let Rakesh into the room, and he destroyed the fragment that was left of her world by telling her he wanted to be with Jaya. Just when Reeva had needed him the most, he'd left her for her younger sister.

It was betrayal upon betrayal, and for reasons Reeva couldn't understand, Sita had taken Jaya's side. She'd found out about Jaya and Rakesh beforehand and had *helped them* cover it all up. When Reeva had confronted her about it, she hadn't even apologized. She'd told her to move on. "I know it's not easy, but you can't be selfish, Reeva. It's not just about you. Jaya's family—you need to forgive her. What are you going to do, never speak to her again?"

That had been exactly what Reeva had planned to do, and she'd kept it up for four years. She'd ignored all of Jaya's calls and texts for the first year, mostly deleting them without reading them. Slowly, they'd petered out. The last time Reeva had heard from Jaya was at the end of the second year, when she'd asked if she was ready to talk about what had happened. Reeva had not been ready—how could she be after Jaya had ripped her past, present, and future apart?—so she hadn't replied. She hadn't spoken to Jaya since, until ten minutes ago, when she'd had the naked audacity to *hug* her.

Reeva closed her eyes and focused on inhaling and exhaling deeply. She felt herself come back to the present moment. She wasn't in Udaipur having her heart ripped out of her body. She was in Leicester. She tried to remember everything her therapist had told her. Rakesh choosing Jaya did not mean that Reeva was not worthy. She was enough. She was not going to be abandoned again. Their relationship ending had given Reeva an extra four years to live her life on her own terms, to grow, and to realize who she was without a man. She was a stronger person now than she'd ever been with Rakesh because she'd finally learned to take care of herself. And in times when she couldn't, she had someone else who'd always be there for her. Someone she couldn't believe she wasn't on the phone with right now.

Reeva pulled her phone out from her pocket and speed-dialed Lakshmi.

She answered instantly. "Reevs! Tell me everything!"

Reeva lay back on the light brown duvet and looked up at the faded cream ceiling. Just hearing Lakshmi's voice already made her feel more like herself. "Well, right now I'm lying on my dad's bed. Because I have to sleep in his bedroom."

"Seriously? That's so creepy. What's it like?"

Reeva craned her neck to look around. "Double bed. Pine wardrobes. Matching bedside table with a white lamp. So far all I can make out is that Dad did not like clutter. Or artwork. Or basically any decoration at all. But he's really into pine. It's just a . . . normal, basic three-bed-one-bath house."

"You need to go through all the wardrobes and cupboards," advised Lakshmi. "To find out more."

"Okay, chill, Poirot. I've only been here half an hour. During which time Sita has already accused me of being a pushover and Jaya has *hugged* me."

Lakshmi's piqued cry made Reeva laugh aloud. She might have terrible sisters, but at least she'd lucked out in the friend department. She had no idea what she would have done if the scarily confident, sexually aggressive trainee in the slightly too-short skirts hadn't decided to befriend her.

"That's fucking *typical* of Jaya," fumed Lakshmi. "We should have predicted it. And Sita's just a bored housewife with nothing better to do than bitch at everyone. But remember who you are, Reeva. Hotshot lawyer, dating a sexy man, with a cute cat and the best friend a girl can ask for. You are incredible and strong, and unlike them, you're a good person. So don't let them get you down. You've got this."

"Thanks, Lux. I needed this pep talk."

"I'll voice note it for you so you can listen to it whenever you need it. I should go now though."

"Wait, just quickly, how are things with the Sherwood-Brown case? Have you asked the judge to appoint an independent social worker to conduct a full investigation into the ex's substance abuse?"

"We're on it. But you do not need to be thinking about this stuff right now, okay? Just . . . deal with your own shit."

"Okay, thanks. But keep me posted, all right? We can't let her take their kids to America—it'll ruin their lives!"

"Reeva, I'm on it. Anyway, I've got to go. I've left the duke on hold."

"Only you would leave nobility on hold." Reeva shook her head in admiration. "This is why you're going to be partner.

You've got boss bitch energy. You don't even *need* the playlist—you're a living embodiment of it."

"You know my mantra: If you do it with confidence, you can get away with anything. Just channel that with your sisters and you'll be fine."


REEVA, SITA, AND Jaya sat in silence around the wooden kitchen table, sipping Sita's sweet, milky chai. Reeva had been the one to suggest making tea after rooting around the kitchen cupboards and finding ready-made chai masala. But Sita had walked in on her adding teaspoons of the powder to three cups of English breakfast and visibly balked. "That's not chai," she'd said, forcing Reeva out of the way as she put a pan on the hob so the tea bags could steep in the ground spices (she even grated a chunk of nutmeg, which was obviously just to make a point) before adding—despite Reeva's protestations—copious amounts of whole-fat milk and sugar. The resulting tea did admittedly taste exactly like it was straight from a chaiwallah in Mumbai, but Reeva wasn't sure it was worth the hassle. Or the extra calories.

"So," Reeva finally ventured. "What did I miss last night?"

"A lot," said Sita.

Jaya nodded in agreement. "It was intense."

Reeva refrained from rolling her eyes. "Right. Could I ... get a bit more info? Who was there? Did you learn anything about Dad? What did they do?"

Sita sighed. "It was the first night of prayers. They did bhajans and spoke in Gujarati the whole time. I understood a fair bit because obviously Nitin's family's Gujarati, but Jaya had no idea what was going on. You wouldn't have either had you been there."

Reeva wanted to snap back at her sister that it wasn't her fault—unlike both of them, she had a proper job, which meant she couldn't get away until today. Plus, they'd all had the same mum who'd never been home to teach them Hindi, let alone Gujarati. And unlike her sisters, she could speak passable French and even better Spanish.

Instead, she took a deep breath. She was the oldest sister. It was up to her to set a positive example. "Right. And who was there?"

"Obviously the lady who led the bhajans," said Sita. "I think Satya Auntie hired her. And she brought a guy with her who played the tabla while she sang. They seem to be big on the funeral scene. Everyone knew them, and they said a lot of appropriate, meaningful mourning comments in between songs."

Reeva tried to imagine what an appropriate, meaningful mourning comment sounded like. She drew a blank. "And what about the guests? What kind of people came to grieve our dad?"

"Loads of old people," said Jaya. "Well, like, Dad's age. I feel like he knew the whole of Leicester. They kept coming and going. It was, like, a never-ending stream. There must have been about forty or fifty of them, but not at the same time. And I have to say, there was a real lack of respect for the start time; it became more of a drop-by situation."

"You act like you've never been to an Indian function before," said Sita. "And thank god they didn't come at once; imagine trying to fit them all into this living room."

"So it was just singing and prayers?" asked Reeva. "There was no ceremony or anything? Or . . . I don't know, speeches?"

"Satya Auntie said something at the end," said Sita. "About how we'll all miss him but death is a part of life. And we'll always continue to be his family no matter what. But obviously the main speeches will all be at the funeral."

"It was seriously moving," said Jaya sincerely. "She's amazing. And there was a lit diya in front of Dad's portrait the whole time. It was so powerful, everyone sitting around a lit flame and singing together. It's kind of like that bit at the end of an acoustic gig where people get out their phone lights and sway."

There was a long silence after this as both her sisters stared at her. Reeva broke it. "Okay. Um. I'm still not fully sure who these crying women *were*. I'm guessing they're not family? Did Dad have any family? Apart from Satya Auntie? I know his parents died when we were kids—unless, wait, was that a lie too?"

Sita shook her head. "Nah, that was real. Other than that, it's just the usual where everyone's related somehow but no one knows exactly how. Second cousins. And then just . . . friends, I guess. He had some colleagues from work. The sad one with the pink lipstick. His best mate, Dhilip Bhai. Some neighbors. Shilpa Ben from the local mandir. She seemed to know everyone—she's the one that did the flowers and most of the admin. It seems Dad was quite active religiously."

"Wow," breathed out Reeva. "It's so crazy to think he had this whole world here. I mean, of course he did. He was isolated from us, but all along he was part of a real community. And he was *religious*."

"Uh-huh," said Jaya. "And they all looked pretty sad he was dead. Which is a good sign. If people like him that much, he can't be that bad."

"Did people say anything about him?" asked Reeva. "Like, give an idea of who he was? Or shed any light on his story?"

Sita shook her head in annoyance. "You swan in the next day

and expect us to have done all the work and solved the whole secret? What did you think, we went up to Dhilip Bhai and were like, 'Um, hey, sorry to interrupt you grieving your best friend, but do you know why no one ever told us our dad was alive?'"

"Not in those exact words, but something could have come up," said Reeva. "Seeing as basically everyone he knew was there."

"It was way too awks," said Jaya. "We would have had to explain everything, and that's, like, a lot of drama for some prayers."

"You can ask them yourself tonight," said Sita. "And every night until these fourteen days are up."

"You mean thirteen," said Reeva.

"No, it's changed."

"Yeah, the priest can't do the kriya on the thirteenth day," added Jaya. "He has, like, a prior commitment or something. So he said he'd do it on the fourteenth day instead. Apparently it's not a major issue."

"Yep, because the soul is going to wait an extra twenty-four hours to depart just to suit his schedule," said Sita. "Utter bollocks in my opinion."

"So . . . we're going to be together for an extra day?" asked Reeva.

"Yep. Lucky us," said Sita.

Reeva sighed. She knew it was only one day, but when she was with her sisters, every second felt like a year. "Right. And what do all these people think of us? Did they know he had daughters?"

"They knew we existed and were in London," said Sita. "He clearly hadn't pretended *we* were dead. Which seems to be a first in our family."

Reeva wrinkled her brow. "Okay, but what did they think about our relationship with Dad? Did they think we had one, or did they know we didn't know about him?"

Jaya shrugged. "I guess the first. They were all like, 'Oh, you must be so busy in London! Your dad would be so proud of you if he could see you now.'"

"I get the sense he pretended we had a normalish relationship," explained Sita. "Only he made us out to be shit daughters. You know, selfish and too busy with our lives to come visit him."

"So like Mum then," said Reeva drily.

Sita snorted, then cleared her throat. "Yeah. Well. We went along with it, to not make things awkward. What's another lie after thirty-odd years of them?"

Reeva nodded slowly. "And did they know anything about Mum or his relationship with her?"

Jaya shook her head. "Nope. I mean, they know we have one, who lives in London. But they don't seem to know it's Saraswati, the famous singer. A few of the women asked how our mum was doing, as though she was sick or something. Who knows what Dad told them."

"This is crazy," burst out Reeva. "All these lies. It's so dramatic. Everyone in Mum's world thinks Dad's dead. And everyone in Dad's world has no idea who Mum is. They're acting like they're mafia overlords."

Jaya nodded seriously. "I already considered that, but we'd know if Mum was a major criminal; there's no way she'd be able to not boast about it."

Reeva turned to Sita. "What about this Satya Auntie? Surely she knows everything. As his sister."

Sita raised an eyebrow. "Because that automatically means they're close?"

Reeva flushed.

"She doesn't give much away," said Jaya, oblivious. "I think she's a Buddhist. We bonded over this unreal temple in Nepal—it's so cool, I'll show you a photo later. I've never met someone else who's been there before."

"We need to get it out of her tonight," said Sita firmly. "She's coming an hour early to meet you. We figured you can do it."

"Me?" Reeva looked at her sisters in alarm. "Can't we . . . all do it?"

"You're the lawyer," Sita reminded her. "Not all of us managed to go to Cambridge. Shouldn't you use that education?"

"Cambridge really wasn't all that. And it's not like you guys didn't go to university!"

"Yeah, but we were never going to get into *Oxbridge*," said Jaya. "Not after all the trauma we had, with Mum going off to India, and us getting abandoned at school."

Reeva stared at her. "That happened to me too."

"Yeah, but you're older. It didn't have the same impact on you as the oldest. That's what my therapist says anyway. She thinks I had it worst because I was the youngest."

"You're three years younger than me," cried Reeva. "And Sita's only two ye—"

Sita interrupted. "Some of us got married and had children. I've been raising a family and supporting Nitin's business. I didn't exactly have the time to frolic around the world like Jaya or throw myself into my career like you."

Reeva's mouth dropped. "Okay. I did not know that's how you saw everything. But it's not exactly fair, considering—"

"I don't *frolic around the world*," interjected Jaya. "It's really hard being an influencer. I got into a very competitive photography course to make my content stronger this year. And there are a lot of business skills that go into building a brand."

Sita crossed her arms. "Are you both done?" Her tone sounded exactly as it did when she spoke to her five-year-old daughters.

"Because in case you've forgotten, we're here because of our dad. We need to get to the bottom of our family history—not attack each other's life choices. The fact is that Reeva's a lawyer, and so she's the one who needs to get the truth out of Satya Auntie. I mean, that is your job, isn't it—to ask loads of questions and trick people into saying things they didn't want to? I've seen *The Good Wife*."

"I'm a family lawyer," replied Reeva slowly. "It's mainly just paperwork and a lot of awkward conversations."

Jaya shrugged. "Last time I checked we were a family. And judging by this"—she gestured to the table and its three occupants—"we're going to be having way more awkward conversations. Am I right?"

Reeva looked down at her cold chai. "Guess I'm speaking to Satya Auntie tonight."

## CHAPTER 4

### Day 2

REEVA SAT SELF-CONSCIOUSLY at the back of the living room trying to subtly massage away the pins and needles in her feet. She was surrounded by dozens of her dad's closest friends, legs crossed, hands clapping, torsos swaying, crooning along with the bhajan singer, who was playing the harmonium as she sang, accompanied by a young man on the tablas. But Reeva was too busy reliving her earlier humiliation to be fully present. At seven p.m. she'd stood with her sisters, greeting all the guests. But while her sisters—dressed in casually chic Indian outfits—had seemed to know exactly what to do, saying "Jai Shree Krishna" with hands in prayer gestures to a middle-aged woman in a baby-pink outfit with matching pink lipstick who had worked at Specsavers with their dad and complimenting Dhilip Bhai ("DB! Love the shirt!"), Reeva had felt like an idiot in her jeans, awkwardly waving hello. She'd tried to be hospitable, offering tea and snacks to everyone, but they'd all vehemently rejected her offers, while embracing her sisters like they were family. Which, Reeva remembered, they were. It was only when the guests had all sat down that Sita had leaned over to whisper in Reeva's ear—with obvious relish—that guests didn't consume food or drinks in the house of a dead person until the funeral. Apparently, it was considered impure, and it was rude to even offer. So could she please stop?

Now she was sitting there feeling like a complete imposter. Everyone was singing or at least swaying and clapping to the music. Dhilip Bhai and Kalpana Ben were crying, while Shilpa Ben was simultaneously weeping and loudly singing. Reeva didn't know how to join in. She didn't have any grief to cry out via group chanting; she didn't even know the lyrics. She forced herself to at least sway in time with the music and distract herself by looking around the room. Jaya had been right; their dad was clearly well loved in the community. All these people had shown up for him, and they'd organized everything. Shilpa Ben had started the evening by giving a little speech, introducing the musicians as well as the sisters. They hadn't expected it, but Sita had dragged them up so they all stood at the front of the room, smiling graciously at the guests, acting the part of dutiful daughters. It was kind, but Reeva had felt like a liar. She didn't know her dad, and after spending a whole day in his house, she still knew nothing about him.

Reeva looked at her new aunt, Satya, sitting at the front of the room, looking composed and calm in her white cotton kurta and jeans as she sang along to the bhajans. She caught Reeva's eye and gave her a tiny wink. She was everything Reeva could have wanted in a long-lost aunt: warm, kind, inspirational, and *cool*. She'd rocked up to the house in a bright flowing coat with her long dark hair falling loose and wavy around her face. Her nose was pierced with a tiny little diamond, and she looked almost as young as her nieces. Reeva had worked out that she was in her late sixties and made a mental note to ask her about her skin care regime—she wanted whatever Satya Auntie was on.

But the best thing about Satya Auntie was her story. She was Hemant's older sister, and while he'd followed his parents' expectations every step of the way, getting into a British university and studying optometry, she'd done the exact opposite. At twenty-one she'd eschewed higher education and, even more shockingly, marriage. Instead, she'd gone traveling. To Reeva, her life sounded like a series of endless gap years. To Satya Auntie, it was "a path of self-discovery." She'd worked in an ayahuasca retreat in Peru, meditated in Bali long before *Eat, Pray, Love*, and, upon "recognizing the separation between herself and her ego," joined a Buddhist monastery in Nepal, where she'd stayed for over a decade.

She'd been an actual nun until she'd left the monastery to go and reconnect with her optometrist brother in England. She'd become estranged from her whole family when she'd left India to travel, even her brother. None of them could understand her life choices, not least her refusal to marry a suitable boy. But Satya Auntie had always loved her younger brother and had decided to leave her life as a nun to reconnect with him out in the real world—aka Leicester. From what Reeva could tell so far, it had been a success. She seemed to be a much-loved member of the local community as well as the only one who could lay claim to ever having been a Buddhist nun.

"WHEN ARE YOU going to speak to her?" hissed Sita as everyone around them sang and clapped to a well-known bhajan. "We told her to come an hour early so you could get answers about Dad, not quiz her about her life story."

"I'll do it afterward," Reeva whispered back. "I can't make her miss her brother's prayers. And it felt weird to interrogate her when she was just trying to get to know her nieces." The three sisters were sitting cross-legged at the back of the room, strategically positioned next to the kitchen door. Their choice of location had received some raised eyebrows from guests who wanted to know why they weren't sitting at the front where family should be, until Sita had charmingly shaken her head, cast her eyes down to the ground, and said, "We want the people who saw him every day to sit there. You all meant so much to him. We're so grateful." It was firsthand insight into how Sita handled her in-laws.

"I don't think she'd care," said Jaya, without lowering her voice. "What? I can't whisper. It's a thing. Look, just ask her. Satya Auntie!"

Satya Auntie—and a handful of other guests—were now looking over at the sisters with blatant curiosity. Reeva, trying to ignore the heat rising on her cheeks, gestured to the kitchen. *Can we talk a moment?* she mouthed. She hated that she was giving in to her sisters so easily, but the truth was that she wasn't sure how much more of these prayers she could stand. It was so much worse than sitting through school assembly as a child; at least then she'd felt like she had a right to be there.

Her aunt gracefully stood up, making her way through the seated guests, before following Reeva through the swirled glass doors.

"I'm so sorry," apologized Reeva when they were both in the safety of the small kitchen. "I hope it's okay to take you away from the prayers for a moment. My sisters were . . . anyway, I just wondered if we could have a chat."

"Oh, I was as desperate to leave as you were," said Satya Auntie, heading straight to the kettle. "Tea?"

Reeva laughed in surprise. "Uh, yes, please. How come you wanted to leave too?"

"I could say I'm just used to praying in my own way, and I'd prefer to do it alone rather than following a lot of rituals. Which is true. But what's even more true is that I was a little bored."

Reeva laughed again. Her aunt was not what she expected. "I didn't think Buddhist nuns could get bored. I mean, sorry if that sounds ignorant. I just thought you were too enlightened for that."

"Oh, I'm a long way from enlightenment," said her aunt, smiling as she opened the exact cupboard to pull out two beige mugs. "I'm still very much a human being with all the same feelings everyone has. I suppose the difference is that my spiritual education means I can recognize the difficult feelings and work to let go of them. But that doesn't mean I always *enjoy* them."

"I can't believe you have shitty feelings too— Sorry! Difficult feelings. I always thought you didn't get them if you became spiritual." She sighed theatrically. "There goes the Buddhist backup plan."

Satya Auntie's eyes twinkled. "I'm afraid that's not exactly how it works. If you want to get rid of the shitty feelings, I recommend feeling them."

"What do you mean?"

"The quicker you embrace the shitty feelings, the quicker they go. Sort of like pulling off a bandage quickly. It works, but it's more intense."

Reeva's brow furrowed. "How do you embrace them? I don't get it."

"You sort of let yourself sink into the depths of the feeling so that you're right there in the pain, and then you breathe through it," explained her aunt. "Relaxing into it rather than resisting it. Easier said than done, of course. But when you do manage it, everything becomes a lot more bearable." She came over to the table and put down the two cups of tea. Reeva felt vindicated to see that she'd just added a dash of chai masala to normal English breakfasts—with no saucepan or grated nutmeg in sight. "Shall we sit?"

Reeva nodded and pulled up a chair next to her. "Thank you. And for this chat. I'm sorry to pull you away from the prayers. I mean, I know I also saved you from mild boredom. It's just . . . I felt really out of place." She flushed with instant shame at her honesty. It normally took her months to open up to people—in the case of her family, they were thirty-four years in, and she still hadn't gotten there—but something about Satya Auntie inspired confidence. Maybe it was her total lack of judgment. Or maybe it was her nose piercing.

"That makes sense," said her aunt. "You don't know any of these people, and you're going through a lot with your dad. Not just the normal grief, but the confusion. It must be so hard to suddenly hear of his existence along with his sudden lack of existence."

Reeva nodded emphatically. "Yes, exactly. And it's too late because he's gone." She paused, then gasped. "Wait! You know that we didn't know Dad existed?"

"Yes," admitted her aunt. "I'm sorry."

"You don't need to be sorry," cried Reeva. "This is perfect! You can tell us everything. I have so many questions. We've all been so confused. Everyone here seems to think we had a normal—albeit very distant—relationship with Dad. His friends have no idea we thought he was dead! It's so strange. We just want to know what happened. Why our parents lied to us." She looked at her aunt expectantly, but the hope slowly slipped off her face as the silence grew.

"I really am sorry, Reeva," said Satya Auntie finally, looking straight at her. "I hate to disappoint you when you were clearly counting on me for answers, but the truth is that I don't *know* what happened. Your father never told me. He refused to speak about any of it with me, and I wasn't allowed to ask. It was one of the conditions of us being back in each other's lives."

The remaining sliver of hope fully left Reeva's face, and she slumped into her chair. "He didn't tell you anything? At all?"

Her aunt shook her head. "No, and I wasn't there when it all happened. Because, well, I wasn't part of the family." She looked down at the table sadly. "You know your parents married a year after I'd left home? They met in Mumbai before Hemant went off to London to study—I actually met Saraswati then too, though I didn't know how serious they were about each other—and then kept up their relationship in secret while he was away. When he went back to India after his studies, they got married—without either of their parents' permission. They asked for forgiveness afterward but didn't get it, so they decided to move to England to make a life here."

Reeva nodded politely; she knew all this. What she didn't know was why they had then split up and told their daughters Hemant was dead. But it looked like Satya Auntie needed to tell this story more for herself than for Reeva. "Then what happened?"

"Well, they came over to India a couple of times after that. Our parents—Hemant's and mine—ended up forgiving them when your mum fell pregnant. You all met your grandparents when you were babies; it's just such a shame they passed away when you were young." Her voice softened. "But it's even more of a shame I didn't meet you all until now. It's my biggest regret, you know. That I was estranged from my family. I did try to get in touch with my parents, but they weren't open to it. It's easier to forgive a son than it is a daughter—especially one who does something so unusual for the times. I wish I'd reached out to Hemant and Saraswati though. I just . . . I thought they were as angry with me as my parents were. But maybe they would have understood, considering they'd also had to break expectations."

Reeva frowned. She'd never really thought of her parents as rebellious teenagers with a love story before. This version of Saraswati—a romantic who put everything on the line for love— did not match up to the superficial mother she knew who'd once refused to sit in economy with her young daughters when there hadn't been enough space for them all in first class. An eleven-year-old Reeva had been forced to stop Sita and Jaya from squabbling for an entire eight hours while their mum slept in luxury. All she'd wanted was to read her Harry Potter book in peace, but she'd barely managed a chapter.

There were so many parts to her parents' story she didn't fully understand. And the one person she'd thought could explain it to her couldn't because she'd been estranged from them for decades. Reeva spent most of her life dealing with messy families, but hers was proving to be the messiest. "What about since you came back?" she asked, not even trying to hide her desperation anymore. "You said that my dad told you this topic was off-limits. What was that conversation like? How did he talk about it all?"

"Well, it came up soon after we reunited, because obviously I asked about you all. And your dad said that he wasn't in your lives anymore. I remember thinking that was an interesting way of phrasing it—that he wasn't in your lives, rather than you weren't in his life. I asked him what had happened, and he said he couldn't talk about it. He'd promised your mother to never speak about it to anyone, and it was the least he owed her."

Reeva crinkled her brow. "The least he owed her?"

Satya Auntie nodded. "He always said it wasn't her fault. That was the one thing I understood very clearly about all of it—it wasn't her fault. He was very protective of her. Never let me say a bad word against her."

"I like that you tried." Reeva gave her aunt a sad smile. "But— is that it? He didn't say anything else? Didn't you ask why he never saw us?"

"Oh, all the time!" cried Satya Auntie. "Don't forget, I was desperate to meet you all too. But Hemant said it wasn't an option. In the end, he had to admit that you all thought he was dead. I was completely shocked. I couldn't think why they'd told you such an extreme lie."

"Tell me about it," sighed Reeva.

"But the more I demanded answers, the more Hemant closed up. He could be quite obstinate at times. He just refused to tell me, and after a while, he made it a condition of our new relationship. I had to accept that we couldn't talk about this. And if I didn't, then it was best if I went back to Nepal."

"Wow, Dad was harsh," observed Reeva. "Did you have any theories about what happened?"

Satya Auntie smiled gently. "I try not to believe any thoughts that aren't rooted in reality. Otherwise they're just fantasy. So, yes, I'd have theories from time to time. But I let them all go, and, Reeva, I don't think I should share them with you. There's no point. They're not real."

Reeva sighed. "Okay. So that's the only clue—that Dad always said it wasn't Mum's fault. Great."

Satya Auntie placed her hand on top of Reeva's bare forearm. The silver metal of her (many) rings cooled Reeva's hot skin. "I know it hurts to not have the answers. But maybe it'll be easier for you to accept that rather than desperately hunt for them."

Reeva looked up, puzzled. "But . . . don't they say it's the truth that sets you free? That's all I'm looking for: the truth."

"Yes. But the truth right now is that you don't know. That's the reality. Accepting that is what sets you free."

"I can change that!" insisted Reeva. "By finding out the answers."

Her aunt exhaled. "Yes. And you should do whatever feels right. I suppose I'm just trying to protect you. And what I've always found is that acceptance is better than resistance. If the answers are going to come to you, they'll come in the right time. It's just about surrendering."

"I feel like that only ever happens in books. Where Dad would have written us a secret letter that arrives in chapter twenty-four and everything finally makes sense. But real life isn't like that. There aren't any secret letters because he died so suddenly, and if we want to know what happened, we have to find out ourselves."

Her aunt smiled sadly. "If he'd known he was dying, he probably would have written you a letter."

"But he didn't."

"No. And there might not be any letters, but the answers we need are almost always inside of us. If you can't find them externally, perhaps go inside. Chances are you'll find the truth."

Reeva was trying to think of a more suitable response than "Sorry, what?" when she noticed that the singing next door had completely stopped. "Oh god, we've missed the whole prayers! Am I a terrible daughter?"

"Only if you choose to see yourself that way. To be honest, Hemant probably felt like a terrible father at times too."

Reeva paused. Just thinking that her dad had felt that way made her feel more connected to him. They both knew what it was like to feel you'd let people down.

"We can grieve Hemant anytime, Reeva," said Satya Auntie gently. "You don't need to feel bad. And I think he'd like to see us getting to know each other. It's funny, a little part of you really reminds me of him."

"Really?" Reeva's eyes widened. "Which part?"

"I get the sense that both of you are quite stubborn. But then again, I could be completely wrong. Biscuit?"


"ARE YOU KIDDING?" demanded Sita. "There's no way Dad didn't tell her why. She's got to be lying."

Reeva hugged her knees to her chest, pulling her cashmere cardigan tight around her. "I don't think she is. She doesn't strike me as the kind of person who lies."

Sita, sitting in a chair opposite the sofa her sisters were occupying, looked at Jaya. "What do you think? Hello? Oh my god, do you have to be on your phone all the time?"

"Uh, yes, it's my job." Jaya, sprawled out on the sofa, continued scrolling through her phone. "And I don't think she's lying either—she's a *nun*. She probably took an honesty vow or something."

"Plus she told us that stuff about Dad saying it wasn't Mum's fault," said Reeva.

"I bet Mum manipulated him into thinking that," said Jaya, still scrolling. "So she could go and be famous. You know her parents cut her off when she married Dad. Leaving him was the only way to get back into the fold and use their support to get success. It makes total sense. If I'd moved from a mansion in Mumbai to an average house in England, I'd also be up for faking my husband's death to go back."

"Not everyone's as shallow as you," retorted Sita. "So was that it? She didn't say anything else?"

Reeva shook her head. "No. I just don't know what Dad could have done that was his fault that's big enough to make Mum tell us he was dead."

"An affair," said both her sisters in unison.

Reeva stared at them. "What? No."

"It makes total sense," said Jaya, finally looking up from her phone. "He cheated on Mum, then she lost her shit, because, hello? She's Mum, and there is no way her ego can handle anyone cheating on her. She made him fake his death and get out of our lives forever."

Reeva felt her stomach twinge uncomfortably. Hearing Jaya talk about affairs was not an enjoyable experience. "Okay, but isn't that a bit dramatic? Even for Mum. I think a divorce would suffice."

"Too dramatic for our mother?" asked Sita. "I don't think that exists."

"Totally," agreed Jaya, the thin strap of her black lace pajama top sliding off her shoulder. "She would definitely think death-faking is an appropriate punishment for cheating on her."

"I don't know," said Reeva uncertainly. "I can't imagine Dad having an affair."

"You're so naive," said Sita. "You always want to think the best of people, but remember, you never even knew our dad. None of us did."

"Yeah, who knows how many secrets this man had?" asked Jaya. "I mean, look at his house. It's so bare. He could have been a spy. A spy who had an affair!"

Sita sighed in frustration. "We're not in a Bond movie, Jaya."

"I actually once worked on a divorce case where a man abandoned his wife and family," said Reeva. "Turned out he was a spy who just took off one day! The kids never heard from him again. We still got him to pay pretty decent child support though."

"See?" cried Jaya.

"Are you seriously telling me you think our dad was a spy?" demanded Sita.

Reeva sighed, shaking her head. "No. Obviously not. I just . . . I can't believe he had an affair. There's no evidence to support it."

"It won't be hard to find it," said Sita. "Now we have an idea of where to start, I say we hound Dad's friends tomorrow and ask about anything linked to an affair. Let's all do it this time. Clearly Reeva's not as skilled at questioning as we'd hoped."

Reeva swallowed her irritation. By the time she'd left the kitchen with Satya Auntie, most of the guests had already rushed off home, and she hadn't had a chance to speak to Dhilip Bhai or Shilpa Ben. Her sisters, however, *had*, but they'd chosen to ask them only about the best local restaurants. Which was why they'd had a delicious saag paneer for post-prayers dinner but knew nothing about their dad. "Right, well, I'm going to take my poor questioning skills upstairs. I need to call Nick."

"Nick? Who's Nick?" asked Jaya. "Oh my god, are you dating someone? You kept that quiet! Tell us everything! I love hearing about people's love lives."

Reeva froze. She hadn't meant to bring up Nick. She couldn't talk about him right now. Not to Jaya. Not after everything Jaya had done to her. She just couldn't. She looked at Sita in total desperation.

Sita looked away from Reeva and turned to face her younger sister. "Leave it, Jaya. We're not fifteen years old at a sleepover, staying up late to gossip about boys. You're as bad as the twins."

"Um, excuse me for taking an *interest*," replied Jaya, pulling herself up onto her forearms to glare at her sister. "It's more than you've done. Do you even know how many followers I have now?"

"Do I look like I care?"


REEVA COULD STILL hear her sisters bickering as she gratefully closed the bedroom door behind her. She'd needed to get out of there. The idea of her dad cheating on her mum had made her feel physically sick. She knew she didn't know this man, and there was a strong possibility he wasn't a nice person—contrary to her sisters' thoughts, she wasn't so naive as to think her parents had faked his death over a polite misdemeanor—but Reeva hated the thought of an affair being the cause. She knew what it felt like to be on the receiving end. And this was her dad! He lived in this unassuming house. He worked at an average optometrist's office. He had old religious friends who wore saris. He did *not* seem like the type to cheat.

But then, neither had Rakesh.

Reeva shook her head and pushed that thought away. Nope. She wasn't going to go there. Her therapist had taught her how to deal with intrusive thoughts. She needed to count to three and come back to the present moment. And the reality was that there was zero proof to suggest her dad had cheated, so there was no point thinking about it. Instead, she could think about Nick. He'd already been at the back of her mind all day, mainly because she hadn't heard from him. Not once. She knew he was busy, but he had said he'd call. She pulled out her phone yet again, and the lack of missed calls and notifications made her heart sink. She'd been there so many times before. She'd be dating someone, she'd start to let herself sink into a sense of safety, and then . . . silence. They'd start canceling, texting useless apologies, and eventually fading from her life. The thought of this happening with Nick was categorically not an option.

It was why she wanted to take her therapist's advice and be a grown-up. Instead of just waiting for his call like a tragic woman in a rom-com, constantly checking her phone and falling asleep with its outline imprinted on her face, *she* could call *him*. That way, she could straight-up ask him why he hadn't called. Direct, honest communication was the way forward. So why did it feel so hard? Reeva took a deep breath and shook her head. The last time she'd seen Nick, he'd had his head between her legs. That was way more intimate than a ten p.m. phone call. She needed to get over her insecurities and just call.

It went straight to voice mail. "Hi, this is Nick. Sorry to miss you. Feel free to leave . . ." Reeva sighed as she hung up. He must be busy. Maybe he was on the tube home with no signal. Or he could have lost interest in her and this was his way of letting her down gently. She felt her anxiety rising. Lakshmi. She'd instantly remind Reeva that this was not a big deal. And calling her would be even better than Nick—she wouldn't have to worry about sounding cool or try to make her family seem more normal. She could even tell Lakshmi her sisters' theory about their dad.

But the call went straight to voice mail. Reeva's stomach sank in disappointment.

**Sorry! Can't talk! But look how cute we are.** The text from Lakshmi flashed up on Reeva's phone screen, followed by a photo. It was a selfie of her and FP touching noses. Reeva felt a pang in her chest. FP had never rubbed noses with her before. Had Lakshmi initiated it, or had FP done it of her own accord? Reeva shook her head. There was codependence, and then there was plain crazy. She needed to calm down. It was positive that Lakshmi was bonding with the cat and FP was learning to like people. By the time Reeva came back to London, it was very probable that she'd give her nose kisses too.

Her phone flashed again with another message. It was Nick. She opened it eagerly. **Sorry darling. I wanted to call, but work has been mad. Hope you got there safely. I think it'll be too late to call when I finish up here, so I'll ring you first thing tomorrow. Sleep well xxx.**

Another flash. **PS. What's your address? I want to send flowers.**

The anxiety in Reeva's stomach finally settled down. Being around her sisters was turning her into a nervous wreck. But everything was fine. Nick had replied. He was still at work. Plus he'd called her "darling," put three kisses, and wanted to send flowers. It was still a shame he wasn't free for a chat—she really needed to talk to someone about everything that was happening—but at least things were going in the right direction. Surely people didn't send flowers if they didn't see a future with the recipient? Reeva quickly typed out a reply to him, put her phone on sleep mode, and got out her lavender silk eye mask and Bach calming flower drops. She used the pipette to drop a generous dose of herbal remedy into her mouth (the bottle said two drops, but Reeva figured four was more appropriate for her situation), tied her mask gently around her eyes, and turned off the light. She was officially ready for today to be over. After everything she'd been through, she deserved—no, she *needed*—a good night's sleep. She just hoped her dead dad wouldn't mind her doing it in his bed.

## CHAPTER 5

### Day 3

REEVA HAD NOT had a good night's sleep. Instead, she'd spent the whole night plagued with nightmares. She couldn't remember what they were about, but they'd forced her awake at four a.m. drenched in a cold sweat. The dreams had disappeared instantly, but the fear—palpable, chilling, real—had remained. It had taken another two hours of scrolling through Insta and downing more Bach remedy to fall back asleep. Reeva had eventually woken up late, dazed and groggy, even less ready for the day ahead than she'd been the previous day. She wished she could remember what the nightmares had been about, but it didn't take a psychologist to tell her they were probably linked to the person whose bed she was in.

She yawned at her reflection in the stark black-edged mirror up on the wall. The bags under her eyes looked terrible, and the yellow halogen lights made her brown skin look sallow. But that was nothing compared to the bald patch on the side of her head glaring at her in all its hairless glory. She pulled her ruler out of her toiletry bag, trying not to panic. Everything looked worse with wet hair. It couldn't be as bad as she thought. This would get better. The tonics would work. They had to; they'd cost £350. It would be fine.

Seven point two centimeters.

It was not fine. The patch had grown more than half a centimeter overnight. This was a complete disaster. Reeva stared at her horror-stricken face in the mirror. Seven point two centimeters of her scalp stared back at her.

"Auntie Weeeee!" The door burst open, and a small child rocketed toward Reeva. "It's meeeeee!"

Reeva flung her wet hair back over the patch and crouched down. "Amisha, baby! How are you?" She wrapped her arms around her five-year-old niece, dressed in tracksuit bottoms and a green T-shirt.

The child drew back. "Um, I'm not Amisha."

"I'm Amisha," announced a quieter voice. Reeva looked up to see her other niece standing shyly in the doorframe, with an equally messy ponytail, clad in identical tracksuit bottoms and T-shirt. She frowned in confusion. Not for the first time, she wished that one of them had a distinguishing facial mole.

"Oh, I'm sorry. I guess I haven't seen you in a few weeks."

The twin nearest her burst into loud cackles. "It's a trick!!! I am Amisha!"

"And I'm Alisha!"

"You guys are the worst!" cried Reeva. "I knew I was right."

Both twins jumped onto their aunt as she fell back onto the floor, laughing. "Love you, Auntie Wee."

Reeva's heart felt like it was about to burst out of love for these tiny creatures. They were so perfect; she had no idea how they'd come out of Sita. It had not been easy continuing to see them after her mum's wedding. She'd had to make charged small talk with Sita while the twins gurgled on FaceTime. But as the years had passed, and the girls had begun grabbing the phone to show Reeva their death traps and secret dens, she'd barely even needed to speak to Sita. And when she drove down to Virginia Water—the bougie part of Surrey they lived in—or Sita drove them up to Reeva, their exchanges were mainly done through the girls. It was essentially what her divorced clients did with their kids, and it seemed to work just as well for divorced sisters.

"I love Auntie Wee *more*," said Amisha.

"I love you both the *mostest*," replied Reeva, tickling them. "My precious little peanuts."

The twins howled with laughter over this. *"You're* a peanut!"

"Auntie Wee?" asked Alisha, after a moment. "Can I ask you an important question?"

"Of course, angel."

"Is your daddy dead?"

Reeva blinked. She had no idea what Sita had told the girls about death. But she didn't want to lie. "Uh, yes."

"Cool!" cried Amisha as Alisha's eyes lit up.

"It is?"

"He's going to get to eat *all* his favorite foods and never eat dhal bhat shaak again," said Amisha.

"And he'll get unlimited iPad time and all the cucumbers!" added Alisha.

Reeva stared at her nieces. "Where did you hear that?"

"It's *heaven*!" said Amisha. "Everyone knows. We learned it at the Sunday indoo classes Mum takes us to."

"Indoo?"

"Indooism," clarified Alisha.

"Ohhhh. I didn't know your mum was that religious."

"*She* doesn't go," said Amisha. "Only us. So can we go visit your daddy in heaven?"

"Um, I'm afraid not. That's not . . . uh, an option."

"Can we FaceTime him instead?" asked Alisha.

"Can we see his dead body?" asked Amisha.

Reeva laughed. "I wish we could, but sorry, darlings. That's not quite how it works."

The twins' faces fell. "Please? Even if we're good?"

"You're always good, my most gorgeous girls. But no, I'm sorry. You can't see people once they've died." The twins' faces looked so distraught that Reeva panicked. She had no idea what Sita had told them about death. But she could remember what she'd believed when she was the twins' age and had been told her dad had died. "I mean, you can't see people *physically*. But you can feel their presence. And see them in your mind. You can talk to them as well and have imaginary conversations. It's actually great because they'll always understand you, and you can tell them anything because they'll keep all your secrets."

"Cool!" cried the twins, starting to run around the room. "We can talk to dead people!"

"Great, so you've turned my kids into *The Sixth Sense*," said Sita, materializing in the doorway.

"Oh my god, you need to stop coming out of nowhere!" cried Reeva. "Can you wear some shoes so I can hear you creeping up on me?"

"I like my feet to breathe," said Sita. "And can you not call the girls 'gorgeous'? We don't want them growing up feeling their worth is based only on their beauty. Oh, and next time you tell my kids your theories on death, you might want to check with me. You know, as their mother and everything."

Reeva flushed with shame. "Sorry. Yes." This was where the similarities between being a divorced parent and a divorced aunt ended; when it came to raising the kids, her opinion didn't matter.

"Auntie Wee, your dad says he wants cucumbers," announced Alisha.

"*Lots* of cucumber," clarified Amisha.

Sita rolled her eyes. "There's some downstairs. I already chopped it up. I imagine he's also requested you eat it for him, so go ahead."

Reeva raised her eyebrows as the twins raced down the stairs. "Cucumber?"

Sita shrugged. "They fucking love it. Are you planning on coming downstairs at some point?"

"Yeah of course, I just had a bunch of work calls to do," lied Reeva. She was embarrassed for her sister to find out she'd woken up after eleven a.m. "Hey, where's Nitin?"

"He already left," said Sita. "He has work to do, so he's gone back to London. He'll be back for the funeral. And I've spent the whole morning making lunch and cleaning the living room. So maybe you could—"

"*Reeva, door for you!*" Jaya's voice cut through their conversation. "*Reevaaa!*"

"I, uh, think it's flowers," explained Reeva, grateful for the excuse to slip out of the room. She could hear Sita muttering something about it being "all right for some" as she made her way down the stairs. After just one night in the same house as her sisters, Reeva's life in London—like her quiet, spacious flat where absolutely nobody ever barged into her room—felt increasingly far away.

"Surprise!"

Reeva halted mid-step. It was Nick. In the actual flesh. Her—actually, he wasn't her anything because they hadn't used labels yet—was standing in the narrow hallway with three-day stubble, dressed in a light blue shirt with rolled-up sleeves showing his tanned forearms, grinning at her with his warm hazel eyes. Reeva felt her ovaries drip with desire, and then suddenly became acutely aware of the fact that Nick was standing uninvited in her dad's house and she was standing there with dripping-wet hair, zero makeup, and a T-shirt with no bra.

"Oh my god, Nick! Uh, what are you doing here?" asked Reeva, crossing her arms over her chest, while simultaneously trying to fluff up her hair so she looked less like a drowned rat.

"I wanted to be here for you. I hope . . . I've not overstepped a mark?"

Reeva shook her head in a daze. "Uh, no. Of course not."

"This is so cute!" cried Jaya. She was still standing by the door, with a face of full makeup, dressed in a stylish floral dress. Reeva shot her a look of pure irritation. How had her sister, who never got out of bed until midday, known today was the day to get up early and look *Love Island*–ready? She felt an irrational burst of anger at Nick for not thinking to call before turning up. Did he not realize it would take Reeva at least an hour's prep to get ready for his arrival—from hair removal on her body to hair maintenance on her head? She wasn't Jaya, who was permanently in "cute girl" mode. Reeva needed advance warning to make sure she looked, and thus *felt*, good. It was why she was of the firm opinion that spontaneous surprises were not conducive to healthy relationships. Not that she was going to tell Nick that anytime soon. "You must be Reeva's boyfriend! I'm Jaya."

Reeva looked away in panic. This was getting worse by the

second. She should have spoken to Jaya about Nick the previous night and stressed that they weren't an official couple yet. But instead, she'd run out of the room like a scared schoolgirl. She felt her cheeks burn up, but Nick just smiled and casually reached out a hand to shake Jaya's. "Yeah. I'm her boyfriend. Nick. It's great to meet you."

"Nice of you to tell us your *boyfriend* was coming."

Reeva spun around to see Sita standing behind her. Again. "It was a, uh, surprise. I didn't know he was coming." Up until a second ago, she hadn't even known she had a boyfriend.

"Well, lunch is ready," said Sita, walking past them all and going into the kitchen. "I guess I'll lay an extra place. Jaya, come help."

Reeva smiled clumsily at Nick. "Sorry about her. That's . . . Sita. And the less rude one is Jaya. Oh, she introduced herself already, didn't she? I'm being weird. Sorry. I just . . . did not expect to see you here!"

"Hey, come here." Nick held his arms wide open. "I've missed you."

Reeva walked into his arms and let her eyes close as he hugged her tight. It felt so good to be held. By her boyfriend! She couldn't believe he'd finally used the label. And he'd driven all the way to Leicester to see her. Reeva opened her eyes. Shit. He was in Leicester. In her dead dad's house. With her family. Who had zero concept of boundaries.

"How, um, how long are you going to be here for?" she asked. "Sorry, I mean, how long can you stay for?"

"Well, I was hoping to stay a night. If you can put me up, of course. But if not, I'll head back tonight; it's not a problem. Whatever works for you."

Reeva forced herself to smile breezily. "Of course you can

stay. I'd love that. Just, uh, let me pop upstairs and freshen up."
With her wet hair plastered onto her head, Reeva was panicking
that her patch was visible. She tried to nonchalantly rest her left
forearm on top of the patch as though it were completely normal
to wear her arm like a hat. "I'll be right back!"

"Sure," said Nick. "Sorry, I've caught you in your pajamas."

Reeva flushed. Her cropped T-shirt and wide-legged palazzo
pants were not pajamas—she'd actually thought she looked quite
cool—but Nick was used to seeing her in work clothes, so his
confusion made sense. She forced herself to smile brightly. "Right,
I was about to get changed."

"Cool. In the meantime, I can get to know your sisters."

"Great. That's . . . *so* great."

"I HATE DHAAAL!" screeched Amisha.

"No, I hate dhal," echoed Alisha.

"You will both eat it or you will get no more cucumbers,"
snapped Sita. "Here." She dolloped a spoonful of dhal onto her
daughters' plates, before doing the same to Jaya's, Reeva's, and
Nick's.

"Sorry," Reeva mouthed to Nick.

He winked at her and looked straight at Sita. "This looks delicious, thanks so much. I love dhal."

"Oh, you know Indian food!" cried Jaya. "That's so great.
Have you ever been to India?"

Nick nodded. "I went to Goa once—so beautiful. Reeva tells
me your mum's in India now."

Sita sighed loudly. "As always, yes, she's managed to handily
escape being a mother just when we need one."

"She's not even answering any of our messages," added

Reeva. "Which means we're no closer to finding out the big family secret."

"That must be hard," said Nick. "Especially as you're here, organizing your dad's funeral and everything. It's a really strange situation to be in."

"You don't say," muttered Sita.

"*Auntie Wee*, I want to see your *hairband!*" cried Amisha.

Her mum glared at her. "Masi, not Auntie."

Amisha rolled her eyes in a perfect impression of her mother before trying again. "*Wee Masi*, I want to see your *hairband*."

Sita nodded in approval, while Reeva stared at her niece in speechless shock. When she'd left Nick to go and freshen up, she'd realized she didn't have time to choose a new outfit *and* dry her hair, so she'd stuck a wide velvet leopard-print hairband on instead. Taking it off would almost definitely reveal her patch.

"It's, uh, not a very interesting hairband, baby," said Reeva finally. "But I'll show you later if you want."

"Please?" asked Alisha, her eyes somehow growing bigger. "Pwetty please?"

Reeva's stomach tensed. She looked beseechingly at her nieces, trying to convey the truth via her eyes. "What about later? If you wait, I'll let you guys have it! Or I'll get you your own! Wouldn't you like your own hairbands?"

"*Noo!*" screeched Amisha. "I want to hold *yours!*"

"Oh my god, can you just give it to her?" exclaimed Jaya. "This screeching is giving me a headache."

"Surely that's not the best way to teach them manners?" Reeva turned desperately to Sita. "Maybe if they eat their dhal first?"

Sita snorted. "As if I have the energy to teach them manners on top of everything else. Just give it to her. She'll get bored of it in a second."

"Why is Auntie Wee being mean?" asked Alisha.

Reeva felt a wave of guilt wash over her. She felt terrible. She was choosing vanity over being a good aunt. But she knew if she took off the hairband, everyone would look, and Nick would see the patch. She couldn't cope. It was too much. "I'm sorry, angel," she said miserably. She was too embarrassed to look at Nick to see his reaction. She knew she was coming across as seriously unhinged. "I'm not trying to be mean. I promise I'll show you later. You can try it on and you'll look so beautiful!"

Amisha started banging her spoon against the table. "Hairband! Hairband!"

"Seriously? Can't you just give it to them?" asked Sita. "And I've asked you to stop with the 'beautiful angel' crap. Would you say that to a boy?"

"I . . ." Reeva looked down at her dhal in despair.

"Hey, why don't I show you girls my watch?" asked Nick suddenly. Reeva slowly lifted her head to see him wave his slim black watch at the girls. "Look, it's waterproof. Why don't we try and put it in a glass of water and test it?"

The girls looked at him, transfixed. Reeva sent him a silent prayer of gratitude.

"What's waterproof?" asked Alisha.

"It means if you put it in water, it won't damage the watch. See? Water . . . proof."

"Cool!" cried Amisha, grabbing the watch and dropping it into her dhal. "Dhal . . . proof?"


REEVA SAT CROSS-LEGGED on the bed and looked at Nick, who was leaning against the headboard answering e-mails on his phone. "I'm really sorry about earlier. I know my family are a lot. And, uh, I guess I owe you a new watch."

He laughed and put an arm around her, pulling her into his warm body so she could rest her head against his chest. "It's absolutely fine. I'm used to kids. I'm a godfather to about five of them."

"Really? I didn't know that! I'd love to meet them one day."

"Sure. So long as you refrain from sexist language around them."

Reeva flushed until she realized Nick was grinning. "I feel so out-of-date. I'm like the ancient old-fashioned aunt."

"If you're ancient, what does that make me? Decrepit?"

A rumble of low chanting came up the stairs. "The bhajans," explained Reeva. "They're in full swing."

"Are you sure you don't want to be downstairs?" asked Nick. "I didn't feel like it was my place to be there, but I don't mind waiting up here on my own. It's honestly not an issue."

Reeva shook her head. Part of her did feel a little guilty for avoiding the bhajans again, but she really didn't want to be there. She hated the way everyone assumed she knew and loved her dad when the truth was so much more complicated. And she felt like such an imposter. Nick didn't get it. He thought because she was Indian, this was her world. But she felt just as out of place as he did. Probably even more so *because* she was supposed to fit in.

They'd initially sat downstairs for the prayers, listening to Satya Auntie thank people for coming. Nick had squeezed Reeva's hand, and she'd felt her whole body go warm. She'd imagined what it would be like to permanently have a plus-one in her life. She could even see herself going to Jaya and Rakesh's wedding if she had Nick by her side, holding her hand. Maybe they'd even have a wedding of their own one day . . . She'd found herself daydreaming about it while Shilpa Ben spoke in Gujarati for seven very long minutes. But when the speech ended and the bhajans began, Nick had turned to her and interrupted her reverie. He whispered in her ear that he was going to head upstairs because he had no idea what was going on. Reeva had felt a deep pang of disappointment. She had no idea what was going on either, and now she was going to have stay without her plus-one holding her hand. But then she'd forced herself to see sense. This was newer to Nick than it was to her. Besides, it gave her the perfect excuse to slip away. She could stop grieving for a man she never knew to spend quality time with a man she did know. A man she was starting to hope that she'd know for the rest of her life.

"Honestly, it's fine," she said. "I'm kind of grateful I don't have to be there. It's so much nicer being here with you. Especially after a full forty-eight hours with my sisters."

"Sure? I felt like a bit of a bell-end sitting there, to be honest, with no idea what was happening, but I know this is your world, so please go down if you need to."

Reeva smiled tightly at the mention of her "world" again. Just because she was brown, it didn't mean she understood any more than Nick did. But there was no point trying to explain—Nick was white. He wouldn't get it. "It's cool. Honestly."

"Good. I'm really glad I came, Reevs."

"Me too," said Reeva, relaxing as she realized it was true. "I so appreciate you coming up. Thank you."

He kissed her gently. "You know, I wasn't sure if it would be a bit much. Considering we're quite early days, and we haven't really spoken about us yet as an 'us.'" He paused. "Maybe we should speak about that now?"

Reeva sat up straight, trying to control her excitement. "Really? You want to have, um, that chat? Now?"

He nodded. "Yeah, why not? I like you, Reeva. And I think we have a good thing going. I haven't been seeing anyone else since we met, and I'm hoping you haven't either?"

Reeva shook her head. "Nope."

He exhaled in relief. "Cool. Yeah, great. Cool. Then, uh, perhaps we should just call it what it is. You know, if something looks like an orange, smells like an orange, and tastes like an orange, then, well, it's an orange. So, yeah."

Reeva nodded slowly. She had no idea what he was saying. They were . . . an orange? Did that mean they were in a relationship like he'd suggested to Jaya? Or that he was trying to take that all back, and say that when they were properly in a relationship, they'd know? She opened her mouth to ask him. "Great."

Nick beamed. "I'm so glad we're on the same page."

Reeva's thoughts ran wild. What was she doing, acting like she knew what he was going on about? She needed to say something now. Before it was too late and the moment passed. Were they in a relationship or were they in an orange? And if it was the latter, what the *fuck* did that mean?

"Um, though, if you could maybe clarify?" she ventured. "Like, what you mean?"

Nick blushed endearingly. "Yeah. Sorry. I get a little awkward with these conversations. The teenage me comes out. I guess I'm trying to say I'd like us to be in a relationship. If that works for you."

"It does." Reeva leaned over to kiss him, trying to not grin excessively. This was the conversation she'd been dreaming of ever since Nick had made a Jane Eyre reference on their second date. And it had finally happened. After everything she'd been through with Rakesh, and then years of bad dates, good dates that never went anywhere, and dates so bad they didn't even make funny stories, Reeva was in a relationship with someone she liked who *liked her back*. She couldn't help but think that this was her reward for all the heartbreak—wasn't that how it worked in rom-coms? And that would make Nick her happy ever after.

Nick kissed her back passionately and pulled off her T-shirt. Reeva reciprocated, surprised. She hadn't intended to initiate anything sexual—not in her dad's bed. But she didn't want to reject Nick after the conversation they'd just had. And it wasn't that big a deal. She could be intimate in her dad's bed. She'd had plenty of sex in IKEA beds; what was one more?

"You're so sexy," whispered Nick, as he ran a hand through her hair. Her hair! It was going to be so much harder to hide her patch during sex now that it was getting bigger. She should have kept the hairband on. Or tied her hair up so it wouldn't move. Oh god. Reeva continued kissing him, desperately trying to think of a solution. Would it be better if she was on top? Or perhaps if she just stayed in missionary and tried not to move her head? Nick ran his hands through her hair again and Reeva balked. She couldn't do this.

Reeva pulled away, then caught Nick's confused expression. She didn't know what to say, so instead, she pulled down his boxer shorts. He moaned in surprised pleasure. Reeva took her chance to rearrange her hair and when she looked up, Nick was staring straight at the ceiling. She was safe. But she was also painfully, unusually aware of everything she was doing—every movement, every sound, every sensation. Normally during sex, she was caught up in the moment. Right now, she was not. Mainly because *she was giving her brand-new boyfriend a blow job in her dead dad's bed.*

Reeva prayed desperately that her dad's ghost had not chosen this moment to look down on his three daughters fulfilling his dying wishes by praying for his soul. There was no way her current actions could be mistaken for prayer. Even if she was on her knees.

"Hey," gasped Nick. "Stop."

Reeva looked up at him questioningly. "What is it?"

"I . . . well, I just don't feel comfortable, um, well, finishing in your mouth while you're grieving your dad. It doesn't feel right."

Reeva tilted her head. "Uh, I'm sorry, I think I misheard you. Did you say you *don't* want to do that?"

"Yeah. Not while your family is singing prayers for your dad downstairs. I . . . don't really think I should finish at all. Sorry."

As Nick spoke, Reeva felt a thick, hot wave of shame spread over her. She sat up and pulled her top on quickly. She didn't understand; why had Nick initiated sex stuff if he hadn't wanted to? Had she been the one who'd accidentally started things? Did he think she'd *wanted* to do this in her dad's bed? "No worries," she said, wishing she was brave enough to say all of this aloud. "I get it."

Nick reached out an arm and hugged her. "Good. Not that I wasn't enjoying it; I very much was."

"Of course," said Reeva, suddenly wondering if he'd stopped her because he *wasn't* enjoying it.

"Perfect. Shall we just watch a movie? I can pull something up on my laptop, and we can cuddle. I'm more in the mood for that anyway."

"Uh-huh."

Reeva plastered on a fake smile as Nick scrolled through his laptop. She felt shame burning into her skin. Her brand-new boyfriend had wanted an innocent Netflix and chill, and her depraved mind had taken things in the opposite direction. What was wrong with her? She was a terrible girlfriend—and an even worse daughter.

## CHAPTER 6

**Day 4**

"That does sound bad," agreed Lakshmi.

"Thanks. Aren't you meant to be reassuring me that everything is okay and not as bad as I think?" Reeva adjusted her earbuds and wrapped her puffer jacket tight around her. It was miserable outside—gray, cold, windy—but it was still better than being cooped up with her family indoors. She'd left the house under the pretense of doing errands, but she'd just needed some space. And at least this way she could get to know the city her dad had called home.

"He stopped you from giving him a blow job. That's never a good sign in my book."

Reeva sighed morosely outside a pound shop. So far, she couldn't see the appeal of Leicester. "Great. Well. Guess that relationship's over before it began. Twelve hours is a real record for me."

"Oh, calm down; I'm not saying you guys are *over*. He went out of his way to ask you to be in a bloody clementine with him."

"He didn't specify what kind of orange it was."

"I don't care if it's a satsuma or a bag of Easy Peelers; he likes you enough to be in a relationship with you, Reeva. And he drove two hours to spontaneously surprise you while you're going through a hard time. That's practically a marriage proposal in my book."

Reeva laughed despite herself. "A guy taking you out to dinner is practically a marriage proposal in your book."

"I just don't see why we need to sit through three courses and have them judge me on how many carb-based sides I order when we could go for drinks instead. And you know I don't want to be tied down."

"Yes, but you know I do . . . I love the thought of being married to someone I love. I always have."

Lakshmi groaned. "I have no idea how you can be so traditional with a mother as progressive as yours. No wonder you get on so well with my mum."

Reeva felt a warmth spread over her at the thought of Lakshmi's mum. She was everything Saraswati was not—soft, affectionate, caring—and Reeva had spent most of the last decade wishing they could swap mothers.

"I know you're fantasizing about my mum," said Lakshmi. "Stop it; it's creepy."

"Sorry. I just can't get over the Nick thing. I feel so . . . rejected."

"Hey, he didn't reject you. He changed his mind because he realized the weirdness of the situation. Let's take him at face value. He didn't want to come in your mouth during such an emotionally challenging moment for you. That makes him polite. It's cute. You can chill."

"Okay, you have gone full circle. And how am I meant to be

chill when it's midday, he left at six a.m., and I *still* haven't heard from him?"

"Because that's only six hours ago. I know you've got an anxious attachment style, but you need to try and calm down."

"That is very much easier said than done. How would you feel if it was you?"

There was silence as Lakshmi thought about it. "I just can't imagine a man ever stopping me during oral sex, sorry. It's literally impossible. Oh, hey, Lee. Just chatting to a client. Yep. Sure." She lowered her voice. "Got to go, babe. Call you later."

REEVA OPENED THE bedroom door and stopped. The duvet was covered in a giant heap of stuff—clothes, books, old toiletries—and her sisters were on either side of it, carelessly chucking more stuff onto the bed. The bed she was going to have to sleep in later that night.

"Uh, what are you doing? And whatever it is, why are you doing it on my bed?"

"Dad's bed," corrected Sita. "Good of you to finally show up and help."

"Help . . . destroy his room?" asked Reeva.

"We're looking for clues," explained Jaya, who sat cross-legged by the bed going through its drawers. "There must be something in here somewhere to help us figure out what happened."

"We left the wardrobe for you," said Sita, who seemed to be emptying the contents of a chest of drawers—old wallets, batteries, and . . . was that a rope?—onto the bed.

"Right." Reeva sighed, making her way over the bulging wardrobe. She wrinkled her nose at the musty smell. "What exactly am I meant to be looking for in here? Other than mothballs."

Sita shrugged. "Anything. And you can put the clothes in charity bags while you're there. We may as well start clearing the house out while we hunt for secrets."

"Oh-kay," said Reeva, rolling up her sleeves and resigning herself to following her younger sister's orders. So much for her planned day of catching up with TV shows and reading the new literary thriller that was all over social media.

For a while, the sisters worked in semicompaniable silence and Reeva lost herself in her task. The more she inhaled the scent of her dad's clothes—the mustiness combined with laundry detergent and an unfamiliar scent that must have been his own smell—the more he became a tangible person in her mind. It felt surreal to think he'd actually worn these pale blue shirts, navy polos, and gray jumpers. When she came across a faded, well-worn jumper with a hole under the armpit, Reeva found her eyes tearing up. She couldn't explain why, but there was something so sad about it. She wished she'd known him so she could buy him jumpers for Father's Day and mend his clothes. She turned away from her sisters and buried her face in the jumper. The longing in her chest felt unbearable. She so desperately wanted to know the man who'd worn these clothes. What had he been like? Would he have loved his daughters? Would he have loved Reeva?

"Can we not hire someone to do this?" asked Jaya. "Like, pack up his stuff and get rid of it?"

Her sister's complaint broke through Reeva's reverie. Jaya was anxiously checking her long shell-pink nails as she gingerly folded sheets: the epitome of influencer cliché.

"If you want to pay for it, sure," said Sita. "Be my guest."

"I can probably get it for free if I post about it," said Jaya, her face brightening. "I could do a whole thing: 'Uncovering Family Secrets, hashtag Who Is My Dad?'"

Sita turned to glare at her. "You'd better be kidding. This is our private family business. We're not telling the world about it."

"I agree with Sita." Reeva could not remember the last time she'd said those four words. She shook her head and tried not to overthink it. "We should definitely keep this quiet. Especially when we know so little. Our parents clearly hid it from us for a reason, and I'm not sure I need anyone else to find that out before we do."

Jaya sighed. "Ugh. Fine. Guess I'll get back to the sheets. I don't know why he had so much bed linen when he lived alone. Weird, right?"

Reeva shrugged. "I think he just didn't believe in throwing anything away."

"Agreed," said Sita. She held up a wad of papers and tickets. "He kept *cinema* tickets. And these, uh . . . Are these coupons?" She paused. "Our dad . . . cut out coupons in the newspaper."

"You can do that? For what?" asked Jaya, baffled.

"A food processor," said Sita. Her voice was different—softer and quieter. Reeva instinctively turned away so Sita could have her moment in private. She knew exactly how Sita felt; seeing these human details about their dad evoked a triple sense of longing, pathos, and regret.

"Who collects coupons to buy a food processor?" asked Jaya.

Sita scowled at her. "Someone who understands how to budget. It would have been a total bargain if he'd collected the last one. In fact, fuck it. I'm keeping them. I'm going to collect the next one and get the goddamn processor. There's no point coming so far and falling at the last hurdle because—well, because he died."

"That's a nice idea," said Reeva. "I get the sense Dad would have appreciated that."

Sita gave her a rare smile. "Yeah."

"I wish we knew more about him," said Jaya. "Don't you re-member *anything*, Reeva? You were the oldest."

Reeva bit her bottom lip. "I can't tell what are my memories and what I've seen in photographs. I kind of remember his face—mainly his eighties mustache. And I think I remember him hold-ing me. Hugging me. But I'm not really sure."

"He hugged you," repeated Jaya softly.

"I'm pretty sure he hugged you too," said Sita. "Parents do generally hold their children. Seeing as babies can't, you know, do anything without being held."

Jaya's eyes moistened. "It's crazy to think of him truly hold-ing me. Like, now we're here in his house. And I'm folding his linens."

Sita shook her head impatiently, but Reeva nodded. "I know what you mean. I thought about him so much as a kid, but then I just . . . you know, life. He became an idea, not a person. And be-ing here, in his house . . . he's real again."

"Exactly," cried Jaya. "I just want to know who he was. Do you remember anything about what he was like with Mum? If they were, like, relationship goals? Or the couple who should have divorced?"

"I'm guessing the latter," said Sita. "Seeing as they ended up faking his death. Probably because he cheated."

"They did start out with that romantic forbidden-love story," pointed out Reeva. "Eloping and hiding it from their parents. But . . . I don't think that lasted. All I know is what Mum's always told us when we asked about him—that he loved us all, but he wasn't the easiest husband to live with. Which probably just trans-lated to him not letting her spend the food budget in Selfridges."

Sita snorted. "Exactly."

"I wish I could remember more," said Jaya sadly. "I hate how Mum never wanted to talk about him."

"It's typical her—if it's in the past, leave it there." Sita shrugged. "I vaguely remember her saying they argued a lot, but she argues with everyone."

Reeva nodded. "I feel like I have hazy memories of them arguing, but I think it was just normal husband-wife stuff. Oh, and I have one nice memory. Of us all sitting on the sofa watching *The Jungle Book*. And maybe an argument about a babysitter?"

"The one who stole!" cried Sita.

"How do you know that?"

"Mum told me. It's why she always locked her stuff up in a safe."

"Oh my god!" Jaya's face lit up. "Reeva, maybe you're the key to all of this. We could get you hypnotherapy! I bet you know more than you think. You probably overheard them talking about the big secret. His affair."

Reeva rolled her eyes. "Five-year-old me is not the key to this. I barely remember what I had for lunch, let alone our parents' adult conversations from the nineties."

"You never know," said Jaya excitedly. "I vote you do it. We've got nothing to lose, and it's not like we have any other leads."

"Sita, tell her that's a ridiculous idea," said Reeva, looking at her sister. "Sita? Hello?"

Sita turned around slowly. She was holding a large brown folder. "I think you guys need to see this."

Jaya instantly sprang up while Reeva cautiously made her way across the room. "What is it?"

"I don't know," replied Sita. "Let's find out."

The sisters sat down on the carpet and opened the folder. It had dozens of colored dividers inside, all clearly labeled with dates going all the way from before the girls' births to the previous year before he died.

"Look how organized it is," cried Jaya. "Tell me now he's not a spy."

"He's not a spy," said Sita automatically. She pulled out a file, and all three sisters gasped as photos of the three of them as babies spilled out. Photos of their dad holding them. Even a photo of their mum laughing next to him in the sunshine. "It's . . . us," said Sita. "He has photos of us."

Reeva quickly brushed away the tears that were spilling from her eyes. Her dad had photos of them all. He'd kept them neatly organized inside a folder. He'd cared about them all this time.

"They look so normal," said Jaya. "Mum doesn't even have her extensions in."

"Though she is still wearing a full face of makeup to take us swimming," pointed out Reeva.

"I think this is the first photo I've ever seen of Mum actually being a mum," said Sita. "I can't believe they used to take us *swimming*."

"Let's look at the rest," said Reeva. "Like, the later years. Here, give me a file." She grabbed a file from the last decade and cried out loud. "He's got stuff on us as adults! He . . . he knew who we were." She pulled out a headshot of herself as a trainee from her firm's website. One of Sita's wedding photos. A magazine clipping of an article on influencers that featured Jaya. She paused as she saw a printed-out photograph of her old Facebook profile picture—her and Rakesh laughing together at a friend's barbecue—and quickly pushed it back into the folder before anyone noticed.

"Oh my god." Sita held the wedding photo and looked up at her big sister, her eyes wide. "He kept track of our lives."

"I can't believe it," said Jaya softly. "He knew about my career. He knew who we were."

Reeva felt the tears coming again, and this time she didn't bother to hide them; her sisters were just as emotional as she was. She grabbed another file and felt her heart melt as she pulled out its contents. Reeva's GCSE results. And the "Best Improver" certificate she'd been given for gymnastics. Her dad had it all.

"Oh my god, this is a story I wrote in primary school!" cried Jaya, going through a different section. "Look, it's about a hedge-hog."

"He's kept my artwork," said Sita quietly. "And I was really shit at art. If my girls came home with this"—she held up a drawing of five different-colored blobs—"it would be in the fucking bin."

"He must have really loved us," said Jaya. "Mum would *never* keep stuff like this. I don't think she even knows my middle name."

"You have a middle name?" asked Reeva.

"Oh my god, yes!" cried Jaya. "I swear, no one—"

"Look," interrupted Sita. "He's got a file on the girls! Photos of them, ones I posted on Facebook. And . . ." She sniffed loudly. "He's labeled the photo. 'Amisha and Alisha.' He's got their names the right way around."

"Guys, he must have been in touch with Mum," cried Reeva. "To have all this stuff. Our schoolwork. I know he's got most of our adult stuff from the internet and social media, but he had to be in touch with her to get my GCSE results!"

"Unless the school just sent them to him," suggested Sita. "He was still a parent. He could call up and get access to it all."

"Speaking of Mum," said Jaya, holding up newspaper clippings featuring Saraswati's beaming face, "he's got stuff on her too. And her extensions are back."

"Guess he never got over her," said Sita. "If he did have that affair, I reckon he really regretted it."

Reeva frowned. "We can't just speculate. And if he did cheat on Mum, wouldn't there be a photo of her here too? The other woman?"

"Not if it was just casual," said Jaya.

"Or if he threw it away in his guilt," said Sita.

"This is pointless," declared Reeva. "Let's just . . . keep looking. We've only searched one room and we've found so much. By the time we've done them all, I bet we'll be so much closer to finding out the truth."

FIVE ROOMS LATER, the sisters were no closer to finding out the truth. They'd found nothing of relevance—except divorce papers, which proved that Saraswati had not committed bigamy; she and Hemant had divorced in 2005 when the girls were all teenagers.

"Which means they were speaking then." Sita scowled. "She could have had the decency to tell us."

"As if Mum would ever tell us anything," replied Jaya. "Apart from lies. She loved those."

"I wonder why they waited around a decade after the death-faking before they actually divorced," said Sita. "What do you think, Reeva? Oi!"

Reeva looked up. She was sitting at the table going through the folder again—ostensibly in case they'd missed any clues, but really because it made her feel close to the dad she'd never known. He'd kept her piano certificates; she didn't even know she'd been given piano certificates. She'd certainly never seen them before, and yet here they were, carefully filed under "Reeva, 2002–2007." Even the fact that she had her own subsection made her feel special. Her dad had cared about her. He might have even loved her.

"Uh, what was the question?" she asked.

Sita rolled her eyes. "Whatever; we still know fuck all. We should get back to hunting for clues. Whether it's a machete or his mistress's underwear."

"A machete?"

"You never know with our family."

"Fine, I'll redo the drawers under the bed," said Reeva, getting up and closing the folder. She'd look at it properly when everyone was in bed.

"Oh right, you want to recheck the bit I was responsible for," said Jaya, crossing her arms. "Rude."

"It's practical, not rude," said Sita. "There's no point us searching the bits we already did. It's about fresh eyes. I'll do the wardrobes."

"Whatever, it's obvious none of you trust me," said Jaya.

"Uh, I wonder why."

Reeva tuned out her sisters' bickering and sat down by the bed, carefully removing the linens from the drawers. She couldn't stop thinking about the folder. She didn't understand if her dad had done it all alone or if her mum had helped. None of it made sense. The only thing she knew for sure was that her dad had thought about them. And he knew things her mum had never cared about. Like her GCSE results. Her fingers found something hard in the drawer. She reached down. A shoebox. As she pulled the lid off, her jaw fell slack. "Uh, guys, you're . . . going to want to come over."

"Oh my god, what have you found?" squealed Jaya. "Is it a gun?"

"Obviously you found something in the bit Jaya was meant to search," muttered Sita as she crouched down next to Reeva. "So, what is it?"

Reeva showed them the contents of the shoebox. "Around ten thousand pounds. In cash."

Her sisters gasped out loud. "Oh my god!"

"I know," said Reeva. "I need to count it properly. But it looks about right. I mean, it's all in fifties."

"Guys, surely now you see my point?" said Jaya. "About Dad's line of work."

"For the last time, he was not a spy!" snapped Sita. "He's just . . . Indian. He doesn't trust banks. It's what foreigners do. Nitin's parents have solid bars of gold under their bed!"

"Jealous," said Reeva. "I wish I had piles of hidden gold."

Sita turned to look at her. "They do it because when Idi Amin made them leave Uganda, they had to come to the UK as refugees with just the belongings they had on their back. It's a reaction to trauma."

"Oh," said Reeva. "Well, yeah. That's awful."

"So, neither of you think this is suspicious?" asked Jaya.

Reeva shook her head. "A lot of my clients hide money in their homes. I just never expected Dad to have so *much*." She picked up wads of the money and then frowned. "Wait, there's something else. Bank statements."

The three sisters crowded around to read the statements. Reeva ran her finger down the paper, looking for the bit they all wanted to see, and then paused. It couldn't be. She turned the paper over and then turned it back. The figure was right.

"Oh my god," she breathed out. "Dad was loaded."

## CHAPTER 7

### Day 4

THE SISTERS SAT in silence around the dining table. The box of money was right in the middle of them, along with Reeva's laptop. Up on the page was an e-mail from Hemant's lawyers confirming the hefty sum of money he had in his bank account. Money that was going straight to his three daughters.

"I still don't get it," said Reeva. "He was an optometrist. How do you make that kind of money?"

"I wish I knew," said Sita. "Then I could do the same."

"Maybe Mum gave it to him?" asked Jaya.

"That would have shown up on the bank statements," said Reeva. "It looks like he just . . . saved. A lot."

"No one can save that much," said Sita. "I know Leicester is cheaper than London, but the man would have had to live like a monk."

"Unless he did something illegal," suggested Jaya.

"Well, we're about to find out," said Reeva. "Satya Auntie's here."

———

THE SISTERS LOOKED expectantly at their aunt. She put down the bank statement and smiled at her nieces. "Congratulations. That's a lot of money."

"Do you know where it came from?" asked Reeva.

"She means, what did Dad do to get it?" corrected Jaya. "And we're fine with it being illegal. You can tell us anything."

Satya Auntie laughed. "I'm sorry to disappoint you, but as far as I know, Hemant was just very careful with his money."

"You're saying this came from his salary?" clarified Sita.

Satya Auntie nodded. "Yes, I think so. I had no idea how much money he had. But, girls, your dad hardly ever spent anything on himself. His whole purpose in life was to work for you. It doesn't surprise me he accumulated so much."

Reeva frowned in confusion. "But . . . I don't understand. He didn't need to earn money for us. Mum always supported us. And she obviously had plenty of money."

"I think he did need to," said Satya Auntie gently. "It was his way of being a father. It made him feel better, knowing that he was leaving you all with this security. He and I spoke about it once—he sat me down to tell me that his inheritance was going to you three, and not to me. He hoped I wouldn't mind, and of course I didn't. It was his way of making it all up to you—his physical absence."

"It was his way of . . . loving us?" asked Reeva.

"Exactly," said Satya Auntie. "Everyone shows it in different ways, remember?"

"His love language was money," cried Jaya. "This makes total sense now! To be honest, I relate—mine is gifts."

"Wait, but how did he get it all?" asked Sita. "He would have had to have saved everything he earned for *decades* to get this much money."

Satya Auntie paused and dabbed her eyes. "That's exactly what he did. It makes me emotional, because he denied himself everything. He only ever spent money on the absolute basics. He saved it all. For you. For years."

Reeva felt her eyes watering up too. Her dad's old clothes. His basic furniture. He never treated himself to anything—he was saving it all for his daughters. His whole life he'd been keeping tabs on them *and* trying to provide for them.

"Please tell me he still treated himself too," said Jaya, looking pale. "To, like, holidays and stuff?"

"I don't think he ever traveled," said Satya Auntie. "But he had quite simple needs. He was from a different generation and culture."

"The vouchers—the food processer," cried Sita. "Fuck!"

"Did . . . any of it come from Mum?" asked Reeva. "In cash maybe? She does love undeclared income."

Satya Auntie shook her head. "I don't think so. Your dad did say she offered, but he never accepted it. It was his pride. Remember, he grew up in a world where men were expected to provide. This was his way." She paused. "And, well, I think he also did it out of some kind of penance. He had a lot of guilt."

"Because he had an affair?" asked Sita. "An affair that devastated Mum and tore our family apart?"

Satya Auntie looked taken aback. "He had an affair?"

"It's a theory we're working on," explained Jaya.

"Ah," said Satya Auntie. "Well, I can't say I can confirm that. As I told Reeva, he never told me exactly what it was that led to him leaving your lives. I always got the sense there was so much shame surrounding it for him. So he found it too hard to talk about."

"Shame and affairs are massively linked," said Jaya knowingly. "It's a thing."

Reeva found her cheeks burning. She needed to change the topic. "Uh, Satya Auntie, we also found a folder he'd kept. He knew all about us. Did you know about that?"

Her aunt nodded. "Oh yes, he was so proud of you all! He'd share everything with me. 'Oh, Sita's had twins,' or 'Reeva's been promoted.' I was always so glad to hear it, but I wished he could have been in your life to hear it firsthand, not off Facebook."

Reeva felt her eyes water up. Her dad had been *proud* of her. He was turning out to be exactly the kind of man she'd always dreamed of. Her sisters' affair theory was nonsense—their father was far too devoted to his family to risk it all for a bit of passion.

"Why didn't you tell us?" asked Sita, as Reeva shot her a look. "That he kept tabs on us?"

Satya Auntie hesitated. "I . . . didn't want to interfere."

"We are more than happy with you interfering if it means we get to find out the truth, right, guys?" Sita turned to her sisters.

"Chill out," hissed Reeva, before facing her aunt. "I know you'd never lie to us, Satya Auntie, don't worry."

"It's okay," said Satya Auntie, running a hand through her dark hair. "You're allowed to be upset, Sita. I'm sorry. And I really wouldn't lie to you, ever. But I didn't want to talk about how your dad felt about you—it felt like it wasn't my place."

Sita nodded. "Thanks, Satya Auntie. It's all cool. But if you do know anything else, please let us know. The quicker we can find everything out, the quicker we can start to move on."

"Totally," said Jaya. "Like, can you even tell us if you think Dad was capable of having an affair?"

"I . . . don't know," said Satya Auntie helplessly. "Aren't we all capable? On some level?"

Reeva forced herself to breathe deeply. This wasn't about her. "There's no point trying to guess when we don't know. We're going to end up making things up otherwise. It's better to just . . . focus on what we do have."

All four women's eyes turned to the box in the middle of the table, with wads of cash and bank statements spilling out of it.

"Financial freedom," said Sita. "Thanks, Dad."

"The deluxe wedding package," said Jaya. "I can afford it now."

"Proof," said Reeva. "That our dad loved us."

REEVA STOOD AT the door at 6:50 p.m., dressed in jeans and a kurta top (borrowed from Sita). She was ready for the prayers this time. Now that she knew more about who her father was, she felt like less of an imposter grieving him. And more importantly, she was ready to find out more about who he was. The real him—not the cheating husband her sisters had made him out to be.

The doorbell rang, and Reeva rushed over to answer it with her "Jai Shree Krishna" at the ready.

Dhilip Bhai and Kalpana Ben stood on the doorstep, offering namastes to her. "Thank you for coming, come in," cried Reeva. The bhajan singer was already setting up, but she'd been hoping her dad's best friend would be next. As the couple took off their coats she got straight to the point. "Dhilip Bhai. Kalpana Ben. I was wondering if you could tell me a bit more about my dad. I mean, obviously I *knew* him. But I'd love to know what, um . . ." They were both staring at her like she was mad. It was throwing her off. "Sorry. I'd love to know what he was like as a man, not just a dad. You know?"

This time, Dhilip Bhai nodded heartily. "Of course, Reeva. You want to know who your dad was when he wasn't being a responsible father. You want to hear about when we'd all go and watch the cricket together!"

His wife slapped his arm. "No, Reeva doesn't care about cricket, do you?" She carried on talking before Reeva could respond. "You want to know if your dad was lonely, don't you, beta? But you don't need to feel bad for being so busy in London. He was very proud of you and your wonderful job."

Reeva felt a pang of misplaced guilt—she would have loved to make time for her dad if anyone had bothered to let her know he was alive.

"And we never got up to too much trouble, don't worry," said Dhilip Bhai, winking at her. "Especially your dad—he wasn't like us, drinking too much whiskey."

"Whiskey, cricket, all you ever think about," complained his wife. "But don't worry, beta. He wasn't lonely. He liked to spend time alone; you know what he was like. You all were his priority. And he had his friends, and you know . . ."

"Who?" asked Sita, sidling up alongside them.

Kalpana Ben hesitated. "His friend."

"Oh my god, Dad had a girlfriend?" asked Jaya, joining them. "Who?!"

Dhilip Bhai laughed awkwardly. "No, no. He wasn't like that—he was always talking about you girls and your mother."

"Leela is just his friend," said Kalpana Ben firmly. "Come, Dhilip, the guests are arriving. Let's go inside."

Sita crossed her arms smugly. "That's the proof we needed. Dad had a girlfriend."

"A friend," corrected Reeva.

"Oh, come on," cried Jaya. "He and Leela were totally shagging."

"Jaya!" cried Reeva. "Also, even if they were, which I really don't want to know about, that doesn't mean they had an affair. He had almost thirty years of being single—they could have met anytime."

Sita rolled her eyes. "I need to put the twins to bed. Keep an eye out for this Leela."

"I need to call Rak—uh, someone," said Jaya.

The sisters left Reeva alone in the hallway with a growing pile of coats and a deep sense of unease. She didn't agree with her sisters—it was obvious this Leela was someone he'd met recently. A friend. So why did Reeva feel absolute dread at the thought of meeting her? The doorbell rang. Reeva stared at the door with trepidation. She opened it slowly, wondering if this mystery Leela would be behind it.

"Jai Shree Krishna, Reeva." Shilpa Ben spoke authoritatively. "Can I give you my coat?" Reeva took it silently as Shilpa Ben smoothed her sari. "Thank you. Is Seema Ben here?"

"Seema . . . oh! The singer. Sorry, yes. She's setting up. Satya Auntie's there with her."

"Good. I'll just—"

"Hang on!" Reeva reached out to touch her. "Sorry. I just wanted to ask you, um, you knew my dad from the mandir, didn't you?"

"Oh yes. Hemant Bhai was very active."

"Really?" asked Reeva. "Was he always? It's just, um, I don't remember him being really religious when I was younger. And I was wondering when he, uh . . ." She hesitated. "Found God" sounded a bit dramatic.

"He started coming to the mandir regularly maybe five years ago now. For guidance. Something we all need at different points in our lives."

"Was it . . . for anything in particular?"

Shilpa Ben frowned. "Well, I wouldn't normally say. But I mean, he was your dad. It's just . . . it was when your mum found someone new. It all hit him."

"What hit him?"

"His loneliness, I think," said Shilpa Ben. "Isn't that why we all turn to God? To find that sense of connection?"

"So he wasn't, uh, Leela wasn't—"

"Leela? His colleague? What about her?"

"Nothing," beamed Reeva. "Nothing at all. So Dad came to the mandir to find connection?"

"I think so. He lived a quiet life. All those years of sacrifice, working hard for you girls and denying himself so much. He deserved a bit of community, heh nah?"

Reeva nodded. "Definitely. I'm glad he got it."

Shilpa Ben gave a satisfied nod. "Now, we'd better sit down. We'll start soon."

"I'll be right there. I just need to tell my sisters something."

Reeva ran up the stairs and opened the door to Sita's room. She was standing in a corner, trying to shield herself with a giant Star Wars book while the twins threw balled-up socks at her.

"Whoa," said Reeva. "Are you okay?"

"Do I look okay?" cried Sita. "I don't know *why* they're acting like this, but I've had enough. Reeva Masi can deal with you." She turned around, slamming the door behind her. The twins instantly stopped screaming and burst into tears instead.

"Uh, what's going on, girls?" asked Reeva hesitantly.

"Everything," they sobbed loudly.

"Oh-kay," said Reeva, glancing at her watch. The prayers were starting any minute now. "Maybe you can go to sleep while I go downstairs?"

"No!" wailed Alisha.

"You have to stay," demanded Amisha.

Reeva sighed. She really should go down. She'd already missed the previous night. But . . . the twins needed her. And if she was honest, she'd much rather curl up with them than go downstairs and wait for Leela. Even if it was all innocent, she knew her sisters would find a way to make it sound anything but.

"All right," she conceded. "I'll just stay for a little while. But not long, okay?"

## CHAPTER 8

## Day 5

REEVA STIFLED A yawn as she walked through the city center, past familiar brand names and endless Indian restaurants. She really had no right to yawn after falling asleep at seven p.m. with the twins. Her sisters had been furious she'd avoided yet another night of prayers, especially because they hadn't found this mystery Leela. But Reeva had been subjected to another night full of nightmares. And this time she could remember something. A cat. She couldn't recall the details, but seeing as it was a nightmare, something bad must have happened. To the cat. And Reeva had woken in a cold sweat. She presumed it must be linked to her anxiety about leaving FP alone. But considering all the things Reeva currently felt anxious about, she had no idea why her subconscious had chosen her cat. Especially when the photos Lakshmi sent her suggested that FP was having the time of her life without her.

She still hadn't managed to speak to Nick since the Incident either. She'd tried to call—again, it was always her—and he'd replied with a **Sorry Reevs. I know I'm being shit but work is** really busy right now. Sending hugs. Promise I'll call soon! xxx. It was sweet, but Reeva's abandonment fears were in overdrive. She wished she was more like Lakshmi. Her confidence levels were out of this world. She always assumed every man she dated was into her, unless explicitly told otherwise. And even then, she interpreted their rejections as proof they were "going through something." She never took it personally or attached her self-worth to what a man thought about her, which was probably why she was so mentally stable.

Reeva was not. Her patch was at 7.7 centimeters and seemed to be growing by the minute. It didn't help that the three sisters could barely spend ten minutes alone together without arguing. They'd never been this bad before. Even in their twenties, when their lives were completely different, they'd always had fun together whenever they'd been forced into attending their mum's latest premiere. Reeva remembered the time they'd snuck out of an event to go to a club in Mumbai and danced till six a.m. Or the time they'd left to hang out in McDonald's and eat all the food they'd never been allowed growing up. But since their mum's wedding, everything had changed. The tension was so intense that they bickered nonstop. The only way they were going to get through this fortnight was with someone there to help them. And by someone, Reeva meant Saraswati. She was furious at their mum for being AWOL. Not only had she lied to them for their whole lives, she'd disappeared right when they needed her. Again.

Reeva remembered the first time she'd done it—twenty-three years ago. Eleven-year-old Reeva had been so excited for her mum to watch her flute solo in the school concert. She'd spent hours practicing. Only, of course, her mum had never turned up. Deep down, Reeva had always known on some level that Saraswati would miss the end-of-term concert—but she'd never imagined she'd also miss the actual end of term. It turned out she'd gotten the day wrong, so while Sita and Jaya were still at day school in London with the nanny, Reeva had been forced to spend a night entirely alone at boarding school with only the math teacher for company. Her mum had turned up the next day, full of empty apologies and boxes of Ladurée macarons, as though that made up for what Reeva had gone through. Reeva had never played the flute again.

That was an objectively bad memory, but what her mum was doing now was even worse. Reeva was so angry that she was tempted to jump on a flight to Mumbai to confront her mother in person. Only she knew she'd never really do it. If it came down to winning a case for one of her clients, she'd be straight on that flight. But not for personal family drama. She'd never been able to confront her family, and over the years she'd decided this was for the best. They were all so unreasonable that she'd never be able to get through to them anyway. It was best to just continue taking the higher ground, avoid their constant baiting, and take her therapist's advice to breathe very, very deeply.

Reeva kept walking and realized there were cafés all around her with blackboards advertising matcha lattes and vegan lasagnas. She'd walked into the gentrified bit of Leicester—and she was into it. She wandered into one of the cafés to buy herself an oat milk flat white and began paying more attention to her surroundings, with the cobblestone streets and Tudoresque buildings. Leicester was starting to grow on her. Maybe she should take the girls to go and see the sights one day—they'd love the story of King Richard III's skeleton being found under a local car park. Suddenly she stopped. She'd found it. The place she was looking for.

Specsavers.

"Excuse me, can I help you?" A smiling blond employee stuck her head out the door.

Reeva jerked. "Uh. Um. Yes. I mean, no. Can I just . . . browse?"

"Of course!" she beamed. "We love browsers. We're not like those fancy shops that make you feel you have to buy. You're more than welcome to try on every single pair of glasses in here and leave without spending a penny."

"Uh . . . thanks?"

Reeva followed the woman into the shop and looked around. This was it. Her dad's place of work. A very normal-looking optometry office with rows of glasses, big posters featuring diverse families in glasses, and worn brown doors that led into private examination rooms. Reeva realized just how surreal it was that her dad had worked there while her mum had lived a life of five-star luxury. And he'd denied himself every possible luxury available—all for his daughters.

Reeva turned back to the blond lady with a renewed sense of purpose. "Excuse me, does a Leela work here?"

"Leela? Of course! She's just with a customer now, but she'll be out shortly. Unless it's urgent and you need me to rush in there?" Her eyes glowed as if she'd love nothing more.

"It's cool, I can wait," said Reeva. "Um, and did a . . . Hemant Mehta work here? I . . . think I used to know him."

The lady stopped smiling. Reeva squinted (she probably could do with an eye test herself) to read her name badge—Meg. She sniffed loudly and then cleared her throat. "I'm sorry. He did. It's just, well, he . . . he passed away. Recently."

"I'm so sorry. Did you know him well?"

"Oh, everyone knows Hemant! He worked here for years, so

the whole high street knew him. He was so funny—he'd say the most outrageous things. No filters at all. Just hilarious."

"Really?" Reeva had no idea her dad had been funny. "What kind of things?"

"He had a real thing about making sure we'd all eaten our five a day. And he was always going on about the health benefits of mackerel. He had this pot of fish oil tablets in his office he'd try and give us." Meg shook her head, laughing. "Such a funny guy. We all loved him—he was like the granddad of our team—but for some reason, he'd never come out to the pub with us. He was very boundaried like that. Ooh, Leela!" Meg called out to someone behind her. "There's someone here to see you. Sorry, I didn't get your name?"

Reeva turned around slowly and then blinked in surprise. It was the woman in pink lipstick who'd been at her dad's prayers the first night. She'd been expecting another Saraswati. Not this old woman with a tight bun, black rectangular glasses, and a faded pink jumper. She looked so *normal.*

"Reeva," said Leela in surprise. "You're here."

"Uh, yes," said Reeva. "Sorry. To just turn up. I wondered if we could have a little chat?"

"Of course," said Leela seriously. "Let me finish up here, and we can pop outside."

Reeva nodded and realized she'd been wrong to call her old. Up close, Leela must be in her late fifties. It was just that her clothes made her look older. She was actually quite pretty. And she had kind eyes. Reeva found herself hoping that Leela and her dad *had* been more than friends. Not while he'd been married. But he'd spent almost thirty years alone afterward—he deserved some love and company in his life. Especially if it was with someone who looked so kind.

"Sorry about that," said Leela, walking out of the shop to meet Reeva. "It's nice of you to come."

"Of course. I felt bad I hadn't spoken to you at the prayers or anything. I know you and my dad were close."

Leela's face lit up. "Really? He . . . spoke about me?"

"Uh . . . yes." It suddenly felt important to Reeva to make Leela feel special. "He . . . always said how great you were."

Leela pursed her lips and sniffed. "Sorry. I can't believe I'm crying in front of you. I just really miss him."

Reeva pulled out a tissue from her bag—her clients often needed one—and handed it to her. "Please don't feel bad. He would have, uh, wanted us to speak."

Leela dabbed her eyes with the tissue. "Thank you. I always wanted to meet you. But I know Hemant was very private, so, well . . . it never happened."

Reeva nodded slowly. So Leela didn't know that Hemant hadn't been in his daughters' lives. She felt strangely disappointed— she'd hoped that her dad had felt close enough to someone in his life to share his burden. Whatever it was. "Have you known my dad a long time?"

"Oh, years! We've been close since university. We studied to-gether in London. Before he married your mum."

"I . . . didn't know that," said Reeva. "So, you must know a lot about him. Did he . . . ever tell you *why* he and my mum split up?"

Leela fidgeted awkwardly with her glasses. "Not in so many words. I know how different they were. Though it's not my place to speak about your mother."

"But what was the thing that made them break up?" persisted Reeva. "What happened when I was five?" Leela took a step back and Reeva realized she was scaring her. "Sorry. It's just my mum never speaks about these things, and with Dad dying, it's all coming up. I think having some answers would really help us."

"I'm sorry. Your dad was so private. He hardly ever spoke about you three, and you're his daughters!"

Reeva sighed. This was useless. Her dad hadn't told Leela anything. Unless her sisters were right and Leela was the cause of it all. "Leela, I'm . . . I'm sorry to ask something so personal. But . . . were you and my dad ever . . ."

Leela blushed. "We were very good friends."

"Okay. But, um, like . . ."

"Good friends," repeated Leela. "Just good friends."

"Good friends," repeated Reeva. "Cool! Sorry. I . . . yeah. And have you been, um, good friends ever since university?"

"Oh yes," said Leela. "*Very* good friends."

REEVA CLOSED THE door behind her and sat in her car. This was not good. Leela and her dad dating recently was one thing. But them being "good friends" since before his marriage was another thing entirely. Could her sisters be right? Reeva shook her head. No. There was still no firm proof. *Good friends* could mean anything. Though she doubted her sisters would see it that way. She groaned loudly. The last thing she wanted to do was go back home and hear them triumphantly proclaim that their dad had ruined his family by having an affair with an optometrist. Or hear their warped rationale that Reeva should do the eulogy because she was the one who got paid six figures a year to speak in court (they refused to accept she was a solicitor, not a barrister), and could she please just sort out the flowers and the funeral car while she was at it?

But Reeva didn't have to go back to her dad's house and deal with her sisters. There were still five hours before prayers. She could go and do something else. Like hang out with the one member of her family who didn't make her feel like she was undergoing a root canal.

"ROSE PETAL AND ginseng tea," said Satya Auntie, placing a delicate teacup in front of Reeva. She inhaled the fragrant scent and felt a sense of calmness descend over her that she hadn't felt since . . . she couldn't even remember. That couldn't be a good sign. "Thank you. This is exactly what I need. And this place is gorgeous!" It really was. The decor of the Ayurvedic spa was simple—bright wood and pale lemon walls with green plants and warm lighting—but the final effect was one of pure, luxurious tranquility. "It must be amazing working here every day. I feel so relaxed already. And I *never* feel relaxed."

Her aunt—dressed in a soft cream jumper and light blue jeans—nodded sagely. "I know. So few people in the West are ever actually relaxed, and I think it's worse for women. I once heard a woman on the radio saying that she'd never met a truly relaxed woman, and that it was her goal in life to become one. It's one of the best life goals I've ever heard."

Reeva sighed longingly. "Can you imagine? I didn't even know that was possible. None of my girlfriends are relaxed either. It's all so stressful—work, relationships, raising kids, or just getting your eyebrows done and logging your period on your phone. I mean, sure, you can be relaxed for a week or so on holiday. But permanently? That feels impossible. Especially if you've got my—well, our—family."

"It's the society we live in," agreed Satya Auntie. "It makes it so hard. It was a lot easier when I was in the middle of no-where, surrounded by nuns, where the only source of stress was a wayward goat. But even then, I would get moments of anx-iety."

"Really, what about? The lack of people? Or, wait—did they have bad food? I always imagine monasteries would have terrible food, but maybe that's just because I'm still thinking of the me-dieval ones we learned about at school."

Her aunt laughed. "You really are Hemant's daughter. He thought about food the whole time as well." Reeva smiled as she mentally added this to the slowly growing list of facts about her dad. They already had so much more in common than she did with her mum—Saraswati ate only to live. "The problem wasn't the food—one of the nuns was French, so we ate well. It was my mind, as always. Thoughts. About the family I'd left behind, the disappointment I felt at how they'd reacted, then disappoint-ment about how *I'd* reacted, and eventually regret."

"Did you really regret it? I know it must have been so hard to lose your family, but the life you've lived is so *you*. I can't imagine you staying in India and marrying someone normal." She flushed. "Sorry, I can't believe I said that. I mean—"

But Satya Auntie just laughed. "No, you're right; I definitely couldn't have done that. But it's not easy disappointing people you love. It took me a long time to truly make peace with my life choice."

"How did you do it? I can barely make my peace with the last text I sent my boyfriend."

"Compassion," said her aunt simply. "For yourself. It's the only way to move on. It's how I got over my guilt at what I did to my family."

"I'm so bad at self-compassion," admitted Reeva. "It comes

about as naturally to me as being relaxed. My stress levels are so bad that my hair—" She stopped. The only person who knew about her alopecia was Lakshmi, and it had never been an option to *not* tell her—she was Reeva's family. But Satya Auntie was family too (and a marked improvement on Reeva's previous blood relatives). If Reeva chose to share with her, maybe she could accelerate their bonding and make up for the last thirty-four years. She took a deep breath. "My hair's falling out. It's called alopecia areata." She bent her head and moved her hair to reveal the patch. "Seven point seven centimeters and growing."

"Oh, Reeva." Her aunt touched her arm in sympathy. "You poor thing. It happened to me once. I was only eleven, but I remember it being terrifying."

"It happened to you?!"

"Yes. But it grew back after a while, and I'm sure the same will happen to you."

"I'm not so sure," said Reeva miserably. "The doctors say it's linked to stress, and every time I try to destress, something stressful happens. Like my dad dying for the second time. Or having to spend time with my sisters after . . . oh, I guess you don't know, but Jaya's marrying my ex-boyfriend. Rakesh. We were together for years and then she had an affair with him. Sita took her side. It's all, well, incredibly stressful."

Satya Auntie winced in sympathy. "That sounds tough. You must have been devastated."

Reeva nodded, feeling her eyes tear up. Her aunt's sympathy was making her remember just how awful it had been. "Yes, and . . . it's why I'm struggling so much with my sisters' theory that my dad had an affair. But, Satya Auntie, I went to see his friend today. Leela. And . . . she said they've been close ever since he came to England. Very close."

"They were," agreed Satya Auntie. "They spent a lot of time together—I often joined them. I like Leela a lot. But I don't know if they were in a romantic relationship—it's not something Hemant would have spoken to me about. And it definitely doesn't mean they had an affair!"

"But didn't you say anyone is capable of cheating?" persisted Reeva. "Surely that includes Leela?"

Satya Auntie sighed. "Oh, beta. Don't torture yourself over this, especially when we don't know what really happened. These are just guesses. And we're all human. We all make mistakes."

"I don't know if I could handle Dad having an affair," whispered Reeva. "Not with everything else. Things are . . . it feels like they're all falling apart."

Her aunt smiled. "Sorry, I'm not smiling because I'm not taking it seriously. It's just . . . to me, when things fall apart, that's when the growth happens. I know you're in a lot of pain, but it's in these moments that you get strong. Because there's an indestructible piece of you at your very core that refuses to fall apart no matter what."

Reeva wiped away a tear. "But I already did that. Things fell apart four years ago, in the worst way possible. And I found that inner strength then. Do I really need to do it *again*? Because I don't know if I can."

Her aunt squeezed her hand tightly. "It must be part of your path, Reeva. And remember that nothing ever stays the same. Things are *always* going to fall apart. That's the first noble truth in Buddhism—that you're guaranteed to suffer if you believe things are going to last. Impermanence is the name of the game."

Reeva nodded. "You're right. I know everything ends at some point for everyone. But—and I don't want to fall into self-pity— but I feel like things fall apart for me so much more than they do for anyone else. Most of my friends are married now, with kids and perfect families. Like Sita! And Jaya's doing it too. And they all have their hair." Reeva looked down at her empty teacup. "Sometimes I feel I've got the worst luck."

"You never know what's really going on for people. Your life must look enviable on the outside to so many, but you're actually struggling. It's just like your hair—no one can see the patch beneath it. It's the same with all our problems, even the emotional. We're all going through things—the problem comes when we wish life was different from how it really is."

Reeva rested her head on her hand. "I know. Rationally it all makes sense; I just wish I could *feel* it. No matter how many Eckhart Tolle audiobooks I listen to, I can't seem to live in the present reality. I'm always in my head."

Her aunt smiled. "Well, it's not easy to unlearn the messages we grew up with. It doesn't happen overnight. And—you don't need to be so hard on yourself, Reeva. Life isn't an exam you need to get an A in. You can take the easy path."

"I . . . did not know taking the easy path was an option," admitted Reeva.

"Well, now you do!" Satya Auntie leaned back in her chair. "Do you know the meaning of your name?"

Reeva shook her head. "I try not to think about it too often. It's almost like they wanted me to get bullied. *Reevanshi*." She overemphasized the Indianness of the pronunciation, shuddering. "Then they give Jaya and Sita super-cute names that white people can pronounce."

"I like Reevanshi," said her aunt mildly. "It's unusual—even in India. And the meaning is beautiful. It translates to 'someone who has the potential to attain spiritual enlightenment.'"

"Really? That's . . . kind of nice. But I think it just proves my parents chose the wrong name for me. I'm a divorce lawyer who's basically an atheist. I can't even do a downward dog."

Her aunt laughed. "You'll be glad to know that's not necessary for spiritual enlightenment. Now. How do you feel about a treatment? On the house?"

"Oh, no, I couldn't! I should—"

"No excuses, and absolutely no *shoulds*. The word isn't in my vocabulary. I'm your aunt, and I fully plan on treating you to our afternoon Ayurveda package. That should help you start to relax, especially if I ask the therapist to add in some shirodhara. You don't mind a bit of oil on your hair, do you?"

## CHAPTER 9

**Day 5**

Reeva quietly opened the front door and creaked up the stairs. The prayers were in full swing in the living room, but she was in no fit state to join them. Her hair—and her entire face and body—were entirely covered in a thick oil. She looked, and smelled, like a salad. But she felt incredible. The last time she'd treated herself to a spa session like that had been during the influx of hen parties she'd gone to in her twenties. She'd stopped saying yes to them ever since Rakesh had dumped her for Jaya; it had felt too depressing to celebrate other people's love when she was so tragically alone. But after just one afternoon of pampering, Reeva was starting to remember the benefits of spas. How had she ever let her self-care slide so badly? As soon as she got back to London, she'd make up for her poor millennial behavior by booking as many massages as she could afford.

Carefully tiptoeing around the landing, she opened the bathroom door. She started running the bath, pouring in the essential oils her aunt had pressed on her as she'd left—apparently lavender and frankincense were exactly what she needed to lessen her anxiety—and stepped out of her oily clothes. She still felt so calm post-massage. Did other people feel like this all the time? The thought of permanently being this relaxed made Reeva want to cry a little. It was just so different from the constant tension she normally walked around with, and the ever-growing vague sense of panic that something was going to go wrong.

She was just lowering her naked body into the steaming tub when the door burst open.

"Oh my god, get out!" she screeched, rushing to cover herself with outstretched hands.

Her sisters—both standing next to each other in the doorway—ignored her.

"Oh, it's nothing we haven't seen before," said Sita, chucking her a towel.

"Nice style down there," said Jaya. "What is it, an extended Brazilian?"

Reeva wrapped the towel around herself, glaring at her sisters as she got out of the bath. "What are you guys doing?"

"Uh, more like what are *you* doing?" asked Jaya as she locked the door behind her—something Reeva had failed to do in her state of pure relaxation. "You've missed the start of the prayers, and now you're having a bath?"

"Where have you been?" demanded Sita, sitting on top of the closed toilet.

Reeva lowered herself onto the edge of the bathtub. "I went to see Satya Auntie. And she offered me a massage."

"Oh, that explains your hair situation," nodded Jaya. "Ayurveda? Shirodhara?"

"Um, I think so. There was a lot of oil."

"Right, so while we've been here hosting our father's prayers, you've been getting free massages from our aunt?" asked Sita. "Did you manage to also get any more info from her, or did that not cross your mind mid-facial?"

"Ooh, did they give you a facial too?" asked Jaya, peering at her sister's face. "Your pores still look a bit clogged."

"No, they did not," said Reeva, crossing her arms. "And I just went to see her because she's our aunt. I wanted to get to know her."

"Is she the only person you went to see?" asked Sita pointedly. "Because we happened to speak to Leela just now. She was looking forward to seeing you. *Again*."

Reeva shook her head in irritation. "Why didn't you tell me that when you came in? Look, I didn't hide it from you on purpose. I would have already told you if you'd given me a chance. Instead of intruding on me mid-bath."

"Pre-bath," said Jaya. "You still smell kind of weird."

"So tell us then," said Sita. "What did Leela say when you went on your clandestine visit?"

"Just that she and Dad are friends. And . . ." Reeva sighed preemptively, knowing exactly how her sisters would react to what she was about to say. "They've been friends since uni. Good friends."

"Called it!" cried Jaya. "*Good friends* definitely means they're shagging."

Sita smiled complacently. "Mystery solved. They were involved from the start and Mum found out. Lost her shit. Faked his death. Ruined our lives. Case solved."

"Okay, we do not have enough evidence to make that conclusion," said Reeva.

"You legit sound like you're in a courtroom right now," said Jaya.

"Reeva, you know in your gut we're right," said Sita. "You just can't bear it because you refuse to see the bad in people. It used to be you defending Mum and now you're defending Dad." She shook her head. "As always, you're too busy trying to protect our parents when you should be protecting us."

"I'm sorry, what?" asked Reeva. "I'm not defending anyone; I'm just refusing to jump to conclusions. And why should I be protecting you both?! From what?"

"Uh, our family," said Jaya. "You're the older sister. You were meant to be there for us. We really needed you."

"Well maybe I needed you to not cheat with my boyfriend," snapped Reeva.

Jaya staggered back as if she'd been physically hurt. "I . . . you . . ."

"We needed you when we were kids," interrupted Sita. "But all you've ever done is just do your own thing and ignore us. When Mum fucked off to Bollywood, you forgot about us and just focused on yourself. Like you always do."

"I was a kid myself!" cried Reeva. "Why was it on me to save you all? I didn't even know how!"

"Because there was nobody else," shot back Sita. "Most older sisters would have become a surrogate mother if they were in your position. You did the opposite."

"That's not fair," cried Reeva, wishing she didn't sound so much like her teenage self as she said it. "I mean, I was a child. You can't expect that from me. I did what I could. What else could I have done?"

"Speak to us maybe," said Jaya. "And be an actual sister. You never told us what you thought about anything. You always just . . . disappeared."

Reeva stared at her in growing rage. She felt a familiar urge to swallow down her fury—and then ignored it. She didn't know if it was all the massaging or the result of spending four days with her sisters, but something inside her had released. "Okay. You want to hear what I think? Fine. How about, I basically had a breakdown when you went off with Rakesh because I was abandoned by my boyfriend *and* my youngest sister. Not to mention my other sister totally betraying me by siding with her! Jaya, having to deal with you getting engaged to Rakesh is the hardest thing I've *ever* had to do. And . . . and now . . . I have to be here with you both acting like everything is fine while we try to find out why no one ever told us our dad was alive! And the only theory either of you will even consider is the only one that makes me want to curl up and cry. Oh, and to top it all off, my brand-new boyfriend has stopped speaking to me because I gave him a blow job in our dead dad's bed!"

There was a long silence. Sita and Jaya gawped at their sister in shock. Reeva stared back defiantly, but as seconds of silence passed by, the hot fury inside her dulled down. Instead, a cold wave of regret washed over her, settling into a steel lump inside her stomach. What had she just done? How—*why*—had she said all that to her sisters? This was so unlike her. The Ayurveda had gone to her head. She was the one who didn't react, not the one who lost her shit. This was a mess. A disaster. A total fu—

Suddenly Jaya's face twitched, and she burst into loud laughter. "You went down on Nick in Dad's bed?!"

Reeva felt her jaw literally drop. As if Jaya was laughing at her! A choked sound emanated from the other side of the bathroom. Reeva whirled around and saw Sita was doing it too. She could not believe her sisters found this funny. "Are you kidding me? Seriously?!"

"I'm sorry," said Sita, trying and failing to swallow her laughter. "I can't stop imagining you and Nick while we're all praying downstairs. It's so retro. Who even gives blow jobs anymore?"

Reeva stared at her, speechless. And then the laughter caught her too. "Oh my god, I can't believe I'm laughing at this."

"It's *hilarious*," cried Jaya, holding her stomach.

"It's just . . . so . . . inappropriate," gasped Sita.

"You think that's bad," snorted Reeva. "The worst part is that mid-oral, Nick *stops* me. And says, 'Sorry, I don't want to come in your mouth while you're still grieving.' He didn't feel *comfortable* doing it. Oh, and he didn't say 'come.' He said 'finish.'"

"No!" cried Jaya as Sita cackled loudly. "That's the most British thing I've ever heard."

Reeva sat on the bath mat, her shoulders shaking, as her sisters joined her.

"Oh god, we have to be quieter," said Sita. "They're praying downstairs."

"Praying!" Reeva exhaled. "What have our lives become?"

"It's fine, they'll think we're shrieking with tears," said Jaya. "What with our dear dad having just departed and all."

"And instead we're discussing our older sister's sex life. Who knew?" Sita paused. "Though, at least you have sex. That's a long-forgotten dream for me."

"Really? How long has it been?" asked Reeva.

"Years. Too many."

"*What?!*" cried Jaya. "You still have it alone though, right?"

Sita raised an eyebrow. "Maybe once a year. I don't have time for anything more than that; the girls are always there."

Jaya looked at her, aghast. "I knew sex could die down after having children, but I didn't expect solo sex to do the same. Oh my god."

"I wish I'd taken a break from sex," said Reeva glumly. "Then I wouldn't be dying with shame right now. Guys, you should have seen his face when he stopped me. It was this mixture of pity and . . . judgment. I felt like a kid getting told off at school."

"Don't worry; I've done worse," replied Jaya. "I once shat on my ex. Anal. Top tip: Never eat a massive bowl of tiramisu before you do it up the bum."

Reeva's jaw dropped again. "Oh my god. I can't believe that happened—or that you just told us!"

"Nitin and I had sex in Mum's honeymoon suite at the Palace," said Sita. "During the wedding." She cocked her head. "Huh, that was probably the last time we actually had sex."

"That was four years ago," cried Jaya. "And ew!"

"I really hope the hotel had time to change the sheets before Mum and MJ turned up," said Reeva.

"So do I," said Sita. "I'm a squirter."

Reeva shrieked. "No! Why are you telling us this?! I do *not* need to know that."

Sita shrugged. "It's natural. I'm not going to hide it."

"Wait. If we share the same DNA, does that mean I can squirt too?" cried Jaya. "Rak— I mean, I would fucking love that."

"I'm not sure that's how it works," said Reeva. "But what do I know—I've never squirted a day in my life."

Sita shrugged. "It's not as great as it sounds. It just makes the sheets messy, which means extra washing. You know, that's probably the main reason I never bother masturbating anymore. It's all such a hassle. Who has the time?"

"You can make yourself squirt?" Jaya stared at her in awe. "Okay, I'll be right back, guys, I need to go practice."

Reeva made a face at her. "You cannot go off and masturbate. We're at our dad's death prayers."

"Seconded," said Sita. "Save it for after the funeral. Give you something to look forward to."

"Fine." Jaya sighed. "Just make sure you tell me your tips first, okay? Like, everything from technique to soundtrack."

"It feels very wrong to be having this chat while Dad's loved ones are singing bhajans downstairs," commented Reeva. "I can't believe none of us are down there. And I missed most of yesterday's prayers. This is not good. Do you think they're going to judge us?"

"He already made it out like we're the world's most selfish daughters," said Sita. "We may as well continue the narrative."

"And you're allowed to wander in and out of prayers," said Jaya. "It's chill. They'll think we're doing funeral admin or, like, crying or whatever."

"Are you sure it doesn't make us terrible people?" asked Reeva. "Terrible ... daughters?"

"Not as terrible as our parents," replied Sita. "They're the ones who lied to us our whole lives. Sex chats during prayers is nothing in comparison. At least we've had the courtesy to come upstairs and do it in the bathroom."

Reeva nodded slowly. "You know what? You're right. Fuck it. Let's stay up here and chat." She stood up. "You guys don't mind if I get back in the bath while we carry on, do you? I feel inappropriately dirty right now—and it's not just the oil."

"Go wild," said Jaya. "Why don't we make it a bit of a party? Get some drinks and snacks?"

"Is there any booze?" asked Reeva. "I didn't see anything on our clue hunt. Dad clearly wasn't a big drinker."

"I bought some wine," said Sita. "Essentials."

"And snacks?" asked Jaya.

"Sure. So long as you guys like chopped-up cucumber."

REEVA SNUGGLED INTO her dad's bed, her hair freshly washed and dried, feeling oddly content. She wasn't sure if it was the effect of three glasses of wine, or because she'd just had an objectively enjoyable evening with her sisters for the first time in years. They'd spent hours drinking and laughing in the bathroom together—long after all the guests had gone—sniggering over Jaya's fear of foreskin and squealing at Sita's graphic retelling of exactly what happened to her vagina after childbirth. Neither Reeva nor Jaya had known that nappies were so essential for mothers as well as newborns. Jaya had looked so nauseous she'd started retching over the loo, which had naturally made Reeva and Sita howl even louder.

She'd tried to go downstairs to speak to the guests when the singing had stopped, but when she'd peered into the room and seen them all chatting together, a community she had no part in, she'd slipped away again. Sita had texted Satya Auntie to ask her to make the girls' excuses, saying they were just too emotional to be there. And then they'd carried on drinking and laughing until they'd woken up the twins. They hadn't spoken about any of the real stuff—like the Big Betrayal—but her sisters had admitted she was right about Leela. There wasn't enough evidence to act like it was true, and they'd have to speak to her again to find out more. It was the first time Reeva could remember both her sisters telling her she was right.

The only thing still bothering her was the zero contact from Nick. She knew he was busy, but *how* had he still not tried to call her? She didn't understand. He was the one who'd wanted to make their relationship official, but now he'd gone AWOL, just when she needed his reassurance the most. Reeva hated that she was always the one calling him, but she hated sitting around waiting for his call even more. She picked up her phone and dialed his number.

He answered enthusiastically. "Reeva! I was just thinking about you. How were tonight's prayers?"

Reeva instantly felt better. He was happy to hear from her. And he'd been thinking about her. She pulled herself up to lean against the pillows. "Um . . . I didn't actually make it again."

Nick laughed. "Oh, really? I hope that doesn't mean you were busy with another overnight visitor you were doing unsuitable things to instead?"

Reeva flushed at the reference to what was now officially the most embarrassing moment of her thirties. "Uh. No. Of course not. I was in the bath. With my sisters. Not like that. Obviously. Okay, I think I'm drunker than I thought."

"Indian funerals are *really* not turning out to be what I expected."

"I was the only one in the bath; they were just hanging out and drinking wine. We actually . . . bonded."

"Hey, that's great!" cried Nick. "Why *is* it you weren't that close to them before? Just general personality clashes or did something happen?"

Shit. Reeva did not really want to admit to her new boyfriend that her youngest sister had stolen her last boyfriend. But she was too tired to think of something else to say. "Jaya slept with my ex. We'd been together for nine years. And now they're getting married. Oh, and Sita helped her. So . . . yeah."

Nick breathed in sharply. "Reeva, that's *awful*. Being cheated on is bad enough, but with your sister?! Your family really is full of drama."

"Told you," said Reeva glumly. "We're worse than the Kardashians."

"When was that?"

"Four years ago. It's okay; I'm over it now. Just. But obviously it was horrible at the time."

"It's amazing you get on with Jaya now."

"'Get on with' is an overstatement, but . . . after tonight, I think I can tolerate her. Hey," said Reeva, suddenly realizing that there was a massive benefit to speaking to Nick about her history. "I've never properly asked you about *your* exes. Surely now we've had the 'what are we' chat, we should do the 'who are your exes' chat?"

Nick groaned. "You're sure you want to do it now?"

"It's only fair. And I don't really know anything about your ex-wife."

Nick sighed. "Okay. Well, it didn't last long. Only five years and then we called it."

"But . . . why?"

"I think we just didn't have enough in common. Which is funny because we're from very similar backgrounds. I think we just . . . I don't know, got married because everyone else was doing it."

"Peer pressure," said Reeva knowingly. "I've seen so many clients who got married and had kids purely because they felt like they should. Hey, no wonder my aunt hates the word *should*." She shook her head. "Wait, so were you okay splitting up? Did you stay in touch afterward?"

"Oh, I mean, it was hard but fine. You know, just a normal divorce."

"If there's one thing I've learned from work it's that there is no 'normal' in divorce. Did you manage to do it amicably? And why did you decide to split up—was it her decision or yours?"

"Uh, a combo."

"Right," said Reeva, hesitating. Was it just her or was Nick really holding back? "So, when was that again?"

"God, almost seven years ago now."

"It . . . must have been hard."

Nick cleared his throat. "Let's just say it got messy, but I still see her at the occasional dinner party."

"Oh." This was news to Reeva. "Cool. That's . . . very mature. And it's okay when you see her?"

"Sure! She's even introduced me to some of the women I've dated since her."

"Wow, that's . . . I'm not sure I actually have an adjective for that."

Nick laughed. "I know it's a bit different, but we all grew up together. Our circles are quite incestuous, so it's not as weird as it sounds. In fact, you're the only person I've ever officially been in a relationship with who I haven't had mutual friends with!"

"Guess that's online dating for you," said Reeva lightly, trying to mask the fact she was now panicking that Nick would prefer to date someone he had mutual friends with.

"And you are hands down the best thing I've ever found online."

"Wow, what an honor. Maybe you can leave a five-star review for me. So the next guy can see it."

"I'd be delighted to."

Reeva shifted uncomfortably. He was meant to say there wouldn't be a next guy. "Right. So, we were in the middle of—"

"You grilling me about my past?"

"You *sharing* your past with me. We got up to your ex-wife introducing you to your next girlfriends."

"Ah yes. Well, after her I dated a few people but nobody special. Until—" Reeva smiled, waiting for the inevitable. "The person I met just before you."

The smile fell off Reeva's face. "Oh?"

"She's probably the most serious relationship I've had since my ex-wife. And we were only together for a few years off and on."

"When . . . did it end?"

There was a long pause. "Uh, I guess around the time I met you. But it was long overdue. It was all pretty unstable because she's a singer, so her life is quite hectic. And there wasn't any overlap, so please don't worry about that."

"Right," said Reeva, very much worrying about that. "So, when you say *no* overlap . . . ?"

"Well, just the normal. A couple of dates maybe. But I ended it with her the second I started to have feelings for you."

Okay. That was fine. Normal. She would have done the same. "Right. Good to know." Reeva bit her bottom lip. She still had so many more questions she wanted to ask: Who was this singer? Was she famous? Had they worked together? Why hadn't it been stable? Why did it end? Did he love her? Did they speak? Did he still have feelings for her? But she wasn't sure how to bring it all up. Especially as Nick already thought she was grilling him. "Um, is there anything else I should know?"

"Just that I think you're great and I'm very glad to be with you."

Reeva smiled and felt her anxiety settle. Everything was

fine—it was just her insecurities going crazy again. Nick liked her and she liked him too. "Okay. Me too. Very much so."

"Good. Well, I'd better let you sleep. It's getting late. Good luck tomorrow, darling, and you know where I am if you need me."

"Thanks, Nick." Reeva yawned. "Speak soon."

"Sweet dreams, Reevs."

## CHAPTER 10

**Day 6**

REEVA PULLED HER nieces close to her and inhaled their smell. Strawberry shampoo, laundry detergent, and the indescribable scent of their soft, breathing bodies.

"Get off me," cried Amisha as Alisha shrugged off her aunt, reaching for the next Lego piece.

"Sorry, I just really love you both," said Reeva, squeezing them tight. "And I'm so glad you're okay."

Amisha raised an eyebrow at her aunt in an uncanny impression of her mum and turned back to the Lego. They were slowly—very, very slowly—building the *Millennium Falcon* from Star Wars. Reeva was meant to be helping them, but she was mainly just beaming at their small sticky hands and kissing their soft heads. She knew she was being weird, but she'd had another sleepless night with the same nightmare. Only this time she'd remembered something else. Her nightmares didn't just feature Fluffy Panda, they also featured the twins. And all of them—the cat *and* the girls—had been screaming in pain.

Reeva had already FaceTimed Fluffy Panda (via an annoyed

Lakshmi) and had been reassured by the sight of her soft belly rising and falling as she slept. Now she was creeping out her nieces by doing the same to them, but she didn't care; she was just grateful they were okay.

She left them sitting in silent concentration with their Lego and padded out to the bathroom with her ruler in hand. She knew that the stress of her dreams probably meant the patch was still growing, and as much as she wanted to avoid reality, she knew she couldn't. It looked worse in the harsh glare of the fluorescent LEDs, and she braced herself for the result. Eight point five centimeters.

There was a knock at the door. Reeva quickly rearranged her hair to hide the patch as the door slowly opened to reveal Alisha. She was sucking her thumb. "Auntie Weeva?"

"Yes, darling? How's the Lego?"

"Mummy says you have to come downstairs to pull your weight."

Reeva was taken aback. "Right. Okay. To the point. Sure, I'll come down right now. Thank you."

"She did say other things, but then she told me not to tell you those ones."

Reeva smiled. "Well done for not telling me. You're a very good girl, Alisha."

"You're not *allowed* to call me a good girl."

"Seriously? Why not?"

Alisha looked up at her aunt. "Is sexist."

REEVA WENT DOWNSTAIRS, trying not to think about the fact that a five-year-old had just schooled her in sexism. She'd always prided herself on her liberal attitudes, and yet Sita's parenting was officially putting her to shame. She didn't even fully understand why it was sexist to call her niece a good girl—she'd say good boy if Alisha were male—but she had a feeling that it would not be a wise idea to bring this up with Sita. Especially before she'd had a coffee.

"Here she is," said Sita. "The missing masi."

"It's only nine a.m.! I was watching the girls." Reeva pressed the button on the coffee machine, yawning. "And besides, I needed a lie-in after last night. How are neither of you hungover?"

"Genetics," said Jaya. "And youth."

"I don't have the luxury of hangovers," said Sita. "Motherhood doesn't allow it."

"Uh, I spent the whole morning taking care of your kids," said Reeva. "You can't play the motherhood card."

"I pushed two kids out of my vagina. I can play the motherhood card for the rest of my life."

Reeva rolled her eyes and accidentally made eye contact with Jaya. Her youngest sister made a face back, grinning. Reeva turned straight back to her coffee, busying herself with the oat milk. She was not ready to act like Jaya was forgiven just because they'd had a night bonding over Sancerre and cucumbers.

"Anyway," said Sita. "What's the plan today?"

"Ooh, maybe we could go get lunch?" suggested Jaya. "There's a super-cute brunch place down the road. I ran by it yesterday."

"You went for a run?" asked Reeva.

Sita sighed loudly. "I meant what's the plan in terms of finding out more info about Dad. You know, the reason why we're here?"

"Oh, well, we could do what Reeva did yesterday and go stalk Leela?" said Jaya.

"I wasn't stalking her! Let's just keep hunting for information. Like, uh, I don't know—maybe Dad had a journal or some-thing."

"Yeah, because men in their sixties are really big on gratitude journals," said Sita. "Be real."

"You never know," replied Reeva. "Mum suggested he was the type to have written us a letter."

"Which we would have found during our house hunt if there was one," said Sita.

Reeva sat up straight. "Hey. Where's Dad's *phone*? And his laptop?"

"He doesn't have a laptop," said Jaya. "He has an actual com-puter. It's very 2005. It's in my room. I tried to open it and look at his e-mail, but he was logged out and I couldn't get in. And his phone's locked, remember? We obviously tried to open it when we arrived, but we don't know the pin. It's in the hallway drawer now."

"We should try again," said Reeva decisively. "If we need clues, we should be hacking his tech. Not going through drawers and harassing his friends. Why are we being so old-school about this?"

"Uh, because none of us know how to hack tech," said Sita.

"Well, let's try." Reeva ran out of the room into the hallway and began rummaging in the drawer.

"You know we already tried this," called out Sita. "It didn't work."

"We'll try again!" Reeva triumphantly pulled out an old iPhone and walked back into the kitchen waving it over her head. "Got it."

"It's going to be dead." Sita sighed. "Stick it on my charger. Here."

"How are you going to hack it?" asked Jaya. "Or do you have contacts who can do it for you?"

"I love the idea you guys have of divorce law," said Reeva. "It sounds so much more fun in your heads. I'll just . . . try birthdays. That kind of thing. And if it doesn't work, we'll go into one of those shops and pay to get it unlocked. It can't be that hard."

Sita shrugged. "If you think you'll have better luck than us. Go for it."

"What kind of codes did you try?"

"Zig-zag patterns," said Jaya. "They're normally my go-to. We did his birthday too. But nothing."

"Did you try our birthdays?" asked Reeva. "He cares about us enough to keep that file on us. We might be his passcode too."

Jaya shook her head, so Reeva turned on the phone and began trying each of their birthdays in turn, in various combinations. She looked up, disappointed. "Nope. Nothing."

"What about, like, a combo of all our birthdays?" asked Jaya.

"I already tried. It didn't work."

"Told you," said Sita. "It's not as easy as you think."

"Let me try one more." She slowly punched in the numbers 2-6-0-7-6-9. The phone unlocked itself.

"Oh my god!" Jaya shrieked. "What is it? How did you know?"

"Mum's birthday." Sita crossed her arms. "I was about to suggest the same."

"Wow, he must have still loved her," said Reeva in wonder. "Who makes their ex's birthday their passcode? Especially when she's going around telling your kids you're dead."

"Awkward for Leela," said Jaya.

"Come on," said Sita impatiently. "Let's see if there are any messages from her."

Reeva opened up her dad's WhatsApp and started scrolling as her sisters peered over her shoulders. He had more than 160 conversations open.

"Dad was popular," cried Jaya. "Who are these people?"

"Looks like they're mainly the evening prayers crew," replied Reeva. "I recognize their WhatsApp pics."

"What are they messaging about?" asked Sita.

"By the look of it, absolutely . . . nothing," replied Reeva. "They're just sending each other religious memes. And look at these guys, messaging Dad *every day* to say good morning. And not just 'Good morning,' but 'Good morning, I hope you have a day full of blessings.' Oh my god, look. Dad's doing it too—he replied, 'Thank you, Jai Shree Krishna, wishing you a peaceful day.'"

"Old Indian people are *weird*," remarked Jaya. "Mum would never send shit like that."

"Which is probably why they split up," snapped Sita. "Can you get to Leela already?"

Reeva tapped on Leela's name and a stream of messages popped up. The sisters scanned them quickly.

"Why has she sent him a video about a monkey meditating?" asked Reeva.

Jaya frowned. "Why have they attached the video *and* sent the YouTube link? What a waste of phone storage."

"Let me see," said Sita. "Yeah, I already watched that video about the monkey. It's a total anticlimax. What? Nitin's parents send us stuff like this all the time."

"Their chat's so dull," said Jaya. "I guess they're well beyond the honeymoon stage."

"Or maybe they're just friends, like Leela told us," said Reeva. "There's nothing here. He's speaking to her the exact way he speaks to Dhilip Bhai."

"It doesn't mean anything," said Sita. "They're just not big texters."

"She didn't even know we thought Dad was dead though," pointed out Reeva. "I'm sorry, but if they were having an affair, I think the consequences would have come up."

"Yeah, but Dad was really loyal," said Jaya. "He promised Mum he wouldn't tell anyone about the death-faking. Remember, Satya Auntie said he didn't even want to tell her? I bet he wouldn't tell his mistress."

"Could you be any more contradictory?" snapped Sita. "That's a rhetorical question; please don't answer. Reeva, are there any messages from Mum?"

"Let me search for Saraswati . . . oh my god! There's a whole message thread. They've been speaking for ages. And the messages are *long.*"

"Fuck," exhaled Sita, leaning over. "What have they been saying? And from when?"

Reeva scanned them quickly. "I think they're all from a few years ago. Oh my god." She stared at her sisters. "He asked to see us. Repeatedly. And Mum said no."

"Are you fucking *kidding*?" cried Sita. "She said no?"

"Look," said Reeva. "He says that things are different now. He says that he's changed. Time has passed. He's done a lot of work on himself."

"Oh my god, I love that Dad did inner work," cried Jaya. "That's so me."

"He says he wants to . . . he wants to know his daughters before it's too late," continued Reeva, swallowing a lump in her throat. "He . . . he wanted us in his life. Oh my god, read this. 'Who knows how much time we have left? I want to know them while I can.'" She put down the phone and looked up at her sisters. "And Mum said no."

"Fuck," cried Sita. "What's wrong with her? Who says no to a dying man?"

"Well, I don't think either of them knew he was dying," said Reeva. "But that doesn't excuse a thing."

Jaya burst into tears. Her mascara started sliding down her cheeks as she hiccuped loudly. "I can't believe . . . we could . . . have . . . had . . . a dad! Mum took him away from us, and now he's dead, and we'll never get a chance to speak to him."

Both her sisters ignored her, choosing to continue reading the messages.

"Look at her responses," said Sita. "She keeps saying things like, 'You know that's not a good idea. It's not fair on the girls.' As if she ever knew what was right for us or not. She barely knew us!"

"She's the most selfish person I've ever met," declared Jaya, dabbing her mascara away with a tissue. "What kind of person stops a loving, caring father from being in touch with his daughters?"

"I don't know," said Reeva. "It just . . . none of this makes sense."

"It makes total sense," said Sita firmly. "Mum chose her career over Dad, and that's why she wouldn't let us see him. You know that she's selfish, irrational, and self-centered. She does whatever she wants. Always has, always will."

Jaya nodded, all trace of tears gone. "Exactly. Mum put herself first—as per. She couldn't risk us getting to know him in case it came out publicly that he wasn't dead. Imagine if there were pics of him at our weddings or whatever. She'd be known as a liar. Or unhinged. It would have been too much of a risk. When you're a public figure, you have to be really careful with stuff like this. Take it from me."

"We need to ask Mum," said Sita suddenly. "About all of it. Reeva, you're going to have to call her."

"Uh, I've already tried. You know I have. But she doesn't answer my calls, or my messages."

"Well, make something up," said Sita. "You're clearly the only one of us she'd ever answer the phone to. I still can't get over the fact that she video calls you. Just . . . say you're sick or something."

Reeva frowned. "That's terrible. I'm not doing that."

"Oooh, I know!" Jaya grabbed Reeva's phone right out of her hands.

"What? No! Give it back!" Reeva leaned across the table and wrestled her sister, but Jaya fought her off. "Seriously, give it back to me. You're acting like a child."

In response, Jaya bit her.

Reeva stared at her sister in unmasked outrage. "You did not just bite me!"

"Priorities." Jaya shrugged as she started typing quickly on the unlocked phone. "Just . . . give . . . me . . . a second and . . . Sent! Soz."

"I cannot believe you just did that." Reeva scowled at her sister. "You are a complete child. Give it back to me now."

Jaya's eyes lit up as the phone screen vibrated and flashed. "Oh my god, she's just replied. She's calling you this evening. She has a slot at seven p.m."

Sita looked at her younger sister in admiration while Reeva let out a strangled cry. "Nice. What did you write?"

"I said that Reevs is dating a famous music agent who works with Hot Lips and wants to tell her all about it. You know how she loves a bit of name-dropping."

"Wait, what?" asked Reeva. "Hot Lips the singer? Nick works with her?"

"Yeah, of course," said Jaya. "He represents her. They were papped at the BRIT Awards last night. Do you not read the *Daily Mail*?"

REEVA WAS TRYING—and failing—to be chill. Hot Lips was an insanely attractive, insanely successful singer who currently had her arms wrapped around Reeva's boyfriend in a selection of photos on various media outlets. She'd even specifically thanked Nick Trippier in her speech as she won Best Artist at the BRIT Awards. She'd then performed live onstage, wearing hot pants and some kind of leather shirt, alongside a famous rapper she'd once dated.

Before meeting Nick, Reeva wouldn't have been aware of any of this. She barely knew what was at the top of the charts and only ever heard about celeb goss if she was representing one of them in a divorce. But in just a matter of hours, Reeva had become an expert on Hot Lips's career and personal life. According to Wikipedia, she'd dated a number of high-profile actors and rappers—including the one she'd sang with onstage—but hadn't been linked with anyone for the last year. She never spoke about her love life in interviews (Reeva had checked) or posted photos of boyfriends on Instagram (Reeva could also vouch for this). But she did have a very impressive set of abs, loved taking photos of herself in bikinis on yachts, and was only twenty-seven years old. All of which made Reeva feel incredibly insecure.

She called Lakshmi for the sixth time.

"I said I'd call you when I got home," grumbled Lakshmi. "I've barely got through the door. I still need to pee."

"Pee while we speak. I'm still freaking out."

"There's nothing to freak out about! He's a music agent. You always knew he worked with famous hot singers. Obviously, he's going to be photographed with them."

"But he told me the other day he recently dated a singer!" cried Reeva. "What if it's Hot Lips?"

"And what if it's not? You're going to drive yourself crazy for no reason."

"You know you'd also freak out if you were dating someone who'd maybe been in an off-and-on relationship with Hot Lips," said Reeva. She heard Lakshmi clank around the bathroom and start peeing.

"Ahh, that feels good. And no, I don't think I would. I'd be flattered. It would put me in the same league as someone who was voted one of *FHM*'s top ten sexiest women."

"What?" cried Reeva. "I didn't see that! How can I compete with one of the top ten sexiest women? Please tell me we're talking UK, not international."

"You need to chill. You can't imagine Nick has dated everyone he's worked with or you'll die of stress. It's not good for the alopecia. Okay?"

At the mention of her alopecia, Reeva calmed down. She exhaled deeply. "You're right. I just . . . panicked it was her, and that he was cheating on me. It's stupid. I know I have no reason to think that. I was just so shocked seeing all those photos of him with her on the internet. I've never dated someone who's been in the Sidebar of Shame before."

"I know," said Lakshmi. "It's fucking weird. But it is what it is, so *breathe*."

"Okay, okay." Reeva paused. "He wouldn't have dated someone called Hot Lips, would he? I mean, her name is awful."

"Forget it. He's *your* boyfriend now. He drove all the way up to Leicester to see you. He's also going to do it again in a couple of days for the funeral. And he was very polite about grieving appropriately for your father. If he's too much of a gentleman to come in your mouth during your dad's prayers, he's definitely too much of a gentleman to cheat on you while you're at your dad's funeral."

Reeva groaned. "Don't remind me of that. But okay. You're right. Thank you. I think I have PTSD after Rakesh and Jaya."

"I know, but, Reevs, you can't keep projecting your past onto the present. It's not healthy; you're letting your fear fuck up a good thing."

"You sound so much like my new aunt right now. She's always talking about me needing to live in the present."

"She's right. But didn't you just meet her the other day? She's already life coaching you?"

"Yup. I guess it was glaringly obvious that I am very much not living in the present." Reeva sighed. "Maybe I need to swap therapists; I feel like all the progress I thought I'd made isn't much at all."

"You're doing great," said Lakshmi firmly. "You just need to remember that not every man is Rakesh. And if you're so stressed about the Nick thing, why don't you ask him?"

"No! He'll know I'm googling him, and he'll think I'm obsessed with him. It's too much."

"You can tell him you saw the pics by chance and ask if Hot Lips is the ex he was talking about. It's not a big deal, Reevs. And at least that way you'll know."

Reeva shook her head vehemently. "I can't. His favorite thing about me is that I'm strong. I can't let him know I'm freaking out. He'll think I'm an anxious mess and dump me."

Lakshmi grumbled loudly. "God, I wish I could give you some of my confidence."

"I would love some of your confidence. I have no idea where mine has gone. I feel like I'm constantly worried about when Nick last called or didn't call, and why he didn't message when he said he would. I'm exhausted. Not to mention I'm also meant to be finding out whether my dad was a marital cheat, a spy, or somewhere in between. I feel like a nervous wreck. No wonder I'm going bald."

"You've just got a lot going on right now, Reevs. And relationships are exhausting—that's why I avoid them. You should do what I do."

"Um, I'm exhausted dealing with one man, let alone having a couple on the go at the same time."

"It's easier than you think. Especially when you have a secretary."

Reeva laughed. "It's still not for me, but thanks. Anyway. I'd better go and trick my mum into revealing the truth."

"Good luck. Keep me posted."

"I will, and thanks, Lakshmi. Sorry I've been so needy lately; I'm just . . ."

"Dealing with a fuckload of drama. Anyone would be the same in your position. Stop thanking me and go reverse psychology your mum so you can figure out the truth and come home. FP and I miss you."

"Thanks. And I know FP hasn't noticed I've gone, but you're sweet for pretending."

## CHAPTER 11

### Day 6

TIME DIFFERENCE—AND the twenty-minute slot allocated to Reeva in their mum's schedule by her PA—meant the sisters were unable to greet the guests for the prayers. Instead, while Satya Auntie was Jai Shree Krishna–ing all their father's friends, the sisters were crammed into the upstairs bathroom.

"Can't we bring chairs in here?" complained Jaya. "My ass is not enjoying having the edge of the bath poking into it."

"And you think mine is?" countered Sita. "Shut up and deal with it."

"We could all just sit on the floor," suggested Reeva.

Sita gave her a withering look. "We're not twelve."

"I'm with Reeva," said Jaya, sliding down the side of the bath onto the graying mat, pulling the edge of her floral skirt with her. "We may as well be comfortable. Ooh, this mat is springier than it looks."

Sita reluctantly followed suit in her jeans. They left a space in between them for Reeva to fill. She looked down at the formerly cream mat, with its unidentifiable gray stains, and regretted her suggestion.

"Hurry up," demanded Sita. "It's time."

Reeva gingerly lowered herself—and her soft camel loungewear—onto the mat. "Fine. Let's do this."

She pressed call, her heart pounding with anxiety. She knew it was excessive to be so stressed about calling her mother, but it was never easy to have a conversation with Saraswati, let alone about something as complex as this. This time Reeva had a plan. Instead of trying to plead with her mum for answers, she was going to pretend she already knew the secret and hope her mum accidentally revealed something. Her sisters had approved the idea and decided it would work better if they weren't there—or at least if their mum didn't know they were there—which meant it was all down to Reeva.

"She's there," mouthed Sita, nudging her sharply in the stomach.

Reeva shot her a look of annoyance as her mum's face filled her phone screen. "Darling? Hel-loooo?"

"Hi, Mum." Reeva forced her face into a relaxed smile. "How's India?"

"Exhausting," declared her mother. "These actresses are so demanding; we can barely get through a single scene without some complaint or other. I was hoping we'd be wrapped up by the end of the week so I could come home and see you, but it looks like it'll definitely be a full fortnight."

"What a surprise," said Reeva, under her breath. Sita snorted in response.

"What's that, darling? I'm just so tired of it all. Thank god MJ's in the movie too, or I'd be bored out of my mind. Our afternoon breaks are the only things keeping me going."

"Ew," said Jaya. Sita glared at her and put her finger to her lips.

"Sounds fun!" said Reeva. "It would be good if you could try and get away earlier though, because—"

"The music agent!" cried Saraswati. "Tell me *all* about him. I'm thrilled you've finally got a new boyfriend. I knew that waste of space running off with Jaya would be the best thing for you. I always felt you could do so much better than some boring banker. A music agent is much more the kind of person I imagined you with."

Reeva tried to hide a smile as Jaya bristled by her side.

"And what's this about Hot Lips?" Her mum was still prattling on. "Have you met her yet, sweetie? It would be so good for you to have friends in the music industry. You need to get out and have more fun! You know, I actually met her at a benefit last year, though she went by Daniella back then. Of course, she wasn't as famous at the time or she would have been at our table."

"No, I haven't met her." Reeva tried to push away the images flashing up in her mind of Nick with his arms around the beautiful twenty-seven-year-old. "But anyway, Mum, there's something I wanted to ask you."

"Look, I don't like to do favors for music agents, or they'll all be asking for them, but if there's something I can do for your boyfriend to help his career, then of course I'll make an exception."

Reeva tried to keep a straight face as Sita pretended to gag. "Thanks, Mum. I'll keep you posted if I need any music favors. But actually, I don't want to talk to you about my boyfriend right now. Or about Hot Lips. *Definitely* not Hot Lips."

"What?" Her mum's entire face lifted slightly in confusion. "But that's why my PA scheduled this call."

Reeva took a deep breath. It was time. "Mum. I know."

"Know what?"

"The big secret about what happened with Dad." She tried to keep her face neutral, hoping that her expression corresponded to whatever emotion she should be feeling.

Her mum took in a sharp breath. "Oh."

"Yes. Oh."

"How did you find out?"

"Um . . ." Reeva hadn't prepared an answer for this. "Dad kept a journal."

"Of course he did!" cried Saraswati. "That's so him. He was always so emotional." Suddenly she burst into tears. Reeva stared at her in alarm. She'd never seen her mum cry in front of her before. Never. Not even when her own parents had died. She resisted the urge to look at her sisters, but she could feel them tensing up at her side.

"Uh, Mum?"

Saraswati kept sobbing loudly. Tears slid down her cheeks, but her expression didn't change. It was an odd sight. "I'm sorry, Reeva. That this all happened."

"What bit? The death-faking or . . ."

"Yes that, but also the . . . you know. I don't like talking about it. It's too difficult to remember it all."

"Right," said Reeva. "Uh . . . why did it happen?"

"I don't know! I don't think I'll ever really understand it. But it's not just your father's fault—I'm to blame just as much."

"Really? Why?"

"I don't know," wailed Saraswati. "We just argued so much. If I'd . . . or if he'd . . . and we'd . . . oh, I knew nothing back then. I was so young! I know I wasn't a good wife."

"Or mother," said Sita under her breath.

"Ask about Leela," hissed Jaya.

Reeva shifted uncomfortably. "Mum, uh, Leela's been coming to the prayers. You know Leela, right?"

Her mum's tears dried up and she scowled. "Of course. Is she still dressing like a librarian?"

Sita snorted.

"Uh, she looks good," said Reeva. "What's she . . . like?"

"I bet she's been there every day at the prayers, hasn't she? Head bowed, modest as ever. She was always so perfect. If it wasn't for her . . ."

"What, Mum? If it wasn't for her?"

"Nothing," snapped Saraswati. "I thought you wanted to know about your Dad, not Leela."

"Uh . . . yeah," said Reeva. "Even though what happened was, well, really bad, why did you fake his death? Instead of getting a divorce or something?"

"Oh, I don't know." Saraswati sighed. "It made sense at the time. And it's what you all assumed! When I told you he'd gone and wasn't coming back, you girls were the ones who presumed he'd died. I just . . . went along with it."

"Right, so it's our fault," muttered Sita.

"In a way, it felt like the truth," continued Saraswati. "He was gone from our lives. When I told your dad, he accepted it too, and he said it made sense to continue letting you all believe that. He felt bad. We both did."

"What about once he wanted to see us again?" Reeva looked into her mum's eyes as she asked the one question that she knew was true. "He tried. And you said no. Why?"

Her mum's face and voice both hardened. "I did what I thought was best, Reeva. I'm sorry if that makes me a terrible mother.

I'm sorry you were so desperate to see your dad. I would have thought that you of all people would have understood why I did that."

Reeva stared at her in confusion. Why her of all people? Because she understood the trauma of being cheated on? She tried to force herself to focus on the task at hand. Sympathy. Her mum responded well to sympathy. "Look, I know it must have been so hard for you, Mum, and you did what you thought was best. You poor thing, you were so brave."

Her mum sniffed. "Yes. It was hard."

"Definitely. I guess I just wish we could have spoken to Dad about it all before he died."

Her mum let out a strangled cry. "Well, you're with him in death, aren't you? You can talk to him about it now. While his spirit is still with you, before he leaves forever in the kriya ceremony."

Reeva looked at her sisters in desperation. Her mum was being a lot weirder than usual. Jaya shrugged while Sita nudged her. "Get more info."

"Uh, okay, Mum, that's true," said Reeva. "I'll talk to him. Is there . . . anything you want us to say to him for you?"

Her mum shook her head. "No. I just hope you can find it in you to forgive him, Reeva."

"Yeah. I guess we all will."

"Oh, it doesn't matter so much about your sisters. It's you I'm worried about. You were the one who was so affected by it all."

"Me?"

"Of course. My little Reeva. That's the whole point—it's why we did what we did. But I'm glad you're doing so well. My clever girl."

Reeva looked at her mum in a daze. "Okay, it's just, even though Dad's journal explained things, there are still a few holes . . . Can you tell me more about what happened? In detail? It would be really, really helpful to hear your side of things."

Her mum shook her head vehemently. "Reeva, you know I don't believe in going over the past. It's just not healthy. Let's leave it where it belongs and focus on the future, okay? I'm glad you know what happened now—but I cannot relive it. It's too much for me. That's why I was hoping you'd find out without me these two weeks. I just can't bear to talk about it. So let's leave it there, okay? Now it's done; there's no need for us to ever speak of it again."

The plan was backfiring. Reeva looked at her sisters in panic. "But, Mum, I need to—"

"Sorry, darling, I have to go. They're calling for me on set, but I love you lots and I'll see you soon, okay? Stay strong. Oh, and say hi to your sisters for me. You're all getting on okay?"

"Uh, yeah, I guess—"

"Wonderful. Kiss kiss!"

REEVA TURNED TO look at her sisters. "Is it just me or is anyone else more confused than ever?"

Her sisters nodded glumly.

"It sounded like our Leela theory was completely true," said Jaya. "I mean, 'if it wasn't for her.' But what's that got to do with you, Reeva?"

"I have no idea. Maybe it's what you both always say, and it's because I'm the oldest?"

Sita shook her head. "No—something bigger had to have happened. Didn't you hear the way she was talking? It sounds like you're the reason they broke up, Reeva. No wonder you're the favorite—she always felt sorry for you."

"Okay, what?" cried Reeva. "I'm not even the favorite. And what exactly could have happened to me?"

There was a pause, then Sita snapped her fingers triumphantly. "I bet you walked in on Dad and Leela. As a kid."

"What!"

"It happened to a friend of mine," continued Sita. "She walked in on her dad sleeping with some other woman. It scarred her for life. She was only about eleven years old. It would have been even more traumatic if you were five and you walked in on your dad and his lover."

Reeva shuddered. "I . . . don't think so."

"Oh my god, what if we've got this all the wrong way around?" cried Jaya. "What if *Mum* was the one who had the affair? She's way more the type. And then Dad caught her and attacked her lover. Maybe Reeva saw the attack!"

"What?" cried Reeva. "We can't just assume that. And Dad seems so chill—he wouldn't just attack someone."

"Mum said they argued all the time," said Jaya. "And he's definitely intense. Look at the lack of stuff in his house, the fact he went along with being dead, even his folder on us and the money stash . . . It's why I thought he was a spy; he has assassin energy."

"I don't agree with anything she just said," said Sita, pointing at Jaya. "But it is true that Mum says they argued a lot."

"Yeah, he argued with his wife—that's not the same as attacking someone," cried Reeva.

Sita shrugged. "I don't know. There's something in this . . . Mum said it was her fault too. What if they both had affairs?

Either Dad did it first and Mum had one out of revenge, or Mum did it first and then Dad turned to Leela for comfort."

"Isn't that a bit much?" said Reeva.

"Something big had to have happened to necessitate the death-faking, and two messy affairs is definitely bigger than one," pointed out Sita.

"Especially if Dad almost killed Mum's lover," added Jaya.

Reeva frowned. She hated this cheating narrative—it was bad enough when her sisters thought her dad had been guilty of having an affair, but now they were accusing their mum too. "This is ridiculous. I thought you were convinced it was all about Leela."

"She's obviously got something to do with this," said Sita. "Mum's reaction proves that. It's just it could be more than a simple affair."

Reeva shook her head. "There's no evidence for this. All we know is that Dad blamed himself. Mum blames herself. And it affected five-year-old me the most."

"Maybe he abused you," suggested Sita. "Like, sexually."

Jaya and Reeva stared at her in shock.

"Oh my god, Sita, you can't just invent abuse claims," said Jaya.

"I . . . No," said Reeva. Her sister was voicing something that had also crossed her mind. Something so awful she had instantly discarded it. She tried to be rational and see the situation how she would if it were happening to one of her clients. "I would have remembered. Often, people do. They have memories. Or it comes out in dreams and things. If it had happened, I'd know. I know I would. And Mum isn't talking about it like it's that. She would have checked I was okay more than she did if it was that. Well. I hope she would have."

"Okay," said Sita. "But we really do need to consider all options. Not just the affairs."

Reeva's phone vibrated. She looked at it in relief—a message from Nick would be the perfect antidote to this conversation. But it was just Lakshmi. Your cat is needier than you are. I've just had to play laser with her for 30 minutes.

Reeva's face creased in worry. The pet book she'd bought said it wasn't healthy to let cats play with lasers for longer than ten minutes. Was Lakshmi neglecting FP? Should she go back and recuse her cat? Life had been so much easier before she'd had the never-ending responsibility of looking after this damned feline all the time. Reeva was starting to really empathize with Sita's motherhood struggles. Though she decided it was best to not verbalize this aloud.

Her phone vibrated with another message. Lakshmi. But fear not; I've found a genius solution . . .

Reeva tapped on the image below. It was a video of Fluffy Panda playing with something purple buzzing around the wooden floor. Reeva examined it closer then cried out in horror.

Sita peered over. "What is it? Is that your cat?"

Reeva nodded, still speechless.

"Oh my god, cute!" cried Jaya, leaning over. "I didn't know you had a cat. What's it playing with?"

"My vibrator."

REEVA LAY FLAT on the bed, on top of the duvet, going over everything again. It was so frustrating having these snippets of clues rather than the full truth. Especially when it seemed to be all about her. Her sisters seemed fine labeling their dad as a violent man or a cheater. But Reeva couldn't be so laissez-faire. This was her family. Her childhood. And she knew firsthand what cheating was like. Reeva sat up straight as she heard a knock at her door. The guests had left—she was trying to ignore her guilt about it being the fifth evening in a row she'd failed to attend the full prayers—and Sita didn't believe in knocking, which meant it could only be—

"Can I come in? It's me, Jaya."

"Uh, okay."

The door opened and Jaya, dressed in a black lace camisole and matching tiny shorts, tiptoed in. Reeva looked down at her own pajamas—her oversized white nightshirt had looked sexy when she'd first bought it, but it had since gone gray from too many washes, not to mention the large mascara stain on its hem—and decided to start investing in better sleepwear.

"How are you doing?" asked Jaya as she perched on the edge of the bed.

"Okay. You?"

"Fine. I just thought you might feel a bit weird after what Mum said. I wanted to see if you were okay."

"Oh." Reeva leaned back against the pillows. "Yeah, it's a bit disquieting knowing it affected me the most, but I'm fine." She paused. "I didn't expect you to come and ask."

"What are sisters for?"

*Not stealing their boyfriends,* thought Reeva.

"So, how are things going with Nick?"

Reeva looked suspiciously at her sister. They hadn't been alone together in four years, and now Jaya was acting like they were best friends? "Fine. Why?"

"I'm just trying to be a good sister and ask you about your life!"

Reeva scoffed in response. It was a bit late for Jaya to try and be a good sister.

"If you have something to say, just say it," cried Jaya. "I'm sick of these raised eyebrows and annoyed sounds. And it's freaking me out that you've not said anything to me about Rakesh for the last week."

"Excuse me? You're the one who hugged me and has been acting like everything's hunky-dory."

"I'm just trying to do the right thing! I know, I *know*, I did the worst thing back then. But, Reeva, I tried to apologize for an entire *year*. I called you the whole time. And there was that week where I kept showing up to your work?" Reeva remembered; she'd told security that Jaya was a crazy client they shouldn't let into the building. "Then I respected your silence and left you alone. It's not my fault Dad died and made us spend these two weeks together."

Reeva shook her head. Wasn't it obvious that she'd been so broken that year—a year where showering, managing to eat, and showing up to work had taken all her strength—that she'd been physically *unable* to speak to Jaya? When that year had passed and she'd started to slowly heal, Jaya had stopped trying to apologize. As though Reeva had a twelve-month window to get over her nine-year relationship, and after that, sorry, it was too late.

"Please say something," cried Jaya. "I can't bear this anymore."

"*You* can't bear this? I'm the one whose life was destroyed."

"I know. I know. And I am so, *so* sorry." Jaya looked straight into Reeva's eyes. "That's what I've been trying to say to you for the last four years."

"You stopped trying after the first year."

"Because I thought I was making things worse and you wanted

to be left alone! If I'd known you were ready to hear me apologize, I would have hundy-p got the first flight home to come
and see you. Even if I'd been at that amazing resort in the Mal-
dives."

"Right," said Reeva. "Well, I never actually said I'm ready to
hear you apologize. I just noticed that you'd stopped trying."

Jaya raised her chin defiantly. "I'm trying now. And I don't
care if you're ready or not. I've listened to a podcast on how to
apologize, and *I'm* ready to do this." She cleared her throat. "So,
Reeva, I am really, truly sorry about what I did to you. I have
tried to imagine how I would have felt if it had been me, and I
would have literally died. I will never know how bad it was for
you and how much pain it caused you, but if I could take that
away and experience it instead of you, I would. When you said
how bad it had been for you, the other day in the bathroom, it
really hit me what I've done. I mean, I already knew, but this
time, I literally *felt it*. And now you have to sit here watching me
marry him. It must be, like, the actual worst. I'm so sorry. So
fucking sorry. There's no excuse for it. I know that. I just . . . fell
in love."

Reeva felt her stomach churn. She hated being reminded that
Rakesh and Jaya had fallen in love—it was meant to be Rakesh
and Reeva who were in love. But at the same time, a small part of
her felt vindicated by Jaya recognizing just how much pain she'd
caused. It was the first time someone in her family had truly acknowledged the enormity of what Reeva had gone through.

"Well," said Reeva eventually. "I wish you could have felt the
pain instead of me too."

"Totally," cried Jaya. "I would have done *anything* to make it
better."

"Even give him up?"

Jaya hesitated. "Reeva. I . . . I'm marrying him. I hate that everything happened the way it did, but this *is* happening."

"I am very aware of that, thank you." Reeva crossed her arms. She was ready for Jaya to leave. There was too much going on in her life right now (8.5 centimeters of it) to heal a four-year feud at the same time.

Jaya continued, hesitantly. "I know this is probably the wrong thing to say, so don't hate me—well, more than you already do—but were you guys even that happy together? I just . . . I look at you now and you seem way more *you* than when you guys were together. I know it's a very weird time, but you still seem happier. And stronger. You even dress better."

"For god's sake," muttered Reeva. "Just because I've been working on my personal style does not mean you get to assume I'm happier single."

"Well, you're with Nick . . ."

"That's irrelevant. Look, I can't do this right now. I need to sleep. Can you just go, Jaya?"

"Okay." Jaya got up to leave, and then turned back around. "Actually, no. I'm sorry. I'm not leaving till you forgive me."

"I'm sorry, you're going to hijack my bedroom? Was that another recommendation on your apology podcast?"

"No. This is my idea." Jaya sat back on the bed. "You need to forgive me. For *you*."

Reeva looked up to the ceiling. "Please tell me this is not happening right now. I can't deal with this."

"Reevs. I know I've crossed the biggest line. I know what I did is basically unforgiveable. I'm not an idiot, even though I know you all think I am. But, like, we're family. And if you don't let this go, it's going to eat you up forever. It could even cause some kind of, I don't know, disease. I heard of people getting cancer because they couldn't move on from stuff."

Reeva tried not to think about her alopecia. Jaya's theory was ridiculous. And offensive. "Are you trying to tell me I'll get cancer if I don't forgive you? Because that's next-level manipulation. Even from you."

"No! Just . . . please. I am so, so sorry for what I did. I hate myself for it. It's awful. I deserve to be hated for it. I'm a terrible person."

"Okay, you don't need to self-flagellate in front of me."

"What does *flagellate* mean?"

Reeva shook her head. "Jaya, look, I get it. You're sorry. I believe you. And it's good to hear. But I can't just *forgive* you. Too much has happened."

Jaya nodded. "Well, maybe just accepting I'm sorry is enough? Like, properly accepting it?"

Reeva looked at her sister. She still felt so much anger toward her. But it was softening. This was the first time Reeva had heard Jaya apologize properly (and yes, she knew she was partly to blame for that), and it felt better than she could have imagined. It was nowhere near enough to make up for what she'd done, but it wasn't often that one of her sisters tried to see things from her point of view. It felt good, vindicating. Reeva felt something relax inside her—a tight tension she hadn't even really been aware of until this exact moment—and sighed. "Okay. I accept your apology."

"Oh my god, thank you," squealed Jaya. "Thank you, thank you, thank you."

Reeva reached out her hands to stop Jaya from jumping onto her. "Okay, calm down. It doesn't change anything. I'm still not forgiving you; I'm simply accepting your apology."

"No, no, of course not. Well, like, if there's anything you need to talk about or get clarity on, I'm here. If you want to know any details for closure, just ask."

Reeva shuddered. "I will not be doing that."

"Oh, Reeva, I've been waiting for this day for so long! I can't believe you've forgiven me."

"I *just* said this doesn't mean I forgive you."

"Isn't that, like, potato potato?"

"You're meant to pronounce them differently. And no. It isn't like that."

Jaya shrugged happily. "It is to me. I'm going to take this as forgiveness. By which I am also releasing you from hating me. So you can move on too. You're now free. Namaste."

Reeva rolled her eyes. It was impossible to have a normal, rational conversation with Jaya. But she could feel her anger slipping away. Jaya was too Jaya to be resentful of her. She was still nowhere near forgiveness, but she was closer than she ever thought she'd be. "Fine. Sure. But let's not make a massive deal about this, okay?"

"No, of course not," hurried Jaya. "Whatever's right for you."

"Thank you."

Jaya suddenly wrapped her arms around Reeva. "You're the most amazing person in the entire world. The next time I'm interviewed, and they want to know who my role model is, I'm going to say you."

Despite herself, Reeva laughed. Her sister was ridiculous. "Okay, just get off me. And let's stop talking about this."

Jaya dropped her arms and crossed her legs. "Okay. Deal. Sorry. Let's talk about something else. Now that we're friends again, tell me about Nick! He's super hot, Reevs."

"I never said we're friends again. And it is still way too soon for you to call my boyfriend hot."

"Boyfriend?! I thought you were avoiding the B-word."

Reeva was about to shut Jaya's questioning down. Then she paused. She really wanted to talk to someone about Nick, especially because Lakshmi was so busy, dealing with Reeva's Sherwood-Brown case, as well as the duke. Reeva hadn't wanted to inundate her with calls, so she'd been trying to deal with Nick alone, but she was desperate to talk about it. It was crazy to consider confiding in Jaya—even Sita would have been a better option—but this was already the craziest week of Reeva's life. And at this point, she had nothing to lose. She took a deep breath. "I can't believe I'm telling you this. But Nick asked us to be exclusive. He called himself my boyfriend. The other day."

"Oh my god, congrats! I love that for you!"

Reeva hesitated. "Yeah, so did I, but he doesn't always *act* like a boyfriend . . . He doesn't call me when he says he will. He's terrible at replying. And he doesn't share a lot. At all. I tried to ask about his past, and it was so hard to get anything out of him. He always asks me questions, but I feel like he's quite distant. Emotionally. And these photos of him with Hot Lips are all over the press, but he never even *told* me he went to the BRITs with her. Is that not something you'd mention? The fact he's avoiding talking about it makes me feel so anxious. Oh, and he recently told me he dated a singer! So I'm terrified it's Hot Lips. The whole thing makes me so insecure. Like I'm not good enough for him." She stopped suddenly. She'd shared too much. Way too much.

But her sister was unperturbed. "Hot Lips isn't even that cute, and her music is terrible. And who chooses that name? Nick has way better taste than that. And if he doesn't, do you even want to be with him? If Rakesh had dated someone like Hot Lips, I'd seriously judge him. But instead, he dated you, which proves he had amazing taste." She saw Reeva's stony glare and backtracked. "Sorry, sorry. Bad example. All I'm saying is that Nick probably didn't date her, and even if he did, who cares? He's not with her now; he's with you."

"Yes, but he's being so vague lately. Lakshmi thinks it's because I'm away and it's the first time we haven't seen each other regularly for ages. But he's not that *present*, even when we speak, and then those photos . . . I don't know if I'm overthinking things or if he's doing what all men eventually do and bailing. I mean, why doesn't he want to call me every night? Isn't that what most couples do?"

Jaya paused thoughtfully. "It sounds like you're expecting him to be a UCB."

"A what?"

"An uppercase boyfriend. A boyfriend with a capital *B*. One who calls you every night. And replies all the time to texts."

"Of course I am. That's what boyfriends—or uppercase boyfriends—are meant to do. Aren't they?"

"Sure," said Jaya confidently. "UCBs. But before Nick brought up this chat, did you expect the same level of communication from him? Did you expect the nightly calls and regular texts? Or for him to tell you he was going to an awards ceremony with a client?"

"Well, no . . . He wasn't my boyfriend then. He was just someone I was dating. Though I think he could have dropped the BRIT Awards in somewhere."

"Exactly!" cried Jaya, ignoring Reeva's last sentence. "The only thing that's changed is his label. And now you've got expectations that aren't being met. So either he changes, which is also an option, but you'd have to talk to him about it"—Reeva shook her head violently—"or *you've* got to change the way you see him."

"Oh-kay..."

"Just see him as an lcb. A lowercase boyfriend. Take away his capital letters and you'll expect less of him."

Reeva thought about it. Her sister had a point. Even just thinking of Nick as an lcb made her shoulders relax. An lcb didn't have to call every night. Or tell their girlfriend every detail about their exes. And it was okay if they were a bit emotionally distant at times. "Okay. But how long do I have to be with an lcb for? I do want a UCB one day. I want...love."

"Of course you do. And this is the way to get it. It's all about pacing and timing. You're transitioning from dating into a serious relationship. You can't go from zero to one hundred."

Reeva nodded slowly. "Right. Pacing. This isn't a terrible theory—where did you get it from?"

"I made it up! It helped me with Rak—uh, men in the past. And it's helped my friends too. You know, to have fewer expectations and be more present, blah, blah, blah. It's so easy to fall into unhealthy neediness. But I find that demoting someone to an lcb helps."

Reeva looked impressed. "Do you share this kind of thing with your followers?"

Jaya shook her head quickly. "No, no. That's just photos. And one-line captions. It's about creating an escapist fantasy—not real life."

"I'd much prefer to read about this than see hot pics of you on the beach."

"That's because you're jealous of how hot I look on the beach."

"Okay, I said it's too soon for these kinds of jokes." Reeva stood up and shooed her sister away with her hand. "Get out. Go. This has been more than enough for one night."

"Okay, okay, I'm sorry." Jaya made her way out of the room. Then she poked her head back around the door. "Sorry I'm so hot."

Reeva threw a pillow at her face. "Oh my god, out!"

## CHAPTER 12

**Day 7**

SATYA AUNTIE SIPPED her chai in delight. "This is delicious, Sita, thank you. You can really taste the grated nutmeg."

Sita glowed in response and took a self-satisfied bite of her gathiya. They were all sitting in the kitchen having a late breakfast, with Satya Auntie as the guest of honor. The funeral was the next day—which meant they had to go and visit their dad's body that evening to start stage one of the prep. None of the sisters had any idea what this prep actually involved, which was why Satya Auntie had come over to explain what was required. So far, all Reeva had ascertained was that they had to dress their dad in his favorite outfit.

She hadn't been able to take in anything else after that. She was still trying to absorb the fact that the first time she was going to meet her dad as an adult, he was going to be both naked and dead.

"So have you managed to find out any more?" asked Satya Auntie. "About your dad and everything that happened?"

The three sisters all shook their heads morosely.

"We have some theories," said Jaya. "An affair is the top one. But we can't figure out if Dad did it with Leela or if Mum did it with someone else and Dad found them and went cray."

"Or both," said Sita.

"But we don't have any proof for either of them," added Reeva. "It's all conjecture."

"We tried to reverse psychology Mum," said Sita. "But we didn't get much out of her. She's jealous of Leela, which suggests something happened with her and Dad. And that whatever happened is partly her fault for not being a good wife, which is, well, surprisingly self-aware of her. But other than that, it's the usual—that it's too painful to relive whatever it was that happened."

"And that whatever it was happened to *Reeva*," added Jaya, looking pointedly at her eldest sister. "She was the one most affected by it all."

Satya Auntie's eyebrows raised in surprise. "Really? And you don't know what it might be?"

Reeva shook her head. "Nope. It's so frustrating." She hesitated.

"Do you think Dad was violent?" asked Jaya. "Like, for example, if he'd found out Mum had a lover, could he have attacked him?"

"It's another theory," explained Sita as their aunt's eyebrows shot up in surprise again.

"I . . . wouldn't say so," said Satya Auntie slowly. "For me, his flaws were more around him being so headstrong. Like how he didn't contact me—his younger sister—for decades, until I reached out first."

"Sounds like someone I know," said Sita, jerking her head toward Reeva.

"They're completely different situations," cried Reeva.

"But you have to remember that I didn't see him for a long time," added Satya Auntie. "I missed a lot of his life, and those were the years he never wanted to talk to me about. The Hemant I knew wasn't violent—if anything, he was very gentle. Especially with animals. But . . . I do know that there was a lot he hid from me."

Reeva felt a warm glow inside her. Her dad loved animals. And he was gentle.

"Fair enough." Sita shrugged. "If he did lose it, it would have been because of Mum's behavior. No surprise there."

"Well, that's not—" said Satya Auntie.

"It's okay," interrupted Jaya. "We know what Mum's like. Most things are her fault. Even if Reeva likes to think otherwise."

They all turned to look at Reeva. "What?" She'd been lost in yet another daydream about what life would have looked like if she'd grown up with their dad. A daydream she didn't want to leave.

"What are you thinking about?" demanded Sita.

"Just Dad. What he was like. I love that he took care of animals."

"Oh yeah," said Sita. "Reeva's become a crazy cat lady."

"No, I just happen to have a cat. A cat that I love."

"Oh, I didn't know that!" Satya Auntie beamed. "Tell me more."

"Well, she's called Fluffy Panda, FP for short. She also answers to Princess Fluffy Panda."

"Jesus," muttered Sita.

"She's a total nightmare, but I love her," continued Reeva. "My best friend, Lakshmi, bought her for me to help me with my—uh, you know, stress. She hates organic food, people, all other cats, and, often, me."

Her aunt laughed. "Aren't cats amazing? I feel like we can learn so much from their absolute refusal to be anything but themselves. And they're always so at peace. Really, we all need to be more like cats."

"That is so true," cried Reeva. "I've been thinking that ever since I got her. Sometimes I look at her, waving her bum in my face or collapsing in the middle of the empty bathtub like it's her god-given right to do whatever she wants, and I'm almost jealous. I wish I was brave enough to do what I want. Like nap in the office or say no to baby showers."

Sita shook her head. "You sound insane. And where has it all come from? We Indians don't do pets."

"Uh, that's so racist," interjected Jaya. "And not even true. Some of my Indian friends have dogs. Little adorable fluffy ones."

"And I bet they don't let them in their beds," said Sita. "Call me racist if you want, but no Indian is going to treat their dog like a member of their family. Not if they've ever been to India."

"Uh, I definitely treat Fluffy Panda better than a member of my family," said Reeva. "She's the best family I've ever had." Then she realized what she said. "I mean—"

"Whatever, you prefer your cat to your family," said Sita. "We get it. Just don't tell the twins."

Reeva bit her bottom lip, hesitating. "I haven't told you yet, but I've been having really bad nightmares lately . . . like really bad. I can barely sleep. And they're all about FP and the twins. The twins are always screaming."

"No surprise there." Sita shrugged. She glanced over to the open door into the living room, where the twins were sitting in unusual silence, with thumbs in their mouths and eyes transfixed on the dinosaur cartoon on the television screen. "They'll be at it again when the dinosaur dies. You'd think TV directors would know better."

"No, it's not like that," said Reeva. "It's *dark*. Their screams are bad. Last night . . ." She paused as she remembered waking up in the middle of the night dripping in cold sweat. No wonder her patch was now 8.9 centimeters. "I think I saw the cat die. Only it was an all-black cat, not black-and-white like FP. And the twins were holding it, screaming and crying. They were covered in blood."

Jaya's mouth dropped open. "Oh my god! Is it, like, a premonition? Have you checked in with Lakshmi?"

"I got a selfie of them curled up in bed earlier. I'm not worried; it's more just exhausting having all these nightmares."

"You do look tired," said Sita. "Bags. Under the eyes."

"Do you know what the dreams could mean?" asked Satya Auntie. "It sounds like your subconscious is trying to tell you something." She looked at Jaya. "Not . . . necessarily predicting the future, but maybe showing you what's on your mind?"

Reeva nodded. "I figured I must just miss FP more than I thought. Or I'm anxious generally. I mean, that's a fact. I'm always semianxious."

Her aunt reached out to put a hand on hers. "I'm sorry, Reeva. Night terrors are awful. And not getting enough sleep can make us feel terrible."

"True that," said Sita. "I hardly ever slept the year after I had the twins. And I made the worst life choices."

"You should totally get hypnotherapy," said Jaya. "It could help you uncover the meaning of your dreams."

"Oh my god, not this crap again," cried Sita. "No offense, Satya Auntie."

Their aunt suppressed a smile. "None taken. I've never done hypnotherapy."

"It's amazing," cried Jaya. "Like, super healing. Will you do it, Reevs? There's a hypno-influencer I know who does it. I can probably get you a free session if you let me do a post on you?"

"We're not all like you, Jaya—sacrificing our privacy for freebies," said Sita.

"Please, Reevs, will you?" asked Jaya. "I'll pay for it!"

"Uh, no, sorry." Jaya looked so crestfallen that Reeva found herself saying, "But if you send me a link, I'll take a look."

Jaya squealed in excitement.

"I think Hemant used to have a cat," said Satya Auntie unexpectedly.

"*What?*" All three sisters turned to look at her. "When?"

"He only mentioned it a couple of times. I got the sense it was when you girls were young. But if you don't remember it, maybe I've got things wrong."

Jaya shook her head. "It must have been after us. There is no way Mum would have let us have a pet. That would take the attention away from her. Not to mention the molting hair—she doesn't really do germs."

Sita nodded. "Jaya's right. But it's interesting that Dad was a pet person. It's not what I would have expected for him." She gestured toward the room. "What with his whole spartan self-denial vibe."

"I love that he had a cat," said Reeva, picking up her cup of chai. "I feel like we would have got on."

Jaya nodded. "I hear you. The more I hear about him, the more I like him. He sounds *nice.* I know it sounds harsh, but if one of our parents was going to be fake dead, I wish it had been Mum, not Dad."

Sita sighed in agreement. "Yeah, he sounds a lot more normal than her. I bet he wouldn't have shoved us into boarding school. Or made us get our legs waxed at age ten. *And* he has photos of his grandchildren in his house. Things Mum would never do ..."

Satya Auntie smiled. "He was very different from your mum. But I know for a fact they've both always loved you. They just had ... different ways of showing it."

"Yeah, they really did not have the same love language," said Jaya.

"Exactly." Satya Auntie laughed. "Your dad showed his love by providing for you financially, keeping track of your lives, and I suppose by keeping his distance for whatever reason. While your mum ... well, her way is more ..."

"Individual?" offered Reeva.

"Selfish?" suggested Jaya.

"Nonexistent," concluded Sita. "More chai anyone?"


REEVA SAT ON a park bench watching Amisha and Alisha attack each other on the playground. She wasn't sure when she was meant to intervene, but she figured she'd wait till they drew blood. She pulled out her phone and reread her latest message from Nick. I'm so sorry I can't make it to the funeral to-morrow, Reeva. I have to go to LA for a couple of days with one of my clients. Wish I could get out of it. But I promise I'll come see you straight after. Have you got any closer to finding things out? Lots of love, Nx.

Twenty-four hours ago, this would have tipped Reeva into a panic-induced internet trawl as she tried to find out whether he was lying or not—and exactly what Hot Lips's schedule for the week looked like. But after her chat with Jaya, she felt better.

Nick was just an lcb. He didn't have to turn up to her estranged dad's funeral. And she didn't have to freak out about it. She could just . . . reply.

> Oh, that's a shame but I understand. Which client
> is it? A few more clues here, but nothing concrete.
> Call me when you can, and I'll fill you in. Rx

She reread it before pressing send, impressed by her naturally keen-but-not-too-keen tone. It was perfectly lowercase girlfriend, and she hadn't even planned it out in her draft messages. Just ditching the capital letters from their relationship was making everything so much easier. She didn't have to worry so much. She could just let things be.

Her phone rang.

"Lakshmi! I am so glad to hear from you. How are you?"

"I miss you," cried her best friend. "I'm sorry I've been so shit. Work has just been way too much, and that bloody cat takes up any energy I have left over. I have no idea how you take care of her on your own. You know I've had to ask Lee to let me work from home two days a week so I can look after her? I finally get how working mums feel."

Reeva laughed. "Don't let them hear you say that. How is FP?"

"Awful and perfect. She's currently sitting on my foot. Which means I can't move and have had to hold in my pee for the last hour."

"Wow. I can't believe my cat has you so well trained."

"Don't. I've always prided myself on not letting a man tell me what to do, but now I'm bending over backward for a feline. It's shameful."

"Ahh, I'm so excited to see you tomorrow! I miss you. And I

have so much to tell you. You know, I've been having real conversations with Jaya and Sita. And oh my god, Jaya apologized!"

"About fucking time! What did she say?"

"It wasn't bad, actually. Genuine. She'd listened to a podcast on how to apologize."

"Of course she had. And what did you say back?"

"I accepted her apology. I didn't think I would. But I'm sick of hating her so much."

"That's amazing! Well done, Reevs. I mean—I don't think she deserves it. But anything that makes you feel better is a good thing in my book."

"Thanks." Reeva smiled.

"Have you found out anything more yet? About your dad?"

"Just that Mum feels guilty about it, even though Dad says it wasn't her fault. There's a woman, Leela, who the others think Dad might have been dating. I'm not convinced though—they don't seem like the type."

"Well, if there's anything we've learned in our line of work, it's that anything is possible."

"Right." Reeva sighed. "Oh, and Mum slipped that it affected me more than the others."

"What, why? Because you were the oldest?"

"She made it sound a little more than that. It was all quite ominous. I'm hoping it's nothing too bad."

"Surely you'd know if it was?"

"I hope so. Sita thinks Mum had an affair and Dad beat up her lover. And I witnessed the whole thing."

"Oooh, like that Russian couple we did a couple of years ago! Yeah, that could make sense. But your dad could have just divorced her and taken all her money . . . He didn't need to fake his death."

"Tell me about it. I can't think of a single reason that justifies the death-faking. Oh, hang on. Amisha! Stop attacking your sister. Alisha, push her off you! Come on, girl, you've got this. Okay, they've stopped. Bloody hell, they're feral."

"Sounds like Sita's palmed babysitting duties onto you."

"I offered. You know I love them. And it gets me out of the house. Though I'm meant to be using this time to write a eulogy for tomorrow . . ."

"Oh wow. What are you going to say?"

"I have no idea. I didn't know him! And all his friends seem to think we all had a normal father-daughter relationship. It's just . . . awkward."

"Not as awkward as it would be if you revealed the truth."

"Yeah, definitely not something I'm planning on doing. Anyway, you'll hear it tomorrow. Hey, what are you doing with FP in the end? Have you hired a sitter from that website I sent you, or is your assistant going to do it?" There was silence on the other end. Reeva furrowed her brow. "Lakshmi? Please tell me you're still coming tomorrow?"

"I'm so sorry," she cried. "I just— It's work. The pedophile case is in court, and I can't trust anyone else with it. He's innocent, I know he is, and, Ree, his whole life could be ruined if I don't defend him against that lying gold digger."

Reeva sighed. She was familiar with the case. "Surely Lee can handle it?"

"You know he can't."

"But how am I meant to get through tomorrow without you? You're my family more than Jaya and Sita have ever been."

Lakshmi made a guilty sound. "I know, I know. But I can't get away. Please don't hate me. I'll be with you in spirit, I promise."

Reeva exhaled loudly. "Oh, fine. It's okay."

"You will truly be fine, Reevs. I so believe that. And you're practically best mates with your sisters now."

"I would not go that far."

"And Nick's going to be there! Surely you're excited about that?"

Reeva hesitated. "Yeah, I guess." She hadn't meant to lie to her best friend. But the thought of Lakshmi bailing on her court case out of pity was just unbearable. "Anyway, the twins are murdering each other, so I'd better go. Bye!"

Reeva hung up the phone call and saw Nick had replied.

It's with Hot Lips. Not sure if you know her stuff?
She cleaned out the BRIT Awards the other day!
Miss you. XX

Reeva took a deep breath. She could do this. Nick was an lcb. And he missed her. As lcbs went, that was big stuff. She just needed to do what Jaya said and lower her expectations. And do what Lakshmi said and stop projecting her past onto the present. And do what Satya Auntie said and fully accept her reality. Easy.

## CHAPTER 13

**Day 7**

For once, all three sisters were speechless. They were standing in a private room of the local funeral parlor next to an open casket. Their father was inside. His skin was pale and anemic looking. His eyes were shut, his eyelids papery and thin, and there was gray stubble growing on his cheeks. His dad bod was hidden in a graying white T-shirt and checked M&S pajama bottoms—the outfit he'd been asleep in when he died. It was hard to imagine what he would have looked like when he was alive, but Reeva guessed he wouldn't have caused heads to turn in the street. He looked . . . ordinary. The one quality she'd always wanted in a parent.

"I can't tell if he looks so much older than Mum because he's dead or because she's had so much work done," said Jaya. "Do you think she'd be as wrinkly as Dad without all the Botox?"

Sita shrugged. "Probably. But then again, she spends a fortune on her face creams. All I found in Dad's bathroom cabinet was E45 cream."

"If only I'd known, I could have given him some Crème de la Mer," said Jaya sadly. "I have so many samples."

"Uh, I'll take them," said Sita. "Why do you never give me your free shit?"

"Because you make fun of my job about five times a day."

Sita nodded. "Fair point."

"Don't you think he looks like he would have been a nice person?" asked Reeva, who'd been staring intently at their dad. "I know he's dead and all, but his energy seems so calm."

"Hundy-p," Jaya said, nodding. "Serious Zen vibes."

Sita shook her head. "You've both lost it. You can't get vibes from a corpse. And I thought we all agreed Dad was difficult to live with too."

"Yeah, when he lived with Mum," said Jaya. "Which is obvious. MJ's probably in therapy right now."

"All I'm saying is that I think he would have been a good dad," said Reeva. She couldn't stop gazing at his face. "A really good dad."

"Me too," said Jaya. "Even if he did cheat. Or attack Mum's lover."

"Yeah, whatever he did, I'm sure he would have been better than Mum," conceded Sita.

"We need to do this, don't we?" said Reeva. "Get him ready."

Sita nodded grimly. "Who wants to pull his trousers off? I bet you a fiver he's not wearing boxers."

UNFORTUNATELY, SITA WON her £5. The sisters had shrieked so loudly in the process of uncovering this that the undertaker had rushed in, assuming the body had fallen out of the casket. "It happened once," he'd told them. "Almost killed the poor wife when her dead husband fell on top of her."

Their father was now lying in the coffin wearing a pair of boxers with a white shirt.

"I can do the buttons," offered Reeva. "If you guys want to put the trousers on him?"

Jaya shook her head quickly. "I was standing by his waist when we took the pajama trousers off."

"I lifted the boxers all the way to the top," said Sita.

Reeva sighed. "Fine. But help me, okay? Jaya, if you grab that leg, no, the right one, okay cool. And I'll slide these on . . ." She awkwardly maneuvered his right leg into one side of the black trousers. "Sita, can you . . . ?"

Sita reluctantly helped her shove the other leg into the other side. "This is fucking hard," she grunted. "Why does no one talk about this?"

"I can't believe the undertaker isn't doing it," complained Jaya. "I'd definitely pay extra for this."

"We opted out of that service," said Reeva.

Both her sisters turned to her in shock. "What?" cried Jaya. "Why?!"

"Satya Auntie mentioned it, and when I googled it, the Internet said it was a tradition for family to dress their relatives. So I told the funeral parlor we'd do it."

"You *chose* this without asking us?" demanded Sita.

"Well, Dad's will said we had to do the full traditions . . ." Reeva trailed off. "And, I don't know, daughterly penance?"

"I'm pretty sure Dad would rather we'd skipped that one and let the undertakers see him naked instead of his long-lost daughters," said Jaya.

"Yup," said Sita grimly. "You seriously owe us, Reeva."

Reeva looked up. "Uh, bad news, guys." She pointed to the waistband of their father's trousers. "We've put them on the wrong way around. The fly is at the back."

"Oh, for fuck's sake!" cried Sita. "I can't do it again. I mean... will anyone really notice?"

"He's dead!" cried Reeva. "We can't dress him in backward trousers. That's got to be bad karma." Sita shrugged in response. Reeva looked at her younger sister. "Jaya? Back me up here."

"I don't really believe in reincarnation or whatever. I think he's fine as he is. No one will know."

Reeva shook her head in resignation. "You're both awful. Remind me never to let you guys dress me when I'm dead." She started trying to yank the trousers off his legs. "Um, can someone help me?"

Her sisters shook their heads in unison.

Jaya held up her manicured nails. "Sorry. My nails can only do so much. And this was your idea."

"Agreed," said Sita. "This was all you. If you want to do the full Hindu rites, be my guest."

Reeva reluctantly began trying to slide the trousers off her dad's corpse, panting as she did so. "This...is...so...bullshit. Can't we just do a closed casket like white people?"

"We need it open for the ceremony tomorrow," Sita reminded her. "To do all the powder-and-sandalwood malarkey."

"We should be grateful it's Dad, not Mum," said Jaya. "Imagine trying to put a sari on a corpse."

"I can't even put one on myself," replied Reeva. "Last time I needed to for a wedding, I got stuck in a YouTube hole of Indian influencers. And I still ended up begging a random auntie in the hotel bathroom to redo it."

"We don't need to worry about that," dismissed Sita. "There's no way Mum will let us near her dead body. She's probably already got it in her PA's contract that her duties don't end till she's six feet under. Literally."

"Uh, you okay there?" Jaya looked at Reeva, who currently had their father's left leg draped across her shoulders.

"No," grunted Reeva. "But since when was any of this okay?"

Her sisters nodded in grim agreement.

Reeva finally put their dad's body down. "Right. Just need to do these up, and Dad's funeral-ready."

Jaya nodded approvingly. "He looks good. Having his trousers on the right way does actually help."

Sita leaned back against the wall to survey him. "He looks less tragic in a suit instead of pajamas. Still can't imagine Mum being married to him though."

Reeva pulled up a stool and sat down next to the coffin. "He looks quite handsome. And don't forget that when she met him, she was normal too. Pre-Bollywood. Pre-Botox."

"I can't imagine Mum ever being normal," said Sita.

"They looked normal in that wedding photo we found," said Reeva. "And happy." She looked at her dad, trying to imagine him as the strong, smiling man from the photo. "He's changed a lot, hasn't he? And not just because he's more horizontal than vertical right now."

Sita snorted. "Yeah, I think death does that to you."

"I meant more in terms of personality. From what we've heard so far. How he became religious and everything. Sacrificed so much for us."

"I can't believe he won't be at my wedding," cried Jaya. Her eyes started to water. "I hate that I won't have a dad to walk me down the aisle."

Sita shot her a death stare. "I didn't get that either. And you're having an Indian wedding; there is no father-giving-away-the-bride bit. The uncles do it."

"Yeah, but at least Dad was alive for yours! He had a photo of you and Nitin in his folder. He won't even know Rakesh." Jaya burst into loud tears.

Reeva tried not to snap at her. At least her sister was still going to marry Rakesh—the very dream Reeva had lost. Then she remembered she was trying to forgive Jaya. She closed her eyes and breathed through her frustration like her therapist had taught her. When she opened them, she was looking right at her dad. Seeing him there made everything feel so real and final. It felt like such a waste. What was the point in being alive if you couldn't even speak to your children? No matter what had happened, Reeva knew she'd never feel it was worth keeping someone's entire existence hidden from their family.

"Are you okay?" Sita came up beside Reeva. Jaya was still standing on the other side of the coffin sobbing loudly.

"I'll be fine," said Reeva. She brushed a stray tear from her eyes. She didn't want to cry. Not now. Especially when Jaya was crying enough for all of them. "It just . . . feels like a waste, you know? That we never got to know him."

Sita nodded. "I know. It's shit. They probably thought they had years left, but then he died in his sixties."

"It's such a *shame*. If Mum had just let him get in touch with us, I know we would have accepted him. Loved him."

Sita looked at her in surprise. "Loved him?"

Reeva shrugged defensively. "He's our dad. He liked cats. He was kind. And funny. What more do you want?"

"He may have also been a violent, lying cheat," said Sita. "But, you know, nobody's perfect. I should know—I couldn't be further from Mum of the Year."

"What?" Reeva's disbelief was real. "You seem like a great mum. You're so socially aware."

"It's complicated. At least the girls know both their parents are alive though."

Reeva smiled wryly. "Yeah. I wonder if I'll ever contribute toward creating the next generation."

"'Course you will. There's loads of time."

Reeva looked down at her dad. "We don't always have as much time as we think."

Sita hit her sister's arm.

"Ow!" cried Reeva.

"Stop being so morbid," said Sita. "It's depressing me. As is this sad little room. Let's go home and get drunk in the loo."

"Shouldn't we be at the prayers?" asked Reeva. "It's the last night of bhajans before the funeral. I feel like people will expect us to be there."

"Who cares?" replied Sita. "Life is short, remember? Hey, Jaya, stop sobbing. No one's filming you. You up for hanging out in the bathroom again?"

Jaya sniffed. "Okay. Can we get some better food though? I'm over the children's crudités."

"I saw a pizza place on the way," said Reeva. "Let's stop off en route. I could murder a stuffed crust."


"I CAN'T BELIEVE we have to cremate Dad tomorrow," said Reeva. Two glasses of wine in, she was lying on her duvet, which was squashed into the empty bathtub—because if you're going to hang out in the bathroom, you may as well do it properly—munching on pizza. Jaya was sitting opposite her on the toilet seat, with a cushion behind her back, while Sita was perched on top of the closed laundry basket, eating a slice of pizza straight out of the box. Reeva took a satisfied bite of the cheesy crust. Satya Auntie had suggested going gluten- and dairy-free to help her alopecia, but as much as Reeva wanted her hair to grow back, she couldn't face such drastic action during the hardest two weeks of her life.

"Poor man," said Sita. "He doesn't seem to have had the best life."

Jaya raised an eyebrow at her sister. "Uh, there's like thirty people downstairs crying their eyes out over him."

"While his only children—well, as far as we know—are hiding out in the bathroom," said Reeva. "Not really funeral goals."

"And we're eating pizza. Which we're not meant to do until after the funeral," added Jaya. "Remember? We're only meant to eat bland food before he's cremated. We're totally getting reincarnated as flies."

"I thought you don't believe in reincarnation," said Reeva. Jaya made a face at her in response.

"Hey, we dressed his corpse," pointed out Sita. "That's the epitome of daughterly duties."

"Only because his will literally told us to," replied Reeva. "Though, from everything I've seen in my line of work, kids basically only ever do stuff for their parents so they can inherit their money. Which actually makes us a pretty normal family."

Sita scoffed as she downed the rest of her wine. "Normal? Us?"

"Speak for yourself," said Jaya. "I'm quite happy with my life. I'm getting married in the summer to the love of my— Uh, sorry, Reevs. I like my career. I get paid while I travel the world for free. And I'm reconnecting with my sisters!"

"Well congratulations to you," said Sita. "It's all right for some."

"What's so wrong with your life?" demanded Jaya. "You've got two gorgeous girls, a super successful husband, and a posh postcode. Your life is everything you ever wanted it to be."

Sita shrugged. "You wouldn't get it—either of you. But being a mum is not easy."

Reeva looked down at her half-empty wineglass and felt a wave of sadness wash over her. Both her sisters' lives had turned out exactly how they wanted. Jaya was marrying the love of both her and Reeva's life, while Sita's biggest problem was juggling motherhood duties. Reeva had always wanted to be a mother, but having kids no longer looked like the certainty she'd always thought it would be.

She was currently thirty-four, which meant even if things did work out with her and Nick, she probably wouldn't end up trying to have kids till she was at least thirty-seven. If she believed the newspaper articles that said her fertility would fall off a cliff at age thirty-five, that meant she might never get to be a mum. And what if things didn't work out with her and Nick? She'd be back to square one and probably wouldn't end up trying to have kids till she was in her forties. Not to mention that she currently had 9.2 centimeters of scalp showing on her head. That was sure to add a few years to her search to find a man to impregnate her.

"I think we're all really lucky," said Jaya, warming to her topic. "Us Mehta sisters. Reeva's killing it as a lawyer. You have this sick flat in London. A super-cute cat. A best friend who loves you so much she's taking care of it for you. And a seriously sexy boyfriend."

Reeva blinked drunkenly at her sister. "Uh, let me reframe that. I have a lowercase boyfriend who keeps forgetting to call me and is currently in LA with one of the UK's top ten sexiest women, who he may or may not have dated until he met me. My best friend isn't coming to the funeral because she's choosing work over our friendship. My cat prefers said best friend to me, despite the fact that I've spent hundreds of pounds and hours trying to win her love. And I'm going bald."

Jaya and Sita stared at her.

"I'm sorry, what?" asked Sita. "You're going bald?"

Shit. Reeva shuffled down farther in the tub. She knew there was a reason she didn't drink white wine.

"Is it alopecia?" Jaya looked at her sympathetically. "I thought it could be something like that."

"What?!" Reeva jerked upright. "How did you know? Is it showing?!"

Jaya shook her head quickly. "No, no. I just— This one time I thought I saw a patch on the side of your head. I follow someone on Instagram who has it, so I know what it looks like. And, also, you were *really* weird about the hairband with the twins."

"Show me," demanded Sita. "Go on."

"No!" cried Reeva. "I'm not getting my patch out."

"Get it out." Sita slid off the laundry basket and walked over to Reeva.

"What are you doing?" Reeva put her arms up to stop her sister touching her hair. "Oh my god, you weirdo! Stop it! Okay, okay, fine. I'll show you. Just . . . stop trying to pull out what little hair I have left."

Sita retreated to the laundry basket triumphantly as Reeva sat up straight. With careful precision, she moved her hair across to the right side of her head and showed her sisters exactly what she'd spent the last week desperately trying to hide from them.

"Mm, you weren't exaggerating," said Sita, peering over her head. "It's bad."

"Thanks."

"It's . . . so . . . bald." Jaya's voice wobbled as she spoke, and then she burst into full-on tears. "I would die if it was me."

"You've got to be kidding me," muttered Reeva. Then she raised her voice. "Stop crying. It's *my* alopecia, not yours. And if I'm not crying, you're definitely not allowed to."

"It's my alopecia and I'll cry if I want to," sang Sita. "The remix."

Reeva shot her a dark look. "Seriously? Both of you have to be dicks about this?"

"Sorry, sorry," choked Jaya. "It's just really impactful to see it. You know you could get a lot of likes if you put it on social. There really aren't that many alopecia influencers out there."

"What the fuck!" Reeva crossed her arms and glared at her sister. "I'm not exploiting my biggest insecurity for followers. I'm a lawyer, not an influencer."

"Don't yell! I'm trying to *help* you. Sorry if I think it's a good idea to inspire people."

"You're not trying to help me at all; you're just making it all about you, as per usual!"

"How am I making it about me? I'm crying because I *feel* for you. I'm an empath, Reeva. It's actually a gift."

"Uh, bullshi—"

Suddenly Sita spoke. "Nitin and I are over."

Reeva and Jaya both spun around to stare at her.

"Over what?" asked Reeva. "Conservatories? Private school?"

Sita looked down at the linoleum floor with its faux-wood design. "Our relationship. It's done. We hate each other. We sleep in different beds. We're basically separated. But we're still living in the same house because, well, we don't want anyone to know. Not even you two."

"Oh my god," breathed out Jaya. "I can't believe it. You guys are, like, my example of what a happy marriage looks like."

"Not any longer," said Sita. "Maybe you should try the Obamas instead."

"For all I know, they're secretly over too," cried Jaya.

Reeva shifted around in the bathtub so she could face her sister. "Wait, Sita, are you serious? You guys are really over?"

Her sister nodded glumly in response. "It's been two years."

Reeva's eyes widened. "What! That's ages! Why are you guys still living together if you're so sure it's over?"

"You were not kidding about the no-sex-for-years thing," said Jaya. "Damn."

"Look, it works for us," said Sita. "It's how we're doing things. We're fine."

"Wait, so you're not planning on divorcing properly and living apart?" asked Reeva. "But . . . I can help you! You'll get everything. Hundy-p, as Jaya says."

"I'm not taking my husband to the cleaners." Sita scowled. "I don't want anyone to know. I have no idea why I just told you both. But when I saw your baldness I thought, fuck it. If you can share something that bad, I can share this."

"I'm glad my baldness is helping, but I don't get why you want to keep it a secret. It sounds so horrible having to live together if you're not together. How will you ever date again?"

Sita crossed her arms. "I don't want to date. It's what we've chosen to do. So let it be, okay?"

"This is, like, really sad," said Jaya. "You're too young to resign yourself to spinsterhood."

Sita's brow furrowed. "Spinsterhood? Can you try to be less sexist about this? I'm making a decision that's right for me and my daughters."

"But isn't this worse for the girls?" asked Reeva. "They'll pick up on the tension and it'll end up affecting them more than you think. It'll be so much better for them if you guys are happy separated. Divorce is so normal these days, it's not even a thing for kids. They find it weirder when people's parents stay together."

Jaya nodded. "It's so true. And it's not just white people. Bollywood is divorce central these days. Mum is MJ's, what, third wife?"

"I don't care," said Sita firmly. "I'm going to keep holding the fort down so I don't fuck up their lives like our parents did to us."

"Uh, I think so long as you don't tell them Nitin died, you're all good," said Reeva. Sita glared at her. "Sorry! I just think you guys staying together could do the kids more damage than separating."

"I didn't ask you for your opinion," snapped Sita. "Can you all just ease off on this? I'm doing what I want to do, okay? Nitin agrees. It's our choice—not yours."

"Okay, okay," said Reeva, taking another deep sip of her pinot grigio. "Fine. I'm sorry it's happening. And I'm sorry you felt you had to hide it from us."

"You hid your baldness." Sita frowned at her. "And it's not like we really open up to each other. Why would I have told you? We've barely spoken in the last four years."

Jaya nodded sadly. "We're not really a sharing kind of family, are we?"

"How could we be when our mother didn't bother to share anything with us?" asked Sita. "Except for, you know, making us watch the films with her songs in them, or telling us she was marrying a Bollywood star."

"Let's not talk about her," said Reeva. "It's too exhausting to relive. And I don't want to be the cliché daughter who bitches about her mum."

"'Course you don't," muttered Sita. "Because you're her favorite."

"I refuse to dignify that with a response," said Reeva, grandly raising her head. "So, what about you, Jaya? What secret are you hiding then?"

"Secret?" Jaya stared at her. "What secret?"

"Reeva's bald, I'm single. What's yours?" asked Sita.

Jaya blushed deeply. "Oh my god, nothing. Why are you guys being so dramatic?"

"There is something!" cried Reeva. "I was kidding, but there is!"

Sita jumped up. "I'll hold her ankles. You hold her wrists."

"What is wrong with you lunatics?" shrieked Jaya. "You can't just tickle me till I tell you. That's abuse!"

Reeva shrugged and reached out for Jaya's ankles. "Why not? It worked when you were nine."

"Oh my god, as if this is happening!" Jaya tried to fight off her sisters, but they held on to her and began tickling her. She cried out with a combination of laughter and agony before eventually collapsing into gasps. "Okay, okay, I'll tell you. I just . . . Please don't be weird about it."

Reeva let go and grinned triumphantly at Sita. "Go us!"

"Spill," commanded Sita. "I don't have all day."

"Okay. Here's a clue—I've been drinking the same glass of wine all night."

Reeva's mouth dropped open. "No. You're not . . . You can't be . . ."

"I'm pregnant!"


REEVA DIALED LAKSHMI's number again. She still wasn't picking up. The one time she desperately needed to speak to her, and she was AWOL. Fuck! She couldn't process this alone. And who was she meant to speak to if not her best friend? Nick was on a flight to LA, and Reeva didn't want to go to him about this. In an act of desperation, she tried her mum. But the phone rang with no answer. Who else? She had other friends, sure, but they mostly had husbands and families. She couldn't call them at eleven p.m., slightly drunk on a Wednesday night. They'd be asleep. Though they might wake up when she told them her youngest sister was going to have her ex-boyfriend's child. No, Reeva couldn't burden them with this. It was a family crisis, so she'd have to share it with family.

Reluctantly, Reeva messaged Sita. You up?

She replied instantly. What is this, a booty call? But yes. The girls are sleeping, so I'm in the living room watching shit TV.

Reeva left her room and padded downstairs in her thick socks, oversized T-shirt, and the men's boxers she loved sleeping in. They were so much roomier than the female versions.

Sita was sitting on the sofa, wrapped up in a fluffy cream dressing gown, sipping from a mug. The TV was on, with what looked like a gritty crime drama. Sita spoke to her without taking her eyes off the screen. "*CSI* reruns."

Reeva curled up on the other end of the sofa. "Cool." She turned to face her sister. "So. We're both going to be aunts now."

The show turned to ads, and Sita turned to look at her. "Yup. God knows what Jaya's spawn will turn out like."

"It feels odd."

Sita sighed. "Yeah. I thought it might be hard for you. I guess you always thought you'd have kids with Rakesh. And now she's at it."

Reeva nodded. "Pretty much. It also makes me the only sister who isn't going to be married or a mum. And I'm the oldest."

"I'm not really married anymore; just on paper."

"I know. I don't want to fall into a self-pity hole. It's just making me realize nothing in my life is going to plan."

"I thought you were happy with Nick?"

"I am. And I hope that, you know, he and I . . . well, last. He's still a lowercase boyfriend. Meanwhile, Jaya's marrying Rakesh and having a *baby*. I can't believe she's going to be a mum and I'm nowhere near."

"It's still quite early days; she hasn't passed twelve weeks yet. It might never happen."

Reeva's mouth dropped open in shock. "You did not just say that!"

"What?" Sita shrugged. "I'm not saying I *hope* it happens. But it could. It's happened to me. And Mum."

"Really? I . . . never knew that. I'm so sorry."

"It's not a big deal." Sita wrinkled her brow. "Mine was only a year after the girls were born. Blessing in disguise, really; I couldn't deal with three of them."

"And what about Mum?" Reeva looked at her sister. "I never knew she'd miscarried. What happened?"

"Something Mum shared with me and not you," said Sita, crossing her arms. "Guess you're not as much the chosen one as you think."

Reeva gently hit her sister's arm. "Tell me."

"Oh, I can't really remember. But I think she miscarried a few times before she had you. Then the rest of us were in pretty quick succession, so I doubt she had time to miscarry. Yeah, they were all before you, I think. Not fun. It's way more traumatic than they have you believe."

Reeva leaned back on the sofa. "Poor Mum. And poor you. I can't believe I never knew. I'm sorry, Sita."

"Thanks."

"When did she tell you?"

"When I told her about mine. One of the few moments she acted like a mum, to be honest." Sita turned back to the TV screen. "Before she went off gallivanting all over the world again, basically ignoring her grandkids."

"I guess it is her career though. She has to travel."

"As if you're taking her side!" Sita glared at her sister. "After what she's done to us this time, I thought you'd be over that."

Reeva put her hands in the air. "I'm not taking her side. I was just saying."

Sita's expression softened. "Sorry. I suppose I can get quite defensive about Mum."

"Wait, did you just say sorry? Can you do it again so I can film it?"

It was Sita's turn to hit her.

"Ow!" cried Reeva. "That hurt."

"Don't be facetious then." Sita paused. "Nitin's coming to the funeral tomorrow."

"Is that going to be hard for you?"

Sita bit her bottom lip. "Yeah. Probably. But whatever. We're used to it. The show must go on."

"Well, I'm here if you need me. If that's any consolation."

"Thanks, Reeva. I know it's not easy for you. What Jaya did was pretty shitty."

Reeva raised an eyebrow. "That's one way to describe it. But you can't think it's all that bad. You're the one who covered for her."

Sita sighed again. Reeva was starting to notice that she sighed a lot. "What else was I meant to do? Create World War Three by telling you? I told her she had to sort her shit out and confess or make the whole mess go away. I didn't condone her actions, Reeva. I just didn't want our family to blow up."

"Well, you could have been a bit more sympathetic about it all. You took her side over mine!"

"We're not five," retorted Sita. "I just thought—and still think—that the only way to handle a disaster like this is for you to forgive her and move on. Otherwise, the family gets ripped down the middle."

"But our family's always been ripped down the middle."

"Yeah, well, maybe I wished it wasn't. It would be nice to have some support while I'm struggling with my nightmare children and my marriage is falling apart."

"How do you think I felt when my long-term partner went off with my sister? I lost my past, my present, and my future. At once. I'd imagined an entire lifetime with him. I don't even think I'm fully over that loss now."

Sita was quiet. "You're right. I'm sorry."

"You . . . are?"

Sita nodded. "I don't know why I was such a dick about it. I think . . . I've always been jealous of you. And part of me was happy that things weren't going easily for you for once."

"I don't feel like things have *ever* been easy for me."

"You've always done so well! Cambridge, the job, the flat, the perfect boyfriend." She paused. "Until he wasn't."

"You had a perfect husband. Until he wasn't. And house. Kids."

"You're right. Things aren't always what they seem." She cleared her throat. "But look, I know I can't take it all back. I should have been a better sister. Jaya's a lost cause and so is Mum, but you deserved to have at least one sane member of the family by your side. Now that I'm going through this with Nitin, I get what it's like. Fucking *hard*."

It was Reeva's turn to sigh. "Yeah. It is. Thank you for saying that. It doesn't change the past, but the honesty helps."

"Good."

"And you're right. I've gone through what you're going through now. So I'm here if you need me. For support I mean."

Sita gave her a small smile. "Thanks. That's big of you— Oh my god, I'm not being sarcastic! It's genuinely big of you after everything that went down. You know, it's amazing you handled it as well as you did. Especially having to go through it alone. I would have died."

"I wasn't alone—I had Lakshmi. And I can't say I handled it well either—I spent weeks in bed. And then years being sad and crying every evening."

"At least you didn't run away from the pain. And look at you now. You've come through it. And you've got Nick."

"I also have nine centimeters of scalp showing on the side of my head."

"If I had that on top of everything, I'd be having a flat-out breakdown," said Sita. "In comparison, you're fucking winning."

"I'll take that."

"Good. Now can you sit in silence or go upstairs? They're about to find out the sex worker staged her own death."

## CHAPTER 14

**Day 8**

REEVA WOKE UP with a jolt, her breath harsh and uneven. This time she could remember her dream. All of it. It was the same stuff as usual—a cat, twins, and screaming—but this time Reeva had *become* Fluffy Panda. And she'd been murdered.

She lay back on her bed and put her hand on top of her rapidly beating heart. She needed to calm down. It was just a dream. But it had felt so *real*, and living it out from the cat's perspective had made it so much more intense. She (the cat) had been at the top of a staircase when a shadowy figure had pushed her. She could still feel the drop in her stomach as her cat self had fallen down the stairs, until she'd crashed into something sharp. She could hear the twins crying hysterically and see blood everywhere. And then the flashing light of an ambulance arrived, presumably to take the cat to a veterinary hospital. But it was too late. The cat was dead and Reeva had felt every bit of it. She'd always heard that you could never feel pain in dreams, but she could now attest otherwise. Reeva had physically experienced all the cat's agony; it had felt like being stabbed in the head. She rubbed the side of her head as she reassured herself that it had just been a stressful dream. It wasn't real. There was nothing wrong with a bit of stress. No harm done.

Until she remembered that stress was so harmful it was making her bald.

Reeva jumped out of bed and ran straight to the mirror. She pushed her hair over to the right side of her head and anxiously examined her reflection. She exhaled loudly in relief. She wasn't sure what she'd been expecting, but the patch looked largely the same as it had the day before. She pulled out her ruler and measured it. Nine point five centimeters. It wasn't great, but it wasn't as terrible as it could have been. Maybe the alopecia was slowing down and would finally start to heal. Reeva gently pushed her hair back so that it covered the shiny patch and began running her fingers through her hair to tease out the knots. Then she froze. It couldn't be. It just couldn't.

A large lump blocked her chest. She tried to breathe it away with deep exhalations, but it wouldn't move. Reeva tilted her head, pushing the hair away from the back of her scalp with her fingers. It was fine. Everything would be fine. She felt around until her fingers made contact with the one thing she'd feared most: the soft, hairless skin of her scalp. It was not fine.

Reeva stared at her horrified reflection as the lump inside her throat expanded, squeezing all the oxygen out of her lungs. She had another bald patch at the back of her head and judging by what she could feel, it was . . . at least six centimeters wide.

She ran out of the bedroom and into the corridor. "Help! I need help!"

There was silence from Jaya's room, but Sita's door burst open. "Mummy said we can't shout if it's before eight o'clock," announced Amisha, standing proprietarily in the doorway. "Bad Auntie Wee."

"It's an emergency!" Reeva pushed past her niece into the bedroom. Sita was lying in bed with Alisha sprawled across her, playing with what looked like toy soldiers. Even in her state of crisis, Reeva felt a pang of envy. Her sister had two tiny beings who adored her. While all she had was two less-than-tiny bald patches. But now wasn't the time to dwell on her empty womb. She scrambled onto the bed, brandished her ruler, and looked wildly into Sita's eyes. "I need your help. I think I have more bald patches. You need to measure them."

Her sister opened her mouth as if to say something sarcastic, then closed it again. She took the ruler. "Okay."

"Alisha, can you budge over please?" asked Reeva. "Mummy needs to check something for me."

Alisha obediently rolled over to the other side of the bed, watching wide-eyed as Reeva sat in front of her mum, who began methodically parting her hair. Amisha came and sat next to them to join in the viewing of the unusual seven a.m. event. "Auntie Wee has nits?"

Sita let out a snort. "Worse, Meesh. She's—"

"Don't tell them!" cried Reeva. "I don't want anyone to know."

"Reeva, they're only five years old."

"Yeah, which means they'll tell everyone! In fact . . ." She sat up straight. "Can you ask them to leave?"

"No, I cannot! You're being irrational, Reeva. Calm down."

"Calm down? How can I calm down?! I'm losing my hair! Oh god, I said it out loud, and now they're going to tell everyone, and Nick will find out—though how can he not when it's literally so obvious, and—"

"Reeva, breathe," said Sita. "You look like you're about to have a heart attack."

Reeva looked miserably at her. "Just tell me how bad it is. Go on."

"Well, the one at the back is seven centimeters. And the other one is four centimeters. And I think there's another tiny one, but it's really small. Only like one point five centimeters. Then there's obviously the big one you know about. Which is nine point five centimeters."

"What?!" Reeva grabbed Sita's shoulders. "Are you telling me I have *four* bald patches? That's . . . twenty-two centimeters of baldness!"

Sita lowered her eyes. "I'm sorry."

Reeva burst into tears. She hadn't cried like this since everything ended with Rakesh, and now she felt like she'd never stop. She was exhausted. Weeks of tonics, creams, and monitoring her patch daily—only for it to multiply across her entire head. She couldn't cope anymore. "I'm so tired," she sobbed, pulling the duvet up to her face and wiping her eyes with it. "I've tried so hard, and it's . . . all . . . going . . . wrong."

Sita looked at her, aghast. "I . . . Reeva. It's . . . okay." She reached out an arm and awkwardly patted her sister's shoulder. "It'll be okay."

"It won't," she wailed in response. "I'm losing my hair. I'm going bald. Nick's going to leave me and I'm going to be alone again. I'll *never* have kids!" Her sobs intensified, and her shoulders began shaking. "And Dad's gone, and I know he would have been there for me. But he's not, and Mum's AWOL, and everything's a nightmare. And I'm . . . so . . . sad."

Sita turned to her daughters. Alisha was sucking her thumb,

calmly watching her aunt, while Amisha was nonchalantly playing with the soldiers. "Girls, why don't you give your Auntie
Ree—I mean Ree Masi—a hug? She's a bit sad."

"Noo," said Amisha. "I'm playing."

Reeva cried louder.

"Why is she sad?" asked Alisha curiously.

"Because I'm going *bald* and no one cares and I'm so *tired* of
trying to be perfect and *failing* all the time." Reeva half shouted
and half sobbed at her niece. "Look!" She tilted and shook her
head. "They're everywhere!"

Alisha looked with interest at her aunt's scalp. "Auntie Wee's
head looks like Eugea Y's head."

"Who's Eugea Y?" sniffed Reeva.

"Uh, just, no one," said Sita. "It's not a thing."

"U-G-L-Y!" shrieked Amisha. She pushed her soldiers off the
bed and dived under the covers, reappearing with a Barbie doll.
Her long blond hair had been hacked off, so she was now bald in
parts. The remaining hair was standing on end and coated in what
looked like glue. She looked like she'd had an electric shock.

"Uh, they call her U-G-L-Y, as in ugly," explained Sita. "They
think it's funny that it sounds like a name. Eugea Y."

Amisha held the doll up next to Reeva's head. Alisha nodded.
The twins spoke in unison: "Same."

Reeva's eyes widened and she burst into tears again.

"Shit," muttered Sita. "I'm sorry, they're just . . . the worst.
Obviously, you don't look like U-G-L-Y."

But Reeva kept crying, and then before she knew it, she was
simultaneously laughing. "It's not . . . funny, but . . . U-G-L-Y?
Really? I look like a Barbie that's had its hair hacked off? A Barbie
so ugly that it's been named *Ugly*?"

Sita bit her lip then swallowed a smile. "I mean, it's kind of a compliment. Barbies still have hot faces."

"Its head looks like a toilet brush!" shrieked Reeva.

Amisha and Alisha jumped up and started bouncing up and down on the bed. "Auntie Wee is a toilet brush!" chanted Amisha, with Alisha joining in.

Reeva stared at them in appalled horror and then started laughing again. "Your children are horrible!"

Sita joined her in laughter. "The apples don't fall far from the tree."

"Can you try not to sound so proud of it? They're calling me a toilet brush!"

The repetition of the phrase reignited the twins' excitement, and they began jumping higher, screeching, "Toilet brush!" Amisha jumped on top of Reeva, who was now laughing helplessly as she tried to push her off. "Oh my god, get off, you terrible child!"

"I'm *not* a tewwible child!" cried Amisha.

"Am *I* a tewwible child?" asked Alisha.

"You're both tewwible," said Reeva. Then she remembered her hair—or lack thereof—and tears began sliding out of her eyes again. "Sita, Jaya's having a child with Rakesh and I'm going *bald*. What if I lose all my hair? How are things going so wrong? I don't know how I'm going to get through this. Why did Dad have to die *now*? Why couldn't we have met him when he wanted to get in touch?" She sobbed. "Everything is just so bad."

Her sister reached out a hand and pulled Reeva toward her. "Hey. Our family is fucked up, but you're going to get through it. We all will. And if anyone can pull off baldness, it's you."

"But my features are too strong!" wailed Reeva. "I'll look worse than U-G-L-Y. At least the rest of her features tick societal beauty standards. She basically invented them!"

"You'll own it," said Sita firmly. "You'd look great bald. And you live in London. Anything goes there. Just be glad you're not going to try and pull off the bald look in Surrey. Or worse, Leicester."

The door burst open to reveal an angry-looking Jaya. Her cream silk cami was sliding off her shoulders and her hair was pulled into a large, messy topknot with curly tendrils escaping it. "What is going on? It's not even seven a.m. yet!"

The twins looked at her, then at each other. *"Toilet brush!"* they screamed. "Auntie Jaya's hair is a toilet brush."

Reeva and Sita broke into hysterical laughter and fell back on the bed together as Jaya fumed.

"To be fair," Sita whispered to her older sister. "They've got a point."

TWO HOURS LATER, Reeva was standing in the living room with her family, clad in head-to-toe black, with a large fascinator clamped to the left side of her head. She looked like a badly dressed wedding guest, but with so many bald patches cropping up, she'd been left with no choice but to accept Jaya's offer of spare headwear—though she'd drawn the line at the detachable black veil that came with it. Sita was next to her, wearing smart black trousers with a matching leather jacket and ankle boots, while Jaya was in huge YSL platform heels and a long-sleeved low-cut dress. The twins were in black leggings with multicolored jumpers. They all looked like they were going to completely different events.

"We have the sandalwood paste?" The priest standing in the center of the room looked at the three sisters. They stared at him blankly. He turned to Satya Auntie. She nodded, looking elegant in her loose white silk dress, and handed him a small pot.

All four of them, as well as Amisha and Alisha, who were firmly clutching U-G-L-Y, stood in silence around Hemant Mehta's dead body. His coffin was in the center of the room, lid very firmly off, revealing his lifeless corpse. Reeva congratulated herself for bothering to put his trousers on properly. It was the least she could do for her departed father.

The priest began slathering a thick yellow paste over her dad's hands and feet. Reeva watched in alarm. She understood only a smattering of his mixed Sanskrit and Gujarati and now had absolutely no idea what was going on. Judging from the expressions on her sister's faces—Jaya was eyeing up the paste with barely disguised disgust, while Sita was trying not to yawn—they were just as lost. The only one who seemed to know what was going on was Satya Auntie.

"What's he doing to Bapuji?" Alisha tugged her mum's sleeve. "Why's he making him yellow?"

Sita whispered back. "We can google it later, okay?"

"I want to see the dead man!" cried Amisha, ignoring the priest's frowns. "Can we see him?"

Reeva looked at Sita, who shrugged. She picked up her niece so that she could see into the coffin. Amisha's eyes widened. "He's so gray."

Reeva put a finger over her lips. "Ssh, beautifu— I mean, ssh, babycakes. Is that okay?"

Sita rolled her eyes in response.

"Can I see?" asked Alisha quietly.

Sita picked up her daughter. "I really hope I'm not scarring them for life."

"Wow," breathed out Alisha. "A dead man."

Reeva tried not to laugh as she caught Satya Auntie's eye.

Her aunt was chanting along with the priest and trying—but failing—to ignore the domestic scene right in front of her.

"What's that slimy stuff?" asked Amisha. "Can I see?" She stuck her hand out in the priest's direction. He carried on chanting "Om Namah Shivaya," ignoring her.

"It's just ghee," whispered Reeva.

"But why is the old man putting it all over Bapuji?" asked Alisha. "It's for cooking."

"I guess because they used to burn the bodies," said Reeva. "I don't know why they still do it though."

*"You're going to burn Bapuji?"* cried Amisha.

This time the priest stopped chanting.

"Great," sighed Sita.

"No, no," said Reeva desperately. "It's just, um, an old tradition. We're not going to burn him. It's all good, gorge—uh, peanut."

"I'm not a peanut," cried Amisha.

Jaya frowned. "But we are cremating him. That's burning."

"I just didn't think the girls needed to know that detail," said Reeva.

"You can't lie to them," said Jaya. "Think about the damage our parents' lies have done to us!"

"Burning him is so cool," cried Alisha as Amisha nodded fervently. "Burn! Burn!"

Sita glared at her sisters before turning back to the priest. "I'm very sorry. Please continue."

The priest continued slathering different pastes onto their father's feet as the twins watched in utter fascination. Reeva observed them and thought how sad it was that her dad had never had the opportunity to meet them. He'd never even known his own daughters. It was all so *sad*. She felt a pang of emotion at the pointlessness of it all. Life. Pain. Sacrifice. And then this—lying in a coffin in the middle of a semidetached house with a family who barely knew you while a Hindu priest covered you in paste.

"Girls?" Their aunt's voice cut through the rumblings of the priest's chants and all three sisters whirled to attention. "Do you want to get the flowers and start to scatter them in the coffin?"

Reeva nodded mutely. They'd already prepared some flowers to put in the coffin—a selection of roses and tulips. She doled them out between herself and her sisters, giving a few fistfuls of petals to the twins, then they all approached the coffin.

"Reeva, you can go first," said her aunt.

Reeva gently placed a flower into the coffin at her father's feet. He seemed so small and peaceful. She felt a chill run through her body as she realized that one day, that would be her too. A lifeless corpse, dressed in her favorite outfit, with a handful of people chucking flowers into her coffin. She closed her eyes briefly as she lowered the rest of the flowers into the coffin, going in a circle around her dad's body, internally saying a Sanskrit prayer she'd been taught as a child. It felt appropriate to at least try and honor the rituals happening around her.

*Bye, Dad,* she added to the prayer in English. *I'm sorry we didn't get to hang out. I'm sorry for the way it all turned out. But . . . I'm grateful to you. For the fact that you obviously cared about us all these years and saved all your money for us. I know it was your way of saying you loved us.* She paused, feeling her eyes water. She didn't even care anymore if her dad had cheated. Or attacked her mum's lover. Or whatever. None of it was relevant. He was her dad. And he was gone. *I wish I'd had a chance to know you. But I . . . I love you. I love you, Dad.* She brushed away a tear and walked away from the coffin so her sisters could take their turns.

"Lift me!" Amisha tugged on Reeva's dress. "To do the flowers."

Reeva obediently took her niece over to the coffin.

"There!" Amisha flung a handful of petals right onto her grandfather's face. "Better!"

"Uh . . ." Reeva looked up to the priest, who glanced at her in irritation. "Um, I guess I'll just take those off his face . . ." She gently brushed the petals into the silk coffin lining. His skin was so cold. And so thin. It felt as delicate as tissue paper. The expensive kind from Smythson.

"Me now," said Alisha as she approached the coffin in her mum's arms. Unlike her sister, she delicately laid out petal after petal around the body.

"Okay, you don't have to do them one by one," said Sita.

"I'm doing it *properly*," she said. "Look, Auntie Wee!"

"Well done, darling," said Reeva. "What? Surely I can say *darling*?!"

"No, it's just you've got sandalwood paste all over your dress."

Reeva looked down to see yellow blotches staining her dress. The only suitable dress she'd brought with her.

## CHAPTER 15

**Day 8**

Reeva sat in the wooden pew of the crematorium feeling both physically and emotionally uncomfortable. This was it. Her dad's funeral. And she felt as awkward as if she were at a stranger's funeral. She adjusted the too-tight and too-short LBD she'd borrowed from Jaya, then looked around the hall, which was slowly filling up with guests, most of whom were wearing white, not black. Yet another tradition the sisters had managed to get wrong. Reeva had already seen most of them at the prayers—though she was well aware they'd be unlikely to say the same, due to her appalling attendance—and the majority were Indian. The only white person she could see was Meg from Specsavers. She was wearing black.

The priest was at the front, preparing for the service, while everyone else was chatting among themselves. Except for Reeva, because she had no one to chat to. Her sisters were busy—Jaya had gone to find Rakesh, and Sita had gone to find Nitin. She pulled out her phone to hide her awkwardness. There were no new messages, but it didn't matter because she could always reread her latest from Nick. He'd sent it in the early hours of the morning, without her messaging or calling him first. It was perfect lcb material—even verging on UCB . . .

> Reeva, I'm so sorry I can't be with you today. But I know you'll be amazing. You're wonderful and I know your eulogy will knock them dead. (Bad joke, but I know your sense of humor is as inappropriate as mine, so hopefully it will make you smile.) I'll call you in your afternoon/my morning. Lots of love, Nick xx.

In a way, it was better than him being there at her side. She didn't have to spend the whole afternoon worrying about him or making sure he was okay; she could just focus on getting through the day while knowing her boyfriend was thinking about how wonderful she was.

"Beta, do you mind if I sit here next to you?"

Reeva looked up to see an elderly Indian woman in a cream sari and brown coat standing in the aisle. "Of course not! Here, I'll move over." She shuffled in the pew—she'd chosen the second row because it felt weird to claim front-row seats for the funeral of a man she didn't remember—and the woman sat down next to her.

"You're one of Hemant's daughters?" the lady asked.

Reeva nodded. "Reeva. His eldest."

"Ah, yes, I know. Reeva. You know who I am? Kaki. Your dad's kaki. But also your kaki. You can call me Kavita Kaki."

Reeva couldn't remember what kaki meant. Aunt? Great-aunt? She smiled brightly in response. "Hi, Kavita Kaki!"

"You remember me?"

"Um . . . no, sorry. I guess I was quite young when I last met you?"

"Oh yes, very small. You were very sweet—a very shy child."

"Really? Uh, thank you."

The woman nodded happily and looked around the crematorium. "And your sisters?"

"Oh, Sita's over there with her husband, Nitin, and her twins." Reeva pointed to the back of the crematorium, where Amisha and Alisha were sitting on the floor, kicking their legs and having tantrums while their parents hissed at them and waved cucumber sticks. "And my sister Jaya's waiting outside for her"—she swallowed—"fiancé."

"You're also married?"

Reeva shook her head. "Nope."

"It's okay, there's still time."

Reeva smiled despite herself. This woman was a complete stereotype of an elderly Indian aunt, with her thick accent and total lack of tact. But Reeva was surprisingly into it. It was comforting, kind, and reassuringly predictable. Things her own family was not.

"Tell me—what is your job? And how old?"

"I'm thirty-four. And I'm a lawyer. A divorce lawyer."

"Very good! And you're slim, trim, and very pretty." Her eyes lit up. "Let me see what I can do for you."

"Are you going to try and get me a husband?" joked Reeva.

Her new kaki nodded seriously. "I have many options. You just need to tell me what you like."

Reeva laughed. She'd always loved the idea of having a traditional Indian relative set her up with someone—it seemed so much easier than having to do it all herself. Her mum had been appalled when Reeva had mentioned this to her in a low post-

Rakesh moment: "We're modern Indians, Reeva! Can't you just go on Hinge like everyone else?" It was typical that the first opportunity she'd had for a traditional setup had appeared just when she was still basking in how great her lcb was. But beggars couldn't be choosers.

"Well," said Reeva, hoping Nick would find all this as funny as she did. And if he didn't, at least she'd be left with a backup boyfriend. "I do know exactly what I want. I need someone intelligent—they don't need to have a first in their degree or anything, but natural intelligence would be good. As would a degree. Also, emotional intelligence. I've done too much work on myself to date someone who can't talk about their feelings. And a good sense of humor, obviously. You know, someone open."

Kavita Kaki nodded in spirited agreement. "Yes, yes, I have many men like this. What else?"

"Wow. Okay. Um, someone kind, please. That should probably be top of the list, actually. Oh, and handsome would be great. Oh, sorry, hang on." She was interrupted by Leela and another woman she'd never met before—a smart, well-dressed Indian woman wearing a white blazer and loafers.

"Reeva, we just wanted to pay our respects," said Leela, with tears in her eyes. "We're so sorry."

"Oh, I know you are," cried Reeva. "Please, you don't have to pay your respects. I know you're grieving too. I hope you're both coming to the house afterward?"

"Yes, thanks so much," said the unnamed woman, holding Leela's arm. "We'll leave you to it. Come on, Leela, let's sit down."

Reeva stood up to make space for them to slip past her in the pew. As she did so, Kavita Kaki cried out in shock.

"What is it?" asked Reeva, leaning down toward her. "Are you okay?"

"It's just . . . you didn't tell me. Oh, now I won't be able to find you someone. No more options. Maybe . . . no. Not even Mahesh."

Reeva looked confused. "What's happening? I don't understand."

"You're too tall!" cried Kavita Kaki. "At least five feet eight. How can I find a good Gujarati boy who is taller than you and meets your requirements? It's too hard."

Reeva smiled mischievously. "I'm five feet nine."

"Hai ram!"

"Kavita Kaki, do you know Leela?" asked Reeva. "My dad's . . . friend."

"Of course. Everyone knows Leela."

"They do?"

"Yes! And her . . . *good friend*."

"Her friend?" Reeva was no longer sure if they were referring to her dad or the woman beside her.

"Her *good friend*." Kavita Kaki turned and gave a meaningful glance to the woman in the blazer at the other end of the pew. "Sinu."

"Who is Sinu? I've never met her before."

Kavita Kaki sighed impatiently. "She is Leela's *good friend*. For many years."

Reeva frowned in confusion. "Okay. So they're friends?"

"They're *good friends*," repeated Kavita Kaki.

Reeva gasped. "Wait, like . . . But, isn't Leela *good friends* with my dad?"

"No, no, they're just good friends," said Kavita Kaki with zero emphasis. "For many years. Like family."

"Did Dad have any other *good friends*?" asked Reeva.

"No!" Kavita Kaki looked quite shocked by the question. "Your mother was his only *good friend*."

Reeva smiled slowly. She couldn't wait to tell her sisters they were completely wrong. Leela was in a relationship with a woman, and their father had never cheated on their mother. Her phone vibrated. Still grinning, she turned to read her message. Lakshmi. Good luck gorgeous girl. So sorry I can't be there. You'll be amazing. Sending all my love. Can't wait for all the post-funeral goss! Xxx.

"Always with the phones, your generation," complained Kavita Kaki. "Beep, beep, beep. All the time."

"I'm sorry," apologized Reeva. "It's just a message from my best friend."

Kavita Kaki peered over to look at Reeva's phone. *"Good friend?"*

"Uh, no, an actual friend," said Reeva, awkwardly trying to angle her phone away from her aunt. "It's just a good-luck message . . ."

But her new kaki was still staring at her phone. "You have a cat?"

Reeva looked down. Her phone was showing her lock screen—one of the few selfies she had with Fluffy Panda where the cat had acquiesced to look at the camera without scowling. "Oh, yes!" she exclaimed, angling the phone better so her kaki could see the photo. "Fluffy Panda. Isn't she gorgeous?"

"It's good you have another one. You always loved your cat so much as a child."

"Sorry?"

"Your cat. You loved it so much."

Reeva stared blankly at her newest relative. *"I* had a cat? Don't you mean my dad?"

"All of you! A black cat. Your sisters were babies, but you loved this cat. You chose it—I remember your mum telling me."

"But . . . when? What was it called?"

"I don't remember. But I remember when it died. Very sad. Hemant also cried a lot. You were very little. Maybe the same age as the little girls there. Your nieces."

"I can't believe I don't remember any of this. How did it die?"

Her kaki frowned. "Very sudden. Bad accident, I think."

Reeva's mouth fell open. "Wait. I had a black cat that died in an accident when I was the same age as the twins?"

Kavita Kaki nodded. "Very sad. I think that was the last time I saw you. Then, your mum moved away with you all."

THE SERVICE HAD begun, but Reeva hadn't taken in any of it. She was too busy thinking about what Kavita Kaki had said. She'd had a cat. The cat had died when Reeva was five. And then they'd moved away. It couldn't be a coincidence. Because Kavita Kaki had said the cat had been black. Which was exactly what the cat in her dreams looked like.

Reeva sat and looked around the packed crematorium. The guests were all listening to the priest up on the dais—if listening meant fidgeting, readjusting saris, and whispering to each other. They were all here to say goodbye to her dad—a man they'd all loved—but none of them knew the truth about who he was. Not even Reeva.

She closed her eyes shut tight and tried to think. The facts. What were the facts? Something had happened when she was five years old that affected her more than her sisters. That had led to her parents separating and faking her dad's death. She'd had a cat—something both Kavita Kaki and Satya Auntie had confirmed. Only, when she was around five, her cat had died. A cat she kept seeing in her dreams.

What if Jaya had a point and she'd seen something as a child that was coming up in her dreams? Reeva forced herself to try and remember every detail of her recurring nightmare.

It started with one of the twins holding Fluffy Panda—only it might not be FP. It might be her childhood cat. And . . . what if it wasn't one of the twins?

Reeva started again.

There was a young girl holding a black cat. Then there was some kind of altercation. Shouting. And then a shadowy figure pushed the cat. It was flung down the stairs. Where it crashed into some furniture. There was blood. The girl was crying and screaming. And then there were flashing lights.

Reeva opened her eyes and gasped. Sita turned around from the pew in front and frowned at her questioningly. Reeva didn't know how to explain what she'd just realized, so she blinked helplessly at her sister. Sita rolled her eyes and turned back around to look at the stage, where the priest was still exalting their dad.

But Reeva couldn't take in a single word, and it wasn't just because of her poor Gujarati. She was too busy realizing that she'd gotten her nightmare—her *memory*—completely wrong. It wasn't about Fluffy Panda or the twins. The cat was the same cat she'd had as a child when she'd lived with both her parents. And the young girl she'd assumed was the twins was her.

Reeva's mind spun frantically as she pieced it all together. She didn't want to jump to conclusions, but all the evidence felt glaringly obvious. She'd somehow gotten in the middle of a fight between her parents. She'd been holding her cat. And her dad had gotten angry and taken it out on the cat. He'd thrown it down the stairs. The cat had died.

Reeva felt sick. Her head was spinning and she couldn't breathe.

Was this what a panic attack felt like? She reached out a hand to steady herself against the pew. This couldn't be true. She needed to calm down. Parents rarely murdered pets. Especially not middle-class optometrists with three kids. But faking a parent's death was also extreme, and that was apparently a normal activity for her family. Something major *had* to have happened for their mum to say their dad was dead for all this time—and why couldn't it be that her dad had killed her cat?

She tried to remember exactly what her mum had said on the phone. That it was too difficult to remember. She'd said it was her fault too—but that was classic victim blaming. Reeva felt a wave of compassion for Saraswati, who'd lived with so much violence. She'd said that Reeva was the one who was most affected by it— and of course she was; it was her cat and she'd seen the whole thing. All the clues were adding up. Their mum had specifically said that Hemant wasn't an easy man to live with. That was the understatement of the year. Plus, it explained the dreams she was having. The dreams that had started ever since she'd slept in her dad's bed. And it was *definitely* a legitimate reason for their mum to leave their dad in such a dramatic way; who'd want to stay married to someone capable of killing a harmless little being?

Reeva shuddered as she imagined someone telling her now that Fluffy Panda had been killed. She'd be heartbroken. And appalled by the psychopath who'd done it. Only the psychopath in this situation was her dad. The same dad she'd been falling in love with this past week. Reeva's breath quickened. Her head was pounding. She felt like she was having a breakdown.

She was at her dad's funeral. She was meant to be grieving him. But how could she when she'd just realized that he wasn't the kind, generous, stubborn, lovable man she'd thought he was? He was the exact opposite. An angry, out-of-control man who'd lost his temper in front of his wife and children, taking the life of a little black cat.

It was too much. Reeva felt nauseous. After everything she'd been through lately, this was too much. Her hair was falling out. Her boyfriend was alone with his famous ex in LA. Her sister was pregnant with her ex-boyfriend's baby. And her dad had murdered her cat.

"AND NOW, WE have Hemant's oldest daughter, Reeva, here to do his eulogy." The priest gave Reeva a welcoming smile as he gestured toward the microphone.

Reeva blinked at him, dazed. Surely they didn't expect her to do the eulogy now? She had a few bullet points of a banal speech in her pocket—a speech she'd written back when she was convinced her dad was a fundamentally good man who'd just made the mistake of marrying her mother. But there was no way she could read that out now. It was all a lie.

"Beta, they want you to go up. Go on." Her kaki nudged her.

Reeva stared at her. She had to stop this. She had to tell her sisters what she'd just discovered. But how? The entire hall was silent and staring at her. She didn't know what to do. Sita had turned around to look at her—she was mouthing *What the fuck* and gesturing for Reeva to get up. But she couldn't. Not after what she'd discovered. She was too broken and confused and shocked and . . . angry. She was fucking *furious*.

"Go on!"

Kavita Kaki elbowed her so hard that Reeva winced. She stood up, without really realizing what she was doing. Before she knew it, she was standing at the center of the dais looking out at all the faces in front of her. She recognized most of them from the evening prayers. Her family was in the front row. Sita and Nitin with the twins in between them. Jaya . . . and Rakesh. He was sitting right next to her. She hadn't even noticed him come into the room because she'd been so engrossed in her conversation with Kavita Kaki. But there he was, holding Jaya's hand, looking inappropriately handsome in a black suit with a crisp white shirt. Reeva felt like her legs would collapse. How could he just sit there casually at her father's funeral, giving Reeva a small smile, while his child was growing inside her youngest sister? Reeva had thought she'd be okay seeing him, now that she'd practically forgiven Jaya, but seeing them *holding hands* was unbearable. All she could think was that she should be the one sitting next to him, with her hand in his and his baby inside her.

"Come on," hissed Sita from the front row. Reeva jolted. She'd forgotten she was meant to speak. Fuck. She had no idea what to say. Maybe she should just read the most boring parts of her speech and get it all over and done with. But it all felt so fake. What if she just made something up about being too emotional to do the speech and sat back down again? Or she could always google a vague poem about death and read that out from her phone. That was probably the most appropriate way to get through this.

But Reeva was tired of pretending all the time. Lately it felt like she was constantly swallowing her thoughts and blocking her feelings for everyone else's sake. She'd deliberately forced herself to be the bigger person every single day during this last week with her sisters. She'd tried so hard with Jaya, even accepting her apology—and now here she was, holding Rakesh's hand, rubbing it in her face that she had Reeva's future, while Reeva was left with . . . what? A lowercase boyfriend and no Indian blind dates because she was too tall?

Reeva stared out at the expectant faces in front of her and felt a wave of anger wash over her. She felt tears of frustration gather in her eyes. She brushed them away and heard a ripple of sympathetic murmurs. They were all assuming Reeva was too upset to speak. But Reeva wasn't upset. She was angry.

Why should she keep up the pretense that she'd had a normal relationship with her dad when she'd just found out he was the opposite of normal? She'd dropped everything to come to Leicester to prepare for her dad's funeral—but why? He didn't deserve it. Any of it. He'd killed her cat. Reeva looked down at the open coffin. To think she'd painstakingly dressed his lifeless corpse. She should have let him go to the afterlife with his trousers on backward. The longer she stared at his body, the more she felt waves of irrational rage build up inside of her. She was so done trying to be sensible all the time. She didn't *want* to try to understand why her dad killing her cat could be a total accident. She didn't want to make excuses for him or accept that he might have mental health issues around anger that weren't his fault. She didn't want to ask Satya Auntie about his childhood and see if he was just acting out some pattern of trauma that he'd gone through. She didn't even want to consider the fact that she might be wrong.

Reeva was done keeping quiet to make everyone else happy.

Instead, she was ready to tell the truth.

She took a step closer to the microphone.

"Hello, all. We are gathered here today to mourn the passing of my dad. Our dad, really—me, my sister Sita, and my youngest sister, Jaya. Sitting there in the front row." She pointed at them. "We're his only children, as far as we know." There was a nervous titter of laughter in the audience, but Reeva barely registered it. She was on a roll.

"The truth is that we didn't really know our father very well. Mainly because we didn't actually know we *had* a father for most of our lives." There were murmurs of confusion in the audience, as well as intense angry glares coming from her family in the front row, but Reeva ignored them all. "Let me clarify. We were told that we had a dad. Just that he'd died. When we were still kids. Only, surprise, surprise! He was alive all this time. For the last twenty-nine years of my life, my dad was living here in Leicester, but nobody bothered to tell me. Or my sisters. We only found out when he died last week, and our mother—oh, that's Saraswati, the famous singer—bothered to tell us."

"Reeva, what are you doing?" Sita's voice carried up to the stage, lifting its way over the whispers and hushed conversations spreading through the room, but Reeva refused to look at her. Or Jaya. She was finally standing up for herself, and there was no way she was going to let her sisters stop her.

"Now, this makes it quite hard to do a eulogy for him, because we obviously didn't know him, and what we did know about him isn't true. At all. You see, I thought he was a lovely, normal, cat-loving father. But he wasn't. He was . . . the opposite. I won't go into it because there are children present. But what I am going to say is, I'm now quite glad he's no longer with us today." There were loud gasps of shock, accompanied by whispers that were no longer whispers. Reeva ignored them all and kept going. "I know people normally say rest in peace, but I don't think that's appropriate in these circumstances, so instead I'm going to say— What are you doing?" Reeva turned angrily as someone grabbed her arm. Her mouth fell open in shock. She'd expected it to be the priest or one of her sisters, but it was Rakesh. How fucking *dare* he? "What are you doing?" she cried. "Get off me."

He whispered in her ear quietly. "Hey, look, I know you're upset. Come down and we'll talk properly."

Reeva raised an eyebrow. "Uh, no thanks," she replied at full volume into the mic. "I don't fancy talking to the person who cheated on me with my sister. Oh, congrats on knocking her up, by the way."

Sita appeared on the dais and pushed past her sister toward the microphone. "I think that's enough from Reeva. She's going through a very rough time with grief, so please excuse her. Thanks, everyone, for coming today. We are going to let Dad get cremated now. We all are so grateful you could be here, and I'm sure Dad would be too. It is a real tragedy he was taken from us so soon, but we hope that he will be able to truly rest in peace now. And we hope to see the rest of you shortly back at his house where we'll be serving food and drinks. Thank you again."

As the room started to bustle into movement, Sita turned to Reeva. She stood up tall and stared coolly into her older sister's eyes as she spoke. "I guess you're more like Mum than any of us ever realized."

## CHAPTER 16

### Day 8

Reeva sat upstairs in her dad's bedroom picking on a limp cheese-and-cucumber sandwich. Neither of her sisters was speaking to her, and she was keen to avoid all the other guests, so she'd been camping out upstairs on her own for the last hour with nothing but her sad sandwich for company. She'd tried to get her sisters to join her so she could explain everything to them, but they'd flat-out refused. Reeva could see why they were annoyed. She had objectively ruined their dad's funeral and done the one thing they'd all agreed against: telling everyone the truth. But once her sisters heard the full story, they'd understand.

For the first time in her life, Reeva fully sympathized with her mum's decision-making. Of course she couldn't stay married to a man who'd done something so unnatural. She would have been terrified. If her husband had managed to kill a cat in cold blood, what could he have done to his young daughters? The death-faking was admittedly more dramatic than a divorce, but maybe her mum hadn't wanted to relive what had happened; explaining that your husband had killed the family pet was not exactly your average divorce court material. And Reeva was starting to see why her dad had gone along with it all: it would have been the only way to assuage his guilt.

The problem was that her sisters didn't want to hear any of this. Sita had refused to speak another word to Reeva after her mic drop moment of likening her to their mother (an insult that could have been surpassed only by comparing her to their father), while Jaya had told Reeva that her behavior was "not cool" and it was "seriously rude" of her to talk about her and Rakesh's relationship in front of everyone. Reeva did semi-regret the way she'd outed Jaya. She'd never used the phrase *knocked up* before and was unsure why she'd chosen her dad's funeral as the place to start, but she also felt that Jaya's anger was unfairly disproportionate. She was the one who'd taken Reeva's boyfriend; having that revealed in public was *nothing* in comparison. And yes, Jaya was currently crying loudly in the bathroom, but she cried all the time, and Reeva had spent *years* sobbing after Rakesh had left her. It had been the worst time of her entire life. But when she'd tried to tell Jaya that outside the funeral, she'd stormed off and gotten straight into the car with Sita and the twins, leaving Reeva alone with no way to get home. In Reeva's opinion, it was both unnecessarily immature and a waste of a £15 cab ride home. But no one seemed to care what she thought.

"Reeva?" a female voice called out from behind the door, accompanied by a light knock.

"Yes! Come in!" cried Reeva eagerly. Finally, one of her sisters had seen sense.

"Hi, Reeva." It was Satya Auntie. She gave Reeva a small smile and walked into the bedroom, closing the door behind her. "How are you doing?"

Reeva looked down at the faux-wood floor. She was humiliated that Satya Auntie had seen her Jerry Springer outburst in the crematorium. As proud of herself as she was for speaking the truth, she knew she could have handled it differently. And by *differently*, she meant better. "Um. Okay. I'm . . . I'm really sorry, Satya Auntie. For ruining your brother's funeral. I didn't mean to."

"He's your dad as much as my brother. You don't need to apologize to me."

Reeva hesitated. "I feel like I do need to explain things at least. You see, I worked out the secret. The reason my parents felt it was best to keep Dad out of our lives all this time." She took a deep breath. "He killed my cat."

"What?!"

"Okay, I know it sounds crazy. Like, *really* crazy. But bear with me, okay? I used to have a black cat when I was a child—the one you remember my dad talking to you about. Kavita Kaki told me. And I've been having all these dreams where a black cat gets attacked by someone and ends up dying. I thought it was about Fluffy Panda and the twins. But now I know it was about my cat, and the person attacking it was Dad. I remember it all. The crying and screaming. How hurt I was. Because *I saw the whole thing.*"

Her aunt stared at her blankly. "You saw your dad kill your cat?"

Reeva nodded. "Uh-huh. And now I see it every night in my dreams." She paused. "I know I sound insane. But it's real, I promise."

Her aunt exhaled. "I . . . don't know what to say, Reeva. It sounds like an awful thing to go through no matter what you did or didn't see."

"But I did see it!"

"Is there no way it could just be dreams rather than memories?"

"No, it happened," said Reeva firmly. "I remember it now. Not all the details, but I remember enough. And it's exactly what you said to me; I have the answers within. This must be the trauma that's given me alopecia."

Satya Auntie looked worried. "Have you entertained the possibility that you could be wrong? That your memory might not be what you think?"

"Nope." Reeva shook her head adamantly. "It makes perfect sense. I'm telling you—I remember being there. It's hazy, yes, but it's slowly coming back to me. And why would I have been dreaming this for so long if it wasn't true?"

"There are a lot of reasons why we dream certain things," said her aunt cautiously. "It doesn't mean they're all memories. It could be your subconscious trying to communicate something else to you."

"Trust me, it's a memory. Don't you think it's something Dad could have done? Did you never see him get angry and lose it?"

Her aunt hesitated. "Well, once . . . It was one of the last times I saw him before I left. He'd been out with his friends, drinking, and when he came back, I told him I was leaving. Leaving my family, my future marriage, and my chance of respectability. He was furious and he . . . well, he smashed a portrait."

Reeva cried out triumphantly: "See! That's exactly the kind of thing someone capable of killing a cat would do. And what about in the last decade? Have you seen his anger?"

Satya Auntie shook her head. "No, I honestly haven't, Reeva. I mean we've had the odd disagreement, but he's been very calm these last few years. I think his religion helped him. He learned how to respond rather than react."

"Exactly! He sought redemption after feeling so guilty about his previous actions," said Reeva. "No wonder he lived the sacrificial life of a monk, saving all that money. He wanted to make it up to us." She remembered she was talking to her father's sister and softened her voice. "Look, I'm not saying he was a terrible person. Maybe he hurt the cat during an accidental moment of anger. But . . . he still did it."

"I don't know, Reeva. It's hard to jump to conclusions without him being here."

"But you just said it yourself! He smashed things when he was in a rage. Before he became religious and involved with the mandir lot."

Her aunt looked pained. "Maybe. But would your mum really have left him because of a cat? I seem to remember her buying fur long after it was acceptable. And referring to people's pets as vermin."

"She would have panicked that he'd hurt one of us next," explained Reeva. "Or hurt her. She's seen enough Bollywood films; she knows what abuse looks like. And remember, I saw it all. She would have been appalled that her five-year-old daughter had to watch her cat get killed by her father."

Her aunt's face fell. "Oh, Reeva. I don't know what to say. It's all so awful. But I just don't want you to get it wrong. Things aren't always what they seem. Even in our memories."

"I know what I saw. And I don't care if it was an accident or if Dad had issues," said Reeva stubbornly. "To me, this is unforgiveable. And I know my sisters will agree."

"You haven't spoken to them about all of this yet?"

"I hadn't had a chance. I only figured things out right before the service, when I was chatting to Kavita Kaki. How have we only just met her? She knows so much."

"Her health isn't great, so she hasn't been able to make it to the prayers, but she's always been close to your father and, recently, to me." Her aunt sighed. "Oh, Reeva. I'm sorry it's all unfolding like this. I hoped if you did figure things out, it would give you clarity rather than more uncertainty."

"You don't need to apologize." Reeva took her aunt's hand. "I'm just so grateful you're here, hearing me out and being nice to me."

"I'm always going to be here for you, Reeva, for as long as I can. I hope you know that."

"Thanks, Satya Auntie. On that note, what are your wise words for me today? I need all the help I can get."

Her aunt broke into a smile. "Wise words?"

"Um, yes, you're practically the Dalai Lama in my book. I should start calling you the Satya Lama."

She laughed loudly. "Please don't."

"Go on. Hit me with your wisdom. I can take it. What would you do if you were in my shoes?"

"Well," said her aunt. "I'd try and practice compassion. For myself and for everyone involved."

"That's not exactly my forte," said Reeva. "For myself or others."

Her aunt smiled. "I think the same could be said for society as a whole."

"But . . . does compassion mean you think I should *forgive* him? Even if he killed my cat?"

Satya Auntie exhaled deeply. "I would never tell you what to do, and remember, there is no *should*. But I do believe in the importance of having mercy rather than outright forgiveness."

"Aren't they the same thing?"

"Not to me," said her aunt. "I find that mercy is a lot simpler.

It's just acknowledging that we're all fallible humans who make mistakes, and so we're all deserving of mercy. Like the parable in the Bible—let he who has not sinned throw the first stone. Whereas forgiveness is all very high and mighty. Like, 'I, Satya Auntie, forgive you, Reeva.' It's all a bit grand, isn't it? Who am I to forgive you? I'm flawed too. It's just ego."

Reeva sat in silence and then grinned ruefully at her aunt. "See? Satya Lama strikes again. I get what you're saying. Mercy and compassion are about accepting that we're all flawed. But I'm definitely not there. Because there are so many different levels of flaws. What about murder? What if the cat Dad killed had been a child instead? Surely you don't exercise mercy in the same way for something like that?"

"It's what I said earlier; you do it for yourself, not the other person. It's about letting go, not condoning their actions. It's very healing. Take it from someone who's learned the hard way."

Reeva was curious now. "Who have you had to forgive? Sorry, have mercy toward?"

"My parents. My brother." Satya Auntie paused. "Myself."

"Yourself?"

"I've made mistakes, Reeva. And the only way I've been able to get past them is by having mercy toward myself. Accepting my flaws and understanding where they came from. And that, in turn, helps me do the same with others. That's the thing about mercy; it's just recognizing we're all the same. Flawed humans trying to do the right thing and, most of the time, getting it very wrong."

REEVA WAS LYING in the empty bathtub waiting for her sisters. She'd already been there for fifteen minutes—she'd started in a dignified seated position, but as time had progressed, she'd found herself slumping down until her feet were resting on the taps—and neither Sita nor Jaya had materialized. It wasn't meant to take this long. But then again, her plan was in the hands of two five-year-olds.

When she'd realized her sisters were deadly serious about not speaking to her, she'd persuaded Amisha and Alisha to trick them into coming to the bathroom by sobbing hysterically until they agreed. So far, she could hear very little sobbing. The only sounds were the faint chants of the prayers going on downstairs. She hoped she hadn't spent £20 on nothing.

"What *is* it, Amisha? Why are you so obsessed with dragging us—"

The door swung open to reveal a scowling Sita holding Amisha's hand. Alisha was standing beside her, grabbing Jaya.

"Quick, get them in," urged Reeva.

The twins pushed Jaya in too, then closed the door. Reeva could hear their giggles out on the landing.

"Are you fucking kidding me?" cried Sita. "You just manipulated my kids into getting us into the bathroom so you can lose your shit again?"

"That is really, really not cool of you," said Jaya. She crossed her arms. "What's going on with you today, Reeva? You're acting like a completely different person. And I am not into it."

Reeva stood up and climbed out of the bathtub. She felt like her explanation required it. "Look, I really need you both to hear me out, and then if you're still pissed off with me, I'll shut up and leave. Okay?"

Sita sighed. "Whatever. We're here now. Just . . . say what you need to say."

"Okay, thanks. Well—I know it's going to sound mad. But

here goes." Reeva took a deep breath and began the speech she'd been planning for the last fifteen minutes. "It turns out we had a black cat when we were all younger, and it died when I was five."

"Seriously?" asked Jaya. "You're going crazy cat lady on us again?"

"What's the point of this?" chimed in Sita. "I really don't care about our family pet history."

Reeva decided to ditch her speech and get to the climax. "Okay. Sorry. The cat didn't just die; Dad killed it."

Her sisters stared at her in total bewilderment. Now that Reeva had a captive audience, she explained the whole thing—from her dreams to her conversation with Kavita Kaki and her latest chat with Satya Auntie. Her sisters' expressions slowly changed from confusion to shock to total incredulity. By the time Reeva finished explaining why she was convinced their father was a cat murderer, they were both trying not to laugh.

"It's not funny," snapped Reeva. "It's serious."

"It's completely ridiculous is what it is," said Sita. "I'm not taking your dreams as proof, Reeva."

"Uh, I kind of agree," added Jaya.

"But you've been going on at me to see a hypnotherapist!" cried Reeva. "This is the same thing!"

"Oh, if you'd been through it with a professional, it would be completely different," said Jaya. "But this is just something you made up from a bunch of nightmares. It's not the same thing."

"I did not make it up!" Reeva stared indignantly at her sisters. "This is real. I was there. You have to trust me."

"Not till you get evidence," said Sita. "Don't look at me like that; you know you'd say the same to any one of your clients."

"And what about the affair?" asked Jaya. "There was obviously something between Dad and Leela."

"That's the best bit!" cried Reeva. "There wasn't! Leela's a lesbian. She's been with Sinu for years."

"The one in the blazer?" asked Sita.

Reeva nodded eagerly. "Yes! She and Dad were genuinely just friends. Mum must have been jealous of her because of that."

"Okay, well, as happy as I am for Leela's relationship, I don't think that means we jump to Dad killing cats," said Jaya.

"You thought he was a spy!" cried Reeva.

"For once I agree with Jaya," said Sita. "It sounds like you're grasping at straws here."

"Also, you were still a massive dick," added Jaya. "Even if this somehow ends up being true, which would be totally insane, you didn't have to make the funeral all about you."

"I didn't! I made it all about Dad and how much of a fraud he was. Why do neither of you realize how major this is?"

Sita shrugged. "Even if it was true, I don't think it's that bad. I mean, it's only a cat. And *if* it happened—which it may not have—it was probably an accident."

Reeva's mouth dropped open. "Only a cat? He threw it with all his strength! It crashed into furniture and died!"

"Allegedly. And if he did, it was in a rage," said Sita. "It's not the same as a cold, calculated attack. I'm sorry, but I don't think it's the worst thing in the world. Shit happens."

"If this is the big secret, it's really underwhelming," agreed Jaya. "And why would Mum and Dad have faked his death just because he killed your cat by mistake? As if Mum would even care. She'd probably be relieved that the cat wasn't molting all over her Gucci anymore."

"Mum's selfish, but she's not a monster! She faked his death because this proves he's got major issues. She was worried for us. Because if he could do it to a cat, he could do it to a child. Also, I saw the whole thing!" Reeva fumed. "I honestly cannot believe you're both reacting like this. Sita, what would you do if Nitin did something like that?"

"I've already dumped him."

"Okay, but if you were still together."

"We had bigger problems than him killing a cat. And Jaya's right. No matter what Dad did or didn't do, you were out of order at the funeral. This doesn't excuse anything."

"But I was just speaking my truth!" protested Reeva. "You guys do that all the time. I do it *once*, and you all go crazy. How is that fair?"

"Because the one time you chose to do it, you managed to ruin our father's funeral, upset his friends, and insult his memory," pointed out Sita. "It wasn't even your truth to speak, Reeva. And, I mean, time and place."

"Okay, it wasn't my intention to do any of that." Reeva tried to control herself and her voice. She needed to stay calm or her sisters would outmaneuver her like they used to as teenagers. "It really wasn't. I just . . . I had no idea how to do a eulogy for a man who'd killed my cat."

"Why didn't you just not get up there?" asked Jaya. "Say you were too sad or something?"

"I . . . don't know. This felt right."

"Well, it was unnecessarily harsh," continued Jaya. "You always say I'm selfish, but I think what you did today was more selfish than anything I've ever done."

"You're marrying my boyfriend and having his baby!" exclaimed Reeva. She took a deep breath. She was losing control again.

"Ex-boyfriend, and I thought you'd forgiven me?" Jaya looked hurt. "Whatever, Reeva. I don't know who you're trying to be right now, but I don't like her at all. I miss the old Reeva." She opened the bathroom door and walked out.

Reeva turned to Sita. "You have to believe me."

Sita looked directly into her sister's eyes. "Maybe it's best if you just leave."

## CHAPTER 17

## Day 9

REEVA HAD DONE what her sisters had asked and left her dad's house first thing in the morning, before the twins were up. It hadn't been difficult considering she'd barely slept again. She'd thought her nightmares would subside now that she'd figured out what her subconscious had been trying to tell her, but if anything, they'd become worse. She was still seeing and feeling things from the cat's perspective, but knowing her father was the one behind it all added an extra dimension to the pain. She'd woken in a cold sweat in *his bed* at two a.m., gasping for air. There hadn't even been a message from Nick to cheer her up.

Instead, Reeva had lain awake waiting for an appropriate time to get up, going over recent events in her mind. It had not been enjoyable. At one point, she'd even gotten up to measure her patch. It was too hard to reach the newer patches, but the main one had spread to 10.5 centimeters. Twenty-four hours earlier, she would have freaked out over this—her patch was now in double digits and her head practically had more holes on it than a Connect 4 board. Not to mention that when she pulled her hair into a ponytail, it was half the size it used to be. But this time, Reeva hadn't cried. She'd just felt the dull sadness within her expand even further and climbed back into bed.

By four a.m., the dull ache had transformed into a gaping chasm of loneliness. She'd been so desperate to speak to someone that she'd checked the time difference and called Nick. She'd planned on telling him everything, but when he'd answered the phone in a light, upbeat tone—softening his voice only to ask Reeva how the funeral had gone and to send his love to her family—she'd changed her mind. It felt absurd to tell him her dad had murdered her cat. He'd think she was insane or, worse, react like her sisters and view the whole thing as a joke. Even the best-case scenario—him believing her and being outraged on her behalf—was still bad: He'd end up realizing just how crazy her family really was.

So Reeva hadn't said anything at all. She'd glossed over the funeral and her eulogy, instead making him laugh by telling him about Kavita Kaki's thwarted matchmaking efforts. She'd felt a warm glow as he'd articulated how glad he was that Reeva hadn't ditched him for an eligible Indian. But the glow had worn off seconds later as he told her all about the successful meetings he was having with Hot Lips and various execs. She hadn't asked him anything about his relationship with her, and he hadn't offered up any info, which meant Reeva had been forced to keep her jealousy to herself. It was, all things considered, a very lcb conversation.

The problem was that Reeva was now realizing she didn't want an lcb; she wanted a UCB who'd be there for her. The call had been nice, sure, but what was the *point* of it? Why did she have a boyfriend if she couldn't open up to him about her concerns and insecurities? It had left her craving a conversation with real connection—i.e., a conversation with Lakshmi—so Reeva had decided to leave Leicester and drive for two hours to speak to Lakshmi in person. Which was why she was now standing outside her flat at seven a.m.

She knocked gently on the front door, but there was no answer. She knocked louder. Nothing happened. She quietly unlocked the door and stepped inside. The familiar smell of patchouli and amber hit her as soon as she stepped into the hallway with its double mirrors and fresh flowers. She couldn't help sighing in relief at the sight of her clean, ordered, cozy flat where the decor was as minimal as her dad's, but the effect was more expensive Scandi vibes than former MI5 spy, and most importantly, none of her family was inside.

"Fluffy Panda," whispered Reeva. "FP!" She wandered through the living room and kitchen searching for the cat, but she couldn't find her. Reeva tried her bedroom, gently pushing the door open in case Lakshmi was still sleeping. The bed was messy and, as predicted, Lakshmi was wrapped up in the duvet, her legs hanging out the sides and her mouth semi-open as she snored gently. Fluffy Panda was asleep on the end of the bed, curled up in the exact same position as Lakshmi, her tiny mouth ajar as she breathed in sync with her temporary owner. It took Reeva a couple of seconds to register that they were not the bed's only inhabitants. A hairy white male body was wrapped around Lakshmi's.

Reeva let out a cry of shock, then clamped her hand to her mouth. She backed out of the room, but Lakshmi woke with a jolt.

"Reeva!" She pulled the duvet around her. "Oh my god. I'm sorry. I didn't . . . I mean . . ."

"It's fine," cried Reeva, waving her arms awkwardly. "I'm leaving. You're obviously allowed guests. It's okay. I'll just . . . be in the living room. Sorry. It's my fault. Sorry."

Lakshmi looked at her in pain as the man next to her started to move. He yawned loudly and sat up, bleary-eyed.

"Reeva. Shit," he said. "Well, this is an HR disaster, isn't it? A naked partner and two associates in the same room."

Reeva stared at her boss in shock. Lee. He was in bed with Lakshmi. Her bed. She blinked at them wildly and then walked out of the bedroom, closing the door behind her. There was a meow, and she looked down to see Fluffy Panda. Reeva smiled despite herself; the cat had followed her. She crouched down to give her a much-needed hug, but FP ran away from her. Reeva felt a sharp pang of rejection.

She made her way into the living room and slumped down into a chair. She didn't know why she was so affected by the news that Lakshmi was sleeping with Lee; it wasn't the first time her best friend had chosen an inappropriate sexual partner, and it wouldn't be the last. But this felt different. Was it because she'd hidden it from Reeva? Because it had happened while Reeva was going through the hardest two weeks of her life? Or because it had now planted a seed of doubt in Reeva's mind that Lakshmi's recent success at work wasn't just down to her legal skills?

Reeva shook the sexist view from her mind. No. It was just because she was in shock. Lakshmi didn't even like Lee. She'd spent most of the last few years bitching about him to Reeva on their lunch breaks. It was Reeva who normally ended up defending him when Lakshmi made assumptions about his dick size based on his overpriced cars. But now here she was, wrapped around him in Reeva's bedroom. None of it made sense. But all of it made Reeva feel nauseous. Was there not one thing in her life that could remain stable? Or did everything, from her best friend to her fucking hair follicles, have to let her down?

"Hey." Lakshmi, now dressed in a lilac silk kimono, walked into the living room and sat down on the sofa opposite Reeva. "Lee's in the shower and then he's going to get out of here. I . . . I'm really sorry, Reevs."

Reeva opened her mouth to reply, but nothing came out. It was the first time in her friendship with Lakshmi that there'd ever been an awkward silence. But she genuinely had no idea what to say.

Lakshmi sighed. "I guess I should explain a bit." Reeva nodded mutely. "It started . . . maybe a year ago."

"A year!" cried Reeva. It seemed she'd found her voice. "You've kept this a secret for a *year*? Why didn't you tell me?"

"I couldn't at first. I was embarrassed. You know how we felt about Lee . . . It was too humiliating to tell you. I barely even understood why I was into him; I had no idea how to explain it to you. And then, over time, he specifically asked me not to. HR reasons and stuff. I didn't want it to make things weird at work or, more importantly, make things weird between me and you."

"But not telling me has made it even weirder! You've been keeping it from me for an entire year. I thought we told each other everything. I tell *you* everything."

"I know." Lakshmi had the decency to look truly sorry. "I guess I just didn't want you to judge me."

"Why would I judge you?! I mean, I have a lot of questions, yes. But I'm not going to judge you, obviously."

"Well, you do sometimes. You know you can get a bit sanctimonious about things like this, and what's right and what's wrong."

"I do not! Like when?"

"Like when I've had affairs with married men. Things like that."

"But that's because that *is* wrong. It's a fact."

"Things aren't always so black-and-white," said Lakshmi. "Not in the real world. But they are for you. It makes it hard to open up to you about everything."

"That's not true," said Reeva, stung. "I just know how it feels to be cheated on, okay?"

"I know, and that was the worst, but, Reeva, not every couple is the same. You can't project your stuff onto me."

"I'm not!" She frowned. "Sorry, how are you turning this on me? You're the one who's been sleeping with our boss for an entire year and lying to me. You slept with him on the night of my dad's funeral when I *needed* you."

"I know it looks bad," admitted Lakshmi. "But the court case was real. I had to work. That's why I didn't come; not because of Lee."

Reeva sighed. "Okay. Maybe I'm overreacting. I'm sorry if I am. But it's a lot. I don't really know what to make of it."

"Thanks. But people do fall for their bosses. It's not unheard of."

Reeva's eyes widened. "You've fallen for him? It's not just sex?"

Lakshmi bit her bottom lip. "I don't know. I don't want to sleep with anyone else. He makes me laugh. I know he's . . . Lee, but he can keep up with me in a way no man I've ever met could. I feel like we're equals. And he has a side that he never shows anyone—he's really fucking *sweet*."

Reeva stared at her. "Wow. I'm . . . I'm happy for you? But I can't believe this has been going on for so long and you didn't share it with me. I feel like I don't even know you right now."

"Don't say that. I'm still me! How do my feelings for a man define me?"

"But you've been lying to me for an entire year," cried Reeva. "No, don't try and defend it by saying you've omitted, not lied. You've one hundred percent lied about how much you hated Lee. Why would you let me go on about how annoying he is when you were falling for him? I feel so *stupid*. And you've lied about where you've been and what you've been doing. Oh my god, it all makes sense now—the time you were weird about coming to Katy's thirty-fifth birthday. Why you left the Christmas party early! Why you got the duke case."

"Are you kidding?" Lakshmi stood up. "You did not just say that. Are you seriously telling me that you think my career success is down to me fucking Lee?"

Reeva looked down at the floor. She hadn't meant to say that. But it was too late. "All I'm saying is that I don't know now, do I?"

Lakshmi shook her head angrily. "This is bullshit. You're meant to support me, not slut-shame me. What the fuck, Reeva?"

"You're the one who's been lying to me about Lee!"

"And you're the one being a total bitch about it."

Tears stung Reeva's eyelids. "How can you be so cruel when I'm having the worst week of my life?"

"You're always having the worst week of your life. You can't just turn on the waterworks to avoid confrontation, Reeva. Say what you mean for once."

"Fine," cried Reeva. "Fine! I think you should learn to keep your legs closed. You think you've fallen for Lee, but you obviously haven't. You've hated him for years. You're just . . . I don't know, bored. This is what you do. You sleep with people like it's all a game, and you use everyone. You're selfish, and you're a bad friend!"

Lakshmi stared at Reeva, speechless. As her eyes bore into her, Reeva felt her stomach shift uncomfortably. She couldn't believe she'd just said that. She had to get out of there. Before Lakshmi replied. She ran into the hallway, shame rising inside her, and found FP sniffing her bags. Reeva felt a pang of guilt for leaving her yet again, but then she remembered the image of FP sleeping in bed with Lakshmi and Lee like a big happy family. Her lonely heart hardened, and she walked out of her flat with her suitcase and shame in hand, letting the door slam behind her.

REEVA SAT ON the edge of the bed in the middle of her hotel room, taking in the cheap wooden furniture and officelike gray carpet. The sheets looked clean, and the bed was a decent size, but the decor was depressing. She had no idea why she hadn't just found a nicer hotel. There were plenty nearby. But when she'd walked out of her flat, she hadn't felt worthy of a room at the Dorchester. Or even the Marriott. She'd found the nearest Travelodge and now here she was, surrounded by unattractive furniture in what was essentially a large, dark cubicle. The only window was thin, narrow, and purposely frosted over so no one could see into the room—which also meant no one could see out of the room. The whole thing perfectly matched Reeva's mood.

In less than twenty-four hours, she'd managed to have huge arguments with both her sisters and her best friend. Even her cat was pissed off at her. Reeva didn't understand how this had happened. All she'd tried to do was speak her truth for the first time in her life. It wasn't her fault she seemed to be the only one who thought her dad killing her cat was a big deal. And Lakshmi was the one who'd betrayed her by lying to her for an entire year. So how had Reeva managed to come across as the one in the wrong?

She was aware that she hadn't exactly said the nicest things to Lakshmi. Accusing her of doing well at work just because of her relationship with Lee was unacceptable. As was telling her to keep her legs closed. It was sexist. And mean. But what Lakshmi had done wasn't great either. Her sexual appetite always led her into messy situations that Reeva inevitably had to help her fix, and sleeping with her boss was the epitome of a messy situation. Reeva knew it wouldn't be long before the whole thing spiraled out of control and affected her work life too.

Besides, Lakshmi had called her a sanctimonious bitch. Just after Reeva had uncovered a major traumatic revelation from her past, which she hadn't even been able to *tell* her about because she'd been too busy sleeping with their boss. Not to mention the fact that she now had three more bald patches on her head that Lakshmi didn't even know about. She collapsed onto the bed. It was all so painful. She was just trying to do the right thing and stand up for herself like everyone had always told her to. But it seemed to be making everything so much worse.

Reeva pulled out her phone and mindlessly scrolled down

WhatsApp. She had no new messages, but she kept going down the list of conversations. There wasn't really any point in it; it just made her feel marginally less lonely. After a while she moved on to Instagram. There was a photo of Jaya lying on a beach looking unbearably sexy. One she'd obviously taken months earlier but was only posting now. Reeva's finger hovered over the like button—it could be her attempt to put out an olive branch?— then remembered Jaya saying she didn't like who Reeva had become right now. She kept scrolling. She wished Nick had social media accounts she could stalk so that she could feel closer to him, but he was firmly against them. Maybe she could google him instead; there might be more news articles about his clients or presence at awards shows she knew nothing about. Reeva typed his name into the search bar and clicked on the "News" icon to see if anything came up. Then she cried out.

**Hot Lips Pictured Leaving Agent's Flat at 4 a.m. in a Trench Coat with Nothing Underneath!** read the headline. It had already been reproduced by several international websites with variations of the same words. Reeva clicked on the article, sitting up straight, her heart thumping. There was a photograph of the singer looking impossibly beautiful in a light tan coat. The headline was right; there was no way she was wearing a bra underneath it, but—Reeva zoomed in and scrutinized the photo—she *could* be wearing knickers. Unless the editors had other, more explicit pictures they couldn't publish.

Reeva tried to ignore the twisted-up knot in her stomach and began reading. The general gist of the article was that Hot Lips had left Nick's luxurious Airbnb in the early hours of dawn in her sexy getup. The journalist had somehow managed to squeeze eight hundred words out of this by including information about forty-five-year-old Nick Trippier's career, twenty-seven-year-old Hot Lips's love life, and recent photographs of them at the BRITs. Said photographs were reproduced in the article in all their glory—Nick smiling and laughing, Hot Lips gazing up at him seductively.

Reeva felt sick. She exited the article and sat on the bed shaking. It was happening again. She was being cheated on. A tiny voice in her head suggested things might not be what they seemed. There could be a rational explanation for this. It wasn't like the photographer had caught them naked in bed together. But Reeva knew this hopeful voice was her old naivete resurfacing. The truth was obvious, and if she believed anything else, she'd be lying to herself. Nick had told her that he'd dated a singer, and now here he was, getting cozy with her. Again. And why not? Hot Lips was a hundred times more attractive than Reeva, *and* she had all her hair.

Reeva felt tears collect in her eyes. She'd thought that Nick could be the one, that after years of bad dates, she'd finally found someone she could settle down with who could make her as happy as Rakesh had. She'd been too scared to admit that to anyone, sometimes even to herself, but it was true. And now he was leaving her. For a singer called Hot Lips. Reeva sobbed out loud. It was too painful. Everything in her life was falling apart, and now she was losing the last good thing left—her orange.

Her phone rang, interrupting her sobs. It was Nick. She froze. Part of her was desperate to hear from him, to have him reassure her that it was just a misunderstanding. That he had photos of Hot Lips and loads of other guests inside his flat from that very night; they hadn't been alone together. But the other part of her—the intuitive part—knew that if she believed this, she'd be lying to herself. Because Reeva had already worked out that the photos had been taken *before* she'd spoken to Nick after the funeral. Not only had he failed to mention his late-night guest, but it also meant that he'd been with her while his girlfriend was at her father's funeral.

Even if, in some miraculous turn of events, he hadn't had sex with Hot Lips, Reeva still couldn't handle it. She'd been broken too badly in the past. She needed a nice, stable UCB—not an lcb who hung out with half-naked singers. She couldn't cope with the anxiety, the jealousy, and the insecurity that came with dating Nick. Maybe she was better off with someone less interesting than him; someone who would help her feel safer.

Reeva started sobbing again. She was so desperate to feel safe. She always had been. But, as always, she was left with safety's antithesis: fear. A cold, gray feeling that pinned her entire body immobile and then settled hard and heavy in her abdomen. She'd felt it as a child waiting for her mum who'd failed to show up to her flute recital, her birthdays, and parents' evenings. She'd felt it as an adult when Rakesh had left her. She'd relived it in her past with the cat nightmares. And she felt it again now. There was absolutely nobody she could rely on. Everything was out of control. Her hair was even falling out faster than ever. For all she knew, there were more new bald patches at the back of her head. Reeva ran wildly to the mirror. She parted her hair and studied her baldness in the rectangular mirror. In the harsh yellow light of the room, she looked even worse. Like a Cabbage Patch doll. The grim reality of her ugly baldness made her tears dry up. It was too shocking to cry over it. She grabbed her ruler. She'd last measured her patch that very morning, but she had a feeling it had already gotten worse. With trembling fingers, she placed the ruler diagonally across the circle of hairless scalp: 10.8 centimeters. It had already grown by almost half a centimeter.

A cool numbness spread through her. She'd expected to feel hysterical, but instead she felt eerily calm. Because suddenly she knew what to do.

Reeva reached over to the phone and dialed zero for reception, looking resolutely at her watery brown eyes in the mirror. It was time for her to do a Britney.

## CHAPTER 18

**Day 10**

Reeva woke, bleary-eyed. She yawned and reached for her phone to check the time: 10:30 a.m. She'd slept for more than twelve hours! And for the first time in the last ten days, she hadn't had a single nightmare. Her dreams had been completely cat-free. Reeva sank back into the bed and stretched out happily. Who could have predicted that she'd have one of the best night's sleep of her life in a dated Travelodge? It had helped her relax more than any five-star resort she'd ever visited. She never needed to go abroad again; she could just vacation in this sad little hotel room where no one knew where she was, no one could bother her, and if she turned her phone off, no one would ever find out.

Her phone. Reeva could have sworn she'd seen a notification with Nick's name on it. She grabbed it and saw six missed calls *and* three messages from Nick Hinge. She'd never gotten around to changing his name after meeting him on the dating app, and maybe now she never would.

Hey Reeva, please call me when you get this. I don't know if you've seen the headlines about me, but I need to explain either way. I hope you're okay x.

I'm guessing you're asleep now but please call when you wake up. Don't worry about the time difference; I'll be up xx.

I'm scared you're avoiding me on purpose. Let me explain? Please? Nick xxx.

Reeva exhaled deeply. Even just a day before, she would have been thrilled to see six missed calls from Nick and three texts begging to speak with a total of six kisses. But today she couldn't deal with it. It was all too much. She was so tired of the anxiety and stress. She wanted to pretend Nick didn't exist and go back to being the Reeva Mehta of three months ago—a Reeva who was peacefully single, happy in her career, busy with her friends, not speaking to her sisters, unaware she had a father, and having a full head of hair. Reeva sat up straight. The alopecia. It had started almost three months ago. Just after she'd started dating Nick.

How had she never realized this before? It couldn't be a coincidence. The stress of dating must have triggered her alopecia. And it made sense. She'd been overthinking things with Nick ever since she'd swiped right on him. Unlike all the other guys she'd met online, he'd seemed genuinely interesting. Different. Confident, not arrogant. His messages to her were heartfelt rather than witty and clever. Then he'd taken her to a ridiculously cool private members' bar she'd never heard of for their first date. Reeva had been impressed. After endless dates with men she was—quite frankly—so much better than, she'd met someone on her level. It hadn't taken her long to fall for him. But the more that happened, the more she'd abandoned her true self. Instead she'd tried to be the cool, smart, funny girl she thought he'd like, holding back her crazy and showing him just how chilled she was. When all the time, she'd been feeling more and more anxious. This business with Hot Lips had been the final trigger; it had taken Reeva straight back to the worst moment of her life with Rakesh and Jaya.

Reeva wondered if her alopecia was a sign from her body. Her intuition talking to her. Something within her knowing that Nick wasn't right for her. It had known from the start that he'd do a Rakesh and shake Reeva's fragile world apart. But she didn't have to stay here. They didn't have nine years of history like she'd had with Rakesh. This had been only three months and a week. She could take Satya Auntie's advice and choose the easy path instead of the hard path. She didn't *have* to continue dating Nick and battle the feeling of not being good enough. She could go back to the safety of single life instead—and maybe one day she'd find someone who wanted to be a UCB from the offset and didn't trigger her insecurity. Even if Nick hadn't cheated on her with Hot Lips and there was some miraculous proof, Reeva knew she'd be plagued by doubts from now on. Unless she simply left the relationship and went back to the calm, quiet life she'd had before Nick. She wouldn't have to stress about the BRIT awards ever again—she wouldn't even know they'd happened— nor would she ever have to compare herself to a twenty-seven- year-old singer. She'd just go back to a time when she didn't speak to her sisters but *did* speak to her best friend. A time where she had all her hair.

Her hair. Hadn't she . . . No . . . Reeva turned, fast, to face her reflection in the mirror.

She screamed.

She was bald. Bald as an egg. Her head was completely and utterly hairless.

With a flash, it all came back to her. How she'd gone down to reception to collect an electric razor. How she'd stood in the bathroom and resolutely shaved off every single hair without shedding a single tear. No wonder she felt so much lighter; she'd lost half a kilogram of hair. Reeva stared at her reflection in horror. It had felt like such a good idea at the time. But now every single inch of her being knew it was a very, very bad idea.

What had she done? She did not have a tiny face that could look surprisingly pretty with no hair. Nor did she have a striking face that could pull off such a bold (bald!) look. She had a very strange-shaped face—something she was only now becoming aware of—with oddly angular features and unusually fat cheeks. She looked like a chipmunk. And not the cute kind.

Reeva got up and slowly walked toward the mirror, breathing erratically. She couldn't believe she'd done this. What had she been thinking? It had been far too early to take such a radical measure. She'd had enough hair to cover her bald patches. She could have gone to see a specialist to add in extensions to cover them. There were so many options. Why had she opted for the most extreme and irrevocable of them all? She looked like a cancer patient. She looked *worse* than a cancer patient; she looked like a fraud. Reeva reached out a hand to steady herself against the mirror and then stumbled as the cheap mirror swayed to the side. A few small bald patches were one thing, but her whole head was now an *entire* bald patch. She'd never need to use her ruler again. She already knew exactly what the measurement would be: $\infty$.

———

REEVA SNUCK FURTIVELY out of her car in a pair of oversized sunglasses, making sure no one was looking at her. She felt like a celeb trying not to get papped—probably how Hot Lips had felt leaving Nick's place. But unlike Hot Lips, Reeva had no hair. Nor did anyone on her leafy street bother to look at her, let alone try and take photos. No one even gave the black T-shirt clumsily wrapped around her head a second glance. Reeva liked to think it was because she'd succeeded in her goal of making it look like a chic silk scarf, but deep down, she knew it was because nobody wanted to make eye contact with the crazy woman with a T-shirt on her head.

She made her way into her building and unlocked the front door to her flat. Lakshmi had messaged earlier to say she'd left, having given FP breakfast but no lunch (that was all she'd written; no kiss, no question, no mention of the drama that had passed between them), but Reeva was still cautious as she crept into her home.

"Hello? Fluffy Panda? Oh, hello, baby!"

The cat stalked up toward Reeva. "I've missed you," she cried, reaching out to stroke her. But Fluffy Panda instantly retreated with a loud meow and ran into the next room. Reeva sighed. FP's rejection wasn't surprising, but given recent events, she couldn't help but view it as symbolic. She tried to distract herself by unpacking her bag, chucking everything into the washing machine to erase the memories of the last week. And then she saw it: a handwritten note on the table.

Reeva dropped the dirty knickers she was holding and raced over to pick it up. Lakshmi had left her a note; an olive branch that would repair their friendship. She read it eagerly.

Instructions for FP:

1) *She now likes the Chicken Princess sachets for breakfast and dinner. But if she doesn't eat it immediately, leave it out and stick dry food on top. She'll eventually finish it.*

2) *We've gotten into a routine of me giving her a full body massage every night—normally around 11 p.m.*

3) *She sleeps on the bed through the night. She likes to be on the right side, so you'll have to swap to the left.*

4) *The vibrator is her new favorite toy. If I were you, I wouldn't use it for intimate purposes again.*

5) *It's best if you leave the radio on Classic FM. She's not a fan of anything contemporary.*

6) *She likes to watch birds on YouTube every morning. You'll find it under "Cat TV."*

Reeva stared at the list in growing fury. This was ridiculous. To think she'd thought Lakshmi had written an apology note. Her cheeks flooded red. She couldn't believe Lakshmi had called *her* sanctimonious when this was the most know-it-all advice she'd ever seen. Who was she to give Reeva instructions for her own cat? She'd only taken care of her for nine days. Reeva had taken care of her for weeks; she already knew her cat loved a massage! Well, on the few occasions she'd let Reeva touch her. And she could have easily had her eating Chicken Princess if she'd had a few more days of trying. In fact, it was obviously down to the groundwork she'd already done that Lakshmi had got her onto organic.

Reeva scrunched up the list into a ball and threw it in the bin. She was sick of people disappointing her. First her parents. Then her sisters. Her boyfriend. And now her best friend. She needed a break from all of them—even the ones who were already taking a break from her. And she didn't need to do it for £69 a night in a Travelodge. She could do it right here at home. She still had another week of bereavement leave booked off work, and she very much doubted Lee would mention her return to London. Her sisters didn't want to see her. And now that she wasn't speaking to Nick or Lakshmi, there was no one else who cared where she was. The only person who might worry was Satya Auntie, but once Reeva called her to explain what she was thinking of doing, she'd doubtless be on board. Because Reeva was going to turn her home into the retreat she'd been craving. There was no need for her to go to a Buddhist monastery in Nepal; she could re-create the relaxing vibes right here. She'd just turn her phone off, put on some spa music, and enjoy the solitude. For the first time in her life, Reeva was ready to be completely and utterly alone.

REEVA WAS LYING on the sofa, ordering wigs on the internet, and eating ice cream out of the tub, determinedly *not* thinking about her loss of hair, boyfriend, sisters, and best friend, when her intercom buzzed. She frowned. It was probably just a delivery driver, with a parcel for her ASOS-obsessed neighbor, but she wasn't in the mood to see anyone. Especially while she still had a T-shirt around her head. The buzzer rang again. Reeva reluctantly got up to answer it, then paused. This was *her* retreat. The whole point was to finally put herself first. She didn't have to be a people-pleaser anymore. She could be selfish instead. This revelation felt revolutionary. Every member of her entire family—and every guy she'd dated—had been living that philosophy for years. But it hadn't ever occurred to Reeva. Until now.

She selfishly sat back down on the sofa, turned up Taylor Swift (it was more cathartic than spa music), and, determinedly ignoring the persistent buzzer, carried on wig shopping. She'd decided to order a whole selection with immediate next-day delivery. Even though she was planning to be alone in her flat, she couldn't bear the sight of her baldness in the mirror. She needed some hair, stat.

"Hello? Reeva?"

There was a knock at the door. And the male voice sounded familiar. Surely it couldn't be . . .

"It's me. Nick."

He was meant to be in LA! What was he doing here? And how had he gotten through the front door of her building?

"Are you there? One of your neighbors let me in."

Reeva panicked. She couldn't see him like this. The T-shirt was just about acceptable to get from her car to her flat—but not to have a face-to-face conversation with her ex-boyfriend. Shit. He didn't even know he was her ex-boyfriend.

"Uh, I can hear your music, Reeva. Look. I know you don't want to speak to me and you've blocked my calls. But I really want to talk. Could you let me in?"

Reeva closed her eyes. She could do this. She had to. It wasn't fair of her to ghost him without an explanation. God knows she'd been on the receiving end of it often enough. She needed to break up with him like the adult she was. She just needed to do it without him seeing her.

"Is that 'We Are Never Ever Getting Back Together' in the background?" asked Nick. "Please don't tell me you're dumping me via Taylor Swift."

Reeva turned off the music. "Sorry. Uh, yeah, I'm here. Obviously. But, Nick, I'm really sorry; you can't come in."

"I just want to talk, Reeva."

She winced. "I'm sorry. I just . . . I really can't see you right now. Can we talk through here?"

"Through the door?"

Reeva nodded then remembered he couldn't see her. "Sorry, yes. Like . . . Pyramus and Thisbe." She paused. "I guess that was a wall, not a door. But still."

Nick laughed ruefully. "Wow. Okay. That's a lot to not even want to see my face. I'm assuming you saw the photographs."

Reeva stood closer to the door. "Yes. All of them. I am fully up-to-date with all recent Hot Lips gossip."

"I promise it's not what it looks like, Reeva. Nothing happened between us. Absolutely nothing."

Reeva felt her heart tighten as her stomach simultaneously lurched. That was exactly what Rakesh had said when she'd found the photos of Jaya on his phone. Only he'd been lying. She couldn't believe Nick was putting her in this position again. Was she destined to be cheated on forever? Was there something intrinsically wrong with her? She squeezed her eyes shut and swallowed her sobs. It was fine. It didn't matter. She was done with Nick anyway. She'd already decided—she needed to be with someone less complicated. Someone who called her when he said he would. Someone who didn't entertain ridiculously attractive twenty-seven-year-olds in trench coats.

"Reeva, please say something. Or let me explain."

"It's fine. It doesn't matter. It wasn't working anyway. Between us, I mean. We should just leave it here. It was good while we lasted, but it wasn't going to work long-term."

"What?" Nick sounded pained. "But why? I thought we were working really well. Please don't let this ruin everything."

Reeva didn't know what to say. How could she explain everything to him without admitting how unsafe and anxious she felt around him? He'd think she was crazy and insecure. Which she was. But she didn't want him to know that. She'd have to tell him about her bald patch. The fact that deep down she felt she wasn't good enough. How she'd lie awake agonizing about him not calling when he said he would. It was all so private and embarrassing. If he knew, she'd come across as a tragic Bridget Jones obsessing about his every move, all while he'd been happily hanging out with half-naked pop stars.

Nick sighed. "I guess it's on me to explain everything first. God. I just . . . I feel like such a knob saying it's complicated, but the truth is that Daniella—that's her real name—only came over to talk the other night. I know it looks bad, but I swear to you that nothing sexual or romantic happened. It was just a chat. As friends."

Reeva felt her heart start to crumble. She reached out a hand to steady herself. This was exactly the conversation she'd been hoping to avoid by deciding she was done with Nick that morning. But now it was happening anyway, and the agony was unbearable. She wanted to believe Nick, just as much as she'd wanted to believe Rakesh. But she couldn't ignore the voice of reason in the back of her head. She leaned against the door and slid down until she was slumped on the floor, clutching her knees tight to her chest. "How am I meant to believe you, Nick?" she whispered.

She heard Nick sit down on the other side of the door. "I know it looks bad. I do. But you have to trust me, Reeva. I know you've been hurt in the past, but I'm not like your ex. I really,

really like you. I wouldn't fuck this up by cheating on you. Especially with someone like Dani—uh, Hot Lips. I wouldn't. Please believe me."

A tear rolled down Reeva's cheek. Her hard resolve to dump Nick was melting. She liked him; she really, really did. But she still knew she couldn't believe him. She wouldn't let herself. She couldn't go through this all again. She couldn't date a man who made her feel like she wasn't good enough.

But she *could* ask questions. "Okay, well, why was she there then? Wearing absolutely nothing?"

"She was actually wearing underwear," said Nick. "But, uh . . . it was just to talk. I'm sorry I can't go into details of why exactly she was there."

Reeva frowned. "Wait, are you kidding? She was there in her underwear. And you won't tell me *why*?"

"I don't want to betray her confidence. I mean, I can't. But essentially, she was going through some really hard stuff and she needed me as a friend."

Reeva's mouth dropped open in shock. "You're not going to *tell* me your excuse?"

"I'm sorry." Nick sounded miserable. "I'm really, really sorry. It's not my place to talk about it. It's her story, not mine. I can't betray her confidence. But it was just friendship—I can promise you that."

"So you're telling me that she came over to yours in her underwear and left at four a.m. because she needed to talk about some hard stuff she was going through, but you won't tell me what? And I'm meant to just believe this and be, like, 'Okay, cool, no worries'?"

"I don't expect that, but please believe me, Reeva. I know it sounds mad, but this whole industry is mad."

"How naive do you think I am?" cried Reeva. "You can't just blame your job. And, what, are you going to tell me nothing's ever happened between you two before? She's obviously the singer you were dating, and you're not even telling me. Why would I believe you when you're not being up-front about any of this?"

Nick exhaled unhappily. "You're right; I'm sorry. It was her. We dated off and on for a couple of years. I should have told you straight from the outset, but I thought it would just make a lot of drama. When I've told other women, they've been really insecure and not wanted me to work with her, but the truth is that I have to. It's my job. She's one of my top clients."

Reeva felt a pang in her chest. She hated how right she was. And she hated that she was just as insecure as all those other women. Other women. Even that hurt. "Well, I guess it looks like your plan to avoid drama didn't work," she said flatly. "You kept this from me, and I had to figure it out because you weren't brave enough to tell me. It's just . . . it's really shitty, Nick. How am I meant to trust you now about not cheating on me with her? You've hidden things from me all along."

"Nothing has happened between me and her since I ended things with her, which was just after my second date with you. I promise. Things had been on their way out between us anyway. I have no desire to be with her at all—she's completely . . . well, that's another story. I want to be with *you*, Reeva. Please believe me."

Reeva felt the tears come again. She wished she could trust him, but she couldn't. "Nick, you're not even telling me why she was there and what she wanted to talk about. You're choosing to keep her secret."

"Only because it's the decent thing to do. Reeva, I know it's a fucking mess. But please believe me. Open the door. Let's talk properly. I didn't cheat on you."

"I can't. You're just too much of an lcb. You're not sharing with me. Not in the way I need."

"Huh? A what?" Reeva didn't reply, so he carried on. "Look, I know I should have told you we dated. I'm really sorry. I guess I also didn't want you to judge me."

"Why does everyone think I'll judge them!" cried Reeva. "You're the one who lied to me! That's the only thing I'm judging you for."

There was a pause before Nick spoke. "I didn't want you to think I'm the kind of guy who sleeps with young singers. I know how it looks. Fortysomething agent with twentysomething client. It's bad. All the headlines are basically telling me that right now. And you're . . . you're so smart and successful. I could see us working together. Having a real, normal relationship. I like being with you, and I want you to respect me. I didn't want you to think I was weak for being with Dan—uh, Hot Lips when you're so strong."

More tears slid down Reeva's cheeks. She couldn't let herself believe the nice things Nick was saying to her; it would make everything hurt more later. He was just coming up with generic platitudes to make her feel better since he'd betrayed her. It was exactly what Rakesh had done.

"Please give me another chance, Reeva," begged Nick. "I've never felt so safe in a relationship as I do with you. You're such a great girlfriend."

So Nick felt safe with her. Of course he did; she wasn't a Hot Lips who had the whole world desperate to shag her. She was plain old Reeva Mehta. She was dependable. Practical. Hardworking. Supposedly strong when on the inside she was falling apart. There was no chance of her having a wild affair or abandoning him. And yet . . . she couldn't say the same back. She was always anxious that Nick was creating distance between them or judging her. She didn't feel safe with Nick because she never knew where she stood with him.

"Reeva? Say something."

She opened her mouth and then shut it again. She didn't know what to say.

"Reeva?"

She squeezed her eyes shut. "I'm sorry, Nick. I can't do this. It's too hard. All of it. Even if I manage to believe you haven't cheated—which feels impossible right now—I don't think I can cope with the rest of it. How different our lifestyles are. How you have a twenty-seven-year-old pop star as an ex. It's just not me."

He sighed. "I can't erase my past or my job. But you know who I am when I'm with you. I'm just . . . me."

Reeva closed her eyes tight as tears slid out of them. When she spoke, her voice was low. "The problem is . . . I'm not entirely sure *I* can be fully *me* when I'm with you."

"What?" Nick's voice was pained. "I'm so sorry you feel that way. I had no idea. Do you . . . think that can change at all? That it will get easier with time? With some work? From both of us, I mean. I'll do anything I can."

Reeva shook her head. "I don't think it will. I'm sorry."

# CHAPTER 19

## Day 11

REEVA WAS SAD. Really fucking sad. She'd never gone through a breakup without Lakshmi before. Nor had she ever been bald before—with or without Lakshmi. A lot of things were objectively going wrong, and there was nothing she could do. Except cry. So she was doing that to the best of her ability. She'd sobbed ever since Nick had left, with breaks for food and naps. She'd had yet another sleepless night, only this time there hadn't been cat nightmares; instead, she'd been plagued by thoughts alternating from the enormity of what her parents had hidden from her to what had happened with Nick. Their conversation kept replaying in her mind. Had she done the right thing? Should she have been more honest with him? Or had she been too honest? She wished Lakshmi was there to tell her.

Reeva despondently pressed the button on the coffee machine. This at-home retreat was not working out as planned. Maybe she should have just hidden out at the Travelodge. Lakshmi could have stayed with FP for longer; it wasn't like the cat seemed to care Reeva was back. She basically ignored her unless

Reeva was dumping Chicken Princess into a bowl. And the warm post-turning-her-phone-off afterglow of freedom had faded, and she was now itching to turn it back on. It wasn't even that she was desperate to speak to anyone in particular; she just missed the sense of being connected to the outside world. She was so used to the constant possibility of communication, the fizzing hope every time her phone vibrated, and the endless scrolling on Instagram. But now she only had herself.

She'd thought about turning her phone back on—it wasn't like anyone had set these rules for her. But Reeva couldn't bring herself to do it twenty-four hours after she'd decided otherwise. In fact, if she was being precise, it was only . . . twenty-two hours. Time was moving slower than ever now that she was alone with zero plans. She sighed as she poured cold oat milk into her coffee without even bothering to use the frother. She was just experiencing withdrawal symptoms from her phone addiction; it was normal. Besides, what would she even find if she turned it on? An angry message from Lakshmi? A sad message from Nick? Hateful messages from her sisters? Or—a hundred times worse—no messages at all?

There was no way Reeva could face seeing zero notifications after (almost) an entire day of not looking at her phone. Instead, she walked back into her bedroom and climbed into bed with her coffee. She'd be safe there. And why couldn't she treat herself to (another) lazy day in bed? She'd spent all her life working insanely hard—and for what? To end up bald and lonely? The more Reeva thought about it, the more she realized she'd never really let herself do absolutely nothing. She'd lived her life with a relentless pressure to work hard, and then an inevitable guilt that would plague her if she didn't. It was pointless. Especially when it was all self-imposed.

It had been happening since she was at *primary school*—like that time she'd stayed awake all night, crippled with anxiety after forgetting to revise for a vocab test. She'd been six! No other child she knew cared about things like that. Her sisters had partied their way through school and then university, while Reeva had taken it all so seriously. It was different now in that she at least worked hard for a job she loved, but she still said yes to extra hours when she could be having fun. Or sleeping. Why had she wasted so much time trying so hard? It wasn't like her mum had ever noticed—"An A for your coursework, darling? Lovely! Remind me what coursework is again?"—and Lakshmi was on track to be made partner before she was. It was partly why Reeva hadn't put herself forward for the role; she knew her best friend would beat her. And it wasn't even because of Lee. The truth was that Lakshmi did less than Reeva, but her solid self-assurance made her more effective every time.

With a growing resolve, Reeva decided things needed to change. *She* needed to change. It was time for her to stop trying so hard. No more trying to be the perfect employee, sister, friend, daughter, girlfriend—not that any of it had even worked. It was time for Reeva to simply be herself as she was right now: a bald, miserable mess.

BY THE EVENING, Reeva was starting to enjoy her retreat. Now that she'd given herself permission to let go, she was reveling in her freedom. She'd ordered enough food on Deliveroo for four on the basis that she could eat the leftovers the next day—and then she'd eaten all of it. She was still in her pajamas and hadn't showered, she'd opted out of making her bed for the first time in years, and she'd watched trash TV instead of the "must-watch" documentary everyone was talking about. She had no idea why she'd spent so much time watching intellectual TV shows when she could have just watched half-naked people falling in love.

Her thoughts had occasionally veered back to the shitstorm that was her life, but without her phone there to keep her connected to it all, they'd ended up drifting away. And the more hours that passed by without any contact with her family, Lakshmi, or Nick, the less Reeva thought about them. The pain had already lessened. She was quite proud of herself. People always said time was a healer, but she seemed to be healing by the *hour*. She'd already been through anger, denial, and depression during the past few days—to be honest, she'd been doing them for the past four years, which was probably why she was speeding through this—and now she was moving on to acceptance. Reeva shoved a handful of popcorn into her mouth. She was nailing this grief cycle. By the end of her week's retreat, she'd be on Satya Auntie Zen levels. Nick would be a distant memory, while the drama with her family would feel like proof that she'd been on the right track before, when she'd avoided her sisters at all lengths.

The intercom buzzed.

Reeva reluctantly stood up, crumbs dropping off her pajamas. But it was worth it this time because her wigs had arrived. She'd ordered three. Two were variations of her natural style. But the third was her favorite. It was big, curly Beyoncé-esque hair that was dip-dyed from dark brown on top to luminous blond at the tips. It was the kind of hairstyle she never would have opted for—it shouted self-confidence—but the new bald Reeva was done overthinking. And she may as well enjoy this positive aspect of her alopecia: she could live out her Beyoncé fantasy.

She opened her front door and craned her head out into the corridor. "Hello-oo? I'm up here. On the fourth floor. There's a lift." There was silence. Reeva sighed in irritation. Why was the delivery driver taking so long? "Hello?"

The lift pinged, doors opening to reveal stacks of piled-up Gucci luggage. There was no one in there. Reeva walked over toward the lift in confusion. Who in her building was fancy enough to have that much designer luggage? And where was the delivery guy?

"Reeva! Don't let the doors close! You need to get the suit-cases out before they go all the way down again. I couldn't find the porter, so I had to get my driver to load up the lift. You really *must* tip the porters extra."

Reeva turned in slow horror, praying that she was hallucinat-ing. But there, waving a large handbag to match the Gucci suit-cases, dressed in a perfectly ironed cream trouser suit, with a large pair of sunglasses resting on big, blow-dried curls, was her mother.

Saraswati screamed. Loudly.

Reeva started in shock—wasn't *she* meant to be the one screaming?

*"You're dying!"* Her mum ran up to Reeva and flung her arms around her. "My poor beta. Why didn't you tell me?"

Reeva struggled out of her mum's arms. "What are you talking . . . Oh." She'd taken the T-shirt off her head.

"Oh, Reeva, I can't believe it!" wailed her mother, trying to stroke her scalp. "Why didn't you tell me you had cancer? My poor baby!"

Reeva freed herself and took a step back. "It's not cancer. I'm fine. I . . . just . . . shaved it off."

Saraswati recoiled in unadulterated horror. "On *purpose*? But . . . why? It looks terrible!"

"Mum." Reeva frowned. "What are you *doing* here? You can't show up unannounced and tell me how terrible I look!"

"But, darling, you can't surely think you look good with no hair? You don't have the right bone structure."

"Mum!" Reeva glared at her. "Seriously! What the *fuck* are you doing here?"

"You swore! You never swear. Reeva . . . what's going on? Are you having a breakdown? Do I need to call the Priory?"

"Tell me what's going on!" cried Reeva, her Zen vibes long gone. "Why are you here?! You can't just turn up like this!"

"To see you, of course! I had a feeling you'd need me. And clearly I was right." Her mum started rummaging in her handbag. "It's okay, darling. Raj will fix everything. He can source amazing wigs from human hair. I'll get him to find a girl with hair exactly like yours. Well, like yours but a bit thicker and shinier, so he can make a bespoke wig for you. I'm sure if he pays her enough, she'll be happy to shave it off. Hair grows back, after all. Don't look so worried! He'll get it professionally cleaned first. You can get any-thing in India, remember? Where's my phone? I'll call him now."

IT TOOK REEVA another hour to get a proper explanation out of Saraswati. Even then she had to listen to half an hour of Bolly-wood gossip before she got to the point: The movie had ended early because one of the stars had been found in bed with the director. His wife, who also happened to be financially backing the movie with her father's money, had not been impressed. Everything had come to an instant halt while they tried to find a solution, so Saraswati had spontaneously flown to London. Because she couldn't get through to Reeva, she'd decided to get a taxi straight to her door.

"But . . . why didn't you go to the house in St. John's Wood? *Your* house?"

"I was worried about you!" cried her mum. She was now lying on Reeva's sofa with a cashmere wrap flung over her shoulders because *This flat is so chilly, darling; you really need underfloor heating.* "You didn't answer your phone, and when I messaged your sisters, they said you'd stormed off back to London."

"Wait, you came here because you were *worried* about me?"

"Of course! I don't think you've ever not answered a call from me before. I presumed the worst."

This was typical Saraswati. She thought her charm would mitigate the drama she brought into everyone's lives and persuade everyone to do whatever she wanted. Reeva had fallen for it in the past, but she was determined not to get taken in by it this time. "Right. Well, as you can see, there's no need to worry. I'm very much alive."

"Barely! You're bald!" Her mum shook her head despondently. "I can't believe it. But Raj's wig will be here soon. It'll be all right. You'll just have to stay at home till then. No wonder you're here all alone."

"Well, I actually wanted to be alone. That's why my phone is off."

Her mum's eyebrows tried to lift. "But you're always alone. You live alone. Why do you need *more* alone time? If anything, you need to party more, Reeva. Why don't you let me call my friends to take you out? The gays would love to show you a good night out."

This time Reeva couldn't help rolling her eyes. "Seriously, Mum?"

"Why do you keep saying 'seriously' like that? You sound like Jaya."

"I don't want to talk about her," scowled Reeva. "Or anything, really. Look, if you want to stay here, I'll make up the bed in the guest room. But you'll be more comfortable back at yours. I can call you a cab if you want?"

Her mum tutted. "You can't get rid of me that easily, Reeva. We need to talk."

"We already have, and I agree with you; I have zero plans to leave the house till I have some hair."

Saraswati crossed her arms. "What happened with your sisters? Why did you leave them?"

Reeva put her chamomile tea down. "I really don't want to talk about this."

"Tell me or I'll call them and make them tell me. Whose version do you want me to hear—yours or theirs?"

"Oh, for god's sake! Mum, you're worse than a child." Reeva shook her head. "You know what? Fine. I'll tell you. What does it matter anyway? I'm sick of secrets. Especially other people's. And you know it all anyway." She took a deep breath. "I figured out what Dad did."

"I know. You told me."

Reeva frowned and then her brow cleared. "Oh! I forgot. I lied to you back then. When we spoke on the phone, I was pretending. I hoped you'd let it slip."

"Wait, so . . . you don't know?"

"Nope. We thought Dad had had an affair with Leela and that you'd gone mad and made him fake his death."

Saraswati snorted. "Leela! She's a raving lesbian!"

"Yes, I know that now," said Reeva. "Though I'm not sure you can really say it like that. But she seemed so close to Dad, and . . .

you seemed to be jealous of her. Also, you said 'if it wasn't for her,' so we assumed the secret was linked to her."

A look of naked fear flashed across Saraswati's face, but it was gone so quickly that Reeva thought she'd imagined it. "Darling, you know I don't do jealousy," she laughed lightly. "Especially not with someone who buys their clothes in supermarkets."

"But why did you say that then?"

"Oh, you know what your dad was like!" Saraswati had the decency to blush when she realized what she'd said. "I mean . . . he was always so *suburban*! He always wanted to talk, eat meals at home, and watch sports together. I can't do any of those things! So Leela did them with him. And he idolized her for it. You know, he once had the audacity to ask me why I couldn't be more like Leela!" Saraswati shook her head in delicate disgust. "He always did have terrible taste."

Reeva frowned. "Wait, so did something happen between them? Did you always know she was gay?"

"Well, no." Saraswati smoothed her trousers. "She hid it from everyone, because that's what people did in those days. Except Hemant. For some reason, he was her confidant. But I had no idea because nobody bothered to tell me, and when I'd ask him what they were speaking about late at night, he'd refused to tell me! Of course I became suspicious."

Reeva felt a desperate spark of hope that Nick had been up at four a.m. speaking to Hot Lips about her sexuality. And then she remembered the singer's dating history—men, men, men.

"Not that I could imagine him ever preferring Leela to me," continued Saraswati. "But you know what men can be like. So, well, we did argue a lot about it, especially when he'd been, well, you know. That's what we were arguing about when . . ."

Reeva's face cleared. "Oh my god. You were arguing about

Leela when it happened! That's why you said, if it wasn't for her. She's the reason Dad got so angry."

Saraswati flushed. "Well, it doesn't matter now, does it? It's all in the past."

"Uh, it kind of does," said Reeva. "Because I've spent the last week practically pulling out my hair trying to figure out why you and Dad faked his death and ruined our lives." She paused as she realized her unfortunate choice of phrasing. "Look, Mum, I only figured things out at the funeral. With Kavita Kaki's help."

Saraswati tutted. "Oh, that busybody still loves a gossip, doesn't she?"

"Well, it's thanks to her that I worked everything out. In full. What Dad did. When I was five." Saraswati inspected her manicure, deliberately avoiding Reeva's eyes. "Mum, I'm not mad at you for what happened. It's all Dad's fault. But I'm mad you kept it a secret. I wish you'd just told us the truth."

"How could I!" Saraswati dramatically looked up, her hands lifted up to the ceiling in full Bollywood matriarch mode. "You were all so young!"

"Well, when we were a little older then. It's not like Sita or Jaya would have even cared. Neither of them thought the truth was a big deal."

Saraswati gasped. "No! Reeva—tell me you are joking. What's wrong with them?! I knew they were self-centered, but this is ridiculous."

To her surprise, Reeva found herself agreeing with her mum. "I know. They think *I'm* selfish, but they're the ones who've put themselves first at every opportunity. You know Jaya's pregnant? With Rakesh's baby?"

Her mum shrugged. "She did say something, but I never

know with her. I couldn't tell if she was saying she was trying or she was already pregnant. She's not very articulate, is she?"

Reeva shook her head imperceptibly. "Okay. Well . . . she is pregnant."

"Don't worry; it's unlikely it will get her genes—Rakesh's seem much more dominant. And he's so hairy and *rectangular*. I don't think it will be a very pretty baby."

Reeva let out a shocked laugh. "Mum! You can't say that!"

"What? It's my grandchild. If I can't be honest, who can?"

"Well, anyway. That's what's happening. And she's furious with me because I told everyone at Dad's funeral. About her and Rakesh. I didn't go into details about Dad, but . . . I kind of told everyone there that he wasn't a nice person."

Her mum sighed loudly. "He had his problems. A lot of them. But despite his issues, he did love you. All of you."

"It doesn't matter. How can I forgive him? What kind of monster hurts a harmless tiny being like that?"

"I know." Saraswati looked down at her diamond rings. Her voice was quiet. "It was awful to watch."

"I can imagine," said Reeva, moved by her mum's subtle emotion. "The poor cat."

"Oh, that bloody cat," snapped Saraswati, sharply looking up again. "If it wasn't for the cat, we'd all be fine."

Reeva's mouth dropped open. "Mum! It's not the cat's fault that Dad decided to kill it."

Saraswati snorted in annoyance, waving her hand in the air. "Don't be so dramatic; he wasn't trying to kill the cat." She halted, her hand slowly lowering. "But he never should have . . . He didn't realize you . . . It was . . . It was all a terrible, terrible accident."

"Well, even so, I don't know if I can forgive him for it." Reeva wrapped her arms around herself, pulling her knees up toward her chest. "Hurting a cat is unforgivable."

Her mum stared at her in silence. When she finally spoke, her voice was softer than Reeva had ever heard it before. "Reeva, beta. It wasn't the cat he hurt. It was you."

## CHAPTER 20

**Day 11**

REEVA WAS SITTING on the sofa in disbelief. Her mum had dropped her bombshell—and then gone to answer a phone call from MJ. She was now in the kitchen talking to him, making *mwah-mwah* sounds, and acting like a teenager in love. It would be inappropriate at the best of times, let alone when Reeva was still trying to process the fact that her dad had not killed her cat; he'd almost killed *her*.

"Mum! Mum, can you come back into the living room? We need to talk!"

"I'm on the phone! Don't be rude, darling."

Reeva had had enough. She stood up and walked into the kitchen. "You're the one being rude. We were in the middle of the biggest conversation of my entire life when you answered your phone. And we need to go back to it."

Her mum sighed theatrically. "MJ. Reeva needs me. I'd better go. I love you, baby. Call me when your flight lands at Heathrow— I hate that I must spend a night without you . . . I know, at least it's only one night. Hmm, yes." Reeva cleared her throat loudly.

Saraswati rolled her eyes. "Okay. Reeva's making me go. Yes, I'll tell her you send your love. Bye, baby. *Mwah-mwah.*" She hung up the phone. "There. Happy now?"

"Not really. I've just found out my dad almost killed me."

Saraswati's eyes softened with something that looked like sympathy. "He didn't mean to, Reeva. He hated himself for it. But I hated him for it too."

"Mum, I'm so confused. I need to understand what happened. You need to talk me through it all."

Her mum fidgeted with her shawl. "I know. I just . . . Be patient with me, please. It was the worst night of my life."

Reeva closed her eyes. "Okay. I get it. But, Mum, please try. I really need to know what happened. This is my *life.*"

"You're right." Saraswati turned around and started opening cupboards at random. "I'll just make us some chai and then I'll tell you everything."

"*You'll* make us chai? Do you even know how?"

"Of course I can make chai. Well, I could if you could show me how to turn this ridiculous cooker on—I can't use these electric things."

"You press the on button. Yep, that one. The one that says 'On.'"

Ten minutes later, Reeva and Saraswati were sitting across the kitchen table, blowing on steaming, freshly brewed sugar-free chai with oat milk. Reeva had to admit it tasted a lot better than simply adding masala to her mug. But that wasn't the point. The point was that her mum was about to finally tell her everything.

"So . . . ?"

"So let me have a sip and I'll tell you!" Saraswati took a long, slow, deep sip of her tea. And then another. When she tried to take another, Reeva's glare stopped her. "All right! So, okay, what do you want to know?"

"Um, what happened the night Dad almost killed me?!"

Saraswati looked taken aback. "Right. Yes. There's no need to shout. Well. Okay. Your . . . your dad had been out. To the pub. Which was the problem."

Reeva's brow furrowed, and then she gasped. "He had an alcohol problem?"

Her mum nodded. "Yes. A bad one. When your dad wasn't drinking, he was the kind, lovely, annoying, but thoughtful man I fell for. Only, when he was drinking . . ." Her mum's face took on a dark expression. "Reeva, he was very, very difficult."

Reeva thought back to all the alcoholics she'd met in her line of work and the stories she'd heard. She felt a wave of sorrow enter her body. "Oh, Mum. I . . . I'm so sorry. That must have been so hard to live with. I can't imagine." She bit her lip as she thought of the flippant comments her sisters had made about her mum calling their dad difficult—they'd been so wrong.

"Yes, well . . ." Saraswati looked down at her tea. "It wasn't easy. He'd become a different person when he drank, and toward the end, well, he was drinking every day."

"Had he always had a problem with alcohol?"

Her mum shook her head. "Oh, no. Well, actually, that's not true. I suppose he could always get quite angry when he was drunk—even in the early days. But back then, he hardly ever drank, so it just wasn't an issue. It was only when things got difficult that he started drinking. And it got worse and worse. The amount of whiskey he'd drink . . ."

Reeva closed her eyes. It had never occurred to her that her dad was an alcoholic. But he'd been drinking whiskey every night while he had three small kids and a wife in the house. It was . . . seriously depressing. "Did anything spark the drinking?" asked Reeva, opening her eyes to look at her mum.

Saraswati shifted uncomfortably, wrapping her shawl around her shoulders. "Well. I suppose the money problems were a big issue. But to be honest, Reeva, I always think the real reason was because he missed his family. I don't think he ever really realized how hard it would be to leave them behind forever, and as the reality of our life set in—never having enough money, three young kids, a disappointed wife—he probably came to regret his choice. Only by then it was too late. So he drank."

Reeva thought back to how she and her sisters hadn't found any alcohol in the house—at all. "Did he ever stop? Or get help? He wasn't drinking when he died, was he?"

Saraswati hesitated. "I don't think so. I haven't seen him for decades, Reeva. But he never could stop when we were together. He'd try to give it up—and then he'd always go back to it. And when he did, it was worse than before."

Reeva leaned back in her chair. There was so much to absorb. She sighed loudly. "I can't believe it all. I'm sorry, Mum. But . . . tell me about the night he hurt me. What happened?"

Saraswati fidgeted with her shawl again. "Well, we were arguing."

"About what? I'm going to need full details."

Saraswati winced visibly. "Okay. All right. Well . . . we were arguing about the usual. Money. There was never enough of it. We both blamed each other. And I . . . well, Reeva, I'd grown up in privilege. It was hard to adjust."

Reeva nodded slowly. She'd seen it happen to enough of her clients. For one of them, a £10 million divorce settlement hadn't been enough—and Reeva had agreed with her. It was all relative.

"That night I was shouting at him to leave his job and do something better paid. Leela came up in the conversation somehow . . . Yes, he said *she* supported him, so why couldn't I? I made a nasty comment about her. And her, uh, relationship." Saraswati picked up a teaspoon to stir her tea, resolutely not meeting Reeva's eyes. "I'm not proud of it, Reeva. But Hemant, well, he started shouting. And that's when . . ."

"When what? What happened?"

"Well . . ." Saraswati sighed loudly. "We always tried to keep our fights away from you girls. But we couldn't keep them from you, Reeva, because you'd always turn up, trying to fix everything." She looked frankly at her daughter. "I hated it—I wished you'd stay away like your sisters."

"I was *five!*"

Saraswati nodded quickly. "Yes, that's *why* I hated it—you were so tiny and precious, and it made my heart break to see you turn up, your little face all damp with tears. I couldn't bear it! What we were doing to you!"

Reeva looked down at her chai, fighting a strong urge to cry. She was starting to understand what Satya Auntie meant about having compassion for herself. "So, I turned up that night? Trying to fix your fight?"

"Yes. You . . . you turned up on the landing, holding that silly black cat of yours. Catty."

"Katie?"

"No, you named it Catty. Because it was a cat. It wasn't the most original name; I always worried you wouldn't get any of my creative genes." Saraswati's face cleared and she smiled brightly. "But at least you got my brains! Unlike your sisters. I have no idea why Sita felt the need to quit her job to be a full-time mum. *I* never felt the need."

"Okay. So, I was holding Catty and . . . ?"

Saraswati's shoulders slumped slightly, but she continued talking. "You kept trying to get your dad to stop shouting by showing him Catty. You thought it would cheer him up to stroke her, because *you* loved stroking her so much. It was bizarre how much you loved that cat. Scrawny little thing, but every time you held it, you came to life." She sat up straight and laughed. "I was so relieved; we thought you might be on the spectrum, but when you were with the cat, you became almost normal. That's the only reason I put up with its fur molting everywhere."

"Right." Reeva tried to keep her expression neutral. "Could we please get back to what happened on the landing? When you and Dad were arguing?"

Saraswati shifted uncomfortably on her chair. "What is this made of? You need some cushions for the chairs, darling. All right, yes, yes." She cleared her throat. "So your dad got annoyed when you kept coming up to him with Catty. I tried to gently guide you away, but you wouldn't leave. And then, Reeva . . ." Her mum's voice became tight. Tense. "Your dad, he was gesticulating, waving his hands around, and because he was drunk . . . he didn't realize you were still right there . . . and he accidentally must have pushed you . . ." She took a deep breath. "And . . . well . . . you went flying down the stairs. You crashed into the cabinet at the bottom. You were so small. And so still. I thought you'd died. It was . . ."

"Oh." Reeva stared at her mum. She had no words. All this time she'd thought that had happened to the cat. But it had happened to *herself*. That tiny little Reeva. Her dad had accidentally pushed *her* down the stairs. "Oh my god."

"I know." Her mum was silent, and then she flung off the shawl impatiently. "But it was all that bloody cat's fault! Because you were carrying her, you didn't put your hands out to protect yourself! The doctors said it's human evolutionary reflex; we're trained to think of cats like babies, and so you didn't drop the cat when you were holding it on the stairs. You tried to save her life, which meant that you almost died."

Reeva's mouth dropped open. "Did it work? Was the cat okay?"

"Of course she was okay!" cried her mum. "Nine lives, remember? We gave her away to our old neighbors."

Reeva closed her eyes. This was all too much. She couldn't believe she'd been so upset when she'd thought her dad had killed the cat; the truth was so, so much worse. "But . . . was I badly hurt?"

Saraswati's voice dropped so low that Reeva could barely hear her. "Yes. You were in the hospital for a week. They didn't know if you'd make it. They put you in a coma for a few days."

"I was in a coma?!"

Saraswati spoke as if in a trance, staring at the middle of the table. "It was horrific. Your dad was beside himself; he kept crying and blaming himself. He was practically suicidal."

Reeva realized her right hand was shaking and clamped her left hand on top of it. This was more intense than anything she could have imagined. It was even more intense than anything *Jaya* could have imagined. "But I was okay? Everything was fine?"

"Yes, thank god," said Saraswati, turning to look at Reeva but still speaking quietly. "The doctors saved you. You had a head injury and internal bleeding. But they did surgery, and you were okay."

"I had a head injury?" She knew she was just repeating her mum's words, but she couldn't stop. Her mind was circling in overdrive. "And surgery?"

Her mum nodded uneasily. "Yes. Trauma."

A flicker in Reeva's brain registered the irony of the word.

Trauma in all the ways. "Did social services not get involved? I was a textbook case for abuse."

Her mum winced, then shook herself back to composure before she replied. "Yes. I . . . was terrified I was going to lose you. All of you. If they'd known the truth, they might have blamed me too. For staying with an alcoholic. There are so many horror stories—I couldn't risk the truth. Instead, we lied. We said you'd fallen down holding the cat. And . . . they believed us. We were a respectable middle-class family. You'd gone to Montessori. I had a Chanel handbag. They believed it was all a terrible accident. Which, in a way, it was."

Reeva closed her eyes. She knew how biased justice could be—especially back then. "I still can't believe this, Mum. Did anyone else know?"

Her mum shook her head apologetically. "No. But, Reeva, darling, can we leave it here? I've told you all I know and . . . I just can't talk about it anymore. I can book you in for some sessions with my therapist? You can go over it with her instead of me; she knows everything anyway. She'll be much better than me!"

Reeva felt the familiar anger rise inside her, and then she remembered: trauma. Her mum had experienced her own trauma just as much as Reeva had. "I know it's hard for you. I get it. But, Mum, I need to know everything before I can ever have a chance at letting go. You know that."

Saraswati sighed in resignation. "All right, all right. What else is left?"

"Um, how about the fact that after all of this, you and Dad decided the best thing to do was fake his death?"

"Ah. Yes."

"I mean . . . how was that the natural next step? Why didn't you just get a divorce?"

"It was all a mess." Saraswati looked out the window. "We were so relieved you were alive, and so scared and worried. When we finally got rid of social services, we were both wrecks. Hemant more than anyone. He was . . . Reeva, he was broken."

Reeva felt a twist of pain in her stomach. "But . . . it was an accident. He was gesticulating. It's not like he did it on purpose. It could have happened to anyone."

Saraswati shook her head, her curls swinging against her face. "But it happened because he was drunk, Reeva."

"What was he like when he drank? Did he become violent? Did he . . . hit us? Or you?"

Saraswati looked shocked. "Oh no. He loved you all a lot. Too much sometimes. He was very overprotective. I found it all a bit much to be honest, because I'm more of a fan of hands-off parenting."

"Okay, the drinking?"

"Oh yes. No, he wasn't violent. But he could become . . ." Saraswati looked into the distance and then nodded triumphantly as she came up with the right word. "Volatile, that's it. He was unpredictable and irrational. That's why our arguments could be so bad."

Reeva looked down at the plate of biscuits. She had no idea how to process this latest news. "So . . . it was his fault?"

"*I* think so," said Saraswati. "It wouldn't have happened if he was sober. Although I blame myself too, because I shouldn't have let you get so close to us when we were arguing. I should have seen it coming!"

Reeva shook her head. "Mum, don't blame yourself. You were as much a victim of it all as I was."

Saraswati tried to raise her eyebrow doubtfully. "I don't know. But your dad really blamed himself, Reeva. It's why he hated himself so much after that. He couldn't believe his actions had led to you being in the hospital, and he was terrified of it happening again. He was terrified of himself."

Reeva wrapped her arms around her body. She felt really, really small. "Okay . . . So the death-faking was his idea?"

"We didn't exactly plan it . . . He wanted to leave our lives, and I agreed. I was so angry. We'd have these intense hushed conversations in the hospital—it was so soon after it all happened—and we decided him moving out was the best solution. And not speaking to you all ever again. We didn't plan on faking his death *per se*, but then when I told you girls he was gone forever, you assumed he'd died."

"Okay, you can't blame us! We were so young."

Saraswati shook her hair. "No, I know. I'm not. It's just . . . I remember I heard you telling your sisters he was in heaven, and it sounded so innocent compared to the truth. And in a way, it *was* like he'd died. I thought you'd be happier with that version of events. I could hear you chattering away to him in heaven, full of love for him. You'd completely forgotten everything after the head trauma. And I thought it was better that way. When I told Hemant, he agreed. He felt it was the least he could do for you all. Leave your lives forever in case he ever hurt anyone again."

Reeva reached out a hand to steady herself. This was completely crazy. But somehow it kind of . . . made sense. "Okay. But what about later? When he got in touch? And you said he couldn't meet us?"

Saraswati sighed. "I . . . I was scared, Reeva. Of uprooting your lives and changing everything. And he said he'd changed, but how could I believe him? I mean, he was telling me he'd worked things through with a priest. He'd found God! I thought it was all rubbish. I couldn't believe he had genuinely stopped drinking."

"What if he had?" asked Reeva in a small voice. "Mum, I have so many questions. I wish I could have met him just once to ask him."

Saraswati's voice faltered. "I know. I . . . I regret that. I'm sorry, Reeva."

Reeva raised an eyebrow. "Did you just apologize? Of your own accord?"

"Yes," cried Saraswati indignantly. "I always apologize when I've made a mistake."

"Uh, that is not true. You never apologize."

"Because I never make mistakes," replied her mother smugly. "Now, how about more chai?"

## CHAPTER 21

**Day 11**

"Reeva?" The door flung open to reveal Saraswati in a sexy lace nightgown that looked like something Jaya would wear. "I can't find my earplugs. I must have left them on the plane. Do you have any?"

Reeva blinked in confusion. She'd fallen asleep hours before, exhausted from her mum's revelation. "Uh, what?"

"Earplugs!"

"Um, FP's chewed them all up."

Her mum's face recoiled. "How disgusting. Well, can we ask the porter to pop down to the shop and get me some?"

"Uh, I don't *have* a porter. And even if I did, there's no way you could ask them to do that."

"But, Reeva, is it safe to live in a building without a porter?! Why can't you move back to the house and have Minu take care of you?"

"You have spent way too long in India. And I don't need a housekeeper to take care of me."

Her mum sighed. "Fine. So, what time are we leaving for Leicester tomorrow?"

Reeva sat up straight. "'We'? I'm not coming."

"But, the kriya . . ." Her mum's face tightened in anxiety. "It was his last wish."

Reeva frowned. "Uh, he also wanted us to spend two weeks at his house attending his bloody prayers and packing up his stuff. The man wanted *a lot*."

"But . . ." Saraswati walked closer to Reeva's bed, wringing her hands together. "You being at the kriya was his real last wish."

"Real?" Reeva's eyes narrowed. "Mum, are you not telling me something?"

Saraswati hesitated and then shrugged. "Oh fine. I made all that up. There was no clause in the will at all. You and your sisters get everything equally. I made my lawyers invent the stuff about you having to be there for the prayers."

Reeva's mouth fell open. "You lied?!"

Saraswati raised her chin defiantly. "Yes. For the greater good."

"Excuse me?"

"I thought it would be a good way to get you and your sisters in the same place together. I'm so sick of you all hating each other. You need each other. Especially you."

"Why especially me?!"

"You love your sisters—you always have no matter how much you pretend you can go it alone. You need them in your life."

Reeva crossed her arms. "No, I don't. They're selfish, and I'm happier without them. And I cannot believe you tricked me into spending a fortnight with them! That's really, really not okay, Mum."

Saraswati waved her hand dismissively. "They're not selfish;

they're just insecure. Jaya feels her only worth lies in her looks—she's too scared to show more of herself to the world in case she's rejected. And Sita is too scared of people's judgment to leave Nitin and live her own life."

Reeva was privately impressed by her mum's perceptiveness but refused to show it. Instead, she scowled like the rebellious teenager she'd always wanted to be.

"They need you too, Reeva," continued Saraswati. "You're stronger than them. You can help them find the courage to be themselves. And I know this wasn't right of me, but it felt like the best way to help you all. And it worked, didn't it? At least for a while..."

"Mum, this is a new low even for you."

"But, Reeva, I was just trying to help! And you need to come to the kriya tomorrow—it's important. It's what your dad wanted. And forgiving him will help you to let go of all of this and just move on."

Reeva shook her head resolutely. "I'm sorry, Mum, but you can't just manipulate people into forgiveness. Whether it's with my sisters or my dad."

"But at least come—"

"I'm not coming to the kriya," interrupted Reeva. "I already said goodbye when I was five years old and I thought he'd died. I'm not doing it again."

## Day 12

Reeva was alone again. Her mum had left the flat earlier that morning in an expensive flurry of luggage, chauffeurs, and Le Labo. It had been a scene worthy of one of her movies; she'd refused to get into her illegally parked car unless Reeva got in with her, all while cars in a growing traffic jam honked their frustrations. In the past, Reeva would have acquiesced purely to avoid the drama. This time she stood her ground, refusing to go to her dad's kriya.

She couldn't. It was all too much. She was still trying to process how she felt about what he'd done thirty years ago. It might have been an accident, but her dad had almost *killed* her. It was the stuff of Greek tragedies, not lawyers in London. Every time Reeva thought about it, she felt like she was watching a movie rather than tapping into her own memory. It didn't help that her memory was warped and had somehow made it all about Catty. In a weird way, things had been easier to process when she'd thought the victim was her cat. She could just feel pure concern for the little animal and total fury toward her heartless dad. But knowing that it had been her and not the animal had flipped everything around and twisted up her emotions. She still felt empathy when she thought about a younger Reeva, but it wasn't so simple. There was another layer of pain there—a dark, heavy feeling Reeva couldn't place. And her anger toward her dad wasn't so straightforward anymore. It was less intense and more . . . sad. She was starting to miss the uncomplicated rage she'd felt at his funeral.

She wished she had someone to talk it through with, but there was no one she could call. Her sisters, Lakshmi, Nick. They'd all gone—even though in the case of the latter, it was admittedly because she'd told him to. Reeva still felt desperately alone. Even her therapist was away. She could practically feel her abandonment issues throbbing into life again, and with them came the familiar self-pity. Maybe this was all her fault. She was the only common thread in all her recently ruined relationships.

What if she deserved to be abandoned? What if her dad's actions were her fault too? Her mum had said that Reeva never left them alone and always put herself in the middle of their fights. No, that was ridiculous; she'd been only five years old. Nothing was ever a five-year-old's fault.

Reeva squeezed her eyes shut and forced herself to think straight. She needed to find her own Reeva in this situation—someone who would listen, understand without judging, and then say the right thing. Of course—Satya Auntie! Reeva jumped up to grab her phone, then paused. If she turned her phone on, she'd be breaking her self-imposed silent retreat. She'd get caught up in all the drama of her life again, thinking about Nick and Lakshmi and even the Sherwood-Brown case, and would end up even further away from processing everything that had happened to her. No. Reeva needed to stay with herself. Everyone else might have abandoned her, but she refused to abandon herself.

With a newfound determination, she stood up, grabbed an unused notebook from her desk, and sat down to write.

*Dear Diary? Is that still a thing? I don't remember the last time I journaled, but whatever, I'm back. I just need to get this all out.*

*What Dad did to me.*

*I should probably write it out properly.*

*How my dad accidentally pushed me down the stairs and I ended up in a coma.*

*I know he didn't mean to. He was gesticulating and didn't see me. But he was drunk. And I was in his way. I fell all the way down the stairs. Oh god, I'm crying now.*

*My dad was an alcoholic and his problem almost killed me.*

*I always thought he was the good parent. With Mum being so . . . Saraswati, the one I idealized was Dad. The number of times I dreamed about what it would be like if he were still here! I thought he'd be my savior. I always imagined him to be this calm, stoic presence. And the more I found out about him in the last week, the more I began to feel that my fantasy of him was true. He had a normal, stable job, he cared about us enough to have kept track of us over the years, his friends loved him, and people said he was kind and caring. Funny even.*

*Only—it was all a lie. Because he had a dark side too. Where he drank to escape his feelings and hide from his regret and disappointment and struggles. And when he drank, he'd become volatile—that's the word Mum used—so volatile that I ended up in a coma.*

*You know, this journaling is actually quite helpful. The more I write it out, the more it's sinking in that my coma was my dad's fault. And that it was very much me who was hurt— not the cat. I think I made it all about the cat because it was easier. I'm not very good at feeling sorry for myself. I'm not like Jaya—I find self-pity awkward. That's why it was easier to feel sorry for the cat. But all along, I was the cat.*

*I guess all the love I felt for the cat needs to go to me instead. Basically what Satya Auntie's been saying all this time: I need to be compassionate to myself.*

*Why does that make me cry so much? Why does it feel so hard to be nice to myself?*

*Part of me feels like I don't deserve it. Which doesn't make sense. But I guess as a child I didn't let myself cry or feel grief— I just repressed it, and somehow that's led to me thinking it was all my fault. I don't think I even cried when Mum missed my flute recital and I spent that night at school alone. I know I was devastated—but I just swallowed it all down and distracted myself with a book.*

*Did I cry when Dad "died"? Maybe. But I don't even remember. The only tears I remember from childhood are Jaya's. Even Sita cried more than I did.*

*But I'm making up for it now. I cried for weeks—months— when Rakesh left me. I cried after every shitty online date that made me feel more alone than ever. I cried when Nick left—yes, because I made him leave, but what was the point of trying when it was all just a fantasy? I've opened up more to this cheap notebook in two pages than I ever did while I was with Nick.*

*I don't know why I'm like this. But I suppose it doesn't really matter. I just need to be kind to myself. Oh god, I'm crying again. But fuck it. I'm not going to stop myself this time. I'm going to let myself feel it all. To make up for all those years where I forced my feelings away. All the times I tried to be strong when I really just needed to sob and wail about how let down I felt. How let down I feel.*

*By Mum. By Dad. By my sisters. By my weeklong boyfriend. By my past.*

*I'm sad, Notebook. I'm really, really sad.*

## CHAPTER 22

**Day 12**

"Thank you again for coming to my flat on such short notice," said Reeva, her face swollen from all the tears she'd shed.

"Oh, you're welcome, honey! Any friend of Jaya's is a friend of mine. And you're her sister, so you get extra-special treatment." The brunette Australian sitting on Reeva's sofa beamed at her. Reeva smiled back hesitantly. She wasn't sure she was ready for hypnotherapy to make her as upbeat and positive as Marissa.

She still couldn't believe she was doing this. But after the last twelve days in Reeva's life—particularly the last twelve hours—she was ready to do things differently. She knew that the key to her healing lay in that memory of what her dad had done, and the only way she was ever going to access it was if she faced it head-on. Which was why she'd temporarily broken her retreat rules by logging onto her e-mail and getting in touch with Marissa. "So, um, what exactly do I need to do?" she asked. "Do you need a cup of tea and a spoon? Or is that just in horror movies?"

Marissa let out a delicate tinkling laugh. "Oh, you're so funny!

This isn't *Get Out*! I'm not a racist who wants to lobotomize you; I'm an Australian who wants to heal you!"

"Uh, great!"

"I'm just going to play some music and sit here on the sofa with you, guiding you through the journey. We'll be speaking to your subconscious, but your conscious will still be here. So, if at any point you need to intervene, let me know, okay?"

Reeva had no idea what any of that meant. "Uh, okay. And how long will it all take?"

"Anywhere from an hour to a couple of hours. I'm in no rush, so we'll just see how it goes. We'll work through the specific memory you've told me about, and all you need to do is answer without thinking, okay? That way, you're letting your subconscious speak—not your normal rational mind."

Reeva nodded nervously. She'd already given Marissa the SparkNotes version of her alopecia-related issues. Now all she needed to do was let her subconscious—whatever that was—give its own version.

"Right then, honey, you've got your water ready? Now get nice and comfortable on the sofa. Yes, lovely, use those cushions and that blanket. And let's begin . . ."

Reeva let herself sink into the cushions and unwind as Marissa's calm voice—accompanied by soothing spa music—guided her into a state of relaxation. She was aware of everything Marissa was saying ("Let your muscles loosen . . . Sink deep down into your heart . . . Let your mind stop working") but it all felt like background noise. Her focus was on how good her body felt right now. Calm. Loose. Relaxed. All the crying must have helped too—her muscles felt less tense now that she'd spent all morning sobbing out the sadness.

"Good. Now take yourself back to where you were at the time

of the memory you want to work on. Just imagine your younger self there—little Reeva watching your parents argue. And tell me how you feel."

With her eyes closed, Reeva saw her parents materialize in front of her at the top of the stairs. A young Saraswati, whose face still moved. Shouting at a young, drunk Hemant, whose face was contorted in anger. Reeva felt a chill run through her body. When she spoke, it was as if she was on autopilot. "I'm sad. Scared. Anxious."

"Can you attach a color to your emotions?" asked Marissa. "And tell me where it is inside your body?"

"I . . . have dark blue in me? In my heart. It's indigo. Is that . . . Am I . . . doing it right?"

"Perfectly. You don't need to question it, Reeva—just keep answering without thinking. And your parents. What color are they?"

"They're both sad. My mum is . . . blue. Like the whole of her! Her entire body is indigo. And Dad is . . . dark red." Tears started streaming down Reeva's face. "They're both yelling. I'm so scared."

"Okay, well, let's get you some support. Why don't you—adult Reeva—go and join little Reeva. Stand next to her. Is there anything you'd like to say to her?"

Reeva was still crying, but she calmed down as she visualized an adult version of herself standing next to her younger self. "I . . . I want to tell her that it's not her fault. She hasn't done anything wrong."

"Good," said Marissa. "You can tell her now. Anything you want."

"It's not your fault, baby," whispered Reeva. "You have done absolutely nothing wrong. You are perfect. I love you. You're safe. I'll take care of you."

"Tell her how much you've taken care of her—in the future."

Reeva nodded. "I've made you a lovely, safe life. You're so loved. We're so safe. We have our own money. Our own home. Another cat. We're safe and we don't have to ever be with crazy people again. We have each other."

"That's beautiful. How is young Reeva now?"

Reeva took a moment before she replied. "She's not crying now. She seems a bit better."

"Can you give her some of your strengths—your current powers or tools—to help her in this situation? And maybe help create a different outcome from before?"

Reeva saw her adult self giving her child self a big hug. A warmth spread into little Reeva and the fear faded. She smiled. "I've given her some confidence. And resilience. She's . . . not so scared anymore."

"Wonderful. And has little Reeva still got dark blue in her heart?"

"Yes. But there's . . . there's green there now too! More green than blue."

"Can little Reeva use this green feeling to talk to her parents? Is there anything she can say to them?"

Reeva frowned. "Okay. Yeah. She's telling them not to feel guilty. That it's not their fault. She's pressing her hand against each of them and giving them some of the green feeling. And they're listening and not shouting. Little Reeva's walking away. She's walking down the stairs with Catty in her arms—she's not falling. She's okay!" Tears streamed down Reeva's face again. But she didn't feel sad this time. She felt lighter. Happier. Safe. "She's safe. She didn't fall down the stairs. She's okay."

"You're so safe, my darling," said Marissa. "You have this wonderful green feeling in you. Everything is okay. You are okay.

Now. You have a choice. Do you want to just accept this little bit of blue inside you? Or do you want to work through it and turn it to green?"

Reeva felt her inner perfectionist desperate to work through the blue. But then she remembered she didn't have to always take the hard path; she could honor her progress and rest.

As if she could hear Reeva's thoughts, Marissa said, "You don't have to do it. There's no pressure. You can take the green feeling and let this small bit of blue be a reminder to you of what you've been through—a souvenir of your travels. Or you can keep going on this journey with me and transform all the blue into green."

Reeva let her subconscious answer for her. "I'm actually okay. With the bit of blue. It's . . . not so sad now. It feels stronger."

"Does it remind you to do anything for yourself?"

"To stand up for myself. To speak up."

Marissa smiled. "Good. Okay. We're going to slowly come out of this relaxed state now and let our rational mind wake up again. So start to let your body wake up. Wiggle your fingers and toes. Then, when you're ready, you can open up your eyes."

Five minutes later, Reeva slowly opened her eyes and saw Marissa beaming gently at her. "How do you feel?"

"Uh . . . good actually," said Reeva. Her shoulders felt lighter. Her entire body felt less rigid. She felt exhausted—like she'd run a marathon—but also weirdly peaceful. "I feel really good. I know it wasn't real—that in reality I did still get pushed down the stairs. But I feel like I've accepted that a bit more. Does that make sense?"

"Perfect sense. Our work doesn't change reality, or even your memory. It just changes how you feel—which is the most important thing."

Reeva smiled. "Thank you."

"You're so welcome. Was there anything that surprised you?"

"Well, I . . . didn't realize how sad my mum was," said Reeva slowly. "I knew it must have been awful being in that situation with my dad being so out of control. But I *felt* it." She thought back to the blue of her mum's body. The feeling of despair. A cold, hopeless sorrow. She shuddered, then shook her head. "It must have been so hard for her. It makes me feel more forgiving toward her, well, Saraswati-ness. Her life wasn't easy."

Marissa nodded. "That's lovely. We're all so much more than our behaviors. And how did you feel about what you learned about your dad?"

Reeva swallowed. "I . . . yeah. He was so red. There was a lot of anger, frustration, and impotence. I felt his powerlessness. I felt . . . I felt sorry for him too. In a different way from my mum, but my god, he must have been in so much pain to behave that way." She hesitated. "I . . . didn't feel like forgiving him though. Is that wrong?"

"Of course not! It's all a process, Reeva. You'll get to where you need to get in the right time, and everything we did today was perfect. You're right where you need to be."

"Thanks," said Reeva. "It feels good to know I didn't fall short. I'm so used to feeling like I needed to do more and what I did wasn't enough. But I can't believe little Reeva changed color! From blue to green!" She paused. "I also can't believe we have colors inside us. Is that an actual thing?"

Marissa smiled mysteriously. "There's a lot more inside us that we realize. The beauty of spirituality is taking the time to look inside and see what's going on."

Reeva took a sip of water and looked uncertainly at Marissa. "There's something I wanted to ask you. Why did I need to tell my younger self—little Reeva—that it wasn't her fault? I was five. Of course it wasn't my fault. That's just victim-blaming. And yet, when I told her that it wasn't her fault, I felt so much weight fade away. Almost like I'd forgiven myself. But I obviously didn't need forgiving."

Marissa reached out to put her hand on top of Reeva's arm. "So often we can carry feelings that aren't rational, but we carry them anyway. It sounds like little Reeva has been feeling guilty all this time, and the only way out of that wasn't to try and persuade her she's wrong; it was to accept her guilt and forgive her."

"Do you . . . think that's why my hair is falling out?" asked Reeva, looking up into Marissa's eyes. "Because I hadn't forgiven myself for all those years?"

"I have no idea," she replied softly. "It could be. These things can be linked to internal stress—and often that's fear, guilt, anger. The big three. It's wonderful you were able to connect with the fear and guilt in your younger self, and tell yourself what you needed to be able to move on and let that warm green feeling in."

"And it's not bad I left a bit of the blue?"

"Of course not. It's your choice. It's still serving you. And that doesn't mean you can't let go of it one day either. Whether it's in hypnotherapy again or just on your own. I'm going to give you a selection of hypnotherapy meditations you can listen to in your own time so you can strengthen the effects of what we've done."

"Thank you," said Reeva sincerely. "For all of this. I'm so grateful. And I really do feel so much better."

"I'm so glad." Marissa beamed. "You deserve it."


REEVA WAS STILL basking in her green feeling as she got ready for bed. The hypnotherapy had been more powerful than she'd imagined. It wasn't that it had helped her uncover some hidden memory, like it did on TV, or even that she'd lost control of herself and was fully at the mercy of Marissa. It had simply guided her through her most traumatic memory, allowing her to forgive herself as well as begin to have empathy for her parents.

Marissa had stayed an extra hour to chat with Reeva over tea—it wasn't officially in keeping with her solo retreat vibes, but considering both Nick and her mum had already broken her no-contact plans, Reeva had let it go. And it had been intriguing to spend time with someone so different from her. Most of Reeva's friends were people she'd met through work, and even though they were from a range of diverse backgrounds, none of them saw the world like Marissa did. She was kind of like a younger Satya Auntie, except she dressed like Jaya, and her LinkedIn described her as a former marketing exec rather than a former nun. They'd gotten on so well that they'd swapped numbers and agreed to stay in touch. Reeva couldn't imagine her ever getting to Lakshmi-levels in the friendship scales, but she loved that they'd been able to talk so freely.

She'd ended up telling Marissa absolutely everything about the last twelve days. Marissa had listened with empathy, hugged Reeva in all the right places, and put her hand to her heart in touching solidarity when the story became painful. She'd added her own insights to Reeva's theory about Catty too—that her younger self had transferred her trauma onto the cat because it gave her some distance from it all and allowed her to move on. It was a coping mechanism that had served her up to a point. But now that Reeva knew the truth, she was ready to honor little Reeva and finally give her the care she deserved.

Their chat had even inspired Reeva to come up with her own potential breakthrough. What if her desire to protect Catty was reflected in how she wanted to protect people now? She was always the responsible one—the ultimate big sister—whether it was with her sisters, Lakshmi, or even her mum. But maybe it was time for her to let go a little and just allow everyone to protect themselves. It was something Satya Auntie had said to her once: *We're all responsible for ourselves.* It was so obvious, but it hadn't ever really occurred to Reeva before. She'd thought she was responsible for everyone.

The doorbell buzzed. God, who was it going to be now? Nick, for a second Pyramus-and-Thisbe chat through the door? Her mum, ready to physically drag Reeva to the kriya? Or Lakshmi, ready to build bridges? As Reeva raced to the intercom, she realized she desperately wanted it to be the latter.

"Hello?" she asked eagerly. "Who is it?"

"It's us. Hurry up, it's raining."

No. It couldn't be. They wouldn't have come all this way to see her. Not when they were so angry at her. They hated her, and she hated them. That was the way things had been for the last four years, and bar a few nights in the bathroom, that was the way they'd always be. They wouldn't just—

"Oh my god, can you let us in? We're not, like, serial killers. We're your sisters."

## CHAPTER 23

**Day 12**

Reeva sat on the sofa in stony silence facing her sisters. They were both damp from the rain, but while Sita's hair was now plastered on her head, Jaya's had gone curlier than usual and looked annoyingly cute. She reached out a hand to check that her wig was firmly in place and crossed her arms again. "So? Are you going to tell me why you're here?"

Jaya turned to Sita, who furrowed her brow before speaking. "Mum came. She told us everything."

"It was so crazy!" cried Jaya. "I can't believe he almost *killed* you. That is way worse than him being a spy. Obviously. You poor thing, Reeva—I can't even imagine what you're going through."

Reeva frowned; Jaya looked almost sincere.

"So, um, how are you doing?" asked Sita. "After the big, uh, truth reveal?"

Reeva shrugged. "I'm okay. Surprised you guys care enough to ask when the last time we spoke you basically said you never wanted to see me again."

"Well, that's because you lost your shit when you thought

Dad had killed your cat," pointed out Sita. "Him putting you in a coma is a bit more legit."

"I was uncovering my childhood trauma!" cried Reeva. "Surely I can be forgiven for verbalizing it imperfectly?"

Jaya put a hand on her heart. "You forgave me for what I did, so yes, I forgive you."

"Okay, I wasn't actually—oh, whatever." Reeva sighed. "Thanks for coming to check up on me."

"Of course," said Jaya.

"You've obviously been through a lot," said Sita. "We all have, to be honest."

"Definitely," agreed Reeva. "You know, I couldn't ever acknowledge that before—I always wanted to minimize what I'd been through. That's why I made it all about the cat, because I was trying to—"

"Oh god, not with the cat again," muttered Sita.

Reeva glared at her. "Seriously? You're not going to let me even finish my sentence when I'm talking about how I've processed Dad almost accidentally killing me?"

"We obviously want to hold space for you," said Jaya quickly. "But, um, maybe later? You see, we're actually here to talk about something else." She looked pointedly at Sita. "Something. Else."

"Okay, go on," said Sita.

"No, you need to do it!" cried Jaya. "I'm terrible at doing things like this. And I'm more triggering for her. It's better if it comes from you."

"What are you guys going on about?" interrupted Reeva impatiently. "Just tell me."

"Why do I always have to be the bearer of bad news?" asked Sita. "But fine. You're not going to want to hear this, but . . ."

"You're scaring me. Tell me. Now."

"Satya Auntie is dying."

The color drained from Reeva's face. "No. You're joking. It's not . . . what? What do you mean?!"

Sita's expression softened. "She has cancer. A brain tumor. She's had it for ages. But she's got the incurable kind. And it's catching up with her. The doctors say she doesn't have long."

"No." Reeva shook her head vehemently. "It can't be true. She would have said something."

"It's true," said Sita. "Sorry."

"But . . . I have so many questions! What about surgery? Chemo? And what does 'long' even mean?!" Reeva looked frantically from one sister to the next. "Is she okay?! I need more info!"

"She's in the hospital," explained Jaya. "She came over this morning to meet Mum and she collapsed."

"Why didn't you tell me earlier?" cried Reeva. "I would have come immediately!"

"Your phone is off," said Sita. "We've been trying all day."

Reeva's face paled. Why hadn't she tried to call Satya Auntie that morning? She'd been speaking to a bloody notebook and a hypnotherapist while her aunt was dying. "Oh my god. Why didn't you e-mail me?"

"Because I'm not your goddamn secretary," cried Sita.

"Sorry," said Reeva. "It's my fault. All of it. Okay, well, we need to go. To Leicester. Now."

Sita put out a hand to stop her. "Just . . . calm down. The doctors said she's stable. We were with her all day. She's not allowed visitors this late, so it's best if we just go first thing tomorrow morning." Reeva sat mute, feeling like a child as Sita calmly told her everything she needed to know. "She already had surgery and chemo when she was first diagnosed around a decade ago.

It's why she quit the nunnery and came to Leicester to see Dad. She wanted to repair their relationship before she died. She didn't expect him to die first."

Reeva closed her eyes and dropped her head into her hands. "This is so fucked up. Why is everyone dying?"

Jaya looked at her in sympathy. "I know, babe. But the doctors are seriously impressed with Satya Auntie. Apparently, people with her condition normally die in fewer than five years. And she's almost doubled that."

"But can't they do any more for her now? More surgery or chemo or whatever?"

Sita shook her head. "It won't make a huge difference. And Satya Auntie's against it. She doesn't want to spend the end of her life in pain. Especially when it's not going to save her life."

Reeva leaned back against the sofa, feeling a wave of anger wash over her. "Fuck. *Fuck.* I fucking *hate* this!"

"Uh, are you okay?" asked Jaya cautiously. "You're shouting."

"No, I'm not okay," cried Reeva. "I only just met Satya Auntie and now she's *dying*? This is bullshit! First Dad, now her? I've only known she existed for, what, twelve days, and now she's going to die? It's not *fair*. It's not enough time. I need more time with her."

Sita nodded. "I know. She's the best person we're related to, and she's leaving us. Now that we know the whole secret, I kind of understand why Mum kept Dad from us—even though it's a massive overreaction and they went on with it for way too long—but keeping Satya Auntie from us was flat-out idiocy. She could have saved us years in therapy."

"She's just so wise," said Jaya sadly. "I don't know what we're going to do without her." A tear slid down her cheek.

Reeva closed her eyes. She wanted to cry too, but she was too angry. She had so much she wanted to talk to her aunt about, and she wanted years to do it all in, not weeks. Months? Years? She opened her eyes. "Wait, exactly how long do the doctors think she has?"

"They won't say," said Sita. "It's fucking annoying. But reading between the lines, they think a few months is a really good outcome. So it could still be less time. But knowing Satya Auntie, it could be another year." She hesitated. "It's doubtful it'll be more than that."

Reeva's face crumpled. A year. That was the maximum amount of time she had left with her aunt, and even that was unlikely. She felt her shoulders shake as the anger turned into excruciating sadness and she began to sob.

"Hey, it's okay. You'll be okay. We'll get through this."

Reeva looked up in surprise. Both her sisters had moved to sit on either side of her. Jaya was stroking her back with her right hand, while Sita was murmuring reassuring things to her into her ear. She couldn't remember the last time they'd sat so close to each other by choice. She cried even louder.


THE THREE SISTERS were sitting on Reeva's bed in their pajamas eating hummus, crisps, and breadsticks while sipping herbal tea in solidarity with Jaya, who had admitted she was sick of pretending to drink wine. She'd changed into her cream silk cami and tiny shorts, while Sita was wearing one of her old maternity tops ("They're so much comfier than normal clothes") and Reeva was in a button-down cotton PJ set that made her both look and feel like a child. They'd contemplated taking their midnight feast to the bathroom for continuity's sake, but snacking inside a shower cubicle—even a large walk-in rainforest one—hadn't lived up to lounging in a bathtub.

"It feels weird that you guys are here," commented Reeva. "I never imagined you being in my flat. Or on my bed. It's all very *sisterly*."

"Yeah, I'm not sure how I feel about it," said Sita. "I don't want us to start making a sisters' WhatsApp group or some bollocks. And I refuse to be your bridesmaid, Jaya."

Jaya looked awkward. "Um, I, like, didn't know you'd want to be. So, I already asked Svetlana and Saskia—my best friends? But I can maybe—"

"Are you kidding me?" interrupted Sita. "There is *no* way I would want to be your bridesmaid and wear some tiny skimpy thing that makes me look like a whale next to you. Let your Russians do it instead."

"How did you know they're Russian?" cried Jaya. "Do you follow them on Insta?"

"Dear god," breathed out Sita. "How are we related?"

Reeva laughed. "Honestly, I have no idea. But considering our parents both seem to be clinically insane, it makes sense we're all quite, um, different."

"I think we should talk about Dad," announced Jaya. "My therapist always says it's important to get stuff out in the open, and I feel like we never do that."

Sita spread her hands. "Fine. Let's talk."

"I just can't believe he was an alcoholic," said Jaya. "We never even thought of that. I guess because he'd stopped drinking by then."

"Yeah," said Sita. "Almost killing his youngest daughter is definitely a rock bottom."

"It was an accident though," said Jaya. "He didn't see her. It's not like he shoved her down the stairs on purpose."

"It was his fault," said Sita. "He should have been more careful, but he wasn't because he was drunk."

"He punished himself enough for that," said Jaya. "And it's not like Reeva died."

"Uh, guys?" said Reeva. "I'm not sure I'm really into you both analyzing this whole situation in front of me like this."

"Sorry," they apologized at the same time.

"Uh, thanks," said Reeva, surprised. "I should really tell you what I think more."

"So, how do you feel about it?" asked Jaya. "I mean, you ended up in a *coma*. You could have *died*. It must have been *seriously traumatic*."

"Uh, yeah. I guess I'm just . . . trying to make my peace with it."

"If I were you, I'd be hanging out in the anger stage of that grief cycle for decades," declared Sita. "Fuck acceptance. Your dad almost killed you."

"It's actually a lot healthier to work through all the stages of the cycle," pointed out Jaya. "I read a meme about the dangers of getting stuck in anger."

Sita raised her eyes to the ceiling, muttering, "'Read a meme'?"

"Why do you always need to put me down, Sita?" snapped Jaya. "Just because I'm more emotionally intelligent than you are."

"Hey," interrupted Reeva. "Let's not argue about this. I kind of need to talk about it. Properly. It's not exactly the kind of thing I can casually share with people. Although I journaled earlier."

Jaya clapped her hands together in glee. "Yeah, it really helped me accept what happened. That I almost died because I got caught up in Mum and Dad's argument. It's really not ideal parenting."

"No shit," muttered Sita.

"I am angry," admitted Reeva. "It's not fair that happened to me. But at the same time, I can't fully blame Dad. I mean, he must have been in so much pain to drink that much. I'm starting to realize nothing is black-and-white. It's all just very gray. And blue. Or red."

"I'm sorry, what?" asked Sita.

"Uh, it's hypnotherapy stuff."

"Oh my god," shrieked Jaya. "You did hypnotherapy! With Marissa?! Please say yes! How was it?!"

"If you say 'I told you so,' I will kick you out of my bedroom right now," warned Reeva.

Jaya mimed zipping her mouth shut.

"Fine, well, I did it. And . . . it was good. It helped me understand a bit more about why he did it."

"So, you did an hour of hippy crap and what? You forgive him for almost killing you?" asked Sita. "Just like that?"

"More like three hours," said Reeva. "And no. I definitely do not forgive him. I'm just starting to realize that I need to understand why it happened—you know, context. Otherwise I'll repress it and end up blue. Or worse, red."

"What's with the primary colors?" asked Sita.

"Long story. It just means I don't want to end up like them. Mum and Dad. She used to be really sad and angry too. I never realized how much she must have struggled."

"And here we go, defending Mum again," cried Sita. "Did she not tell you that she lied to us all about the will? The money was always ours, whether we went to his prayers or not. She hasn't changed; she's as manipulative as ever."

"But, Sita, she lived with an alcoholic," said Reeva gently. "I know she's been a terrible mum at times, but she's also had her fair share of trauma."

"I know," admitted Sita. "And it's not okay. But it still doesn't excuse her manipulation. She didn't need to trick us into giving up the last two weeks of our lives."

"I haven't minded these two weeks so much," said Jaya mildly. "It's been kind of fun. Trying to figure out if Dad was a spy or having an affair. Hanging out in the bath. I've had worse fortnights."

Reeva and Sita both turned to look at her. "Seriously?"

"Yeah! I was once promised a free trip to a five-star resort, and when I got there, it was *very* four-star. This has been amazing in comparison."

"Well, I don't know about fun, but these have definitely been the most eventful two weeks of my life," said Reeva. "I'm not over how many things have happened. Finding out Dad's secret, that Sita's separated, that Jaya's having a kid with my ex—I'm not having a go at you, I'm just saying! I had a fight with my best friend. Got a boyfriend and broke up with him. Found out I have an amazing aunt and she's dying. It's a lot."

"What?" yelped Jaya. "You broke up with Nick?! Was he shagging Hot Lips? Oh my god, I'm going to kill him!"

"He says he wasn't. He admitted they used to date—after I practically forced him into it," explained Reeva. "But I just don't know if I can believe him. And even if I could, it's too hard to be with him. Everything he does ignites one of my old insecurities."

"So ditch your insecurities, not him!" cried Jaya.

"Maybe I don't want to," said Reeva stubbornly. "Why can't I date someone easier? Why does it have to be so hard?"

"It's always fucking hard," said Sita.

"But surely it would be easier if I dated someone who didn't travel the world to hang out with hot celebs all the time," argued Reeva. "You know, someone normal. A plumber or something."

"Plumbers are always having sex!" cried Jaya. "Do you guys not watch porn?"

"Uh, no. I barely have the time to brush my hair let alone masturbate," said Sita.

Jaya shook her head. "How are we related?"

"The point is he wasn't a UCB," said Reeva. "It's okay to have an lcb for a while, but really, I want more."

"Coming to see you to win you back is pretty UCB," said Jaya. "And don't forget he came all the way to Leicester to see you. He really likes you."

"Yes, but I don't just want a boyfriend who likes me and makes big gestures—I want someone I feel safe with. Someone I can stay up late talking to about my feelings. I want real emotional communication, whereas Nick won't even tell me why Hot Lips was in his room. Or why he divorced his ex." Reeva exhaled. "I'm not blaming him—I know men in his generation weren't raised to share about their feelings. And I know I've made mistakes too. But . . . things are better now that I've ended it. I feel so, so much calmer."

"Yeah, because you're avoiding life," said Jaya.

"I'm taking control of my life! Sita, surely you see my point?"

Sita shrugged. "What do I know? My marriage is a disaster and you two are the only ones who know."

"Give her some advice," urged Jaya. "She clearly needs it."

"Oh, fine. If you love him, then make it work. Even if it's hard. It's worth it."

Reeva looked at Sita in surprise. "But . . . you always say that love isn't enough! That you need the teamwork and partnership and all the practical things in common too. That's, like, your mantra."

"All that comes later. You can figure it out so long as you have a strong foundation of love. Work on that and you'll be okay. Logistics can be sorted."

Reeva looked at her dubiously. "Even when the logistics involve your boyfriend sleeping with a practically teenage pop star? I don't think so. Besides, it's too late. We're over. And I feel better for it."

"Sure," said Jaya sarcastically. "So much better that you've turned your phone off and hidden away from the world. Really healthy behavior, Reevs."

"Hey, it's my detox retreat. I'm healing."

"And fighting with your best friend?" asked Jaya. "Doesn't sound so healing to me."

Reeva looked defensively at both her sisters, then sighed. "Okay, so I'm hiding away a bit. Surely that's okay considering absolutely everything that could go wrong in my life has just gone wrong?"

"You're allowed to take some time," said Sita. "Fuck knows I'd like to. But you've got to face up to shit too."

"I know. I am very aware I can't just live alone inside my flat for the rest of my life."

Jaya studied her suspiciously. "Hey. How come your hair looks so good? It's bouncier than usual, and you've got a cute fringey bit. Did you get extensions?" She gasped. "Oh my god. It isn't a . . . ?"

Sita caught Jaya's eyes. "You get her wrists. I'll get the wig."

"No!" shrieked Reeva as both her sisters lunged for her. "You can't do this! No!"

"You did it to me," said Jaya, as she wrestled her. "Come on, Sita, I've got her."

Sita sat astride her sister's chest, ignoring Reeva's muffled cries, and triumphantly pulled off the wig. "Fuck me! You're bald."

Reeva pushed her sisters off her and frantically tried to cover her head. She stuck a pillow on top of it. "Go away! I can't believe you did that. You're the worst. I hate you both. Just . . . get out of my room. Get out of my flat!"

"Babe," breathed out Jaya. "Where did your hair go?"

"Looks like she shaved it off," said Sita, craning her neck to look at the back of Reeva's head. "Which isn't the worst idea I've ever heard. I probably would have done the same if I were you, Reevs."

"I definitely would *not* have," said Jaya. Sita elbowed her in the stomach. "But, um, yep, love that for you, Reevs!"

Reeva sniffed and slowly lowered the pillow. "You don't think I look hideously repulsive?"

"Nah," said Sita. "It's efficient. And the wig suits you. Better than your normal hair, really."

Jaya nodded. "Uh-huh. Ooh, if you let me do a post about you, I can get you loads more wigs gifted for free. Oh my god, it would be so—"

"No fucking way," retorted Reeva. "I will never let you post about me in any context, so you may as well stop asking."

Sita looked at Reeva, impressed. "You know what? Being bald suits you. You seem different. Stronger. Less . . . mouselike."

Reeva crossed her arms. "I was never mouselike. And I'm not

planning on staying bald, okay? I only did it because I was sick of waiting for it to happen. It was my way of taking back control."

Jaya turned to Sita. "You're so right. Bald Reeva has fierce energy. I'm into it! Yes, girl!"

Reeva looked from one sister to the other and shook her head slowly. "Yeah, I really have no idea how we're related."

## CHAPTER 24

**Day 13**

"So you're sure you're going to be okay with her?" Reeva looked anxiously from Fluffy Panda, who was yawning regally on the windowsill, to Sita and Jaya, who were both huddled around mugs of coffee at the kitchen table, yawning far less regally. "She's a very particular cat. You know she doesn't like anyone touching her except me— Oh, well, I guess she accepted Lakshmi. But she won't like you guys touching her because you're complete strangers. To her, I mean. And remember if she—"

"We get it," interrupted Sita. "We are her slaves and she is a cat god. We will do whatever she desires and nothing less."

Reeva scowled. "You don't need to be sarcastic. I worry about her. She's been through a lot of upheaval lately." She paused. "I mean I've been through a lot of upheaval lately. God, I really need to stop transferring my shit onto the cat."

Sita shook her head. "You've got issues."

Jaya frowned at her, mouthing, *She's bald.*

"I can lip-read," said Reeva. "And you don't need to be nice to me just because I don't have any hair."

"We're not!" cried Jaya. "But don't worry, we'll take amazing care of FP. I think I found your vibrator in the bedside drawer, so we'll get that out for her if need be."

"No! No more vibrators. Just . . . dry food for lunch, and Chicken Princess for breakfast and dinner. And I still don't know if I'll be home tonight or tomorrow."

"You should at least stay the night," said Jaya. "Even if you skip the kriya. We'll be up tomorrow morning."

"And if you stay, you can check on the twins for me," added Sita. "Check Mum hasn't almost killed them. We don't want history repeating itself or we'll have to fake *her* death this time. What? Why are you both looking at me like that? Black humor is a healthy coping mechanism."

Reeva rolled her eyes. "Okay, fine. I'll try and stay the night, but *only* for Alisha and Amisha. In that case, make sure you feed FP a wet sachet for breakfast, and then put her dry food in the automated container so she has lunch and dinner. Even if I miss the kriya, she'll need her lunch ready, okay? And—"

Sita shot her a death stare. "Reeva. I have two children. I can handle a cat. Now go."

"Okay, okay." Reeva grabbed her bag and turned around one last time to look at her cat—who did actually seem quite godlike up on the windowsill—and her sisters, who were slavishly bent over their coffees. "Bye!"

"Good luck," called out Jaya. "Send Satya Auntie our love!"

"And let us know if you'll come back tomorrow or not," said Sita. "So we can feed the cat accordingly."

"I just said leave enough in her container regardless!" cried Reeva. "Oh. You're kidding again. You know it's not funny to joke about starving a pet."

"Cats can live on nothing in the wild for weeks," said Sita. "Nine lives and all that."

"The nine lives thing is true?" asked Jaya. "That's so crazy."

"Oh my fucking god," muttered Sita.

"I'm leaving," said Reeva. "Please don't kill the cat. Or each other."

REEVA DROVE DOWN the M1 in the rain. It was a journey she was now getting used to. The first time she'd done it on the way to her dad's house, following the signs north, she'd felt sick with nerves. All she'd wanted to do was turn around and head back toward the comforting signs to the south. But now Reeva couldn't wait to get to Leicester. She was desperate to see her aunt, especially as she had no idea how long they had left together. And she was grateful to her sisters for offering to cat-sit. As annoying as they both were and always would be, they were her family, and Reeva was beginning to see that this came with benefits, not just endless responsibilities.

They'd stayed up late the previous night, talking about everything from her fight with Lakshmi (Sita thought she'd overreacted; Jaya thought she'd underreacted) to what their mum had told them. None of them had realized how toxic their parents' marriage had been, but it all made sense. Of course their parents had fought nonstop. Saraswati had left behind her famous, wealthy, well-connected family to live with an optometrist in a country where she knew basically no one. And Hemant had found himself with a demanding, dramatic wife instead of the calm, supportive spouse he'd been hoping for. It was a match made in hell—especially with the addition of Hemant's addiction—and their separation was the best thing that could have happened. Even Sita acknowledged that Saraswati's poor parenting had to be linked to the reality of being married to an alcoholic. They were all still furious at their mother in very different ways, but now there was a softer edge of understanding around their rage.

Reeva couldn't say the same about her dad. Her feelings around him were messy. She knew he hadn't meant to hurt her—but she couldn't stop seeing her fuzzy nightmare of him standing at the top of the stairs as she and the cat lay at the bottom, covered in blood. She'd done a bit of googling about alcoholism, and she knew that he could very well have had his own traumas that led to him becoming an addict, but she still felt hurt, abandoned, and betrayed. It was like half of her felt sorry for him, but the other half hated him. It was why she really didn't want to go to the kriya.

Her sisters thought she'd regret this. "We've been tricked into two weeks of this shit; we may as well see it through to the end," said Sita pragmatically. Jaya's perspective was more, "I have a *lot* to say to him about the emotional damage he's caused. And I think the kriya is the perfect place to do it." Reeva had listened to her sisters in a way she normally didn't—they were the only people who understood how she felt—but she still couldn't see herself peacefully wishing farewell to her dad's soul. Not when he'd betrayed her on so many levels. Besides, as Satya Auntie said, she could always make her peace with him in her own time instead of the designated ceremony. Like in her journal. Or in hypnotherapy.

But right now, her full focus was on Satya Auntie. Reeva had fallen asleep researching cancerous brain tumors. It was worse than she'd thought. The internet declared that a positive outcome—something just 10 percent managed—was living for around five years post-diagnosis. To Reeva, this was *not* positive. Her aunt had already lived for a decade post-diagnosis. Given this statistic, the doctors' hopeful prognosis of one year seemed impossible. Reeva felt her eyes water at the thought. She hadn't cried this much since she'd found out about Jaya and Rakesh.

Satya Auntie's cancer put all that into perspective. Reeva had wasted so much time worrying—and for what? Nothing would change what her sister and her ex had done. And instead of cutting herself off from her sisters, she could have forced them to make it up to her with cat-sitting and chai-making. In a way, Sita's harsh comments all those years ago had been right; the only way out of this mess was for Reeva to forgive them and move on. Then there was her alopecia. She'd stressed so much about losing her hair, when all along her aunt was losing her *life*. Reeva couldn't believe how much she'd made everything about herself lately. Even the drama about her parents felt less serious now. The truth was completely insane, but it didn't really change anything. Her dad hadn't been in her life before, and he still wasn't, while her mum had always been a narcissist and still was. It was the way things were.

It was harder to be so Zen about Nick. Her sisters' words were still in her mind. She knew she'd never be able to get back together with him the way her sisters suggested, but part of her wished she could. She already missed him. He was the smartest, funniest, most handsome, confident man she'd met since Rakesh. He was probably more of those adjectives than Rakesh had ever been—she just wished they could talk as openly as she had with her ex. When she'd turned her phone back on that morning, there'd been nothing from Nick. Endless missed calls and messages from her sisters and mum—which had made Reeva feel guiltier than ever—but Nick was obviously respecting her decision, which was partly a relief and partly more painful than she'd imagined. But worst of all was the fact that there was nothing from Lakshmi. Reeva knew she could reach out first, but with everything going on, it would have to wait. She wanted to concentrate on spending as much time with her aunt as she could before she followed in her dad's footsteps and died on her.

"REEVA!" SATYA AUNTIE looked exhausted, lying in a hospital bed, hooked up to machines, but her face lit up at the sight of her niece.

Reeva's eyes welled up again. She'd prepared herself for the sight of her aunt in the hospital, but seeing her in a white gown in a white bed just made her cancer even more real. "Hi."

"I like your hair!"

Reeva's brow furrowed and then she laughed. She'd forgotten she was wearing her Beyoncé wig. "Thanks. I'll explain later. How are you?" She walked up closer to Satya Auntie's bed and took her hand. "Tell me everything."

"I suppose your sisters have told you the basics?"

Reeva nodded as she lowered herself into a plastic chair. "They said it's bad. How are you feeling?"

"I'm okay, thank you, darling. Bit tired, but all right. And, well, you know I try not to define things as good or bad. It's just the path that's been chosen for me. Who am I to label it?"

Reeva grinned as she wiped away a sudden tear. "I should have known the Satya Lama would say something like that. But . . . this does seem pretty bad to me. No offense. They said you're *dying*. And . . . they don't know how long you have."

Her aunt clasped her hand tight. "Oh, but I'm so grateful to have had all these years! I've done so much with my life. I was able to reconnect with Hemant. I was able to meet you! And your sisters. I'm so lucky to have even a little more time with you all. Whether it's a matter of weeks or months."

Reeva was crying too much to speak.

"You don't need to be so sad for me," said Satya Auntie gently. "I've made my peace with going."

"But I'm sad for *me*," cried Reeva. "I can't bear the thought of you not being here. I'll miss you so much. I don't know how I'll cope. And I'm so angry we've missed all this time we could have had together. Even if it was only the last ten years. It would have been . . ." Reeva imagined a world where Satya Auntie had supported and guided her through her twenties, her career, her breakup. She choked back a sob. "Really, really great."

Satya Auntie looked down at the white bedsheet. "I think a lot of that was my fault. I'm sorry, Reeva. My ego stopped me from getting in touch while I was estranged from my family. You know? If they didn't want me, then they wouldn't get me. Not even the kids." She smiled at Reeva. "It's why I'm so impressed by you. Even when you weren't speaking to your sisters, you were still always there for your nieces. The aunt I wish I could have been."

Reeva gave her a watery smile back. "Thanks. But it was different for me because I'd met them pre-drama. I already loved them. You'd never met us."

"You're kind for trying to make me feel better, but I've already accepted my mistake. It's okay—I'm not beating myself up about it. It was just the way it was. And when I came to England to make my peace with Hemant, I didn't really know how to keep him in my life *and* reach out to you three. The situation was so messy. I didn't want to jeopardize my relationship with Hemant, and the topic was so painful for him that I avoided it. But, Reeva,

I have thought about you all. A lot. It was my greatest wish to meet you before I died, so no matter how long I have left, I'll always be grateful that happened."

Reeva shook her head slowly. "It's such a shame that one incident led to so many broken relationships. I don't blame you. It just breaks my heart that families can cut each other out. Imagine how different things would have been if your parents hadn't cut you out, if our mum hadn't cut Dad out, or . . ." She paused, grinning ruefully. "If I hadn't cut out my sisters."

Satya Auntie laughed. "Families are complicated. But I'm proud of you for making up with your sisters. If there's one thing I've learned, it's that life is short. Fix everything while you can."

"Right," said Reeva softly. Her mind flashed to Nick and Lakshmi. "Do you feel you have? Do you feel . . . ready to go? You're still so young."

"I do. I haven't done anything perfectly, but that isn't the point, is it? I've lived my life on my own terms, and that feels like true success to me."

Reeva nodded. "I love that. I've aimed for perfection for so much of my life, but it's so pointless. It doesn't exist. I should have been like you and aimed for authenticity instead."

"You can always start now—" said Satya Auntie, breaking off to cough.

Reeva's brow creased. "Are you okay? Oh, I hate to see you like this. You don't deserve this, Satya Auntie."

Her aunt sipped from a glass of water and cleared her throat. "I'm okay. And it's not about deserving things or not. This is just my path. It's my time."

"It's come so early," said Reeva quietly.

"Only because we had expectations that it would be otherwise. I'm okay surrendering to it all. And you'll be okay once I'm gone, Reeva. You don't need to suffer."

"Um, of course I'll suffer!" cried Reeva. "I love you!"

"I love you too—so, so much." Her aunt squeezed her hand as tight as she could. "It's normal that you'll feel pain—it's the price of love, as they say. But suffering isn't necessary. That's just born out of our thoughts."

"You're going to need to explain that."

"Well, thoughts like 'I'll never be happy again' or 'This is the worst thing to ever happen to me' or 'No one understands.' These are the thoughts that cause suffering. If you learn to question them and realize they aren't true, the suffering can go. Then you'll be left with the pain, which is hard, yes, but it's also beautiful. And it doesn't last. Nothing does."

Reeva looked at her aunt in despair. "How am I going to survive without you telling me these things? Nobody else in my life thinks like you do."

"I'm not in a coffin just yet!"

Reeva gave her a teary smile. "Sorry."

"Now," said Satya Auntie, straining to sit up. Reeva rushed to put a pillow behind her back. "Your mum came to see me yesterday and told me everything. About your dad. And the coma . . ."

Reeva's face fell.

"How are you feeling?" her aunt asked.

Reeva smiled brightly. "Oh, it's fine," she waved her hand dismissively. "I want to talk about you. You're the one who's dyi— I mean, in the hospital."

"You can say the word *dying*. I'm not scared of it." Her aunt laughed. "But, Reeva, I think it's important we talk about this. It'll be helpful for me too—I had no idea my brother had a drinking problem."

"Did you really not know?" asked Reeva. "Didn't you once say he got really angry and smashed something when he was drunk?"

Satya Auntie nodded. "Yes. Before I left. But I never saw him touch alcohol when I came back. Not once in these last ten years."

"So do you think he was sober for all that time?" asked Reeva softly. "He only told Mum he was a few years ago."

"Maybe. Or maybe he was secretly drinking until recently. There are some things we'll never know."

"I can't believe I was the one who almost died—not the cat. And that it was because of him. I just . . . I don't know if I hate him or if I feel sorry for him."

Satya Auntie nodded. "I understand. But does it need to be one or the other? This is a big thing—it makes sense you're feeling big feelings. Contradicting ones too. Maybe there's space for you to feel them all."

Reeva looked down at the bedsheet. "Yeah. I guess you're right. How do you feel? Knowing he was your brother and he did this?"

"I feel sad. That he had so many problems and I wasn't around. That his actions led to such devastation. And that he never felt he could speak honestly about it all."

"It's crazy he never told you. Or anyone, actually."

"I hope he was able to confide in people at the mandir," said Satya Auntie. "Or at least in God. Because I know that while Hemant made some serious mistakes, he lived with a lot of guilt afterward. And everyone deserves forgiveness."

"But does that mean I need to forgive him? Because I really don't think I can."

Her aunt shook her head. "You don't need to do anything other than listen to yourself and do what's right for you."

Reeva sighed. "I wish I knew what that was. I don't even know if I'm doing the right thing in not going to the kriya. I don't even know if I should try again with Nick—it's a long story. Or maybe it's not—I broke up with him because I didn't feel I could be myself with him. I just . . . I'm realizing more and more that I don't actually know anything."

Her aunt smiled. "Well, that is the very first step on the path to enlightenment. Realizing that despite the ego's self-will, we actually know nothing. At all."

"I can't say I feel very enlightened," said Reeva, raising an eyebrow. "If anything, I feel like a total mess."

"I hear you, beta. And I know that it can feel overwhelming to make decisions when you're in that space. But remember that you're right where you need to be. You're perfect as you are— with your flaws, your imperfections, and your wounds."

Reeva felt tears prick her eyes. "Thank you. But I don't feel perfect. I shaved all my hair off. I'm bald."

"That's wonderful!"

"It . . . is?"

"You're showing your vulnerability to the world! It's beautiful. I'm proud of you."

"Well, I'm currently hiding it with a wig, but . . . thanks." Reeva bit her bottom lip. "I just don't know what to do, Satya Auntie! With my dad, with Nick, with Lakshmi . . ."

"I've always believed everything we do comes from either love or fear. So every choice we make ultimately comes down to—are we giving in to fear or are we choosing love?"

Reeva nodded slowly. "Fear or love. Okay. I guess most of my choices right now are because I'm scared. Of getting hurt. But I'm also scared of making the wrong choice."

"Don't worry so much about right and wrong. You don't need to judge yourself, Reeva—or take things so seriously. Remember, life isn't an exam."

"You're right. I need to work on not being so hard on myself. More homework."

"It doesn't need to be homework." Her aunt laughed. "It's just listening to your feelings and coming back to yourself. If you're suffering a lot, then you've probably made a choice that's taken you further away from yourself. If you feel good, you've probably done something authentic. It's the same thing we've been talking about all this time with truth. The meaning of life is to be authentic. To live it all as yourself. To do what feels right for you. That's it. Exam passed."

Reeva looked down at her aunt's hands. They looked bare without her trademark silver rings. She was dying, yet didn't seem to be outwardly suffering anywhere near as much as Reeva was. Which suggested that unlike her aunt, Reeva had already made many, many decisions that had taken her away from her authentic self. "What do you do if you've done the opposite? The inauthentic stuff?"

"You exercise compassion and start listening to your intuition. Now." Her aunt sat up in bed and clapped her hands together. "Let's ring the buzzer and get that lovely nurse to bring up some hot water so we can make tulsi teas. It'll help us both with inner balance. How does that sound?"

"How many tea bags do you have?" asked Reeva. "I think I'm going to need them all."

## CHAPTER 25

## Day 13

REEVA BUZZED THE front door of her dad's house for the third time. "Hello? Can someone let me in? Oh my god." She banged on the door with her fists. "I can hear music! Let me in!"

The door was flung open to reveal Saraswati with Amisha (or Alisha) on her shoulders. MJ was just behind her with Alisha (or Amisha) on his. Their faces were covered in animal paint. One of the twins looked like a lion, the other had elephant tusks on her face, MJ looked like a zebra, and she was pretty sure her mum was meant to be a tiger.

Reeva's mouth dropped open, then she quickly rummaged around in her bag. "Don't move! There's no way Sita and Jaya are going to believe this unless I have evidence. Maybe we really do need a sisters' WhatsApp thread."

Saraswati looked up in confusion as Reeva pulled out her phone. When she heard the click of the camera, she shot her hands up to cover her face. "Reeva! No! You cannot take a photo of me without my permission! I haven't even got my eyelashes on. You'd better not post that anywhere."

"Don't worry, it's only going to Sita and Jaya. And Jaya's two hundred thousand followers."

As Saraswati shrieked, Reeva slipped past her into the house.

"We're *wildlife*!" shouted the twin on her mum's shoulders. Definitely Amisha. "I'm a lion. *Roaaar!*"

"And I'm an elephant," said Alisha. "Look!" She kicked her legs and made MJ run around the living room.

"Hi, Reeva!" he said. "It's all go around here. You'll have to take shelter or you could get hurt in the elephant stampede."

"*Stampede!*" yelled the twins in unison.

Reeva laughed. "Okay. Wow. Hi, everyone. I'm going to just head up to my room and, uh, avoid the stampede."

Her mum stood in front of her. "Oh no, you're not getting away that easily." Reeva took a step back; the orange and black had blended on her mum's face, and she looked savage. "We need to talk."

"Again?!"

"Can't a mother talk to her daughter?"

"But you hate talking. The last time I wanted to talk to you, I had to book in a half-hour slot with your PA."

"She's an EA," said Saraswati, grunting as she dumped Amisha on the sofa behind her. "Let's go upstairs. MJ, look after them both."

"Yes, ma'am," he said, doing a mock salute. "Who wants a break for cucumber slices?"

Reeva escaped the room as the twins began running around in crazed circles. "You're not in your dad's room anymore," said Saraswati, following her. "I can't imagine what your sisters were thinking, putting you in there. No wonder you had so many nightmares. You're staying in the single room—the one Jaya was in." Saraswati paused suddenly. "I hope that doesn't give you nightmares too."

"I'll be okay; I think I forgave her. Where are you guys sleeping?"

"That'll be because of my plan to make you spend all this time together," said Saraswati smugly. "And we're in your dad's room, and the twins are in theirs. It's all perfect."

Reeva turned back to face her mum. "Uh, isn't it weird for you to be in your dead ex's bed with your new husband? I thought you'd be in a hotel as soon as you could."

"We can't just abandon the poor man in death. I know he was difficult and troubled, but he was family."

Reeva refrained from pointing out that Saraswati had done exactly that for most of her life. Then she remembered she was done refraining from speaking her truth. "But you abandon us all the time."

Her mum looked taken aback. "Well, yes. I've made mistakes. I'm the first to own up to them. But I'm here when it matters. Like in death."

"I would have thought the bit that matters most is life?"

Her mum waved her hand impatiently. "There are many lives in Hinduism. What's important is to grieve death properly. So I hope you're coming tomorrow to the kriya."

Reeva frowned. "Mum. Why are you so insistent on me being there?"

"Because it was his last wish—I told you!"

Reeva looked into her mum's wide, slightly manic eyes. "Mum. What else is going on? You can tell me."

Saraswati flung her hands into the air. "Oh, fine—I feel guilty! Okay? I feel guilty!"

"For what?" Reeva tensed as she waited for her mum to reply. She couldn't deal with yet another traumatic family secret.

"I didn't let him meet you when he wanted to." Saraswati hung her head low as Reeva's shoulders relaxed. "I will never forgive myself for that. And . . . I know I'm not an easy person to live with."

"Oh, Mum." Reeva tentatively reached out to place a hand onto her mum's shoulder. "I get it. But . . . you can't absolve your guilt through me."

"I . . . can't? Are you sure?"

Reeva rolled her eyes. "Yes, I'm sure. I can't absolve you of your guilt. I do wish we'd had a chance to speak to Dad back when he got in touch, and yeah, I do find it really hard that you said no to that happening. But I accept it. And I think . . . you need to as well. Mum, you need to forgive yourself. What's done is done."

Her mum sniffed. "Have you been spending time with Satya Auntie?"

"Uh, yes, she's amazing! I'm so sad she's . . ." Reeva's voice faded.

"Yes, if she wasn't dying, I'd hire her to be my therapist. She'd probably earn more than she does at her spa."

Reeva laughed despite herself. "You are so inappropriate, Mum. But look, not going to the kriya is my choice, okay?"

"Oh, fine." Saraswati sighed. "But was I not quite clever in making you and your sisters spend these two weeks together? I was so proud of them for coming to see you last night. My darling girls all together again."

"You never used to care if we got on. You used to tell me to pretend I wasn't related to them at school."

"That was for your own good! So you wouldn't compare and despair! And can a mother not learn from her mistakes and try to make amends for the past?"

"Mum, you don't need to be so dramatic, it's not like—"

Reeva gasped loudly. "Oh my god, please do not tell me you're dying too! I cannot deal with any more people dying right now."

"Of course I'm not dying. I have the health—and the womb— of a forty-year-old."

Reeva shuddered. "Please tell me you and MJ use protection. I can just about handle being an aunt again, but there's no way I can deal with another sister."

"What about a brother? I'm joking! Don't look at me like that, Reeva—it was a *joke*. As if I'd risk anything that would give me stretch marks again."

REEVA SAT QUIETLY in the living room. It was seven p.m. and the prayers had just begun. This time she wasn't squeezed into the back, right next to the kitchen door; she was in the front row, sitting right next to the lady leading the bhajans. Now that Satya Auntie was out of action, Shilpa Ben and some other elderly aunts and un- cles (they weren't actually related, but Reeva had been told to ad- dress them as though they were) had taken charge. It was amazing how much they did for the funeral of someone they weren't related to. But her mum had explained that this was normal. When people who weren't prepared for the death of a loved one found themselves with a funeral to organize—read: three millennials from North London who knew more about Jewish customs than their own Hindu ones—a whole load of elderly people in the community stepped in. They helped the family organize the prayers, spread the word, speak to funeral directors, find the right Hindu priest, and do all the religious admin that no one else knew how to do.

Reeva had seen them helping Satya Auntie, but until now she hadn't understood how much they'd all done or really thought about how much organization had gone into setting up the daily prayers. Nor had she bothered to fully attend a single night of prayers until tonight. Her last chance.

The more she thought about it, the more she realized she'd been so wrapped up in her own life that she hadn't really paid attention to the quiet action happening around her. It was enough to make her want to spiral into a hole of self-hatred, but Reeva was taking Satya Auntie's advice to try out compassion instead. She couldn't undo the past, but now that she had a little more support from her family, she was able to focus on appreciating the clockwork support of the community around her. It didn't always feel like one she belonged to, but she was still grateful it existed.

"Om Namo Narayanaya," chanted the bhajans lady. Reeva didn't know the mantra, but it was soothing. She closed her eyes and let the rhythm of the words wash over her. She knew that her mum and MJ were somewhere behind her and that there were dozens of aunts and uncles packed in the room, but slowly she stopped being aware of their presence. She was too busy enjoying the peace of the mantra. She wasn't even averse to the croaking singing of the lady to her left. If she took away the fact that she was meant to be grieving someone who had almost accidentally killed her, she was having quite a nice time.

As the prayers continued, Reeva's mind started to wander. But it didn't go to her anxieties and to-do lists like it normally did. Instead, Reeva thought about what Satya Auntie had said to her about love and fear. She'd been so scared of getting hurt that she'd chosen fear over love every step of the way. It was why she hadn't ever been fully honest with her sisters, Nick, or even Lakshmi at times. She'd been too scared to have an authentic relationship with them in case she got hurt. Only, look what had happened. She'd made everything worse by trying to avoid pain, when pain was just part of life. She'd self-sabotaged with Nick by not being up-front with him—about everything from her alopecia to her neediness—because she was scared. Scared she didn't deserve love and wasn't worthy of him. But now Reeva knew that was just old fear. And beneath it was love. Love for herself. And love for him.

Reeva smiled as her body swayed in time to the music. She felt so much better now that she could see things so clearly. She didn't even feel an urgent need to rush into action or fix everything. She was happy just knowing the truth. All this time, she'd been trying to control her life. But now she knew she'd never have control, and she'd never *had* it either. Control didn't exist. All she had was confusion and uncertainty. But that was okay. That was what it meant to be human. And she could just sit in it with these people by her side, breathing. For the next thirty minutes she didn't have to do anything other than be exactly where she was: in the living room of her dead dad's house, surrounded by the soothing presence of chanting relatives she barely knew, with a growing hope that the smell wafting in from the kitchen meant there was chili paneer for dinner.

## CHAPTER 26

**Day 14**

"Auntie Weeee!" The door burst open and Alisha and Amisha bounded into the room. "You have to—" Both twins gasped at Reeva.

Reeva yawned from the bed. "What's going on?"

"Wow," exhaled Alisha eventually. "Your head looks like an egg."

Reeva blinked in confusion then gasped. "Oh my god! My wig! No! Girls, can you . . . just . . . get out for a moment while I sort myself out?"

Amisha ignored her and jumped onto the bed. "Let me touch it! Please!"

"Amisha!" Reeva tried to bat her niece away. "No! I don't want . . . can you . . ."

"It's so fuzzy!" shrieked Amisha, patting Reeva's head. "I want it! Will you do mine too?"

Reeva laughed despite herself. "Uh, I don't think your mum would be too pleased about that."

Alisha slowly walked toward her. "But where did all your hair go?"

Reeva sighed. "You know I had those bald bits? Well, I decided to just shave it all off. And start from scratch."

"It's so cool," said Amisha in awe. "Look! Come touch!"

Alisha climbed onto the bed and slowly stroked her aunt's head. "I like it. We should do it to U-G-L-Y too."

"And ourselves!"

"Please do *not* do it to yourselves or your mum will kill me. But thanks for the support. Can you pass me my wig?"

"No!" cried Amisha. "It's better now."

Alisha nodded. "I like that it's fuzzy and then some bits are shiny. Like polka dots."

Reeva put her arms around the twins and squeezed them tight, trying not to cry. "You guys are the best. Only you could put a positive spin on my current hair situation. Or lack thereof." She sniffed. "Hey, what were you going to say when you walked into my room?"

"Oh," said Amisha. "Swaswatee says you need to wake up."

Reeva raised an eyebrow. "You don't call her *Ba*? Or *Grandma*?"

Alisha shook her head. "She says it makes her feel old."

"And the whole world calls her Swaswatee, so we should too," added Amisha.

"Of course. Well, you can tell Swaswatee that I'll be down shortly."

"Shall we tell your boyfriend too?" asked Alisha.

"What boyfriend?" replied Reeva.

"The one from before," said Amisha. "With the dhal-proof watch."

"The white one," prompted Alisha.

Reeva's mouth fell open. "Nick? He's here?!" She pushed the cover off her. "I need to go downstairs."

Amisha wrinkled her nose. "Um, maybe you should shower first. And brush your teef."

REEVA HAD CALLED Nick the previous night. It hadn't been easy; she'd spent ten minutes reciting positive affirmations in the mirror before she'd been able to officially choose love over fear. But Nick hadn't picked up. Reeva had forced herself to accept the anticlimax and use the last of her post-prayers courage to leave a voice note.

"Hey, Nick, sorry to call out of the blue! I just, um, wanted to get in touch. Because I realized I ended things the other night out of fear, not love. Wait, that probably doesn't make sense to you. But I guess I've been really scared lately. I got overly in my head about everything, and I made assumptions that weren't necessarily real because I was listening to my insecurities instead of reality. Which wasn't fair of me. So I'm sorry.

"I'm still upset about the Hot Lips thing, and I don't know what to believe, but I should have had a proper conversation with you about it. In fact, there are a lot of things I wish I'd spoken to you about honestly. So if you'd be up for it, I'd love to try that now. An honest chat. If you want to. I'm up in Leicester again, but I'm free for a phone call whenever or to meet in London for a coffee when I'm back. Tomorrow's the last day of all this anyway— the final goodbye ceremony. Not that I'm going. But yeah. Let me know. Thanks. Bye."

Reeva had been both mortified and proud of herself for pressing send. She was not the kind of person who sent honest voice notes— she barely ever sent them to anyone who wasn't Lakshmi—yet she'd just sent one to a man she liked. Loved. And instead of leaving her reeling with anxiety, it had left her feeling empowered. She'd done what she could. The rest was up to Nick.

"You look good, Reevs," said Nick, stopping in the middle of the path in the nearby park to look at her. "More . . . relaxed than usual."

She smiled back at him. She still couldn't believe that yet again he'd come all the way to meet her with no prior warning. But one thing she was learning about Nick was that he had no qualms about driving down the M1 for a face-to-face conversation. "Thanks, I feel it. You look good too." It was true. Even though Nick had bags under his eyes and was wearing an old gray jumper instead of one of his usual pristine shirts, Reeva felt more attracted to him than normal.

"So, uh, I didn't expect to get your voice message. That was a surprise."

Reeva nodded. "I thought it might be. But . . . a good surprise?"

"It was. Though I'm still a little confused." He hesitated. "I didn't realize you weren't being your honest, real self with me, Reeva. I thought things were going well until everything with Hot Lips. I still don't know if we broke up because you think I cheated on you or because you were never happy with me."

Reeva sighed. "Okay. Maybe we should sit down. There's a lot to say."

"Should I be scared?"

Reeva shook her head as she joined Nick on the wooden bench. "Nope, that's my job. Okay. I'll . . . I'll start at the very beginning. Do-re-mi, etc."

"Excuse me?"

"Never mind." She took a deep breath and looked Nick in the eyes. "You know I was really hurt by Rakesh. It broke me. I did not see it coming, and the shock of it all just blindsided me. I've never felt so awful in my entire life. And I've been terrified of that feeling ever since."

Nick nodded. "Of course. I think we all feel that to some extent. Well, those of us who know heartbreak."

"Definitely. It's just . . . I think I've let it take over my life a little too much. Nick, you're the first person I've really liked since Rakesh. And I started to find myself daydreaming about a future with you." She put her head into her hands. "God, this is so embarrassing."

"Hey, it's okay." Nick gently peeled her hands away from her face. "I've had the odd daydream too."

"Really?" Reeva looked at him doubtfully. "Well, it freaked me out. Because . . . I really wanted it to come true, but I was so scared it would end in trauma. Again."

"Because of Rakesh?"

"Yes." She sighed again. "But also because I felt a little insecure with you. In a way I never did with Rakesh."

"Why?"

Reeva looked away, at the families having picnics on the grass and kids running around with balls. She closed her eyes for a second then turned back to Nick. "This is so hard to say. But I think it's because . . . you're so *perfect* all the time. Today's the first time I've ever seen you not wearing a dress shirt. You're way better groomed than me, which is just awkward. And I feel like you're always doing or saying the right thing, but it doesn't necessarily feel real. Also, I was a little bit intimidated by your past.

I mean, you've dated people like Hot Lips. I've just dated normal people."

Nick looked taken aback. "Wow. That's a lot. But . . . I definitely don't *feel* perfect, Reeva. Nor did I realize that was the impression I conveyed. But you know I could say the same to you. That you're intimidating. And very well-dressed, by the way."

She stared at him blankly. "Me?"

"Of course. You're so much younger than me, and your life is so much more sorted than mine was when I was your age—or even mine right now."

"It is?"

Nick laughed. "Yes! You have an amazing home you bought yourself. You love your job. And you're doing it all alone, with this mad family who doesn't see your worth. You've had to build yourself up in a way most people haven't. Reeva, if anyone's feeling insecure here, it's me."

Reeva felt tears pricking her eyelids and brushed them away quickly. "Sorry, I don't know why I'm getting emotional. It's just nice to hear. I feel like we haven't spoken this honestly before and . . . I need it, Nick."

"Why did you never say anything? I would have happily told you this before!"

"Well, because you can sometimes be a bit distant. And I get the feeling you don't want to share or have emotional chats. So sometimes I feel like I'm pushing you," admitted Reeva. "Like when we spoke about your exes. Or tried to speak about your exes."

Nick looked down at the tired bench. "You're not the first person to say that. My ex-wife used to say I was emotionally unavailable. I'm sorry, Reeva. It's not deliberate—I was just brought up in a household where we didn't share a lot. I know opening up is important though."

"Thanks for saying that." Reeva took a deep breath and tried to visualize the green feeling inside her for a boost of courage. "Also, um, lately I haven't felt you've been giving me what I need. You're very good at showing up as a big romantic gesture. But you don't call when you say you will. You go AWOL and it makes me anxious. Then, obviously, there's the fact that you can be a bit distant and off sometimes. So I, uh, demoted you in my head from an uppercase boyfriend to a lowercase one. An lcb. Because you weren't acting how I wanted a boyfriend to act."

He laughed in shock. "Wow. I have no idea what to say to that. I've been called a lot of things in my life but never an lcb." He shook his head. "Reeva, I'm sorry. I get what you're saying. I think I'm just a bit shit sometimes. I'm not used to my actions impacting someone else so much. And I suppose going to boarding school at seven wasn't the best thing for my emotional skills."

"I was eleven when I got sent off, but I can very much relate."

"You went to boarding school?"

"See!" cried Reeva. "How did we never talk about this before? This is the problem. You're distant sometimes, but *so am I*. I'm guilty of the same thing, but for different reasons maybe. I . . . was so scared of losing you that I hid things from you. I put a wall up to keep me safe when, in fact, it did the opposite."

Nick nodded slowly. "It makes sense. And I think I noticed that. Not in so many words. But I did recognize that you weren't always fully open with me. About your family and things."

"And things," repeated Reeva. "Definitely things."

Nick looked nervous. "There's more?"

"Yup." Reeva gazed miserably down at the bench. "I really, really don't want to do this. But I think I need to show you the real me. It's what Satya Auntie would tell me to do. She always says vulnerability is the only way to create connection. And if she can be brave about death, I can be brave about baldness."

"Uh, I'm a little lost. What boldness?"

Reeva closed her eyes tight. "Okay, I'm not going to look. But you can." She slowly peeled the wig away from the adhesive tape on her scalp and pulled it off.

She heard Nick inhale loudly. "Oh my god. Your hair. Where... What... Are you...?"

"Oh god, no!" Reeva opened her eyes instantly. "Sorry, no, it's not cancer. I forget that's people's first assumption. I'm just ... bald."

"Right. Wow. Because ...?"

"I have alopecia," she explained. She felt the tears coming again, but this time, she let them fall gently. "I ... um, I was losing my hair. It's been happening since I met you. As in a week after our first date. I've had bald patches all this time, and, Nick, it's been *killing* me. I didn't understand why it was happening, and the more stressed I got, the worse it got. But I think I get it now. It's about vulnerability. I thought it was a sign that I shouldn't date you, that my body was against this. But actually ... I think it was just my subconscious being scared about opening up to you. Scared of the past repeating itself. Scared about a lot of things."

"Oh, Reeva." Nick put his hand on her arm and squeezed it tight. "I can't believe you've been dealing with this on top of everything and you didn't say anything. You poor thing."

She lowered her voice to a whisper. "I didn't want you to stop fancying me. It's why I couldn't let you in to see me when you came to my flat. My wigs hadn't arrived."

"Uh, this makes me fancy you more."

Reeva stared. "Do you have a bald fetish?"

"No! I just think it's very cool you can get through this. My sister had alopecia once—just a tiny patch. And she didn't handle it well. She spoke about it nonstop for weeks. She wouldn't leave the house."

"I *thought* about mine nonstop for weeks," said Reeva. "And I tried to hide in my house for a week after I shaved it all off."

"It sounds like you faced it head-on and handled it incredibly well."

"I'm not sure I'd say *well*. I have a fair bit of news to catch you up on."

"Look at you, wanting to share your news with me." He punched her arm gently. "Bald Reeva seems bolder."

"No bald puns, please." She looked into Nick's familiar brown eyes with their little green flecks. "But I am sorry for not being honest with you. I wish I had been. It would have made things easier."

Nick nodded. "I know. I feel the same way. I should have told you what was going on with Hot Lips. I fucked up by not telling you we used to date. That was stupid of me, and of course it made you not trust me when the pictures came out. But, Reeva." He took both her hands in his. "Please, please believe me that nothing happened between us."

"Then why was she there? Half-naked?"

"She wasn't okay," said Nick quietly. "She was suicidal. Badly."

"Oh my god."

"I know. I wanted to tell you, but I didn't feel it was my secret to tell. But I trust you. I know this won't go farther than this park bench, and if I want you to believe me, I have to be honest with you."

"Of course. Is she okay now?"

"She's a lot better. She's been struggling with some issues for a while, which I won't share, and they got worse in LA. She had a breakdown that night when she was in bed with a random guy. That's why she came to my flat in her underwear. It was the opposite of a romantic encounter. She was at her rock bottom."

Reeva couldn't imagine someone like Hot Lips ever being in such a vulnerable state, but she knew Nick wouldn't lie about something like this. She brought her hand to her heart. She knew what that felt like—that pain of desperation and misery. "Poor Hot Lips," she breathed out. "I'm so sorry. I hope she's getting the help she needs. And . . . as hard as it's been, I'm glad you were there for her."

Nick shook his head. "God, I can't believe I ever thought you'd react with anything other than total empathy. I should have told you from the start."

Reeva smiled. "That's down to my aunt. She's been teaching me to be more compassionate. Apparently once we give it to ourselves, we can give it to everyone else."

"Your aunt's a wise lady."

Reeva's eyes glazed over. "She really is. She's the one who helped me be so honest. Nick?"

"Yes?"

"Shall we try again?"

Nick's face lit up. "Really? I know you said you didn't feel safe with me . . . I don't want to make you feel like that."

"I think the problem was I didn't feel safe in myself. But that's already changing. And I'm learning to ask for what I need."

He beamed. "Okay. Then let's start over again."

Reeva cocked her head. "You know what, let's not view it as starting again. I don't want to erase the past few months. We've learned a lot, even if it has been messy. But that doesn't make it a failure. It's part of our story. Let's own it—and keep going."

Nick caressed the back of her bald head with his hand. "You're right. Let's keep going and make sure that from now on, we're fully honest with each other."

"Deal. In that case," Reeva said, smiling, "I would very much like you to kiss me right now."

"That's very convenient, because I was just thinking how much I'd like to kiss *you* right now." He leaned in and placed his lips on Reeva's. "Thank you."

"For what?"

"Being your truest you."

## CHAPTER 27

**Day 14**

REEVA KNEW SHE was meant to be happy. And she was. It felt so good—and so right—to have sorted things out with Nick. Especially as he was now in the living room winning over her mum (with excessive flattery), MJ (with cricket knowledge), and the twins (by letting them use him as a human jungle gym). But while Nick was slowly becoming more important to her, he wasn't the most important person in her life. That was Lakshmi. And they still weren't speaking.

It made Reeva feel unbearably guilty. When she'd had her realization about love and fear during her dad's prayers, she'd chosen to reach out to Nick first. It had felt like the most authentic thing to do in the moment—and also the easiest. He'd been in her life for only a few months; the stakes were so much lower. Reeva didn't regret fixing things with him first. But she knew she needed to speak to Lakshmi, and with each day that passed without her doing exactly that, the lump in her stomach grew bigger. She didn't need Satya Auntie to tell her this suffering meant she wasn't aligned with her truth. A truth that was obviously about her love for Lakshmi.

But she couldn't do anything about this, not just because of her fear of confrontation, but because Lakshmi wasn't answering her phone. Reeva had already tried three times. If Lakshmi was screening her calls, how was she meant to reach her? An e-mail? A rom-com-style spontaneous visit—like the ones Nick was so fond of? She supposed she could do it once she was back in London on the weekend. But how would she know where Lakshmi was? The best thing would be to do it when Lakshmi was at work.

Like . . . today. It would mean definitely missing the kriya, but she didn't even want to go. Besides, she'd been to her dad's prayers the night before; surely that was enough? Her mum would be furious, and her sisters would be disappointed, but Reeva knew that didn't matter. She had to do what was right for *her*, not them. She just wished she knew what that was.

"Reeva?" There was a gentle knock at the door.

She opened it quickly. "Satya Auntie! I'm so glad to see you. How are you feeling?"

Her aunt smiled weakly and sat down on the bed. "I'm well, thank you. Much better to be out of the hospital. How are you?"

"Oh, fine, thanks. You look great! But are you sure you're okay to be here? I would have come to get you if I'd known."

"I'm not dead yet! There's no need to fuss."

Reeva colored. "Okay. Sorry. I just . . . if I can do anything, let me know, okay?"

"Of course." Her aunt squeezed her hand. "It was nice to see Nick here. He's lovely. And most importantly, he really seems to see your worth."

Reeva broke into a smile. "I took your advice. I was my

complete honest self with him. I showed him my vulnerability—literally. I took my wig off."

"I'm so glad," cried her aunt. "Well done for being brave. That's true intimacy. 'Into me you see.'"

"I love that!"

"But why do you look so worried?" asked her aunt. "And don't tell me it's just about me."

Reeva shook her head, laughing. "How do you know everything?

"It's what I'm here for. Your Satya Lama is here to help."

Reeva put her arms around her aunt and let her head fall on her shoulders. "Thank you. I'm so grateful for you." She felt her shoulders relax as her aunt stroked her wig. "I just really miss Lakshmi. I've been too scared to reach out, but now I'm desperate to fix things. I've tried to call and message, but she isn't replying. It's stressing me out. I'm tempted to just drive to London and find her. But then I'll miss the kriya. And I know I always said I'd miss it. But . . . the closer we get to it, the more it feels like a very big deal to not go."

"What do you really want to do?" asked Satya Auntie. "What does your heart say?"

Reeva bit her lip. "I guess . . . my heart wants me to be with Lakshmi. I miss her so much."

"Well, there you have it. The head is always rational, but the heart tells us what we always want to do."

"What if I regret missing the kriya?"

"What if you don't?"

"I do feel that even if I stay, I won't be able to be present," admitted Reeva slowly. "I'll just be in my head. About Lakshmi. About what my dad did. But I feel guilty for not doing my duty to, well, my family."

"Oh, duty shmuty." Her aunt dismissively waved a hand. "Duty rips people's lives apart. You only need to watch one of your mum's films to see that. The important thing is to follow your duty to *yourself*—to be authentic to your heart. Not to follow other people's expectations. Otherwise, what's the point in life? You're here to live your life, not anyone else's."

"It just feels so hard sometimes. To do what's right for me."

"I know." Her aunt sighed. "I've been through it too. But at least then, when you get to where I am, nearing the end, you can look back and be proud you've lived your own true life. Rather than people-pleasing and living the life others wanted for you. Or, worse, straddling them both and not really living a life at all."

Reeva looked alarmed. "That sounds terrible. I definitely want to live my life—or at least *a* life."

"Then off you go."

"Just . . . leave? Can I really? I should say bye first. Shouldn't I?"

"No such thing as *shoulds*."

Reeva hesitated. "If I told them, they'd probably try to stop me. Could you tell them? And Nick? I'll call him on the way as well."

Satya Auntie nodded. "Of course. Good luck, Reeva. I'm proud of you, you know."

"You are?"

"Yes. It's beautiful how important your friendship is to you."

"Lakshmi's more than a friend; she's family."

REEVA RACED DOWN the M1 southbound—again. But this time she was alive with excitement. She knew her actions were irrational, and only Satya Auntie would understand why she couldn't wait till the next day, but she didn't care. She could not pretend to herself for another second that she was fine with not speaking to Lakshmi. It had been weighing on her for days, and the more time passed, the more she was convinced it was all her fault. Lakshmi was not a perfect friend, and it was true she did often take Reeva for granted, but the way Reeva had handled their last conversation had been downright offensive. There was no excuse for judging a friend. Which was why she was desperate to redeem herself by giving Lakshmi her unconditional blessing to date Lee or literally any other man she ever wanted and, most importantly, to say sorry.

Her thoughts were interrupted by her phone ringing loudly just as she hit traffic. She answered the hands-free call without looking at the dashboard. "Hello?"

"Reevs, it's me. What's your dad's address again?"

Reeva jolted. "Lakshmi?! Is that you?"

"Yeah, of course. I need the address. What is it?"

"But why? And where have you been? I need to talk to you!"

"Yes, I know we need to talk," said Lakshmi, like she was talking to a child. "Hence, I need your dad's address so I can talk to you in person."

"Uh, why? I'll text it to you later."

"Later isn't going to work. I'm about five junctions away from Leicester, so I need it now, please."

"What! But . . . I'm on my way to London to see you."

There was silence. "Are you serious? Now?"

"Yes! I left about forty-five minutes ago."

"But what about the kriya?"

"I wanted to see you. I need to fix things with you. I just couldn't wait another moment. And it felt weird to sit and do a family thing when you weren't speaking to me. You're my family, and you should be there. Or I should be with you. Whatever."

"You're so weird." Lakshmi sniffed. "You could have come to see me any day, not kriya day."

"Oh my god, are you *crying*? You never cry!"

"Shut up, of course I'm not. God, that traffic looks terrible."

"Wait, where are you? I'm in traffic right now. There's some police and an accident."

"Shit! Then I must be passing you now. But the other way, obviously."

"Well, let's get off," said Reeva. "At a services or something."

"Uh, but the services are different on the different sides of the motorway. I love you, but I'm not walking across the M1 for you."

"Just . . . go wait at the next services. I'll get off now and turn around and come find you."

"This sounds complicated. Are you sure?"

"Yeah! Just WhatsApp me your location. We'll be fine. I'll see you in five minutes."

THIRTY-FIVE MINUTES AND five stressed-out phone calls later, Reeva finally pulled up next to Lakshmi's car at the Watford Gap northbound services.

"Well, this is glamorous," said Lakshmi, as she wound down her window. "Shall we at least go for a coffee? There's a Costa over there."

"Let's do it. And I can get you some apology flowers from M&S; I didn't have time to do it beforehand."

"Perfect; I'll buy yours too," said Lakshmi, getting out of her car. "Oh my god! Reevs! Your hair! You look like Beyoncé. I'm obsessed."

"Thanks." Reeva smiled at her over the top of her Mini. "It's a wig."

"But I was meant to go wig shopping with you! We always said if your alopecia got so bad you needed to go bald, I'd treat you to . . . Oh my god! It got worse?"

Tears pricked Reeva's eyes as she nodded.

Lakshmi walked over and hugged her. "Oh, baby. When?"

"The day of the funeral. Sita found three extra bald patches on my head. So that night . . ." Reeva looked down at the tarmac. "After you and I fought, I lost my shit and did a Britney."

Lakshmi gasped. "Are you kidding me? That's the most bad-ass thing I've ever heard! I just revenge-ate your expensive chocolates. And used your entire Jo Malone bath oil. Sorry."

"Jealous. I had to wash my bald head with Travelodge toiletries."

Lakshmi looked at her admiringly. "You're so brave. Can . . . I see it?"

Reeva hesitated, then shrugged. "Fuck it." She pulled off the wig. "My bald head in all its glory. Or my vulnerability, as Satya Auntie calls it."

Lakshmi burst into tears. "God, I'm such a bad friend. You've been going through so much. I should have been there for you!"

"No, no, no!" cried Reeva. "I do not deserve this apology. I was driving to see you because I need to apologize to you! I was a sexist bitch. I was judgy and mean. There is no excuse for it, and honestly, Lakshmi, I feel *terrible* for what I said. I was just taking out my feelings on you, okay? I was projecting."

Lakshmi wiped tears from her eyes. "No, but you were right. I do always get myself in dramas and involve you in them. And it wasn't cool of me to sleep with Lee while I was cat-sitting. I didn't tell you this, but . . . FP saw us, Reeva. She saw us *in bed.*"

"Okay, and?"

"A cat shouldn't have to see that! And . . . she *licked* my fingers afterward! I'm so sorry."

Reeva gagged. "Okay, that is disgusting. Please can we never talk about this again? But, Lakshmi, it's fine. You're allowed a sex life when you have a cat. I think."

"I should have tried harder to go to the funeral." Lakshmi looked down. "I could have come after court. Only Lee was free then. And . . . I chose to see him instead."

Reeva felt her stomach tighten and a familiar defensive wall creep up around her. But then she remembered she was someone who told the truth now. "Thanks for telling me that. But it does hurt to hear. I really needed you, and it makes me feel . . . unimportant that you picked Lee over me."

"I'm so sorry," said Lakshmi in a small voice. "I know I let you down. But Lee isn't more important than you. You're the most important person in my life. I just followed my vagina instead of my heart."

Reeva brushed away a tear. "That's very good to hear because you're the most important person in *my* life. And to be honest, I've put my vagina before you too. I fixed things with Nick before I fixed them with you."

"Really? But I didn't even know there was anything to fix with Nick! I'm so out of the loop."

"I think we have a lot to catch each other up on. Like . . . your entire last year with Lee!"

"I know. I haven't been honest with you lately. I'm sorry, Reevs—I was just scared of the judgment."

Reeva nodded slowly. "I get that. And I'm sorry. I know I can be a bit moral sometimes, and it's not fair of me to judge you.

You're my best friend, and I want you to be able to tell me anything." She paused. "But while we're being super honest, I need to tell you that sometimes I don't feel like there's always space for *me* to be frank about how I feel in our friendship."

"What do you mean?"

"You're so confident that sometimes I feel my opinions get lost over yours," admitted Reeva. "It's probably my own insecurity issues more than anything. But it's hard sometimes."

Lakshmi exhaled. "Wow. Okay. I feel fucking horrible I've made you feel like that."

"Please don't! I know it's not deliberate. I just needed to say it out loud so that you know. It's on me too, and I know I've been selfish lately. I'm . . . I'm sorry for everything, Lux."

"I'm sorry too. I love you."

Reeva put her arms around her friend and squeezed her tight. "I love you too. God, Satya Auntie is so right; being honest is amazing."

"I need to meet this Satya Auntie. In fact, oh my god! We need to go!"

"Where?"

"To the kriya! We're going to miss it."

"But I'm missing it anyway. I left to find you. It doesn't matter."

"Yes, and you found me only forty-five minutes from Leicester. So . . . let's go."

Reeva hesitated. "I don't know if I want to. Lux, I found out the secret about my dad."

Lakshmi squeezed her hand. "I know, Reevs. Your sisters told me."

"What?!"

"They called me yesterday. They seemed to think you needed

me. It was quite sweet, actually. I mean—they're both fucking insane. They could barely get through a sentence without contradicting each other. But they do seem to care about you."

Reeva stared at her. "I . . . did not expect that."

"I know, me either. I'd been wanting to reach out for a while anyway, only my pride stopped me. But when they told me what you'd been through, my pride fucked off and I got in my car. Because I should have been at the funeral with you and I wasn't. So I'm going to be at the kriya with you instead."

"But I don't know if I can," whispered Reeva. "Lux, I started to think I *loved* him last week; then, when I found out what he did, it all changed. I was so angry when I thought he'd killed my cat—don't laugh, I know it's weird. But when I found out it was me, I just felt so . . . lost. And betrayed. And kind of humiliated? I just . . . I hate that he wasn't the dad I dreamed he'd be."

"I know. I mean, I don't. But I can imagine. And I've done some research. I've been listening to some podcasts on alcoholism and Al-Anon."

"What is that?"

"It's a twelve-step program, like AA, but it's for people who are affected by alcoholics rather than the alcoholics themselves. It sounds kind of amazing, Reevs—you should totally go. But their message is all about realizing you're not responsible for someone else's issues and letting go of any resentment, because holding on to it is just going to hurt you."

Reeva's brow creased. "I don't know if I can let go though. It's all I think about."

"Of course you do; you only just found out," said Lakshmi. "It's a whole process—a twelve-step one. You don't have to let go overnight. But I do think they have a point in everything they're saying. There's a quote about how when our loved ones don't meet our expectations, it's our expectations, not our loved ones, that have let us down."

Reeva laughed. "Wow. Satya Auntie would love that."

Lakshmi squeezed her hand. "Look, it's your choice. But I think it might help you to let go. To say bye. You don't have to forgive him or anything—it's just a way for you to say whatever you need to say to him and get closure."

"I just wish I could have done that while he was still alive."

"His soul *is* still meant to be on earth for another . . . twenty-five minutes, approx."

Reeva laughed. "It's only a Hindu ceremony. It's not like I believe in the soul stuff. What's he going to do, have a father-daughter reunion from beyond the grave?"

Lakshmi frowned. "I think it's more about you and telling him how you feel. Rather than what he says to you. You know?"

Reeva felt her resolve waver. "I don't know anything, Lux. I just . . . I don't even know what I'd want to say to him. And I'm scared."

"Hey, I'm right here. By your side. The whole way."

Reeva nodded. "Okay . . ." She glanced at her phone. "But even if I wanted to go, it starts in twenty-five minutes. And we're at least forty-five minutes away."

"Oh, Hindu priests are always late. We'll text them. Get them to hold off on the soul-leaving bit till we get there. They can just do the preamble. And what have you got to lose?"

"My sanity?"

"Overrated! Come on!"

Reeva hesitated. She tried to think of what Satya Auntie had said to her about love and fear. Her desire to not go to the kriya was pure fear. She was terrified of how she'd feel and all the emotions that could come up. But going to the kriya . . . In a way, it could be the loving thing to do for her younger self. She didn't have to go to forgive her dad—she could go to forgive *herself.*

"Okay. You're right. I'm going to go—but not for anyone else, not even for my dad. I'm going for me. Little me."

## CHAPTER 28

**Day 14**

REEVA AND LAKSHMI pulled up in tandem outside her dad's house. She supposed she should stop calling it that at some point—maybe after his soul had officially departed Earth. Lakshmi had sent her a podcast to listen to about Al-Anon and Reeva already felt like a slightly different person. There was a whole community of people out there who'd been hurt by their loved ones' alcoholism in completely different ways. And they weren't focusing on the alcoholic; their whole program was about focusing on *themselves.* If they chose to forgive, it was for themselves. If they chose to be radically honest, it was for themselves. And if they chose to see their part in it, it was all for themselves. It was surprisingly empowering.

"Come on!" Lakshmi was already out of her car, rapping on Reeva's window. "Get out."

Reeva rolled her eyes as she turned off her car. "Okay, okay. What's the rush? I thought they were waiting for us?"

"I need to pee. Hurry up!"

They pressed the doorbell, but there was no answer. Reeva knocked loudly on the door.

"They'll all be in the garden," said Lakshmi, crossing her legs tightly. "Shout through the letterbox."

Reeva obediently crouched down to open the letterbox. "Hel-looooo? Is anyone—"

The door swung open, leaving Reeva face-to-face with Rakesh's crotch.

"Oh! Hi." Reeva quickly straightened up, flushing. "I . . . didn't realize you'd be here."

"Yeah, Jaya asked me to come. Close family and all."

Reeva shook her head imperceptibly. It made no sense to her that Rakesh was part of her family without being a part of her life. "Makes sense."

Lakshmi waved her hand and pushed past him. "Hi and bye. Sorry to interrupt the awkward hellos but I need to pee. And check the priest waited."

"Oh, don't worry, the priest isn't even here yet."

"Should have known." Lakshmi sighed. "Indian timing." She disappeared in the direction of voices, leaving Reeva standing with Rakesh in the hallway.

"Uh, congratulations on the baby," said Reeva.

"Thank you," replied Rakesh. He shuffled awkwardly. "Look, I . . . I'm sorry, Reeva. I never meant—"

"It's fine," interrupted Reeva. "You did all this four years ago. I've heard the apology speech. You don't need to do it again."

"I know, but we haven't spoken since, and I'm going to be your brother-in-law. I feel like we should talk."

Reeva winced. "Can you please not call yourself my brother-in-law?"

"Sorry. Of course." Rakesh looked expectantly at Reeva. "So . . . can we talk?"

Reeva had no desire to do this. All she wanted was to walk away from her ex—or say whatever was necessary to make him leave her alone. But just as she was about to reassure Rakesh that everything was fine, she stopped herself. That was her fear. And she was done letting fear rule her life. It was time to let love— love for *herself*—run the show. She looked directly at Rakesh. "Okay. Well, none of this has been easy for me. You left me in the most brutal way possible—for my sister. It broke me. My entire life fell apart, and I genuinely think the shock of it all trauma- tized me. It was the worst thing I've ever been through, and I still have no idea how I got through it."

Rakesh hung his head. "I know. I'm sorry."

"I know, but just saying sorry isn't actually helpful."

"Uh, okay." Rakesh looked taken aback. "What is? Helpful, I mean."

Reeva thought about it. "Some empathy would be good. Do you know *why* it broke me so much? I mean, how would you have felt if I'd cheated on you with your brother? And it all came out of the blue."

"I'd be humiliated," said Rakesh instantly. "Furious. Betrayed."

"Sure. But what if you'd thought we'd be together forever and that our happy future was pretty much set in stone? And then suddenly that was taken from you—as well as your brother?"

Rakesh's shoulders dropped. "I'd be devastated."

"Yep. So was I. I felt so safe and secure with you, then you did that, and I lost everything. I had to mourn our future. Our un- born kids. All the things we'd talked about doing. And I lost our past, because when you cheated, you took that away too. I didn't even know who you were anymore. It was like a bereavement. The grief was never-ending."

"It must have been agony. I . . . I struggle to think about it, if I'm honest, because it's just so bad. But I really hate I did that to you."

"Thanks. Thank you. I hate that you did it too. But you know what? I'm learning to be happy now. Without you. By myself."

"You do really seem happy. You look great too. Your hair is amazing."

"My hair? Oh, it's not mine." Reeva peeled the wig off and watched his face rapidly transform from admiration to shock, followed by total horror. "This is mine."

"But . . . what happened? Are you okay? I . . ."

"I'm great, thank you," said Reeva, realizing that she meant it. "And you know what? I do feel better. I guess there were some things I wanted to get off my chest and say to you. Just to have you hear them. Thanks for suggesting it."

"Uh, you're . . . welcome?"

Reeva smiled brightly at Rakesh, dumped her wig on the table, and walked off to find her family.


"NICK?" REEVA STARED at him in surprise. "What are you still doing here? I thought you would have left hours ago!"

He was leaning against the counter with Satya Auntie, sipping chai. The rest of her family was crowded into the kitchen— MJ was playing with the twins, her mum was yawning loudly as Jaya showed her something on her phone, and Sita and Lakshmi were sniggering in the corner. "You're back! And wigless. Nice."

"I'll leave you two to it," said Satya Auntie. "Saraswati looks like she needs rescuing. And you look wonderful, Reeva."

"Thanks, Satya Auntie." Reeva looked around to see the rest of her family's reaction, but no one had even acknowledged her arrival. Obviously. She turned back to Nick. "Uh, you got my message, right?

"Yes, but they persuaded me to stay for tea, and when I was about to leave, Sita got a call saying you were coming back. So I stayed."

"You didn't have to. I didn't expect you to be here for the kriya. It's a proper Hindu ceremony. You might find it . . . a bit much. I know it's not your world."

Nick flushed. "Yeah. I told a friend of mine I'd said that to you, and she made me realize I was a complete dick. I was just being ignorant; I should have sat through my discomfort, like I'm sure you have many times for me."

Reeva nodded slowly. "Thanks. That's really good to hear. Because, to be honest, I did want some moral support. I am Indian, yes, but I don't feel particularly comfortable with any of this either. I've celebrated more bat mitzvahs than Diwalis."

"I hear that. Which is why I want to be here for the kriya. To support you. As your boyfriend."

"That's quite uppercase of you . . ."

"I thought you wanted an uppercase boyfriend?"

"I do," said Reeva quickly. "Definitely. I just . . ." She sighed. "Fuck, telling the truth never ends, does it? Okay. I'm just a bit scared that if you're a UCB, my expectations of you will build up, then you'll let me down and I'll end up massively disappointed."

Nick nodded slowly. "I hear you. Well, how about we talk about what we expect from a partner and then work out where we stand on things? A proper adult chat about what we need from each other."

"I would love that! Yes. Please. Can we do spreadsheets too? Lists?"

"Uh, if you want to?"

"I would *love* to."

Nick laughed. "Okay, well, come here. Let me kiss you. And your bald head."

Reeva bit her lip. "I can't believe I'm not wearing my wig in front of you. Again."

"I love that you're not."

"Oh my god!" cried Jaya loudly. "Reeva, you're not wearing your wig!"

The whole room turned to look at Reeva.

"Uh, yeah, I took it off."

"But . . ." Jaya faltered, looking from Nick to Rakesh.

"I think she looks great," said Sita. "Powerful."

"Definitely!" agreed Lakshmi. "It kind of works with your bone structure too."

"Uh, am I missing something?" asked MJ. "Reeva, is this a new fashion look?"

"No!" cried out Saraswati. "Definitely not. She's just waiting for her wig that's coming from India. You will wear it, won't you, Reeva? Please?"

Reeva laughed. "Sure, Mum. But I'm still going to go bald sometimes too. Mix it up, you know?"

"Love that," cried Jaya. "Like the Buddhist nuns in Nepal. Very cool."

Reeva turned to Satya Auntie. "Wait, did you shave your hair off when you were a nun?"

Her aunt nodded. "Of course. We all did."

"No way! I love that I'm doing what you did. It makes me feel so . . ."

"Nunlike?" offered Jaya.

"I was going to say connected. But sure. I do also feel a bit nunlike."

"Or priestlike," said Nick, gesturing toward the doorway, where Rakesh was now standing next to the elderly male priest with a shiny bald head. "You guys are rocking the same hairstyle. Though yours looks cuter, obviously."

"OKAY, SO ON the kriya, we finish thirteen days of samskara. Though here, is fourteen days. But it's okay. We can be flexible." Reeva stifled a yawn. The priest had been talking forever, in Sanskrit and Gujarati, as he chanted and waved his hands around with incense, but now he was trying to engage his audience by swapping to broken English. Reeva's gaze fell on her family. They were all in the garden sitting in a circle: her mum and MJ, Satya Auntie directly opposite her, Nick, Lakshmi, Rakesh, the twins, and her sisters on either side of her. Nick, Lakshmi, Rakesh, and MJ all seemed politely interested, but the rest of them—the blood relatives—looked unashamedly bored.

"We will offer the rice balls and milk to the deceased, to Hemant Bhai, to show our gratitude for his life. We, his family, are grateful he was allowed to join us on Earth for this time." Having completed his speech, the priest swapped back to Gujarati, not realizing he was now alienating more than half his audience as he chanted his way through the various rituals.

"Guess that's all the English he's got," Sita whispered to Reeva.

"I have no idea what's going on," Reeva whispered back. "When does the soul go?"

"No idea. But at the rate he's going, Jaya will have had her baby by the time it's over."

"What?" Jaya leaned over, speaking in full volume. "What did you say about me?"

"Ssh!" said Reeva. "The priest will get mad."

"Uh, he looks pretty preoccupied," said Sita.

"Mum's giving us evils," said Jaya. "But her forehead doesn't move properly. Oh my god, look."

Reeva laughed despite herself. She caught Nick's eye and he grinned.

"Cute!" cried Jaya. "Sorry, sorry." She tried to lower her voice. "You guys are very cute."

"I told him he was an lcb," whispered Reeva. "He found it funny, but he's also going to up his game!"

"About time," hissed Sita. "You should have told him earlier. People can't give you what you want if you don't ask for it."

Reeva nodded. Her sister had a point. "Well, I think I've finally learned to ask for what I want. At age thirty-four."

"Took you long enough," said Sita.

Reeva shot her a look.

"Hey, shall we go to the bathroom after this?" asked Jaya as quietly as she could. "Take some snacks up?"

"I already hid a bottle of wine in the laundry basket," whispered Sita. "And juice for Jaya. Oh, and I've invited Satya Auntie to join us."

"I wonder what Dad would think," said Reeva wryly. "He wanted us to pray for him and clear his stuff out. Instead, we've just snooped around and gotten drunk in the bath."

"It could be worse," said Sita. "We could have done oral sex in his bed. Oh, wait . . ."

Reeva glared at her as Jaya snorted. The priest glanced over to them and gave them all a warning glare. Jaya widened her eyes and smiled prettily at him, Sita met his eyes defiantly, and Reeva mouthed *Sorry* in apology.

"Let's be quiet now," she whispered. "I feel like I need to actually be here after all the drama of me getting here."

Her sisters shrugged as Reeva closed her eyes and tried to connect with herself the way she had during the previous night's prayers. She found her thoughts going to her dad and what the priest had said about gratitude. It felt odd to feel gratitude toward her father—this complex man whose deep problems had torn their family apart and almost taken her life from her—but Reeva wanted to try. Especially before they said goodbye to him forever.

*Dad*, she said internally, hoping that somewhere out there, he'd hear her. *I'm sorry for ruining your funeral. I wish things had been different. I don't know how to feel about what you did back then. Your drinking, your anger . . . What happened to me.* Reeva paused her internal speech as she felt a tear well up in her eye. *But I'm starting to realize what Satya Auntie meant, about how life isn't an exam to pass or fail. I don't need to feel a certain way—I can just feel how I feel. And I don't need to forgive you or hate you. I can just accept it. What happened. It doesn't mean I condone it. But I can accept that it happened.*

Reeva felt a tightness loosen inside her. She closed her eyes and breathed deeply. *I think I'm starting to get the mercy thing too. We're all imperfect. I've made mistakes too. And, Dad, I respect the fact that you got sober. I know that's not easy. And I'm grateful to you for staying away from us when you didn't feel you were safe for us to be around. I know you cared for us and that you loved us in your way. It's not necessarily what I wanted—I think I've been living in a bit of fantasy about you my entire life—but it's what there is. And, Dad, in spite of everything, all the pain, I hope you're okay in the afterlife. I hope you're at peace. Don't worry about me—I'm not mad at you anymore. I'm . . . I'm letting go. Bye, Dad. I . . . I love you.*

A tear slid down Reeva's cheek. Part of her really did love this man, with his IKEA-furnished house, his folder of mementoes of his daughters, his quiet life, and his odd group of friends who had religiously come to mourn him each night. She didn't love the way he'd acted when he drank. But she didn't have to approve of his behavior to love him. She could accept that he'd changed and done everything he could to make sure he never hurt any of them again. And she was grateful to him. For taking care of her during those early years and for continuing to care about her afterward. Reeva felt herself crying silently, shoulders shaking, as she thought about her father printing out her headshot from her firm's website.

Reeva felt a hand slip into hers from her left side—it was Jaya. A knee pressed itself against her right leg. Sita. Across the circle, Lakshmi blew her a kiss.

She wasn't alone. She had her sisters. Her infuriating, exhausting sisters. But they were family. And she loved them. If she applied the mercy thing to everyone, not just her dad, then there was no space for her to resent anyone anymore. She was equal to everyone in this garden—to everyone in this world. She finally truly understood the meaning of everything Satya Auntie had been telling her all this time. Reeva had been taking the tiny details of life so seriously, but in the face of death, none of it mattered. Her dad was gone. Her aunt was dying. And one day, she'd go too. Would she really care that Rakesh had left her for Jaya? Or that Nick's ex was Hot Lips? Or that her sisters were rude and her mum was a self-centered drama queen? It wasn't like she was perfect either.

Reeva closed her eyes tight and smiled. It was almost funny how much time she'd wasted worrying about things that didn't matter. She had only one life, and she was determined to *live* it. She had no idea how long she'd get to do that—with so much death happening around her, it no longer felt like a given that she'd reach old age. But Reeva knew exactly how she wanted to live the life she had left: as herself. It didn't matter what happened next, whether her hair grew back or stayed bald and patchy forever. She was beautiful and loved, just the way she was. There was no point wishing things were different from how they were. All she wanted to do now was accept the reality that was her life rather than the imaginary one she'd been fantasizing about forever. To be thankful for what had been given to her, what had been taken away, and what had been left behind.

She opened her eyes. MJ was yawning stiffly. Nick looked fascinated by the priest's actions. Saraswati was weeping delicately. Jaya was copying her. Satya Auntie was sitting stoically. Sita was trying to get the twins to sit still and not throw things in the priest's fire. Lakshmi was eyeing up the ladoos off to the side. Rakesh was holding Jaya's hand. Reeva waited for the familiar pang of pain to come, but she felt nothing. The Rakesh she'd known and loved was gone. This Rakesh was someone else— someone who was suitable for Jaya, not her. And she'd changed too. She wasn't the anxious people-pleasing Reeva she used to be; she was simply herself. She knew that she still had a long journey ahead of her, especially when it came to processing everything that had happened, but she felt okay about it. Because for the first time in her life, Reeva Mehta could feel something that resembled inner peace.

## CHAPTER 29

**Day 264**

REEVA APPRAISED HER reflection in the mirror. Her skin was golden after an unusually sunny June, and it looked radiant against her crisp white sundress. She'd paired it all with gold sandals, Satya Auntie's favorite dangly earrings, and a white silk scarf tied in a bow on top of her head. Her baldness no longer shocked her the way it had all those months ago; she kind of liked the way her face looked without the softness of hair framing it. Some of her patches had healed, but new ones had cropped up at the same time, so Reeva had decided to stay bald while her head did its thing.

And she was proud of her alopecia. It reminded her to stay honest and vulnerable, and that healing wasn't a linear thing. Besides, it meant she could look like Beyoncé whenever she wanted to. She took a step back from the mirror, wondering if her outfit needed something else. Lipstick. She reached for the tube and carefully applied a bright, bold red. There. Reeva was officially funeral ready.

"Finished checking yourself out?" Nick wandered into the bathroom behind her, wrapping his arms around her waist.

She smiled back at him in the mirror, leaning against his white T-shirt. "Just about. How's it going downstairs?"

"The priest is still doing the rituals, but your family asked to pause for chai and croissants."

"Naturally. Is the priest as livid as last time?"

"Oh yes. He didn't even accept the pain au choc I offered him."

Reeva turned to look at Nick. "Ah. That'll be because our house is still impure post-death. You're not meant to offer food and drinks to guests yet."

He groaned. "Yet another rule I've broken."

"You'll get the hang of it. Like me learning how to stack your parents' dishwasher the right way."

"I'm pretty sure stacking the dishwasher poorly isn't as bad as offending a Hindu priest."

"I'm not sure your mum would agree."

The door burst open. Sita—her hair piled high in a messy bun—stuck her head around the door. "Can you hurry up? I can't stand watching Jaya take any more selfies with that baby of hers. It's fucking ridiculous."

Amisha and Alisha ran into the room. "Mummy said a bad word!"

"Yes, and she's going to say another one if you don't get downstairs right now," replied Sita. "Go on! Go climb all over your favorite Saraswati. Get her to make you cucumber sticks again. She's got grandma debts to make up for." The twins ran out, thundering down the stairs.

Nick followed them. "I'll try and make peace with the priest. See you downstairs, Reevs."

Reeva turned to Sita. "So how is single-mum life? Better now that Mum is pulling her weight?"

Sita sat down on the edge of the bath, shifting her white cotton kurta so it didn't crumple against her jeans. "Mildly better, but still fucking tiring."

"You are swearing more than usual."

"I know. And this is me on good behavior." She looked up at Reeva. "If you ever have kids, please make sure you know what you're signing up for. I thought everything would be easier without Nitin because he seemed to create problems rather than solve them, but it's not. At least I could dump the girls on him while I washed my hair. Or went to the supermarket. But now, every time I leave them in a room alone, I end up with a paint-splattered couch or one of them covered in bruises. I think my local GP is about to call social services on me."

"I can sort that," said Reeva, sitting down on the closed loo seat. "Do something lawyerly and make it go away."

"Thanks. I might need it."

"But what about when Nitin has the twins? Isn't that easier?"

Sita exhaled longingly. "Yes. Oh god, yes. The best two weekends of every month. Apart from when he calls me every ten minutes asking whether they can eat calamari or some other bullshit."

"Can they?"

"They can eat anything! Whether they *will* is another thing entirely."

"Well, they seem to be doing great. I'm so happy you made the choice to leave Nitin properly."

"Me too. And . . . what about you? You and Nick seem pretty loved up."

"Yep." Reeva couldn't stop herself from smiling. "It feels so good to finally have that intimacy I've always wanted. I forgot how amazing it feels to have a connection like that with some-one."

"Way to rub it in."

Reeva forced herself to stop smiling. "Sorry. But if it helps, it's also not the magic fairy-tale ending I thought it would be. He's not the center of my life—that's still me. And to be honest, I have a lot going on."

"Are you still going to all those meetings? Al-Anon?"

Reeva nodded. "Yeah. I kind of love it, Sita—you should come one day. It's teaching me so much. I feel like I'm learning to focus on myself rather than trying to take responsibility for everyone. And I'm living in honesty, rather than fantasy like I always used to."

Sita raised an eyebrow. "Isn't the whole point meant to be focusing on healing your trauma rather than all this self-improvement crap?"

Reeva rolled her eyes. "It's not crap—it's spiritual growth. And I'm healing my trauma too. It's a process."

"Well, at least it gave you the confidence to finally quit your job and create your own firm. It was about bloody time."

"I know—I'm still not over how good it feels." Reeva grinned. "And I couldn't have done it without you. Thanks for being my first client."

"Guuyyys? Where you at?" Jaya burst into the room in a floaty white maxi dress, her hair falling in perfect waves, with her baby suckling from her left breast. She looked like an Instagram ad for motherhood. "I can't believe you're doing a bathroom hang without me! And Maya."

Reeva felt the same pang of annoyance that hit her every time someone said the baby's name—the name she'd always told her family she'd give her own daughter. But when Jaya shrieked in pain as Maya bit her nipple, Reeva reached out her arms for her. "Oh, hi, clever baby. Who's the most wonderful little creature?"

Sita shook her head. "It's weird how you talk to her like your cat."

"I think it's cute," said Jaya, sitting down on top of the laundry basket. "And at least Reeva wants to hold her niece. You never bother."

"Because I have two of my own. The novelty's worn off."

Reeva looked up from Maya's big green eyes (it turned out Rakesh's genes weren't dominant; Maya looked just like her mum) and glared at her sisters. "Hey. No arguing. Satya Auntie won't like it."

"Do you think she'll mind if I just climb into the bath and nap?" asked Sita.

"Uh, yes," replied Reeva. "Besides, I need you there. Both of you. Moral support. We all remember what happened the last time I gave a speech at a funeral."

Both her sisters shuddered.

"I wish I didn't remember," said Sita.

"Can you, like, not slut-shame me at this one?" asked Jaya.

"No promises. Anyway, we need to go. We've missed practically all the pre-funeral prayers."

"As always," said Sita. "Too busy grieving in the bathroom."

"Come on," said Reeva. "Let's go grieve with everyone else this time."

REEVA STOOD ON the stage of the local crematorium, looking out at a sea of white. It was the norm for Buddhist and Hindu funerals in the east, and though they hadn't quite managed it for

her dad's funeral, she was glad they had for Satya Auntie; it was
so much more hopeful than black. She looked at the front pews
decorated with paper flowers. Satya Auntie was against using
real flowers—she didn't like the idea of killing living things—so
the sisters and the twins had spent the last few days cutting flowers out of recycled paper. It looked beautiful. Almost better than
real flowers, and more touching because those paper creations
were made with pure love. And paper cuts.

Reeva smiled down at her family, sitting in those very pews.
MJ and Saraswati in matching cream suits; her sisters and their
daughters; Nick dressed in a white linen trouser suit with a T-shirt
underneath; Lakshmi, next to him, in a white wrap dress. The
only missing member was Fluffy Panda, whose white patches
would have worked perfectly with the dress code, but cats weren't
allowed into the crematorium. Reeva had checked.

She looked at the open casket in front of her and winked at
her aunt. She was also dressed in white—a simple cotton sari—
and was rocking the Buddhist nun–meets–Britney hairstyle that
Reeva had made her own. It was part of the last wishes she'd requested for her funeral. As was the fact that Reeva was standing
on the stage about to do a speech.

"Hi, everyone," she said, looking up at the crowd. "I'm Reeva
Mehta, and Satya Auntie was, as you can guess, my auntie. I only
had the pleasure of knowing her for the last two hundred and
forty-one days, but the truth is, they've been the best two hundred and forty-one days of my life. Though that doesn't mean
they've been the easiest. Especially the first thirteen." She heard
a snort of agreement from Sita. "But if Satya Auntie taught me
anything, it's that life is worth living because of *all* the things
that happen, the bad *and* the good. Because we need both. If
things are just good, we start to get arrogant and feel superior,

and we don't even notice that they're good. We need the bad stuff too, to take us back down to reality and teach us humility, mercy, and most importantly, compassion. For ourselves and for others. Because we're all in it together, and no matter what people's lives look like on the outside, we all get our share of joy and pain. I guess what I'm trying to say is that Satya Auntie taught me to live. She taught me to accept everything in life—from loss, grief, and pain to love, laughter, and happiness. She helped me learn to speak my truth, not in a wanky way . . . Uh, sorry. She taught me not to care so much about what people think and to be honest about how I feel. It sounds so simple, but for most of my life, I didn't know how to do that. Until now.

"Which is why I can stand here and say honestly that my heart is breaking to have lost Satya Auntie." Reeva's voice caught, and the inevitable tears started to slide down her cheeks. But she let them fall as she carried on speaking. "I love her so much. She became my best friend as much as my family. Though lately I'm starting to realize the two are pretty much interchangeable." She grinned down at her sisters and Lakshmi. "Her wisdom has completely changed my life. I used to call her the Satya Lama because she was so wise. Part of me hates that I got less than a year with her. It makes me furious. But the other part of me—that part that's trying to be more like the Satya Lama—is just so grateful I got to know her. Because not everyone gets two hundred and forty-one days with such a special person.

"The way she lived her life has taught me to follow my own path and do what's right for me rather than constantly aim for more. I'm learning to ditch my expectations of everything and everyone in favor of just being right where I am." Reeva paused for a second. It still took her a moment to work up the courage to share something vulnerable—but she always got there. "Sometimes I do feel a little lonely because I haven't got married or had kids like my sisters, in the way that society expects, but then I remember that my path is my own. I can't control anything, and life will happen for me the way it's meant to. All I can do is surrender. And no matter what happens, I always have the choice to enjoy the ride, stop stressing so much, and relax into my reality. I'm starting to sound like her, aren't I?" Reeva laughed through her tears as her family nodded emphatically.

"Anyway, I know we're here to speak about Satya Auntie, but I feel like I should also say something about my dad, because if any of you were at his funeral, you'll know I didn't do such a great eulogy for him. So I just want to say thanks for bringing us all together, Dad. I'm so sorry we didn't get to know you in life, but in death, you've done so much for us. You brought me and my sisters back together, you helped me stand up for myself, and you gave us the imperfect perfection that was Satya Auntie. If it wasn't for you, we wouldn't be the family that we are today. So thank you. And please take care of Satya Auntie wherever you both are. Though, if your relationship with her was anything like the one we all had with her, she'll probably be the one taking care of you. Thanks, everyone."

"Darling, you did so well," cried Saraswati as she flung her arms around Reeva and air-kissed her like the Bollywood royalty she was born to be. "We were in floods."

"Thanks, Mum," said Reeva, flattening herself against the wall as the twins raced past her into the crowded house, brandishing cucumber sticks. "It was definitely an improvement on the last time."

"I wish I'd seen that one too. Sounds like it was worthy of one of my films."

Reeva laughed. "Yeah, one of those tragedies where everything goes wrong and the audience sobs the whole way through."

"Well, I'm proud of you," said Saraswati. "And so is my therapist. We think you've come such a long way. You're finally standing in your light and not letting your sisters walk all over you."

"Uh, thanks?"

"And it's lovely to see you so happy with Nick. But I'm mainly just proud of you for being so strong. Your aunt would be proud too."

Reeva put a hand to her heart. "Mum. That's . . . so nice of you. Thank you."

"Well, you always were my favorite." Her mum's eyes twinkled. "Don't tell the others."

"Hey," said Lakshmi, sidling up to Reeva while Saraswati began signing autographs for funeral guests. "Please can you pretend you need me urgently? I'm trying to escape Lee."

Reeva raised an eyebrow. "I thought you guys were loved up."

"Oh, we are," Lakshmi said, smiling. "I had four orgasms this morning. But he still drives me crazy."

"Sounds like how I feel about Reeva," said Nick, emerging from the crowd carrying a plate of canapés. "Minus the four orgasms. Well, three."

Reeva took the plate from him. "I'm taking these as an apology."

"I queued twenty-five minutes for those!"

"She just did a killer speech; let her eat some samosas," said Lakshmi. "And by 'her' I mean us."

Nick shook his head in mock annoyance. "Guess I'll go back to the queue."

"He's so much better than Rakesh," said Lakshmi as Nick walked away. "Thank fuck you got dumped for Jaya."

Reeva swallowed her samosa. "I know. In hindsight, it's the

best thing that ever happened to me. It's just that there's no way I would have believed it had you told me at the time."

"I did. Constantly."

Sita joined them and picked up a samosa off the plate. "Thank god you've got food. I can't be bothered to queue. What are we talking about?"

"How Reeva's way better off without Rakesh."

"I thought we figured that out years ago."

"Oh my god!" Jaya cried out indignantly, appearing behind them. "Why do you guys always hate on Rakesh? It's so rude."

Reeva bit her lip apologetically. "Sorry. But in my defense, they were the ones saying it, not me."

"Ugh, whatever," said Jaya. "Does anyone have any wine?"

"Aren't you breastfeeding?" asked Sita.

"Are you drink-shaming me?" countered Jaya.

"There's a bottle waiting for us in the laundry basket," said Reeva. "Bathroom?"

They all nodded in relief.

"Fuck yes," cried Sita. "I'll get samosas."

"I'll get some glasses," said Jaya.

"Guess I'll do dessert," said Lakshmi. "If you're sure it's okay to go up now?"

"Of course," said Reeva. "What else would we do at a funeral?"

## ACKNOWLEDGMENTS

Writing this book felt very different from writing my other books—I found it more challenging, but also so very rewarding. I've learned so much writing it, and along the way, I fell in love with Reeva and her slightly dysfunctional family.

I'm so grateful to everyone who has helped me write it, particularly in the early stages—which means Kate Seaver, my editor at Berkley, and Eli Dryden, my former editor at Headline. You both really helped me work out exactly what story I wanted to tell, and amazingly, neither of you balked when I said I wanted to write a comedy about death. Thank you so much for all your work and support on the book. Thank you also to Sherise Hobbs at Headline for stepping in and adding so much valuable insight.

As always, none of this would have happened without my agent, Madeleine Milburn, so thank you so much, Maddy, for making it possible for me to write yet another book. Thank you also to the teams at both Berkley and Headline—you all work so hard and I'm so grateful.

Thank you to Sarah Walker for your support—you always tell me everything I've written is the best thing I've done yet, and I'm slowly starting to believe you. Thanks also for the family law insight!

I'd also like to thank my relatives who shared their traditions of funerals and prayers with me. I know it all differs so much between families, so what the Mehta sisters do is very much just one (imperfect) experience.

Thank you also to all my wonderful friends who listened to me throughout the ups and downs of the process—I love you all. Thank you to myself for sitting down and actually writing this book—I love you, too. And finally, thank you to you, reader, for picking this up and reading it!

# I WISH WE
# WEREN'T
# RELATED

## RADHIKA
## SANGHANI

---

READERS GUIDE

---

## QUESTIONS FOR DISCUSSION

1. Reeva is anxious about her relationship with Nick through-out the book. Do you think those are just her insecurities coming out, or is Nick at fault too? Is her decision to "de-mote" him from UCB to lcb a good one?

2. Saraswati is not a stereotypical mother. What do you think of her parenting style and the different ways her three daughters handle their relationships with her?

3. Satya Auntie gives Reeva so much of what she's clearly look-ing for—in terms of being an unconditionally loving figure, but also with her wise words. Are there any messages of hers that really resonate with you?

4. One of Reeva's big journeys is learning to speak her truth—but also learning *when* to speak her truth. How important do you think it is to be fully honest with people?

5. Reeva, Jaya, and Sita are all so different. Which sister do you most relate to—if any?

6. Even though this is a book about sisterhood and family, Reeva's friendship with Lakshmi is one of the most important relationships in her life. Do you think friendships can be just as important as family?

7. Reeva's alopecia inspires her to go on a healing journey whereupon she uncovers childhood trauma. What do you think of the way her healing is depicted in the book? How much does she change?

8. Reeva and her sisters are British Indian, but don't know a lot about their culture. What did you think of the way British Indian traditions and cultures are described in the book? Did you learn anything you didn't know previously?

9. What do you think of Saraswati and Hemant's decision to let their daughters believe he was dead? Did you understand it at all?

**Radhika Sanghani** is an award-winning journalist and author based in London. She writes features for publications like the *Daily Mail*, the *Daily Telegraph*, *The Guardian*, and *Grazia*. She is the author of *Virgin, Not That Easy*, and *30 Things I Love About Myself*. Radhika is also a body positive campaigner and founded the #SideProfileSelfie movement to celebrate big noses.

## VISIT RADHIKA SANGHANI ONLINE

🐦 RadhikaSanghani
📷 RadhikaSanghani
ⓕ RadhikaSanghani

Ready to find
your next great read?

Let us help.

**Visit prh.com/nextread**

Penguin
Random
House